T0128260

1942

1942

DAYS OF DARKNESS

ROGER GALLAGHER

iUniverse

1942
DAYS OF DARKNESS

CREDITS: The U-boat picture is courtesy of C.J. Christ.
The shrimp boat is courtesy of the Versaggi family and C.J. Christ.

iUniverse books may be ordered through booksellers or by contacting:

iUniverse
1663 Liberty Drive
Bloomington, IN 47403
www.iuniverse.com
1-800-Authors (1-800-288-4677)

ISBN: 978-1-4917-8623-9 (sc)
ISBN: 978-1-4917-8622-2 (e)

Library of Congress Control Number: 2015921493

Print information available on the last page.

iUniverse rev. date: 05/27/2016

This story is dedicated to C.J. Christ, a nationally-known authority on German U-boat activities in the Gulf of Mexico, who told me about his search to clear up persistent rumors that some American citizens may have collaborated with the Germans by providing supplies to U-boats operating in the Gulf of Mexico during the early days of World War II

... but if a man lives many years, and rejoice in them all, yet let him remember the days of darkness, for they shall be many ...

--Ecclesiastes--

PROLOGUE

Abbeville, Louisiana, present day.

Reggie Arcenaux was impatient. He had gotten a haircut in preparation for the celebration and was in a partying mood. It was the first day of the Delcambre Shrimp Festival and he was the festival king. He had planned to leave early and attend the gathering at Smitty's Bayou Club, until an old woman named Marie Dugas hobbled into his office to answer the advertisement he had run in the newspaper.

He doubted that he would hear anything new. Others had come with stories of Americans collaborating with German U-boat crews during World War II, but after poring over his notes from the family that hired him, no one had proven to be reliable. The accusers were old people whose details and dates didn't fit. A few appeared to be settling old scores by leveling an accusation of treason. Cajun shrimpers from the old culture were like that, nursing old grudges about a competitor who was more successful or who wouldn't divulge a good trawling area. A few claimed to have witnessed suspicious events during World War II, but none had held his attention. He had heard colorful accounts, but what each person didn't know was Reggie had historical facts about U-boat operations in the Gulf that riddled their claims.

Frankly, he was bored with the lies told by people wanting the reward money and an old woman who had trouble walking didn't lift his mood.

But Reggie couldn't refuse Marie. The money was too good and his sagging law practice was buttressed by the $350 an hour he billed for anyone who told their story. Otherwise, he didn't give a damn about the war. Born after the conflict, it was ancient history to him, but the money was a nice bonus over other clients--repentant drivers who sought to avoid a DUI, spouses fighting messy divorces, runaway kids dealing in drugs, or somebody wanting to enroll under an assumed name in Jackson, Mississippi's detox center. The lucrative cases that guaranteed fat retainers went twenty miles up the highway to Lafayette, but he had grown up in Abbeville and refused to move.

*   *   *

The oil and gas industry had largely by-passed Abbeville and that was fine with Reggie. Lafayette's heavy traffic, numerous road projects, and impatient drivers resembled Houston more than the *Cajun Hub City*. Abbeville had retained the old ways--light traffic, friendly drivers, and a slow, comfortable lifestyle. He lived in a century-old house four blocks north of the courthouse and his office was a renovated hardware store on the west side of the traffic square.

Reggie was established and happy, one of thirty-five attorneys in Abbeville, a life-long resident who lived on five acres that his family had owned for three generations. He held the mineral rights, received a monthly check from a producing gas well, and was somebody, instead of being just another Lafayette lawyer among a sea of sharks.

Tall and square-jawed, with dark-rimmed glasses, graying hair and a flat stomach he maintained from walking the fairways on area golf courses, he stood up to greet Marie as his secretary ushered her into his office.

Marie Dugas used two canes to keep her balance and bent over as she shuffled in awkward mini-steps. White streaks battled the remnants of thin red hair that she combed forward to cover part of her wrinkled forehead and, from the looks of liver spots on her hands and her bent posture, Reggie guessed her to be in her nineties. Her face was heavily powdered and her nose turned downward, giving her the look of stubbornness, and deep wrinkles formed spider webs around her brown eyes that fixed upon him. She wore a tan skirt and a white blouse and had taken care to dress for the occasion. Instead of admiring the plaques, certificates and pictures, she positioned herself in a brown leather chair, leaned her canes against the wall, folded her hands in her lap, and waited for him to speak

Reggie knew little about shrimping beyond the trawlers he noticed at Delcambre on his way to New Iberia. He was involved with golf, parties, his law practice, and the Abbeville Chamber of Commerce. But he'd seen the old movie, *Thunder Bay* with James Stewart, on television. Other than that, all he knew about shrimp was how good they tasted and how much they cost when he purchased them off the docks at Delcambre. Though he occasionally went fishing offshore with his buddies, the beer, conversation about LSU football, and stories of their sexual escapades from high school, drew more interest than catching red snapper, sand trout or amberjack. He had gone shrimping with a friend once, and that trip had killed his interest. It took too much time and work and the long spells in a swaying, rolling boat made him queasy, despite taking motion sickness pills.

Being the Shrimp Festival king was political. He was a successful lawyer and, because the crown rotated among the town's influential men, it was his turn. But since the notoriety would bring more clients, he was prepared to listen to the old timers in their white shirts and red bow ties reminiscing about the old days and how hard it had been working in the Gulf without a cell phone, a radio, a depth finder, a GPS, and the weather service to warn them of approaching storms.

Reggie placed his small tape recorder on the front edge of the desk and clicked it on. "You must understand," he began, "that you could face a libel charge if you accuse innocent people of treason. Even today, collaboration with the Germans would expose someone to an espionage trial. There is no federal statute of limitations for treason."

Without allowing Marie to respond, Reggie continued. "Give me your full name."

"Marie Louise Dugas."

"When and where were you born?"

"On May 10th, 1925, in Pat's Landing, Louisiana."

Reggie thought he'd already found a lie. "How could that be? It was only a village then, and no hospital has existed there."

"Young man, times were different then, and you are too young to know," she answered with a smirk. "A midwife assisted at my birth. Effie May Theriot was a family friend who delivered most of the newborns. The doctor seldom came from the medical clinic in

Houma in those days and women depended on Effie May. When it came to delivering babies, she was as good as any doctor and she charged a lot less. I could name you a dozen children she helped deliver," she added, continuing behind the hint of a smile. "Effie May was the great granddaughter of T-Pat Duhon. The town site was part of the marsh until his arrival. But now it's a supply dock and jumping off place for oil companies drilling in the Gulf. Helicopters and boats go out of there every day and the town has a fish processing plant."

Reggie asked. "What kind of fish?"

A startled look filled Marie's face. "Surely you know what a Pogie Plant does." Before he could answer, she added more detail. "Boats net the Pogie fish in the Gulf and the plant processes them into oil, dog food, and fertilizer." She wrinkled her nose. "If you ever smell the plant when they're cooking the fish, you'll never forget that odor," she admitted. "It sticks to your clothes for hours and smells worse than a skunk."

Stifling his frustration, he finally got to speak. "I know about Pogie plants."

Marie brushed one leg of her skirt and look at him. "Well, you asked me about ..."

"Mrs. Dugas," he said in an agitated voice. "You are here to talk about more important things than midwives and fishing."

Bored with the ramblings of an old woman, the third story he'd heard in a week, Reggie hadn't been in the military and didn't care about his client's case, other than the money he earned by listening to the stories. He waved one hand like someone wiping a window. "I'm only interested in my client's concern. Now tell me how you came upon your story?"

"It isn't a story," she corrected him. "I lived it. My father was a shrimper the same as Rene, my husband."

"But you live in Lafayette?"

"I do now. I moved there when the jobs ran out after the war. Mister Higgins' contract expired and I needed to find something else."

"You were employed by the Higgins' Boat Company?" Reggie asked.

"Yes. I wanted to help with the war effort, and I looked for a job to support myself. I could have worked for the Thibodeaux Boiler Works, making artillery shells, but I didn't want to be in a noisy, smelly factory. Office work was clean and quiet."

"What did you do there?"

"I was a bookkeeper, until his contracts dried up after the war and I wasn't needed anymore."

Reggie thought he recognized a reason to cancel the meeting. He was bored with her already and wanted to go to the festival. "If you lived in Pat's Landing, how did you also work for the Higgins' Boat Company?"

Marie explained. "I moved to New Orleans in forty-three. I wanted to get away, and Mr. Higgins hired me. I worked for him until a month past V-J Day." A smile covered her face. "Andrew Jackson Higgins was a very nice man, courteous and a gentleman. He seldom raised his voice to anyone, and he wore a white shirt and bow tie to work every day."

"Then let's begin," Reggie said, separating two sheets of paper and running his eyes down one page. "About a year ago I was asked to represent two prominent families who had sons killed when the Robert E. Lee, a merchant vessel which also carried passengers, was torpedoed and sunk in the Gulf of Mexico, in May of 1942. The families have put ads in newspapers from Galveston to Mobile, offering twenty thousand dollars to anyone who can provide evidence about a shrimp boat crew, or any other American, who collaborated with the Germans during World War Two. People along the Gulf Coast have heard the rumor for many years, and the families of three of the victims want to find out if such a thing happened. But in case you missed my earlier statement, the statute of limitations doesn't run out on the crime of treason. Both families want justice and are willing to pay for it. So whoever was involved—if it was several people or an individual--my clients want to know the truth." Then he pointed at Marie. "A word of caution; if false accusations emerge from your story, you could also be subpoenaed by a court of law and prosecuted for perjury."

She waved one hand to brush away what he had said. "I'm not worried about anything like that."

"Do you have any family members or friends who can back up your story?"

Marie's eyes moistened behind a brief hesitation. "No ... no one. They're all gone." She looked at the floor, her face and voice softening. "I had a son, but he died in Vietnam. He was born in forty-three, after the bad things took place." She then gathered herself and spoke in a determined manner. "But I don't need someone to verify my story, Mr. Arcenaux. What I have to tell you is the truth."

"The families will be the judge of that," Reggie replied. "Now one more piece of advice before you begin," he added. "Please include dates, names, and places. If you don't remember something, don't guess. I want facts."

Marie's face flushed and her voice sharpened. "You needn't worry about that. I knew everyone in the story, so I only have facts," Marie answered, rapping the tip of one cane on the carpeted floor. "I've relived those events ever since they occurred. You're too young to know much about the war. My son, if he were alive, would be older than you. What do you know about the U-boat threat, about lying awake at night and hearing those damnable engines, about drawing the house curtains in the evening, forced to obey the blackout law and live in the dark like moles, about watching a merchant ship explode and hearing the cries of our boys in the water, and attending a funeral when there isn't a body to bury, or worrying if a U-boat might surface and fire at you? Not everyone had a phone then, and we sometimes worried if the Germans might bomb us." She paused briefly and her eyes moistened. "I lived through it all. I'm a significant part of that story and partly to blame for some poor decisions." She choked back her emotion with a cough, swallowed, touched her chin, and stared at the wall behind Reggie. "Let me see; the trouble started for us in the summer of '42."

1

The Gulf of Mexico, June, 1942

Al Dugas was aggravated at his son, Rene, but after bringing the dead mariner onboard, their argument had to wait. He steered his shrimp boat *Miss Jane* around the western tip of Raccoon Island and headed toward the inspection dock at the mouth of the bayou, relieved that the Gulf of Mexico was now behind him. Until he was out of the Gulf waters he couldn't dispel the thought that a German sub might be lurking nearby, ready to take a shot at him. He never relaxed until he got into the channel and was free of the sub threat and of floating debris from a torpedoed merchant ship that might have drifted into shallow water. Whether coming in or going out, it was a constant job to watch for U-boats and to steer clear of floating debris.

The war had changed the risks of shrimping. The U-boat threat and trawling for two weeks, under the guise of the enemy, was like running a gauntlet. May of '42 had also been the worst month for merchant ship losses. One particular U-boat attack on a tanker had been visible by the people on Grand Isle, who watched the vessel burn and sink less than two miles off the beach.

*   *   *

Woody Chauvin came out of his small, unpainted guard shack and waved as Al's boat drew close. One of numerous coast watchers who manned stations every twelve miles along the Louisiana shoreline, Woody kept tabs on every trawler that went out or came in. But he turned his lanterns off at night and kept a rifle for protection, because part of his job was also to keep a lookout for U-boat activity.

"How was your trip, Al?"

"Better than average for this time of year," Al replied, raising a hand in Woody's direction. "We have about four hundred pounds of shrimp onboard, thirty gallons of gas left and maybe a fifth of our ice." He pointed toward the rear of the boat. "We also caught a man on our last drag. He's behind the wheelhouse."

After Al stopped the boat at the small dock, Woody stepped onboard and they went to the canvas that covered the body. Woody carefully uncovered the corpse and stared a few seconds, shaking his head.

Moving quickly away, Rene leaned over the railing, put his head down, and threw up.

"Where'd you find him?"

"About five miles south of here."

"That's no man. He doesn't look much older than Rene." Woody observed.

"I think he's younger," Al added quietly, tightening his throat to keep from gagging.

"The Merchant Marines take kids from fourteen up," Woody commented.

"That's too damn young," Al answered.

Woody studied the body. The skin on the boy's face and chest was encrusted with a black scale, the hair was burned to its roots on one side of his head, and he was barefoot.

"He's still wearing a life vest," Al remarked.

Woody made a note on his pad. "The crewmen can't submerge with their vests on so they take them off before jumping. Maybe this boy couldn't swim and kept it on, but that made it impossible for him to swim under the flames."

"I haven't checked for his identification."

"We don't need it," Woody answered. "The sheriff will handle that. I'll radio ahead." He glanced at his watch. "You'll need about two hours to reach the dock, won't you?"

Al nodded and closed his eyes. "Yeah."

Woody wrote down the time. "We've been cautioned to be on the lookout for a trawler coming back with no shrimp onboard. Personally, I think the government is nuts to worry about Americans collaborating with the Germans." He motioned one hand toward the body. "This is what concerns me, not if any American is being friendly to the Germans."

Al replaced the tarp over the body and started toward the wheelhouse.

"Don't forget to tell Jane hello."

"Okay. I'll come back out Monday morning."

After Woody stepped onto the dock, Al eased away, but Woody called out. "Did you see any signs of U-boats this week?"

"We picked up an oil can and saw a large fire two nights ago, and an oil slick the next day," Al answered.

Woody shook his head. "After so many ships were lost during May, these damn U-boats give me the willies. I hear their engines but I never can tell exactly how far away they are. Sometimes I lay awake for two or three hours, just listening." He looked toward the open water. "If I ever see one, I'll empty my rifle at it," he declared, his voice growing lower. "Seeing that boy reminds me of the cousin I lost when The *Munger T. Ball* was torpedoed and sunk."

"At least you have a radio to call the Coast Guard," Al said. "None of Savoy's trawlers has one. We may as well be alone out there."

"I don't know what good my radio would do," Woody replied. "I've never seen a Coast Guard boat or an airplane out here at night. If you ask me, we need more airplanes and ships to patrol before the U-boats sink every tanker coming out of Texas. Anyway, have a good trip. I'll look for you Monday. And kiss Jane for me."

He waved at Al and turned toward his lookout shack, which was barely large enough for two people. Designed with no frills, the only window faced the Gulf.

* * *

Clear of the dock, Al aimed into the mouth of the bayou and returned to the argument with his son. He hoped to make Rene come to his senses and stay home. Al had done his part in the first war and figured one conflict was enough for any family, and the prospect of losing his only child was something he didn't want to think about. After spending time over the young mariner's body, the idea of Rene enlisting and not coming home made him weak in his legs.

3

With Rene being fresh out of high school and full of himself, Al realized he had an uphill battle because no one could stop him from enlisting.

His concentration shifted back to the boat as Al searched for the metal signs in the bayou that marked safe passage to the village of Pat's Landing. The triangular red and white markers stood out against the brown water and green foliage that grew to the water's edge in clumps so thick that it was difficult at times to determine where the bank began. Avoiding mud bars and sand flats was routine after twenty years of shrimping, but Al never took the bayou for granted. He recalled the old adage that a waterway changes its mind without warning, just like a woman. A wet winter or a hurricane could shift the mud and fill in part of the channel, enticing an inattentive skipper to run aground and place a boat out of commission for a month, which also meant no income for the crew. For that reason, the shrimpers were grateful that the Coast Guard routinely plumbed the channels and moved the signs that warned of shallow water.

Al didn't want to damage the boat and have another confrontation with his boss, Tom Savoy. Besides accident-prone skippers, many other things angered Savoy. While he could be tolerant, Savoy had no patience with a man who grounded his shrimp boat. During earlier years, clearing the channel had been a family thing when Tom Savoy's father had first monitored the canal during the Great War, so despite the Coast Guard managing the bayou now, Tom took it personally if any captain failed to maneuver safely. Two different skippers who had run aground were fired that same day. One left for New Orleans, but the second had a wife and two kids and was forced to work in the warehouse for half the money he had earned as a skipper.

Working for Tom Savoy was like being in the military. You toed the line or you went looking for another job.

Lined up with the markers now, AL's concern shifted back to Rene. Since the war was only seven months old, Al hadn't made a conclusion about its future outcome. After the attack on Pearl Harbor, Rene had listened to the news on the radio and had talked about little else, but Al stood by his decision that Rene had to finish school before enlisting. And now that he'd graduated, the idea of his only son leaving for the war filled Al with dread.

After surviving World War One and the Depression, he had lived deliberately and avoided risks. But the new war and the threat of U-boats operating within the Gulf of Mexico, weighed on his shoulders each time he cleared Raccoon Point and headed offshore for another two weeks. Though the shallow water along the coast mostly prevented U-boats from operating closer than three miles from land, two shrimp boats had been fired upon in the last few months, with no survivors, and a handful of cargo ships had been torpedoed within five miles of the shoreline.

The shrimpers and fishermen had been warned to report sightings of U-boats and to remain inside the ten-mile limit, where shallower water posed less of a threat. A few shrimpers who ventured past the boundary were admonished by the Coast Guard. One intrusion produced a warning; the second brought a fine. Since none of Tom's trawlers had radios on the boats, the first sign of a pending violation was a Coast Guard vessel pulling alongside and ordering you to turn around.

Without radios onboard, shrimping in the Gulf meant being vulnerable most of the time and, in Al's opinion, going to deeper water wasn't worth the risk of being attacked by a U-boat when shrimp were available closer to shore.

Most of all, Al simply wanted the war to leave him alone. He didn't want any part of the present one, especially since they didn't consider him fit for service. The leg wound he had received in France left him with permanent stiffness in one knee. He could bend it and climb stairs but couldn't carry anything heavy, and he hadn't been pain-free since leaving the hospital more than twenty years earlier. During the summer months, the old wound didn't bother him, but a cold snap or a blue norther made the left knee feel like needles were sticking in him. So he had to be content to spend his days shrimping, fishing, and trapping and letting younger soldiers win the war. Still, it was a shame that the Selective Service didn't call for healthy volunteers over forty years old. Older veterans could perform supply and administration work, but the military wanted young guys they could order around. They asked fewer questions, and in a war the one thing not countenanced was backtalk--a habit his son and others of Rene's age seemed to delight in using.

Still, it was wasteful that the draft only accepted men under forty. Older veterans could pull a trigger and handle the dangers of combat better than a young, inexperienced kid.

Setting aside his frustration about the war, he concentrated on the bayou and steered in the direction of Pat's Landing ten miles away, which sat on a peninsula of solid ground originally called "Prairies" by early settlers. Now visible a hundred yards ahead, another of Savoy's boats churned the muddy waters of the lower bayou, and Al maneuvered to a direct line behind the other boat so the *Miss Jane* wouldn't roll much in the smooth water from the other boat's wake.

*   *   *

A common sight on the way in was Tom Savoy's drying platform, which lay a mile to the east, on the bank of another channel but visible through a break in the trees. The platform was no more than a wooden deck ten feet off the ground and supported by cypress pilings where the shrimp were spread out and dried after being boiled for five minutes in rock-salt flavored water that preserved the meat. The drying area was a series of slanted wood planks with a walkway on top, allowing the shrimp to dry in the sun, but they were covered with tarps at night or when it rained. Timing was critical; the shrimp spoiled if they were not dried out after three days.

Introduced by the Chinese after World War One, selling dried shrimp was a secondary financial operation for Savoy. The shrimp were packaged and sold as snacks in bars, hotels, and stores in South Louisiana, but he had plans to expand the business into Mississippi and Alabama.

The drying platform made his operation more efficient since it took in shrimp from the boats and enabled the crews to return to the Gulf, instead of going into Pat's Landing to unload and then losing the running time back to the open water. Those four hours saved could be spent catching more shrimp. The platform crews got paid at the end of each month and returned after three days off. Due to the demanding schedule and isolated working conditions, Tom Savoy favored Chinese workers who were grateful for the job and didn't complain about the pay or working conditions.

Tom was also working on a contract to have the Army put dried shrimp in the K-ration boxes, since they could stay good for several weeks and give the soldiers a basic source of protein. He had presented his idea to representatives of the War Commission Board in Baton Rouge but afterwards complained to Al that it was difficult convincing politicians who were so narrow-minded that they could look through a keyhole with both eyes.

*   *   *

Al was well into the bayou by five o'clock and had time to get to the dock before darkness. If Tom Savoy was in a generous mood and didn't use the lame excuse that his operating costs had gone up, Al figured he and Rene would clear a hundred-twenty dollars.

Al took a hand towel and wiped his forehead and neck, then propped a wheelhouse window open with a wooden dowel. The June heat and humidity were oppressive. A gentle onshore breeze crept over the back deck and circulated through the door but also brought the acrid smell of the boat's exhaust and the decaying odors of bayou reeds, grasses, and an occasional dead animal. The heat came in waves that were practically visible. On hot summer days, the only coolness happened after sunset and before daylight.

Half a dozen seagulls patrolled above the *Miss Jane*, looking for scraps tossed into the water. Their white feathers blended with the tall clouds developing into thunderheads over the beach that stood shoulder-to-shoulder like soldiers, growing into billowing, white columns. By nightfall they'd become storms filled with violent lightning and thunder that rattled the windows and lit up the towns along Highway 90, dropping torrents of rain across the wetlands and drenching Baton Rouge, Lockport and New Orleans in the middle of the night, and finally losing their energy over Mississippi the next morning.

Glad to be ahead of the storms and safely on his way home after another two weeks of work, Al rubbed a crucifix that hung on a chain around his neck and felt Christ's legs, chest and face with his forefinger and thumb. He could still recognize the features, though he had carried the crucifix with him since his time in France. He also caressed the Saint Christopher's medal that dangled from a nearby nail. It had been blessed ten years earlier by a priest, kissed by Jane for good luck, and had ridden in the wheelhouse ever since. Religious medallions accompanied nearly every trawler in the belief that they would ward off trouble, damage from a thunderstorm, large debris caught during a trawl, and U-boats. But they were principally good luck for a full load of shrimp and a safe passage back home.

*   *   *

Al stuck his head through the door of the wheelhouse and looked toward Rene, who was busy running his hands over the netting, looking for holes. When they weren't dragging, there was always something to do, especially with the nets, which was Rene's job whenever he had slack time.

"Fly the flag," Al called out. "The shrimp gave nicely this trip."

Rene stood up and took the small white flag out of a box behind the wheelhouse, unfurled it and placed the wooden dowel in a metal slot by the door. At eighteen he stood an inch taller and was leaner than his father, who carried a small belly over his beltline, despite having a thick chest and broad shoulders from years of physical work.

Rene placed both hands on the door jamb and looked inside. "Are you going to give three toots on the horn?"

"When we get closer," Al confirmed. "No one can hear us out here except seagulls, nutria, and snakes."

"I wasn't sure if we had caught enough shrimp on this trip."

"We're good," Al countered. "Four hundred pounds at this time of year, before the shrimp migrate, is a fine catch. We'll double that later when the lake shrimp complete their run into the Gulf."

Al steered left to maneuver a dogleg in the channel and adjusted the throttle string. Instead of having a power lever at the wheel, the string ran over a small pulley, back to the engine room and downward, where it was tied to the throttle handle. Coming out of the turn, he increased the engine power because it was a straight shot now to Pat's Landing four miles away.

He looked at the bank and recalled locations where he used to catch shrimp so far inland. The shrimping had been better after the Great War. Back then he'd set his butterfly nets close to Houma, forty miles from the Gulf, and catch thirty pounds of shrimp overnight.

But that was before the 1927 flood and the influx of more shrimpers. There were fewer than fifty trawlers to compete with before the flood, but by the start of the war in1941, twice as many boats worked the same area and dozens now dragged inside the ten-mile limit.

The Great War and the flood had changed things permanently. More people now populated the area, built houses, dumped their garbage in the water, and fished out the bayou instead of allowing time for the migrating shrimp to replenish in the lakes and bays. The bayou now wasn't fit for anything but catfish, perch, and trash fish. The old, dependable way of life was disappearing.

*   *   *

Rene stood in the wheelhouse doorway and Al got ready for another argument about the war. Since Rene had a stubborn streak, it was like Al seeing himself in the mirror when he was young, opinionated, and cocksure.

At eighteen, Rene was a year older than several local boys who had already enlisted. While Al recognized his son's dedication, he was torn between encouraging him to go and wanting to protect him. Although Rene was mature in some ways, he remained naïve about war and the gruesome nature of combat, thinking the time in uniform would be a romantic adventure.

As the only son it was possible that Rene would not be drafted. A rumor circulated that Congress would soon exempt them. But if he enlisted, Rene would be accepted like anyone else. The draft board would take any male who signed up and passed the induction physical administered in New Orleans. The local boards seldom met their quotas, so they welcomed anyone who could carry a duffel bag, touch their toes without falling on their face, march, and take orders.

War fever had the country in a dither and the call for volunteers was a daily spiel on the radio and in the newspapers. A boy of sixteen could enlist if his father vouched for him being seventeen and the officials didn't put up a challenge.

Rene moved closer and stared at his father until Al noticed him. "The paper says the Germans might take Egypt."

"What's that got to do with you?" Al asked, keeping his eyes on the waterway,

Rene persisted. "Don't you understand? The Merchant Marines are taking boys as young as fourteen. I don't feel right while others take my place."

Al launched a comeback. "Half of their ships get torpedoed. Except for one deck gun, the Merchant Marines don't even carry weapons, and the U-boats are hitting them like sitting ducks. We've already lost a hundred ships from their attacks. Is that what you want, to be a floating target? Do you want to be shark bait, or get burned to death like the kid we have on the deck?" Al grabbed a *Life* magazine that lay open on the counter and shook it in Rene's face. "Did you think this story about the Flying Tigers would impress me? Is that what you want, to be a pilot and get your picture in a magazine? Half of those pilots will probably be dead in another year. Is that your dream?"

Rene shook his head. "Of course not. I'd rather join the Navy." He raised the magazine close to his father's face. "Look at the pictures. One pilot is only twenty-three." He clenched a fist and smacked the door jamb. "I don't feel right staying home. You, of all people," he shouted, "should understand why I want to go."

Al swept his right arm around the wheelhouse, nearly desperate. "Do you call this doing nothing? We're supplying food for the armies and navies of this country. How in God's name can you do more than this? Believe me, Son; soldiers can't fight if they don't eat. Without food our military will lose." His voice took on an acid tone. "And you say you are doing nothing?" he hissed.

"I know," Rene answered. "But most of my friends have already enlisted. Manny is the only one who hasn't."

"So you and Manny plan to go, do you?"

"I hope so. He promised me two weeks ago."

"Most of your friends weren't shrimping either," Al replied, turning to face Rene, both hands open. "The farmer and the fisherman are just as important as the soldier. Do you realize how vital food is to war? Let's say a bad winter kills off the wheat, or the fish and shrimp die from the red tide we get in the Gulf. Any break in our food supply would be a disaster, and Germany and Japan would wear us down if our military couldn't eat, and then we'd be fighting on our shores."

When Rene looked dubious, Al pointed at him. "Believe me. It could happen. You remember how the Secretary of War warned that

10

small-scale raids on America are within the Germans' capability?"
He looked toward the bow. "It might happen right here in Louisiana."

Rene answered quickly. "All I know is that I'm being left out," he
claimed, his voice becoming severe. "You went to war. No one stopped
you from doing your duty, and I just want to do mine. How can you
deny me something you did yourself?"

"Yeah, I had my turn," Al admitted. "And look what it got me;
a bum leg for the rest of my life." His tone was flat, his words bitten
off. "Do you think war is fun? You want to do your part, do you? Is
that the romantic notion you and Manny have dreamed up? Do you
think putting on a uniform and grabbing a rifle will be like going on
a winter duck hunt?" His voice lost its strength and Al gestured with
one hand open. "You're only looking at those patriotic ads in the
paper that show smiling soldiers. Believe me, those aren't real people.
That's why you see more drawings than pictures. There is no bright
side to war, Rene, only death and misery."

"I know that," Rene began, but Al didn't give him a chance to
continue.

"Sure, I went to the first war. So did Tom and his brother, Emile.
We were all excited. But it wasn't any picnic. We were in the First
Louisiana Infantry." His words came in a caustic tone. "Oh, it was
great. We drank beer and marched down the street to a band and
loaded onto the boat in the New York harbor. The atmosphere was
like a carnival. We were going to be heroes. The girls waved at us and
smiled and two I didn't even know gave me their addresses." Then his
voice and face hardened and the spider webs around the edges of his
eyes deepened. "But it didn't turn out that way." He stared through
the wheelhouse window and continued barely above a whisper. "Our
romantic expectations turned out to be trench warfare where men
were bunched together in narrow slits of mud and filth. We stood up
for lack of space, ate, slept, fought, and died in those trenches. There
were lice and rats living with us, and in warm weather the gnats and
flies were so dense that the gnats bit us and the flies got into our food.
They even covered the dead before we could evacuate the bodies."
He ran one hand through his hair, his jaw clenched. "The artillery
shells shook the ground from their impact and the air smelled rancid.
Smoke obscured our vision at night, so the Huns would sneak up
and toss potato mashers into the trench, or snipers would pick us

off when we stuck our heads up to return fire. We'd go to sleep just as a shell burst nearby and we'd get down in the mud and curl into a ball and hope the shrapnel didn't get us. I heard religious men curse like drunken sailors during the day and pray like altar boys during a nighttime shelling. Many times I joined them and prayed an entire rosary. We kept our helmets on day and night. Even if there had been room to lie down, the trench was muddy and the mud was mixed with human waste because we had no place to relieve ourselves.

"We lived in constant fear of being wounded and dying from infection. A leg wound might take us out of action, but a head wound was sure to be fatal." He scowled and squinted, his words crisp and cold. "After an attack, the dead were often so thick that we couldn't move, so we stood there and peed in place. Put together the rain and cold, the lack of showers, living in your clothes for days, hot food rarely, lice in your hair because you wore your helmet all the time, the mud so deep you had trouble picking up your boots to take another step…" His voice trailed off and he stared through the windshield.

Al rubbed his crucifix again and wiped his face with the towel, dragging it across his eyes. Rene's yearning wasn't a surprise. For several months he had dreaded the moment that had finally arrived. Since it was natural in any kid with an ounce of patriotism, he was proud of Rene. But the feeling in his gut was sorrow, not anticipation. He wanted to shake some sense into him but also hug him and tell him that he understood, and he swayed between protection and pride for him. But if he went, Al feared a telegram would be delivered to Jane and him one day.

The Merchant Marines did take boys at fourteen, but serving on a tanker was risky. The U-boats were sinking as many as one transport in five that tried to cross the Atlantic. Without more deck guns on the ships and additional airplanes to fly cover for the tankers coming out of Houston or Beaumont and sailing around the tip of Florida, the convoys had no options. The Gulf was especially hazardous. Sheltered by the coastline, until they rounded Florida, the lumbering freighters and tankers were running an explosive gauntlet day and night.

The wolf packs were waiting for every convoy that left for Europe so many people considered volunteering for the Merchant Marines to be a death sentence. At ten knots--the top speed most cargo ships and tankers could maintain--the vessels were lumbering targets. Al had heard from other shrimpers who worked near the mouth of the Mississippi that U-boat periscopes were often spotted as close as a mile offshore. The subs didn't have to hunt in that sector; they simply waited for ships leaving New Orleans and coming through the Southwest Pass. Deeper water at the mouth allowed the U-boats to submerge while a coastal patrol plane flew by and then resurface to periscope depth and wait for another ship to come into range.

The entire Gulf was the U-boats' hunting ground. During a recent trawl about seven miles off the beach, when Al caught the wake of a periscope, he didn't point it out to Rene, but instead turned northward and told him to haul in the net, then added full throttle with one hand while gripping his crucifix in the other.

The idea of warfare in the Gulf, with a slow, cumbersome wooden shrimp trawler against a war machine like a German U-boat, made him queasy, the same way he had felt in the trenches.

It just wasn't U-boats that made the war grim. Much of the other war news wasn't good. Tobruk had recently fallen and thousands of British had been taken prisoner. France had collapsed, Britain was holding on by her eyeteeth and Stalingrad was under siege. The outcome could as easily favor the Germans as the allies. It was impossible to imagine worse conditions, unless the Germans overcame England and swept across the Atlantic. According to a recent New Orleans newspaper, three German spies were caught as they swam ashore at Battery Park in New York City. One war-jittery rumor claimed that a person can stand on a street corner in New Orleans and pick out the suspicious-looking men who were no doubt German spies.

The war's impact flooded the newspapers. Every page held reminders that it was patriotic to join or to give ten percent of your wages to the government. Each message delivered a clear appeal--we need every healthy body to win. It was a tossup as to which took up more space, news stories or ads about the war. Local events were pushed to the back pages or reduced to a small section between stories of a battle or of another ship being torpedoed.

It was the same with magazines. *Life* had displayed horrible pictures of the bombed-out sections of London and of women and children walking among the ruins created by the fire bombs that set rooftops and wooden structures aflame.

It didn't matter where you worked and lived; the war news penetrated everyone's life, including the once serene Gulf of Mexico, where shrimp boat crews were being watched by U-boats every day.

* * *

Rene remained in the doorway, his eyes locked onto his father, and Al softened his appeal. "You've learned to do everything from running the boat to arguing over the price of shrimp with Tom, and you're very good at it. But shrimping isn't like an ordinary job. We don't punch a clock or call in sick when we're on the water. We have our freedom and work for ourselves. It's a calling that stays with us our entire life and, if you love it as much as you say, I'd hate to see you lose that."

"I'll come back," Rene answered. "Why should I forget? Joining up isn't like the end of the world."

"It will be if you don't come home alive," Al answered.

Rene laughed. "No German will get me."

Al shook his head. "I knew several guys who said that in 1918 and they all returned home in wooden boxes."

Rene snorted, pressed his lips together and looked away.

Al slackened the throttle and slowed the boat as they approached the southern boundary of Pat's Landing. It was a courtesy to maintain five knots or less when one boat met another.

In a few minutes they'd be at the dock without solving anything between them.

So Al tried one last time. "In a couple of years you'll have your own boat. Then you'll be one more person feeding our armies. If it wasn't for farmers and fishermen sending food to England, the Brits might have starved by now. A month ago the paper said they were living on meat substitutes and potato flour. It's so bad that the women gather up old parachutes and make dresses and blouses with the silk." He slapped the wheel with one hand. "I've seen what war can do, Rene. You never catch up when you get back, and the memories stay with you in your dreams. It's a daily struggle to feel normal and to suppress a whole passel of bad incidents. War changes your whole outlook. It destroys hopes and plans and robs you of time that you never get back. Why throw your opportunity away by leaving and perhaps losing everything?"

Rene grabbed the string that hung from the horn and pulled it three times to signal that they were docking with a full load. "You made it and I will too."

"I was lucky," Al declared. "I can't remember all the friends who got killed," he said, his voice trailing off and his expression darkening.

He wondered if he should tell Rene how he had driven to Houma and visited the draft board to enlist. But they rebuffed him because his bad leg made him unable to serve. All he wanted was to be a watchtower volunteer along the shoreline, or walk the beach with binoculars and scan the water for German submarines. But as a shrimper he was gone two weeks at a time and couldn't patrol the beach because of a bad leg. He was physically unfit to walk the distances required for a coast watcher and his job interfered.

The rejection left him feeling embarrassed, so he kept it to himself, not even telling Jane. If Rene found out that his own father had tried to join the coast watchers, he would take that as an approval, pack his bags, and leave home the same day. Enlisting was not an obstacle for him. The services were short of young men, and the draft boards looked the other way when a kid lied about his birthday and signed up before he was seventeen. As an only son, they would be glad to take him without giving it a second thought, because government officials expected each draft board to meet its monthly quota.

Al's war experiences returned every time his leg bothered him, setting off a running series of fractured memories, of screams, cries of pain, frightened eyes, and miserable days and nights. Although the war was more than twenty years in the past, there were times when his dreams kept him awake, and he would lie still and try not to awaken Jane.

He took comfort in the knowledge that he and Jane had raised Rene to be a decent, responsible kid, but the possibility of losing him was unthinkable.

Close enough to glimpse the village, Al ran his hands over the boat's wheel and a surge of desire formed as he thought of Jane. Much as he loved shrimping, spending fourteen days in the Gulf without her was becoming more difficult to accept. When she had gone with him before Rene was born, working as a deckhand and learning how to handle the nets, lines and boards, each day was pleasurable and their nights were private and loving. But she stayed at home after Rene started school and Al never adjusted to being without her. After twenty years of marriage he still felt the same reservoir of hunger for her that he had from their early months together.

* * *

They met in 1914 during his basic training at Camp Bowie, Texas, a dusty, military training post on the western edge of Fort Worth, then a town of thirty thousand. She worked in her father's drug store and rang up the sales on a large cash register that hid most of her from view, which forced Al to stand to one side in order to admire her. Her soft face, a warm-eyed smile, and her brown hair attracted him right away. And Jane could not help noticing Al because he kept coming back, first to buy a tin of aspirin, then a nickel bottle of coke from the red, top-drawer cooler, a newspaper, and finally a *Collier's* magazine, which amounted to four trips within an hour one Saturday morning. After he worked up the courage to talk to her, nodding his head and smiling sheepishly, she agreed to go walking with him.

That led to a movie at the Roxy Theatre and a Sunday afternoon stroll along the grassy, mesquite-shaded banks of the Trinity River, a favorite place for picnics during warm weather. As they became better acquainted, he bragged about his home and compared the squat mesquite and redbud trees to the graceful magnolias, huge cypress and live oaks in Louisiana, whose limbs sometimes curved downward and formed a bench to sit on. His enthusiasm became infectious, and she was intrigued with his descriptions of swamps and cypress stumps, warm gulf breezes, a mild winter of no snow, and the abundance of seafood that you could catch outside your back door. So by the time he was set to leave for New York City, he proposed during a dance on his last night and she agreed to wait for him.

* * *

Fortune blessed him for six months, until a bullet from a German sniper's rifle ended his war, and he shipped home with a wound that took three months to heal and an impatient desire to get married.

During his convalescence in San Antonio, Jane traded letters with him every day, and they were married a week after his release from the hospital.

Al wanted to go home, but Jane's father offered him a partnership in the drugstore, which he accepted. However, it only took him a month to realize his mistake. Much as he was grateful for the chance to own part of the business, he was an outdoor person, not a store clerk who was kept inside every working day and forced to look at passing traffic and people. In addition to standing all day and setting his bad knee on fire, he hated to wear a white shirt and bow tie and smile at people he didn't know, acting as if they were all his friends while he answered the same questions about finding items in the store, and then waited for a customer to buy something. It was an honest job but he wasn't cut out to wait on other people and take their money when he hadn't earned it. Compared to handling a trawler and being in command of each day, it took no skill to take someone's money and count change, and the drudgery got to him. So he went back to Louisiana, harboring dreams of owning his own boat and being in a world where he had grown up among people he had known since childhood. Working on the water was essential to his personality and it pulled him back to the fishing grounds he had known as a boy. A shrimp boat and the Gulf were his calling, not a store that closed him in for eight hours a day and forced him to breathe floor wax odor, dust, and oily exhaust fumes from cars. His element was on the water, where the rhythm of the days, months and seasons settled into his bones like an invisible tonic that never went away.

He went to work for Pierre Savoy, Tom's father, shrimping the inland bays, bayous and shallow waters of the Gulf that he had hunted and fished from the time he was ten. It wasn't as promising as clerking in the drugstore, because what he made depended on his catch, but he had his freedom and was with friends and neighbors. Louisiana was where he could absorb the subtle turning of the seasons, where he blended with every aspect of life. It was home.

*   *   *

But working conditions changed when Tom Savoy took over after his father's death during the Great Flood of '27, and he instigated a new rule that wiped out one weekend and made it impossible for Al, Jane and other couples to come in and go to Sunday Mass. Even when the shrimp weren't running, Savoy expected his boats to spend two weeks in the Gulf without coming in. With only a weekend off before heading back to work, Al attended Saturday and Sunday Mass. A long weekend and a late Monday morning start were forbidden. The boats had to be moving as daylight outlined the trees and painted the landscape and water. Standing at the docks when the crews launched, Savoy trimmed a crew's share of their next catch by five percent if any boat left late.

Shouldered with a choking work schedule, religion became Al's ally. He never missed a day without saying a rosary and, on Sundays, when he was at work, he said three rosaries, one for himself, then Jane and Rene. And on lonely Saturday nights, when the dark waters of the bay merged with the star-clustered sky, he'd tally up his weaknesses and make a silent confession, an *Act of Contrition* and ask God to keep Jane safe until he and Rene could fill the boat and go back home and enjoy their precious time together. He loved his work, but she made work worthwhile.

When another boat approached Al steered into the right side of the stream but kept space to maneuver. The *Miss Jane* was thirty-five feet long, wooden hulled, with a broad beam and a wide deck and stern. The wheel house near the bow had five windows for good visibility, and there was a small room behind the wheelhouse for two cots, a propane stove, and drawers for storing clothes, canned goods and other items.

Although it was a company-owned boat, Al and Jane treated it like their own by keeping things in better shape than most of the other crews. Jane mopped the wheelhouse, wiped the cabin down and cleaned the windows every time Al docked. He had also recently painted the hull and wheelhouse with a coat of white and accented the roof and railing in bright green.

Though underpowered for the trawler's size, the hundred horse power engine ran problem-free; and as the result of Al's habitual tinkering, *Miss Jane* had gone five years without developing problems with the engine, transmission or power train. Al also took advantage during the wintry off-season by hoisting the boat out of the water so he and Rene could scrape the hull clear of barnacles, giving them a slight edge in speed over the other boats and a five percent greater range over a boat that didn't have a clean hull.

* * *

Al looked out the door as Rene passed by the wheelhouse, holding a needle and twine in his hands and clenched his teeth as Rene slid out of sight behind the wheelhouse. Because they generally turned in the largest monthly poundage, Tom had hinted that Rene could have his own boat in the near future. Having struggled five years before Al got back on Savoy's good side, he was concerned that Rene joining up could open the old wounds with Tom.

Al cursed the war and the problems it brought and his old bitterness surfaced about the armistice from the Great War that should have ended all future conflicts. The the flowery statements had proven to be worthless in the face of new events. But there was one bright spot; Hitler was slogging it out against Russia and Al hoped the Germans would lose their will to continue after the bloody Russian campaign.

If Rene did go, there was a chance that the fighting would end before he got involved in combat. As they drew near Pat's Landing, that hope gave him little comfort in the face of an uncertain future. With enemy submarines patrolling the Gulf, 1942 held more dangers for America than the Great War ever did. The Germans had deadly subs, the airplane had become a lethal weapon, and European cities were being bombed down to their foundations.

As they approached the village, he decided to push the war aside for a couple of days, to make love to Jane, to eat gumbo, and to enjoy a weekend on the bayou.

2

Pat's Landing was more village than a town. Its name came from a pint-sized trapper called T-Pat Duhon, who emigrated from northwestern France after hearing stories about the fishing and hunting in South Louisiana. Since early Acadians got word back to friends and relatives about the natural beauty and bountiful wildlife in the coastal area, T-Pat was intrigued with New Orleans when he stepped off the boat and stayed in the city for two years. He got married and took advantage of a typhus outbreak by becoming a water salesman, catching it upriver and selling it to people in the city. He prospered until being threatened with arrest because he overcharged for his water, and he and his wife fled rather than be arrested. T-Pat chose an open spot southwest of New Orleans along a bayou, built a small cabin and became a trapper, but his life was cut short, and fellow trappers named the camp site after him when T-Pat was bitten on the neck by a water moccasin and died. He had no chance to survive because it was a three-day trip by canoe to New Orleans, where the nearest doctor lived.

T-Pat's wife left after his death, but Pat's Landing developed in the early 1800s on dry ground along a waterway that the early settlers named Lower Bayou. Two miles north, the same stream came to be called Upper Bayou. No one could ever explain why the name was changed at such an ordinary spot on the same bayou. But everyone called it that from then on.

The people who settled the site were befriended by the local Houmas Indians, who at first were friendly, because they figured the whites couldn't populate the vast marsh that extended from Point Au Fer to Grand Isle, eighty miles to the east. Its mystifying complex of ponds and dense undergrowth required several days of travel by canoe and was nearly impossible to cross on foot. However, they were proven wrong sixty years later. By that time the sprawling area of bayous, ponds and lakes held a population of 4500 Cajuns that mixed with Sabines and Houmas and dominated the economy and the landscape.

A dock was built in the village for the small pirogues that were introduced to the settlers by the Indians, who showed the Cajuns how to make a canoe by burning a space in a cypress tree trunk and scraping it out. Shortly thereafter, cabins sprang up along the eastern side of the bayou, and since shrimp and fish were plentiful, Pat's Landing became a steady source of seafood.

By 1942 the village amounted to a collection of three taverns, a grocery store--owned by Tom Savoy--one lawyer's office, a gas station and garage, a restaurant and bar, a combination hardware and grocery store, also owned by Savoy, a Catholic church, two public schools, and the Savoy Shrimp Company warehouse.

Pat's Landing was promised better roads and the rumor persisted from local police jurors that the clamshell and unimproved segment of the road to Houma would be paved in a couple of years. The job was half completed by the time Huey Long was assassinated but then discontinued, so the paved road stopped five miles north of town. The southern section--not as wide as the northern half--followed the same route as the original horse and foot trail and washed out in low places when a heavy thunderstorm doused the area. The clamshells, dug out of Lake Pontchartrain, provided a road base for a couple of seasons before sinking into the marsh. Consequently, fresh loads of shells—cheaper than asphalt--were laid down once again.

With the war raging and ration cards limiting everything from groceries to gasoline, the southern half of the road into Pat's Landing had lost much of its importance.

*   *   *

The weekly *Houma Courier* had been tossed onboard the day before by the company iceboat and lay at Rene's feet. Savoy kept the iceboat on a schedule so the shrimpers wouldn't have to come back to Pat's Landing to be resupplied. Newspapers were always a welcome addition. In an average two-month span, Savoy figured the iceboat paid for itself by saving running time, fuel and days lost by keeping the shrimpers on the water and making him money.

Rene scanned the headlines as the *Miss Jane* slipped past a group of small houses two miles south of Pat's Landing where a few Sabine Indians lived. Designed differently than houses in the village, their structures perched on stilts to avoid high water from a hurricane or storms. The blackened cypress siding and rusty tin roofing gave the houses a deep weather-beaten look. Each house had a fifty-gallon drum, situated to catch rainwater from the roof, and an access pipe that ran from the bottom of the barrel into the house.

After sewing up a hole in the netting, Rene sat against the wheelhouse wall and looked through the paper, folding the front page to counter a mild breeze that fluttered over the deck and brushed his face and shoulders. He rehearsed his plans for the weekend and admired the passing landscape. He'd miss the beauty of the swamp, but with two days to take care of details before leaving for the war, a sense of adventure fluttered inside his chest like butterflies.

Moving from the front page of a story about U-boats, he looked across the deck at an ammunition can. Crushed on two corners, it was black and rectangular, like the cans his father carried when they went bird hunting. It was a foot long and six inches high with a small swastika on the lid. The can hadn't even been in salt water long enough to degrade the paint. Rene had discovered the can and the body of the mariner when he winched up the net in water not more than twenty feet deep.

Returning to the article, it said that enemy submarines were no longer able to operate closer than fifty miles off the coasts of the country as a result of counter-measures taken by the Navy and the Coastal Patrol, a sub-group of the Truman Committee had explained in a two-hour conference with Secretary Knox. The article also pointed out that the secretary was opposed to the use of boats shorter than 110 feet in length, insisting that smaller craft, mostly made of wood, were in danger of burning and did not carry sufficient armament to combat submarines.

Rene wondered what would happen if he and his father confronted a U-boat. The *Miss Jane* was less than half that length and underpowered too. The shallow water gave shrimpers security only because subs required more depth to maneuver. He guessed they needed at least twenty feet to clear the hull, and since shrimpers seldom worked beyond thirty-five feet of water, it would be foolhardy for a sub to come closer to shore when their only prey in shallow water might be an unarmed shrimp trawler of no military importance.

But not far away was an area called Ship Shoal, a long trench where a sub could operate without fear of running aground. Scooped out like a bath tub and shallow on both ends, it was a popular place to trawl for larger shrimp, though the northern sector of the shoal touched the boundary of the ten-mile limit. A U-boat laying in the trench would be too far south to be seen by a watchtower or a member of the coastal patrol, so it could surface, fire its deck gun or a torpedo, and submerge before an airplane or patrol boat could respond.

The Coast Guard kept a close watch on the ten-mile limit, and violators were stopped, admonished to stay in their designated sector, and turned back. During the daytime, some tankers and freighters operated in shallow water in order to avoid submarines lurking further offshore. The Coast Guard also reminded the trawler crews to anchor on the north side of an island at night, putting land between themselves and the open water. The plan was for the shrimpers' safety, though some skippers believed it would be a wasted torpedo for a U-boat to target a shrimp boat and scoffed at the idea of being hit. A couple of fishermen didn't represent a military target. Except for a 22-caliber pistol, a rifle, and a shotgun to kill sharks, they were no match for machine guns and the four-inch deck gun of a German sub.

Rene moved to a story about Nazi successes in the Russian campaign that brought the Germans close enough to see the skyline of Moscow. In another article Japanese forces captured a portion of the Aleutian Islands, giving them a base to attack Alaska. But what held his attention was the summation of the Battle of Midway, about the outcome being closer to a draw than a victory for the United States.

He looked at a quarter-page layout for the Delta Bank and Trust Company of Houma, which showed four artillery pieces spouting a blazing trail over the slogan; "Buy Bonds for Guns, Planes, Tanks, Ships—Bonds for Victory. Fight as hard with your dollars as American Boys are fighting with their lives."

Every page of the paper had slogans about contributing to the war and mentioned that all businesses were supporting the troops, airmen, and sailors.

Rene also read the words of Secretary Patterson and the back of his neck grew warm the way it used to when his football coach chewed him out for not tackling hard enough. "No sacrifice made at home can compare with those in the Armed Forces. We need every man who can fight." He dropped the paper and walked to the starboard railing, where thick marsh grasses on the bank almost touched the boat, and he closed his eyes and imagined what it would be like to serve on the flight deck of an aircraft carrier. Being a member of the launch crew appealed to him, goggled and gloved, pulling the chocks from underneath the wheels of a torpedo bomber or a Hellcat, the wind from the propeller blowing his shirt against him so hard that the fabric felt like part of his skin, the signal to launch after he had cleared the wings, and the plane gathering speed as it accelerated down the deck; another sortie flying into combat that he had helped launch.

From his background of working on shrimp boats, he was convinced he would make a natural seaman. Rather than carrying a rifle in the Army, the sea and boats were his element.

When Al called him, Rene went toward the wheelhouse, still dwelling on the attractive aspects of his plans.

But his father's attitude blew away Rene's mood. "Don't you think you should talk this enlistment idea over with your mother?"

Rene rolled his eyes. "Whatever she says won't change my mind."

Al pointed a finger at him. "Your mother has a right to be heard. Maybe she can talk some sense into your head since you won't listen to me."

Rene threw up his hands. "I'll get the same old reasons from her that I've already heard from you."

"She's your mother!" Al bellowed. "You're not running out like a thief in the night. If you're going to go, you'll leave only after giving us the courtesy of listening to our opinions."

"Okay," he answered. "I'll talk to her at supper tonight."

Al ran one hand through his salt-and-pepper hair, blew out a gust of air and closed his eyes momentarily. "Savoy isn't going to like you leaving."

Rene nodded, "I'll talk to him. It'll be okay."

"He'll be mad as hell."

"I don't see why. I'm just another deck hand. He'll find someone else."

The veins in Al's neck stood out. "You're not just another deckhand. You're my son. And you may not be aware of it, but Savoy keeps an eye on you."

"Why do you say that?"

Al pursed his lips and paused before answering. "He's probably trying to decide if you'll go against him like he thinks I did a long time ago."

"What do you mean?" Rene asked quickly.

Al changed his tone. "Aahh, I shouldn't have brought up ancient history."

A look of curiosity emerged onto Rene's face. "What happened between you two?"

"Forget I said anything."

But Rene didn't back down. "No way. You brought it up and I want to know."

Al searched through the window, checking his position as they neared the dock. "I wonder if your mother will meet us. I don't see her."

Rene moved closer. "What are you hiding?"

"Let it rest." Al said. "You only know him as the boss. I've known him since he and I were boys. He can act like the devil himself sometimes."

"I know that." Rene replied. "I've seen him angry. But he's always been nice to me."

"You haven't heard the whole story," Al countered.

*   *   *

Tom Savoy stood on the dock and watched the *Miss Jane* edge up to an open berth. The Savoy Shrimp Company behind him, the largest building in Pat's Landing, was a hundred feet long, with cypress siding on the walls and a tin roof that formed a ridgeline down the center. Some sections had been replaced, so different shades of rust broke up any hint of a pattern. The outside walls needed paint; several sections facing the bayou were peeling from the constant assault of humidity, rain, and sun.

"Tom and I had our problems. Let's leave it at that," Al said, slapping the wheel and shrugging his shoulders. "I'm giving you my opinion, but you need to make up your own mind."

Al opened the boat's log, ran his eyes down the figures and closed it. Spider web lines around both eyes and deep creases in his forehead etched his profile from working in the sun for more than twenty years.

Rene touched him on one arm. "What haven't I heard?"

Al steered the *Miss Jane* closer to the ice boat, which was twice the size of a trawler and glistened from a new coat of white paint on its hull and wheelhouse. Savoy's 1941 Chrysler was parked at the end of the warehouse, entirely black, except for a chrome strip that ran along the bottom of the hood. The Chrysler sported a radio, an improvement over Tom's previous car, which he had sold to Al. The Chrysler reminded Al of a huge lump of coal.

Al didn't begrudge Tom his new car. He was happy to drive his own '37 Chrysler. The price was right--$250. It had a solid feel and a smoother ride than his Ford pickup that bounced over bumps and leaked water onto the seat when it rained. Tom had added the price of the Chrysler onto Al's house note of $25 a month. He had four more payments to go and Al would own the car, a brown four-door, with black fenders and a tan, cloth interior. Al had no complaints. The paint was in good shape and the engine ran smoothly.

Al shifted his gaze toward Tom's house not far away, a Greek revival, sprawling structure, with wide concrete steps, four white columns in front and a porch that ran the width of the front. Since he enjoyed showing off his new car, Tom seldom walked anywhere. Like his house, Tom's Chrysler was the fanciest one in town. He even drove the short distance to his store, though he could walk there in three minutes.

"Tom complains about money and he's driving a year-old car worth more than a thousand bucks," Al remarked. "I'm lucky to make that much in ten months."

Rene ignored the comment and held his ground, his words coming out hard-edged.

"Don't act like you didn't hear what I said. What are you not telling me?"

"Get ready for docking," Al ordered, steering the boat parallel with the dock and cutting back the engine. "And stand by with a line."

Rene closed his eyes, clamped his lips together and left the wheelhouse, slapping the door jamb with both hands.

3

Tom Savoy stood four inches shy of six feet and had a prominent belly that pushed on his belt buckle and made it disappear beneath the shirt. His short legs were large and muscular and his thick arms pressed against the sleeves of his white shirt, which was soaked at both armpits. Though he never did any significant work around the dock, his face and head were always covered with sweat on a warm day. His thick neck supported a large, fleshy face, a broad forehead and coal-dark eyes, and his black hair shined from too much Wildroot hair oil. Since a no-nonsense expression was permanently etched onto his face, he rarely smiled, and appeared to be in a hurry most of the time. His capacity for anger was well known; he had fired one of his dockhands a year before when the man said the warehouse gang would like a coffee break once in a while.

Tom called to Al in a loud voice as the engine died. "Why are you coming in so early? You still have two more hours of daylight."

Al tossed the bowline to Manny Duhon and answered. "Didn't you get the report from Woody?"

"Yeah, but you still have plenty of time left."

Al pointed toward the rear of the trawler. "That boy needs proper care."

"Why didn't you set up one more drag on your way in?"

"Damn it, Tom," Al replied, "I won't put care for the dead over any amount of shrimp."

"Alright," Tom answered, raising one hand and nodding toward the back deck. "How large is your catch?"

"About four hundred pounds."

"You can head back out in the morning."

Al stuck his head through the door of the wheelhouse, took his logbook, and aimed it toward Savoy. "I don't like one-day weekends. You know that. Rene and I are still the best crew, aren't we?"

"That doesn't matter," Savoy shot back. "We need to catch all we can while the price is stable."

Al put the logbook on the shelf in the wheelhouse, stepped outside, and closed the door. "There's a war on. Nothing will change as long as price controls are in effect and the shrimp will still be there Monday."

"But the Price Commission didn't freeze my operating costs."

Al grabbed his notebook and a small suitcase and answered without looking at Savoy.

"Other than finding that poor mariner, it's been a good trip. Besides, you have half the money on the bayou already."

Tom shook his head. "A man can never have enough while the government has one hand in his pocket and steals his employees. I just lost Moses Oubré this week. He left for the shipyards in New Orleans and didn't say a thing. Just packed up and left. This damn war is ruining everything," he groused, clenching one fist and shaking it. "But I'll raise hell if anyone else tries to leave. How can I hold onto people when the war keeps taking them?"

When Al didn't reply, Savoy turned to his right and snapped at Manny Duhon, who stood near the bow, staring toward the stern. "Manny, get your worthless butt in gear and help carry the body. And drag that water hose over here and wash down the deck after you get him out of there. I don't pay you to sit around doing nothing." He pointed toward Manny's bare feet. "And put your boots on. I'll not have you working in the shrimp with your damn dirty feet." He turned toward Al. "After the shrimp are weighed, we'll settle up."

"Give it to Rene," Al said, stepping onto the dock. "I'm going home for a few minutes."

Tom's eyes hardened, but he didn't object. "Okay," he responded. "Tell Jane hello for me."

Al kept walking without making a reply, and Tom's attention returned to Manny, who hadn't moved. "Damn it, boy, are you deaf?"

Manny glanced toward the boat and then at Tom. "I don't ..."

"You get down there and help Rene with the body if you want to keep your job," Tom roared.

Manny slipped on his white boots, stepped onto the deck and followed Rene, who swept the tarp away. The ambulance driver, who had also gotten on board, tilted one end of a litter to Rene. "I'll take the shoulders, and you two get his feet," he suggested to Rene.

Before touching the mariner, Manny jerked his head to one side and spit twice.

"Come on," Tom said. "We need to get the shrimp unloaded."

Rene bent over the body and waited for Manny to do the same. "Take a deep breath, and hold it."

Manny nodded, took hold of one side, and lifted as Rene raised the other. Then they moved the body to the litter nearby and hoisted it toward the ambulance.

Free of the litter, Manny stepped back and spit again, igniting Tom's criticism. "Hell, Manny, you've smelled rotten shrimp worse than that. Now grab the hose and wash off the deck before you open the hatch to the shrimp."

Dragging the water hose behind him, Manny began at the wheelhouse and worked the water toward the stern. Close to Rene in size, Manny was a couple inches shorter, but with heavy chest muscles and skin as brown as mahogany. Similar to other Sabine Indians, he had a dark complexion and broad cheekbones, but his hair was brown and wavy. He went without shoes unless working on the boats or during cold weather. As a result, his feet were flat and his toes had separated from years of going barefoot. The bottoms were so thick he could walk on clamshells without pain and he could kick a football barefooted as well as anyone wearing shoes.

Manny worked the docks and in the warehouse but was not allowed on the boats without Tom's permission. He had never given Tom trouble by drinking on the job or being late for work but was restricted to loading and unloading the boats, packing the iceboat with supplies, and hosing down the warehouse floor after processing a load of shrimp. The dock hands were generally Sabines and coloreds and weren't trusted to spend two weeks on the water where they had to take orders from the skipper and stay sober. In earlier times, Pierre Savoy had put some of them on his boats, but it hadn't worked out, and Tom continued the pattern.

Manny was the youngest of the dock crew and the best worker. He didn't slow down when the humidity and temperature were high, he rarely complained, and he didn't come to work hung over. He lived with his mother, Bootsy, in a small house on the north side of town, next door to other Sabines and coloreds but separated from the Cajuns. Manny and Bootsy's old frame house sat on cypress blocks. It had a porch that ran along the front and was protected from the rain by an overhanging tin roof. The small front yard was a mixture of marsh grass, weeds and wild plants that turned into a quagmire when winter rains hit after the holidays and often lingered until March. A heavy rainstorm flooded the grass and ran underneath the house, and after a week of wet weather, the yard reeked of rotting vegetation that remained until sunshine dried things out.

Because his mother took in laundry to supplement her job as a cook at Cheramie's restaurant and bar, Manny had strung three lengths of wire from the front wall of the house to a Pecan tree near the road, and his mother seldom missed a weekend to have someone's clothes drying on the lines. Taking in laundry provided Bootsy and Manny with a few extra dollars.

Manny had never known his father, and Bootsy kept her maiden name after Manny's birth, so no one knew if the man lived in the area or if he was still alive, and interest in her gradually dwindled after several years because Bootsy kept to herself and went to Mass regularly.

While Manny's features mostly blended with the other Sabines, his brown hair made him a curiosity. The rumor persisted that Manny was Tom Savoy's son, but Tom treated Manny the same as he did his other dock hands and yelled at him with the same sarcasm.

*   *   *

Manny grabbed the small shovel to scoop up the extra shrimp while Rene took the hatch board and leaned it against the back wall of the cabin. Working in a relay, Manny poured the shrimp into a tub and handed a full one to Rene, who then gave it to one of the dock hands who carried it to the conveyer belt in the warehouse.

"Pick the ice out," Rene cautioned, taking out random pieces Manny had overlooked and tossing them in the water.

"Yeah, yeah." Manny answered. "Maybe I'll stick some inside the shrimp and reduce some of the fat man's money," he said, gesturing toward Tom's office.

But it wasn't possible. The crew also picked over the shrimp and Tom deducted five percent from the weight if noticeable amounts of ice made it to the scales. Al and Rene got a true weight most of the time, but it was rare when Savoy didn't adjust the poundage, something every skipper couldn't challenge. And it was impossible for a man to unload his catch at another dock when he didn't own his own boat.

Manny bent over the shrimp, scraped off a layer of ice, filled the tub, and lifted it above his shoulders to Rene. The hatch opening gave him room to stand but also trapped the strong odor of the catch, filling him with the fresh smell of shrimp. The routine of unloading shrimp was mastered by the time he was fourteen, and few of the crew could match his stamina. In a busy day he could unload several boats without being tired, while the other dock hands took a break after each one.

After finishing the ninth grade, Manny quit school and started working for Savoy, much to the football coach's disappointment, because he was fast and strong. Still attracted to the game, because catching and running came naturally to him, he'd watch the team practice, sometimes throwing the ball to Rene or Ray Anderson, another player, but it only lasted until the coach saw him and made him stop.

When practice was over they'd walk home together during Rene's senior year, occasionally sneaking a bottle of Jax beer at Cheramie's bar and restaurant, a small, weathered building close to the football field. Overlooking the front door was a large, wooden replica of a Jax beer bottle that stood as tall as the rooftop and was visible a block away, while a Regal Whiskey sign on the opposite side of the door invited anyone with a taste for the hard stuff.

Old man Cheramie was a shrimper who had gotten out of the business before the big flood of '27 and now let his nephew run the boat. He sold beer to anyone who had fifteen cents, but to get served, Manny, Rene, Ray and other minors had to go to the back door like the Sabines and colored men, knock on the door and wait for Cheramie to serve them.

His rule to the boys was one beer per person. No seconds.

* * *

The war touched the local boys as much as anyone in New Orleans, Baton Rouge or Lake Charles. Because Manny and Rene were the only sons in their family, Tom had gone to the draft board and asked to have them exempted, arguing that good employees were a commodity. One change he hoped for was the rumor that agricultural deferments would be given to farmers and fishermen, and it couldn't come soon enough to suit him. The draft board was taking nearly every young man who walked through the door, and that threatened his business. He wanted young, strong men, not old ones who were unreliable or got drunk every weekend.

Pat's Landing had already felt the war's impact. Rene's friend, Ray Anderson, one of three boys in his family, enlisted when he turned eighteen, and news came four months later that he had been killed in his first action in North Africa. He was buried in the church cemetery, two rows away from T-Pat Duhon, and people wondered if they should reserve additional spaces for others who go to the war and do not survive.

In the aftermath of Ray's death, Rene had talked to Manny about joining the Navy and planned for Manny to go with him, but he didn't have Rene's enthusiasm.

Rene looked around to make sure no one was listening and then leaned toward Manny. "Are you going to enlist with me?"

"Why are you pestering me about this again?"

Rene ignored Manny's question. "We'll take the bus in the morning."

"For the tenth time, the answer is no."

"Why?"

"Do I have to draw you a picture?" Manny said. "My mother has no husband," he explained, pointing to Rene. "If anything happened to you, your father will look after your mom, but my mother has no one else." He gave a shoulder shrug. "If the Germans come into Louisiana, I'll fight. But until then, I'm staying here."

"German subs aren't more than thirty miles south of us at this very moment."

"And they can stay there."

Rene tried again "The war won't last very long. We'll probably be back in a year," he added. "Think about the places we could see."

Manny stopped working. "What did that dead mariner see?" He picked up his shovel and continued scooping. "You go, if that'll make you happy."

"Fine," Rene returned. "I never figured for you to go back on a promise."

"I never promised," Manny snapped. "I said I'd think about it. I did, and I say no."

"Well, think harder," Rene demanded.

"Stop pushing me."

Rene moved toward the dock with a full tub and handed it to a dock hand. "Stubborn," he hissed as he bent close to Manny.

But Manny didn't say anything.

Rene stopped short of calling Manny a coward, which would have started a fight.

Since Al had been the last boat in, and they weren't pressed for time, Manny took a brief break, peeled off his shirt and wiped his chest with a small towel he carried in a back pocket of his jeans. Streaks of sweat ran off his muscled shoulders and down to his beltline. He wiped the moisture away, stuffed the towel in his pocket, and looked toward the office.

"Are you really going to enlist?"

"Tomorrow or the next day," Rene answered quietly, to avoid being overheard by two dock hands leaning against the wall of the warehouse, sharing a cigarette.

"You haven't told Savoy, have you?"

"Not yet. I want to talk it over with my folks tonight. But I'll tell him tomorrow."

Manny blew a low whistle. "I'd like to see his face. He'll explode like a firecracker."

Rene was unconcerned. "I can't help it."

Manny cocked his head and looked down the bayou. "Marie won't like you leaving."

"I think she understands. It's not like I'm going away forever. The war will end soon and I'll come back."

Manny's eyes narrowed. "I bet Ray and that mariner kid thought the same thing."

"Is that why you won't go? You're afraid of what might happen to you?"

Manny's eyes narrowed and he clenched his jaw. "No. But if I enlisted, my mother would be alone. I'll go if I get a draft letter, not any other way. Can't you understand?"

Before Rene could reply, Al came back to the boat to get his dirty clothes. "Remember to see Tom about our money."

"Okay."

"Supper will be ready soon. Don't be late."

Rene looked toward his house a short distance away and saw his mother walking toward them. She had on her favorite red dress, which she often wore when he and his father returned home. He waved to her and got back to work.

Manny glanced in Jane's direction and broke into a smile. "Two weeks is a long time. Do you think they're going to do it before you get home?" he asked, laughing.

Rene bent down and grabbed Manny's head with both hands and squeezed him, but Manny pulled away, tossed a piece of ice at him and went into a fighting crouch.

"If the screen door is hooked when you get there, you'd better sit down and wait quietly."

*   *   *

After the shrimp had been weighed, packed in ice, and stored in the cooler, Rene started toward the office, while Manny stayed behind to spray down the deck and wash the tubs. It was the height of the lake shrimp season and the warehouse was packed with supplies, making it difficult for Rene to walk a straight line to the office. Boxes of canned goods and sacks of rice, flour, onions and potatoes filled the floor to his right, while on the left were extra tri-nets, collapsed wooden trawls, cans of grease, oil drums, grease guns, rubber hoses, boxes of gaskets, and barrels of gasoline. Cables for the booms and two-inch mooring lines lay coiled on the floor, while dozens of yellow oilskins hung on nails like animal hides in a taxidermy shop. Mushroom and Danforth anchors and boxes of shackles with their pins in place through the openings, were scattered along one wall. All the metal equipment bore an inch-sized dot of white paint to announce that it belonged to the company.

Piled together were orange life vests and rectangular two-man rafts, all Coast Guard requirements. Savoy had argued that since they were necessary, the government should pay for them, but he had no choice if he wanted to avoid a fine. Since the Pearl Harbor attack, inspectors from New Orleans came every six months to check the boats and the safety equipment required for each crew. The boats' logbooks were also studied to make certain each vessel had gone through the inspection station and that the blackout rule was being followed every night the crews anchored in the bays.

Cooperation with the Coast Guard was critical. They could stop Savoy from running his boats or make him work another sector of water, and with the lake shrimp moving into deeper waters during the height of the summer, restrictions would ruin the season for him and create a financial hardship for the trawler crews.

Rene walked past the noisy ice machine, loudly chewing up ice for the boats. The freezer coils and compressor were enclosed in a small room no larger than a closet. The crusher ejected the chips onto the belt and down a metal chute to the dock.

Rene tucked in his shirt and ran a handkerchief over his face to catch the sweat trickling down his nose. The warehouse was so hot in the summer that the only relief came from two fans in the roof at opposite ends of the building. They turned constantly during hot weather, but their effectiveness on the floor was hardly noticed, making it necessary for men in the warehouse to work without a shirt.

Rene knocked before entering the office, a rule Savoy strictly enforced. He fired one dock hand a month earlier that was in a hurry to tell Savoy that the ice crusher had stopped working and had rushed into the office without knocking.

Savoy called out, "Come in."

Rene avoided a rope noose that hung beside the doorway and wiped his white boots on a floor mat underneath a sign which reminded everyone to clean their feet or stay out. A holdover from the Depression, the noose had discouraged speculators who had come to buy shrimp boats for pennies on the dollar. Tom had copied the idea from the Houma Courthouse, where a noose appeared at an auction in 1933. He put nooses on all of his trawlers, and buyers stayed away after two speculators were run off with a shotgun load of salt and pepper fired at them.

Since the Parish Sheriff didn't like outsiders taking advantage of the hard times, nothing was done about the incident, and word spread that the shrimpers would defend their property with guns.

Savoy's tidy office was nicely furnished, in contrast to the cramped atmosphere of the Warehouse. The polished hardwood floor smelled of fresh wax, and Tom sat behind a wooden desk that faced the door. It had belonged to his father, one of the few items Tom had salvaged when he got into the warehouse after the flood of '27 receded. Cleaned, stripped and refinished, the desk bore few signs of wear.

Tom's pear-shaped body took up the entire black leather chair that was on rollers so he could slide from one end of his desk to the other without standing.

A large, framed map of the United States hung behind the desk, dotted with red pins--the eventual distribution points for Savoy Shrimp along the east coast and south to Charleston, Savannah, Birmingham, Atlanta, Mobile, and Beaumont. Besides selling to stores in Houma and Thibodeaux, he sent weekly loads to New Orleans and Baton Rouge. A yard-long oil painting with a nautical theme hung on the wall to Rene's right, depicting an iceboat plowing through the stormy waters of the Gulf. Long streams of gray engine exhaust expanded over the boat's frothy wake, making it appear to be running from a mass of dark storm clouds which threatened to converge on the vessel.

Despite having seen the painting as long as he could remember, the seascape captured Rene's imagination and heightened his desire to skipper the iceboat after he returned from the war. The iceboat had a better schedule than the shrimp boats because the crew got home more frequently and received a regular salary instead of depending on the catch.

A portrait of Huey Long hung on the wall to Savoy's left. Clad in his usual dark suit, white shirt and black tie, his thick hair was combed neatly over his forehead, capturing the image of him when he was a senator. Despite the passage of seven years since Huey's assassination, Tom still kept a border of black mourning ribbon pinned to the frame.

A new picture Rene hadn't seen before, proclaiming the military importance of food, rested inside a wooden frame next to Huey. It showed a paratrooper descending in a white parachute with a wooden food box near him, whose caption said; "where our men are fighting, our food is fighting."

Tom let Rene get a good look before he pointed at the food and the soldier. "I found it last week in *Colliers*. I liked it right away and had it framed. Food is a weapon, and we're bringing in weapons with every boat. The way I look at it, we're fighting this war on our own terms."

Tom noticed how Rene's eyes returned to the iceboat. "You like that painting? You always stare at it when you come in."

"Yes, I do," Rene confessed. "The storm makes it look like a cold day in the Gulf."

Tom chuckled. "I had one of the WPA artists paint it from my idea. A couple of them were in Houma working on the new city hall. If you ever go there, they painted the murals in the lobby. I gave one of them twenty bucks and he worked nights to finish the boat in a week."

"The waves, the smoke, and the storm clouds look so real."

"They do at that," Tom chimed in, "but I wouldn't want to get caught in such a storm, so be careful out there."

"Summer thunderstorms are bad enough for me."

"I have your money ready," Tom said, sliding to his right. He leaned down and opened a small safe on the floor near one of the legs and out of sight from anyone else in the room. "You and your father had another fine trip. If every crew worked as hard as you two, we'd put Louisiana on the map. Your father isn't like some who sleep late and get drunk now and then. You make a dependable pair." He let out a chuckle. "God made the world, Rene, but he gave the mud to Louisiana, and that's what the shrimp love. We've been blessed."

"Yes, sir," Rene answered, anxious to get his money and go home.

Tom opened the safe with one of several keys on a chain attached to a belt loop on his pants. He smiled as he put fourteen chits on the desk, an expression that filled Tom's face whenever he handled money. The brass chits were the size of a silver dollar, their values according to the numbers stamped on one side. Tom set out ten-tens and four-fives. He had no chits for small change. It was more convenient to round the total off within five dollars when figuring a crew's share. He always rounded the total down, and Rene hadn't heard of anyone who had ever challenged Tom's math and kept his job.

Everyone who worked for Savoy was paid in chits. It was a holdover from Pierre's practice and a way to control the employees' expenses. They then had to go by the company store to convert their chits into dollars and pay their grocery bills. Tom held the advantage because the nearest bank was a forty-minute drive into Houma.

A year earlier one man had demanded to receive his salary in dollar bills, and Savoy paid him. Then the man was fired. After Tom put the word out on him, it took the guy thirty days to find another shrimping job, and it was far away in Mobile.

Rene pocketed the chits after adding the total in his head. It didn't pay to make it obvious that he was counting them in front of Tom because he was known to go into a rage when one of his employees questioned his addition.

"By the way," Tom said. "I told your father to take part of Monday off. We need to look at that vibration on the driveshaft. He had mentioned it the last trip in. Was it any worse this time?"

Rene shook his head. "No. It made a racket when we held full power, but we didn't do that unless the drag got heavy."

"Just to be safe, we'll take a look. And while we're going over the driveshaft, break out the caulking and give the hull a quick once-over. It won't take long and you should be back in the water by noon and in time to tie up for the night. That way you won't lose any work on Tuesday."

Tom looked toward the desktop and pressed the flesh of his double chin against the starched collar of his shirt. "Sam said your bill is twenty dollars. Don't forget to clear it up."

"I won't," Rene answered.

*   *   *

Sam Duplantis, Tom's cousin, who managed the company store, was thirty-five, short and slender, with a lean face and a smile for everyone. He wasn't fit for the war because he'd lost three fingers from his left hand when he caught it in the winch on a shrimp boat. Sam had gotten distracted when he reached down for the handle of the power takeoff just as the brake released and his hand got caught in the rotating spool, smashing his fingers and ripping the flesh off the bones.

Sam chewed tobacco from the time he got up until he went to bed and carried a tin can with him to spit in and a plug of tobacco in a pants pocket so he could take a dip whenever he felt like it. He kept to himself and had no family, but on weekends, if he didn't go into Houma for what he called his "nookie time," he could be found at his house north of town, tinkering on his 1938 Lincoln coupe. Other than shrimping for a few days when Kay, Tom's wife, ran the store, he was content to work on the car he dubbed his "stinkin' Lincoln." Sporting a red paint job and chrome strips along the fenders and down the centerline of the hood, horizontal grillwork in front of the radiator, and moon-shaped hubcaps on the wheels, the Lincoln was the most distinct car in the community, except Tom's new Chrysler.

People liked Sam, though he pestered them to pay their bills. He enjoyed telling jokes and seldom raised his voice to people who had a hard time settling their account. A master at making his own wine from grape juice and sugar, it was difficult to tell if Sam had consumed a liquid lunch, because the strong odor of his chewing tobacco enveloped him from morning to night. People avoided criticizing Tom in front of Sam, but he likewise wasn't immune from getting yelled at by Tom, if he failed to keep the money and the ration cards in order.

Rene turned to leave but Tom asked him to stay, and Rene turned around, not knowing what to expect.

"Did you see any signs of submarines this time?" Tom asked.

There was no telling how far that German can had drifted, and all he wanted was to go home. "No, we didn't," he answered, evading Tom's gaze.

"Not even when you brought up the kid's body?"

"It was shallow where we found him." Rene explained. "The current no doubt carried him for a few days."

"You have a point," agreed Tom. "No one's reported any sightings for a week." His face grew into a scowl. "Thank God May is over. The sub threat may be weakening, but Roosevelt still asks us to pull down our blinds and stay inside. The U-boats could still move down the East Coast and increase the pressure in Louisiana waters, but Washington seems not to worry about the activity in the Gulf." He shook his head in disgust. "With Huey gone, I wonder if the politicians in Baton Rouge and Washington care about Louisiana anymore. First the railroad bypassed Houma, and then the flood of '27 nearly wiped us out when Holcombe and those damned businessmen in

New Orleans blew the levee and flooded us. The banks didn't help in the Depression and now the government restricts us by keeping shrimpers out of deep water, thanks to the Coast Guard that patrols the ten-mile limit like they own it." He slammed both hands on his desk. "I wonder if we still count as Americans." He shook a finger at Rene, his eyes angry slits. "And we're the ones who fought in the Great War, then got spit on by Washington after they promised us a veteran's bonus. Well, my time will come. I don't know when, but my brother's death will be avenged. I haven't forgotten how Hoover, Roosevelt, and those spit-and-polish Army generals treated us like we were common criminals and tried to link us with the communists."

Still fuming five minutes after Rene had gone, Tom slid open a small drawer on the right side of the desk, took out a sheet of paper and read it again. Other than a brief message, there was no address, date or signature, and the envelope bore no detail to signify its origin. It was as if someone had sneaked into town and put the envelope in the mail box. But regardless of its source, the message teased Tom's imagination.

It read: "Are you tired of the war? Are you interested in making a bundle of money in a very short time? You will be contacted at a later date."

As he had done the day he received the letter, Tom resisted the urge to tear it into pieces. Instead, he folded the sheet and slid it back into the drawer. Its origin and the idea of quick, easy money intrigued him, and if the note produced something that was to his advantage, he wasn't about to pass up a lucrative payday.

*   *   *

Rene stepped onto the boat and picked up the German ammo can. There was no reason to let Savoy see it. The young mariner had enflamed him enough. Besides, an old can held no threat. He decided to put it with the other two that he kept in his bedroom.

Manny had just finished coiling the hose and wiping his hands.

"Let's grab a beer."

"I can't. I have lots to do before morning."

Manny showed no sign of anger anymore. "Are you still mad at me?"

"No. I just wish you were going with me."

"I can't leave her alone. I just can't. You must understand."

"I do. But I had hopes it would work out for us." He patted Manny on the shoulder and cracked a smile. "Imagine if both of us served on the same aircraft carrier. We'd frighten the Germans all the way back to Berlin."

Manny showed a weak smile but didn't respond, and an awkward silence developed between them.

Rene finally answered. "I'd better get home."

Manny hooted loudly. "I see a girl in your plans and it isn't your mother."

Rene didn't look back. "I'll come around about ten."

"Don't be late. I feel a thirst coming on."

Less than a moment later, the sound of an airplane filled the air, causing Rene to look skyward, as one of the Coastal Patrol planes followed the bayou toward the airport at Houma. The fuselage was difficult to make out until he saw the plane's propeller, a gray spinning circle in the fading light of the pale blue sky. The plane was also hard to spot from the ground because of its white belly, but as it passed overhead Rene could make out the struts supporting the wings and the large tires on the Stinson's main landing gear.

Thinking he saw the pilot wave, Rene did the same, though Joe Christy, his friend who flew with the Coastal Patrol, would have rocked his wings if he had been at the controls.

Joe had enlisted in the Coastal Patrol Volunteers after graduating from high school a year before Rene. The planes and pilots were based at the Houma airport but would soon be flying out of a camp on Grand Isle, a scrub-tree spit of sand and mud thirty-five miles to the southeast. According to Joe, the camp was nearly finished and would be functioning by the Fourth of July. After relocating there, the pilots would gain an hour of patrol time over staging out of Houma, fifty miles away.

Flying was a natural choice for Joe. Since his father had flown during WW I, Joe had grown up around airplanes. After the war his father bought a surplus Curtis JN-4H, nicknamed Jenny, for $250, and started the Southern Spray Company and convinced the rice farmers that planting seeds from the air was more efficient than doing it by hand. He then followed up by spraying the young rice stalks with pesticides. He also laid down nitrates on the cotton crops around Baton Rouge and acreages as far upriver as Vicksburg. It was a demanding job; he was gone most of the time during the warm months, first to the western part of the state for the rice, then north through Alexandria and east to Jackson for the cotton. The only time he stayed home was during the rainy season. He kept a small suitcase in the Jenny during spray season and slept in a bedroll underneath the lower wing of the biplane, saving the expense of a room.

He taught Joe to fly and Joe soloed at sixteen, so he had already logged fifty hours of flight time, more than any other cadet training with him in Baton Rouge shortly after Pearl Harbor. Joining the unit with a pilot's license already was a huge advantage for pilots who joined the Coastal Patrol.

Manny looked at the airplane and shouted at Rene. "Is that Joe Christy?"

"Don't know," Rene answered, "but that's what he flies. It's a Stinson Voyager. He and his dad bought it together." Rene checked the belly. "He must have dropped his bomb."

He followed the airplane until it disappeared beyond the tree line north of the warehouse.

"I bet Joe likes flying." Manny suggested.

"He says he does, but that's not for me. I'll take a boat anytime," Rene answered, continuing toward his house.

"It's better than carrying a rifle and getting shot like Ray did," Manny said. "Joe's up there where no one can hit him and no torpedoes can get him."

"I still think boats are safer."

"You'd better think about airplanes," Manny called out. "No submarine can hit an airplane. You'd be safe as a bird, like Joe."

"It'll never happen. I want a battleship or a carrier. We'll destroy those Nazi subs, if they're brave enough to stand and fight."

The sun was low as he walked along the bayou where branches from Live Oaks were draped with Spanish Moss that resembled giant spider webs. The shadows lengthened and the sky darkened as the sun slid toward the horizon, and the hot and humid air was motionless and damp and thick with the smell of bayou water, the faint odor from a kitchen stove, a dead fish or nutria nearby, all mixed with shrimp odors from the warehouse.

It wouldn't be long before Sam Duplantis made his rounds as the block captain, making sure everyone had pulled down their shades. The presence of a light on flat land could be seen twenty miles away, so the blackout rule had gone into effect in early '42. All the trucks and cars had their headlights covered with a chromed, metallic shield which had a horizontal slit called a cat eye that blocked the headlight beams from shining upward and giving away a vehicle's location.

While the job of block captain didn't pay anything, it was important in south Louisiana communities, and Sam had been chosen by the Bayou Parrish Commission because he was a well-known, dependable person and had been recommended by Tom Savoy, who promised that Sam would be faithful in the job. Tom also filled in as an alternate whenever Sam needed a day off.

The job was simple; violators were warned once, then fined if caught a second time and subjected to having their home inspected without warning by the sheriff, who looked under beds and in closets for secret radios, notes from spies, or anything of a suspicious nature. Block captains had the law behind them if someone didn't cooperate. So prevalent was the paranoia about coastal vulnerability that it only took a phone call and the F.B.I. or the sheriff would be knocking on the violator's front door.

Though they both had given out plenty of verbal warnings, until the practice became second nature to the residents, Sam and Tom had yet to violate anyone in Pat's Landing.

Sam also drove Tom's ice truck on its weekly rounds. He picked up extra blocks at an ice house in Houma and delivered them to Pat's Landing and to homes along the way. Anyone wanting ice left a colored card on their mail box, which told Sam how much to put in their icebox. Red was for a quarter-block, blue for half a block and green for an entire block. The business didn't return much profit, but by having his own truck, Tom served the entire bayou south of Houma.

Having control was as important to Tom as making money.

4

Despite having eaten their red beans and rice, with fried jalapenos on the side, neither parent had mentioned Rene's enlistment or the dead mariner. Rene had spoken to Jane about it before leaving on the last trip, but she had listened without commenting, and he was wary after her greeting this time had been different. She hadn't uttered a word when she gave him a hug. After he had grabbed her hands, pinned them against her waist and lifted her off the floor to kiss her on the forehead, she turned back toward the stove without responding to his joke about the cooking that he had to put up with on the boat.

In the pleasant aftermath of supper, the kitchen was filled with attractive odors of cooked beans, fried onions, and steamed rice, but an air of tension developed in the room.

Rene knew what to expect from his father. For two weeks they had argued nearly every day. But Rene had never been able to talk to his mother as he could his father. She wasn't as straight-forward. She communicated more with her eyes and facial expressions—a neutral glance, or a stare--the unspoken alarms Rene had experienced since childhood. When she was upset with him, silence was her main weapon, and her eyes could practically bore holes in his soul.

While he waited for both of them to say something, Rene remembered the chits in his pocket, so he dumped them on the green porcelain table and Al separated them into a pile, one for himself and one for Rene. Al slid Rene's toward him, but Rene took the top chit and handed it back.

"What's this for?" Al asked. "Did I miscount?"

"No," he explained, glancing toward his mother. "I want to pay for some of the expenses now that I'm going away."

His mother slapped a wooden spoon against a black kettle, wiped her hands on her apron and glared at him. "Are we going through this again?"

Rene struggled to look relaxed and rested one arm on the table. "Nothing has changed from two weeks ago. I simply want to join up."

Jane's voice raised a notch. "I know about that poor boy you brought in. Is that what you want, to end up floating in the water?"

"He was on a tanker. I plan to be on a carrier."

Jane sat in her chair and leaned toward him. "Please understand. You're our only son and we want to protect you. We want to remain a family."

"But I don't need protection."

She pointed toward the front door. "I bet that young mariner thought the same thing."

"I'll be okay. Don't worry."

Her tone softened into a plea. "But you're so young."

"Just about everyone else my age is gone."

"Not Manny."

"I think he's afraid," he responded, then backed off his accusation. "I mean he's afraid for his mother. He doesn't want her to be alone."

For a moment or two they were silent. Then Jane got up, went to the stove and scraped a pan with a wooden spoon, while Al grabbed a chit and spun it, and when it lost its momentum, he spun it again, his concentration fixed on the chit.

Al finally broke the silence. "Have you talked to Tom about leaving?"

"No. I'll do that in the morning."

"Then why are you bringing this up tonight?" Al asked in a stronger voice.

"Because you told me to talk to her first," Rene replied in the same tone.

Jane looked at one, then the other. "Have you two been planning this behind my back?"

Rene shook his head. "No, we haven't, Mama. But I couldn't leave the boat these last two weeks and see you, could I? So I'm talking to you now."

Jane tried again. "But why be in such a hurry? Give us a few more weeks to think it over."

"I want to go now," he said firmly. "The war won't last forever."

Jane shrugged her shoulders. "Then what else is there to say? Why are you even bothering to ask me?"

She turned back to the stove and sat a bowl beside the black kettle to hold the leftovers and wiped her eyes with both hands before spooning out the beans and rice. Moving over and positioning himself behind her, Rene took her by the shoulders and nudged her until she turned around. Twin rivulets of tears ran over the creases beneath her eyes and down her cheeks.

"I know it's my decision," he explained in a gentle manner, "but I want you to agree that it's the right thing to do. Ray went and ..."

Jane flared up, "Don't mention Ray. He's not here anymore."

"Well, I'm no different than he was when he enlisted."

"Yes, you are. You're my son," she insisted, grabbing him in a quick hug and squeezing his shoulders with both hands.

Rene waited until her grip relaxed and then separated from her, his face nearly touching hers. "I'll get by. You'll see. Ray was in the Army. I'm joining the Navy, and I'll be on a battle ship or a carrier."

"War isn't the same as a football game," she answered, gesturing toward Al. "All you have to do is look at your father. The first war got him a bullet to carry for the rest of his life, and now you want to do the same thing, or maybe worse, by not coming back?"

Al slapped the paper onto the table. "One man won't make a difference in this or any other war."

"Maybe so, but I have a right to go."

Al ran his teeth over his lower lip. "Yes. You're old enough to enlist without our signature," he agreed. "But you're being damned foolish."

"Don't curse at the table?" Jane insisted.

"Sorry," Al apologized. "But he's being foolish."

Jane set a refilled glass of tea in front of Rene and stared at him, examining him in a fresh way, both of her hands resting on the table, her faced close to him. "Are you sure this is what you want?"

He put one hand around the glass of tea and didn't meet her stare. "Yes."

"Even if we don't agree with you?"

"Yes."

She ran a hand through a damp ring on the table, her brown eyes narrowing behind her glasses. "Will you still go if it causes problems for your father and me?"

Al broke in. "That's not the issue. We're talking about his life, not ours."

"His life?" she countered. "What about our own? He's part of it too."

"I'll find another deck hand, that's all," Al said. He sipped his tea, drew the glass back from his face and looked as if he'd found something floating in the glass that required his attention. "I'll ask around and get a kid from Houma or Thibodeaux who's working for another company."

Jane smacked the table. "How are you going to do that when Savoy has no competitors any closer than Morgan City?" she demanded. "You remember what he said, and he's not a man for idle statements. I think he'd carry it out."

"What are you two talking about?" Rene asked, looking at his father, then his mother.

"It's time that you tell him," Jane pleaded.

Al waved a hand in the air. "Tom likes to hear himself talk. He won't do anything."

"We could lose the house. He said so."

Rene grabbed his mother's arm. "Why would you lose the house if I leave?"

Jane didn't give Al time to reply. "Tom heard a rumor that you planned to enlist and told your father that he wanted cash for the house if you left."

"Cash?" Rene repeated. "How can he do that when he signed a contract?"

Al and Jane looked at each other before Al answered, already looking tired. "We've been paying on the house for ten years. It was a handshake deal with Tom's father and a handwritten bill of sale; nothing fancy. There were no detailed conditions or anything like that, so it's easy for Tom to do what he wants." Al rubbed one arm. "And we're behind two payments."

"He can't change the rules. Not if it's in writing, can he?"

"The bill of sale doesn't say anything other than we'd make monthly payments on the fifth day of the month."

"But why would he do that because of something I did?"

Jane fixed her concentration on Al, her words locked inside a cold tone. "It's time he knows. Get everything out once and for all."

*   *   *

Al stared at the table and rubbed the knuckles of his left hand as he began. "Tom and I go back to grade school days. We even worked on the same trawler for a year. He always insisted on being the skipper, though Pierre told us to share the work and responsibilities. But Tom never did. He's the type who must be in control." Al paused and looked at Jane. "The trouble may have actually started over Kay," he confessed.

Jane looked surprised, but Al launched into the details before she could say anything.

"The three of us grew up together. Kay and I were childhood friends, but that's as far as it went. She loved to fish and Tom didn't. Sometimes she and I would spend an afternoon fishing and talking, and that drove Tom crazy. She only wanted to talk about Tom, so he had no cause to be jealous. I was just her sounding board."

Jane's voice was tinged with anger. "Why didn't you tell me about her?"

"There is nothing to say. The most I ever did was kiss her on the cheek once or twice. I liked her company. What boy wouldn't like such a pretty girl? But we were just friends."

Al reached across the table and grasped Jane's hands, rubbing them with his own. "Kay was a childhood friend, that's all. You're the only woman I've ever loved. And no matter what happens, you'll always be the only one for me."

Jane withdrew one hand, wiped a strand of hair from her eyes and put her hand back in his. "I've never been comfortable around her. Kay guards her feelings and never opens up. She isn't a warm person. She doesn't make light-hearted conversation and hardly ever smiles."

"That's Tom's influence. She adopted his ways," Al answered, giving her hands a gentle shake. "You're worth ten of her anyway."

Jane patted his hands and sat back in the chair. "She's not the issue here. Rene needs to know why you and Tom don't get along."

"Oh, we get along well enough." Al suggested. "Things just aren't what they used to be."

Jane wasn't satisfied. "You know what I mean. Tell him about Emile and Tom."

"I know about Emile," Rene put in. "He died in an accident."

"But you don't know the details."

Al fidgeted in his chair. "Those things don't apply to Rene. He has his own life now that he's grown."

"Wait a minute," Rene interrupted. "What are you hiding?"

"It was a long time ago," Al pleaded. "Let Rene do what he wants. We'll get along. We always have."

Jane rapped the table with the knuckles of one hand and leaned toward Al. "We're a family, and that man has the capability to hurt all three of us. Rene has a right to know why."

Al exhaled a batch of air, rubbed his forehead and began. "I was your age when I joined up. So was Tom. His birthday is a month before mine, in December. Emile was two years younger. But after Emile got Pierre to vouch that he was our age by signing for him, we all went in together." He gave out a bitter laugh. "Wilson had signed the Selective Service bill that established the draft, but we didn't wait to be called. We were going to save the world." He smiled, but it didn't warm his face. "Pierre was proud of his sons going to fight and put a big sign outside that said 'Death to the Huns.' He gave money to the war effort and matched the quota the government suggested, though I forget how much the amount was. But as I recall, it was fifty dollars per business. That was a lot of money back then."

Al looked at Rene for a reaction but got none and continued. "I felt the same way that you do now. We all did. We couldn't wait to get into uniform. We were full of vinegar and spirit. But the war wasn't quite what we imagined. It was brutal and violent. The artillery knocked down buildings and destroyed trees, bushes and killed everything green. Pretty soon we couldn't see anything but mud, dirt and wire barriers."

He stared at his hands for a brief interval and organized his emotions. "The ads you see in the current newspapers show anxious soldiers itching for a fight, but that isn't the way with war, and it won't be with this one. We lost over a hundred thousand Americans; nine million men, counting all the armies. France lost an entire generation of young men. The only good out of any war are the friendships you make with the guys who survive."

Al gestured toward the bedroom off the kitchen. "I kept a notebook on a dozen boys in my platoon who served with me. It's in the dresser drawer underneath my undershorts and socks. I pull it out once in a while and read their names. When I came home, the only ones in my notebook who were still alive were Tom, Emile and Bob Christianson, from Lafayette. Three men out of thirty."

Al took a drink of tea and Rene cut in. "You never told me about your notebook"

"Why should I?" Al responded, glancing at Jane. "I haven't even showed it to your mother. It's too personal. I haven't looked at it for six months."

"You need to explain about Emile." Jane insisted.

"I'm getting there," Al answered, holding up one hand. "Unlike Tom, Emile got along with me. He didn't try to be the best at everything like Tom did. I was also closer to him, and Tom didn't like being number two.

"Well, one night in France, Emile pulled guard duty for me because I was sick. Dysentery hit most of us in the trenches and I had a bad case. Cramps bent me double. When Emile took my place a sniper shot him in the shoulder. It was a lucky wound; any further over and he would have been hit in the lung or heart and died. Few men survived chest wounds then."

Al rotated his tea glass, staring at it, and then drank again. "Tom blamed me and he's never let me forget it."

"But it wasn't your fault."

"Tom doesn't think like that. I suspect he thinks I should have taken that shot."

"There's more to it," Jane intervened. "Get to the Bonus March."

Al frowned at Jane for breaking his rhythm but returned to the story, his eyes focused again on the table.

"Emile's wound only made things worse between us."

"What about your condition?" Rene asked. "Didn't lots of soldiers have others take their place when they were sick?"

"That didn't matter to Tom. In his opinion, I was responsible for Emile getting shot. Anyway," he went on, "Tom's father had problems finding crews during the war. So many boys had gone to fight that he couldn't keep up, and he lost one of his boats to the bank. So when we got married, I tried your grandfather's drug store business just long enough to know I didn't want to spend the rest of my life in Texas, and we moved here. Pierre had also written to me and wanted me to come back and work for him.

"Tom and I were paired up on the same boat again for nearly a year. Emile was physically limited with his shoulder wound and couldn't work the winch or handle a lot of weight, so he wasn't much good on the boat. As things turned out, Emile didn't like boats anyway, so Pierre put Emile in the company store."

"The one we go to today?"

"That's right," Al said, sipping his drink. "Emile loved to organize things. The floor plan of the store was his idea."

"When things started to look better, Pierre bought another boat that I took over, and I had the best deck hand in the company," Al said, reaching for Jane's hands. "I hired a transplanted Texan who hadn't ever been on a shrimp boat. And was it ever fun breaking her in."

Jane blushed. "We had a good time on that boat."

"We sure did, and most days weren't like work. Oh, sure," Al admitted, "I had to educate your mother about shrimping, but she learned fast." He reached over and punched Rene on his left shoulder. "You're almost as good as she was."

Jane chimed in. "He should be. I taught him how to work the winch, the catcher, and how to take care of the nets, while you were up front playing captain."

"We had a good life then," Al said, smiling and glancing at Jane. "We bought this house from Pierre and he promised to sell the boat to us, but Tom nixed the boat sale too and drew up the bill of sale for the house after Pierre drowned. There was nothing I could do about either agreement. It was a handshake deal each time with Pierre, and Tom didn't honor either one."

Al glanced toward the back bedroom where Rene slept, his face brightening. "You were born right in that room. Effie May, Pierre's sister, was a midwife. She never had any children of her own, but she helped with three or four babies a year. You came out so quickly there was no time to get to the clinic in Houma, and it seems that you've been in a hurry ever since." He chuckled softly. "Back then, the poor shape of the road made the trip a one-hour drive."

"You're taking all night," Jane said, admonishing him. "I want to go to bed before midnight."

Al dropped the animation in his face. "The future was bright. We had the house, and shrimping was so good that we didn't have to go much beyond the beach. Then the flood of '27 hit." He shook his head and stared at his hands. "We received a foot of rain in one day. The levees held, but the officials in control channeled the water through New Orleans and made the river rise so high that it threatened the city. The April storm was the worst in Louisiana in ten years," he said, looking at Rene. "We got rain from January through March. Nothing's ever hit South Louisiana like the storms of '27.

"We planned ahead for high water and thought we were prepared. The shrimp boats were tied to the dock and your mother and I had our flat-bottomed boat here at the house, in case the water got high. But not long after that a crest of water washed down the bayou, and another came higher than the first one. We might have been okay but the third wave washed out the front yard and floated our boat as high as the front door, leaving us no place to go. Our house and everything we owned was here. But we weren't the only ones affected. No one could get out because the road to Houma was blocked by six feet of water. Most people in this part of South Louisiana were marooned."

"I remember some of it," Rene claimed. "We had a leak in the kitchen and you set a tub there to catch the water," he said, pointing to his mother. "We stacked things on the kitchen counter and on the beds." He looked again at his father. "And you turned the sofa on one end and stood it in the corner of the front room."

Al was taken aback. "You were only four then, but do you remember all that?"

"Yes. And I recall how Mom was frightened."

Al released a chuckle. "That's because she'd never seen that much water in her life."

Jane reacted right away. "I saw rainstorms in Fort Worth, just not so much all at once. There are no hills to stop the water like there are in Texas."

The memory of dark, sunless days of storms sharpened Rene's recall. "The rain on our roof sounded like someone hammering. The wind howled and the rain came down sideways. The boats bounced when the wind picked up and the windows in the front room shook." He pointed to his father. "You went to check the boat, and when you came back you were soaked, and Mom gave you a towel to dry off after you took off your shirt and pants. Then we said a rosary to keep the water from destroying our house. I learned the *Hail Mary* that night by listening to both of you and following along."

Jane got up and put her arms around Rene and held him without speaking. Finally, she drew back, her face forming a deep, warm smile.

Al took another drink and wiped his lips with a napkin. "We spent two days on the roof, waiting for the flood to go down. But the water wasn't the worst thing. Pierre went outside during the night to look over the boats, and when Tom got no answer for ten minutes, he checked the dock for him."

Al scratched his left forearm, looked at the table, and his words came out slowly. "We found him two days later, crammed between the pilings and the shrimp boat that I was running that season."

Silence filled the house until a dog barked outside and a car pulled off the road. When a door slammed nearby, Al got out of his chair and closed the back door.

"No doubt that's Sam making the rounds. It's my fault he's here," he confessed. "I shouldn't have left the door open."

A loud rap on the front door sent Al through the kitchen to open the door, and Rene recognized Sam's gravel-like voice, his pie-pan helmet and the two yellow letters signifying Civil Defense (CD) on the black armband that represented a block captain.

"Al, you had a door open. I saw your light a block away."

"You're right, Sam. We were talking in the kitchen and ..."

"You can't do that. You know the rules."

"I simply didn't pay attention," Al answered agreeably. "I lost track of the time after we got to talking."

"Okay." Sam said, softening his tone. "I'm only doing my job. But don't worry. I won't make a federal case of this."

"Thank you, Sam. It won't happen again."

Sam changed the subject. "Are you ready for the blessing of the fleet?"

"We always look forward to it,"

Sam smiled. "I'm taking a boat out afterwards. We ought to catch a load on that day. The blessing always helps. God seems to show us where the shrimp are."

"I hope he'll do the same this year."

"Well, goodnight."

"Goodnight, and thanks again, Sam."

Before leaving the porch, Sam turned back. "I almost forgot; I was told to ask you where you picked up the mariner's body. Do you remember?"

"Who mentioned this to you?"

"I never saw the guy before. He was a government man I think. He wore a black suit and had an official-looking, stern face."

"Woody radioed that we were coming with the body. So why didn't he meet us when we docked?"

"I can't say. But he was interested in your location."

Al rubbed his chin and took his time answering. "We were about six miles due south of the bayou inspection station. We found him among the catch and continued on in. I didn't cross-check my location with the map, but I could make out some details of the island. I drag that area a lot."

"Okay. I'll pass it on."

"Thanks. Good night."

But Sam wasn't through. "Do you have any scrap metal? I'm collecting it tonight too."

"I've got some cans on the boat that I'll give you tomorrow."

"Anything for the war."

"Absolutely," Al agreed.

"I'll see you in the morning."

Jane was agitated when Al came back into the kitchen. "Will he turn us in?"

Al shook his head. "I don't think so."

"He talked long enough."

"Someone told him to ask about the finding the body.

"Was it the sheriff?"

"Sam didn't know him. It was probably a state official."

Jane's voice became tense. "I don't want anyone inspecting our house like we're criminals hiding something."

Al placed a hand on her shoulder. "That rarely happens. Sam's only doing his job. But Tom could have been a problem if he had been on duty tonight. You know how he loves to catch someone with their lights showing. It makes him feel important."

Jane agreed. "At least Sam gives people a second chance."

When they returned to the kitchen table, Rene brought back their conversation. "I can still see Tom's face at his father's funeral. He glared at everyone, and for a long time afterwards, I used to dream about him staring at me."

"Tom thinks the world is against him," Al said. "I've never caught him in a pleasant mood, except when he talks about money. He certainly wasn't happy after the water went down. Some 200 people drowned during high water and Tom lost two cousins in Buras. He agreed with Judge Perez in Plaquemine Parish, that $20 for every person who was hurt from the flood was a slap in the face. The judge wanted adequate compensation for the damage people incurred after they blew the levee to save New Orleans, but the government didn't budge. Some 50,000 people and businesses had property losses. Twenty dollars per case was an insult. All that fresh water also tainted the brackish lakes and nearly wiped Tom out." Al took one of Jane's hands and sought her eyes. "It was a tough year, but our garden got us through."

"That and lots of prayers," Jane added, smiling.

Al returned to his story. "The state government wasn't sympathetic because the southern parishes were big in rum-running and had to be punished. A rumor circulated that Tom may have made a few deliveries himself, but he wasn't charged, and I've never seen evidence that he was ever involved.

"Anyway, Tom rebuilt the warehouse and patched up his boats. We worked from sunrise to sunset for a month, getting things back in shape, and we never heard a peep from Baton Rouge. Tom called every politician he knew, and argued that the compensation was not reasonable, but we didn't get any help. During the flood we used our runabouts to rescue people stranded by the water and never got as much as a thank you. At that time, I felt angry at the state the same as Tom."

Al drew a circle with one finger on the table. "The flood covered two million acres and went as far west as New Iberia. Huey Long argued that the river states should share the cost of cleaning up because the Mississippi drains over half the nation. But the idea didn't go anywhere, and Louisiana got the raw end of the deal. At least Huey tried when no one else did."

Jane broke into a smile. "But we survived. We fished a lot that winter to make up for the lack of money."

Rene joined in. "I remember eating catfish nearly every day."

Al broke into a lighter mood. "We ate catfish in every way possible--fried, baked and deep fried. I thought I'd never want to eat them again."

Jane disagreed. "It wasn't so bad. We didn't go hungry. And I got to be very good at cleaning them."

Al tapped Rene on the arm, a gleam in his eyes. "I even got your mother to eat squirrel gumbo."

Jane shuddered. "The poor little things. We never had that in Texas."

Al tilted back in his chair. "The year things settled down, the shrimp came in such great numbers that Tom even quit griping." Al smiled at Jane. "That was one of our best times, wasn't it?"

"That was a grand summer," she agreed.

"It sure was," he echoed, turning toward Rene. "There's a rhythm of life when you're on the water, the hum of the engine, the boat rocking on gentle swells, seagulls begging for scraps, and the shrimp spilling out of the net onto the deck. At the end of the day we'd eat, wash off and lay down together under a full moon that was there just for your mother and me." His eyes twinkled. "You were probably conceived on such a night like that."

Jane snickered, her neck growing red. "Now why say that to him?"

"It's the truth," Al answered. "And what's more, you and I were the happiest when we were together on that boat. It made us a family. We owe a lot to that old trawler."

Rene cut in. "I still haven't heard anything to make Tom so mad that he'd reclaim our house."

Al poured another glass of tea before he moved on to the Bonus Army.

* * *

Half an hour later, Al had finished the story of how he and Emile had ridden the train to Washington, D.C. while Tom stayed home to keep the company together. It was 1932, the depth of the Depression. Al carried Tom's deposition and demand for the bonus of $700, the amount promised to each man who served overseas during the Great War.

Jane wiped her eyes and sniffed a couple of times as the details unfolded. "Tom shouldn't blame you. It was an accident. Emile tripped and fell. How can that be your fault?"

"I told him how we were run out of the building and how the men became a mob from trying to get away from the cops, tear gas, and clubs." Al held out his left hand. "I kept a grip on Emile until I got hit on the shoulder by a cop's nightstick, and the blow nearly knocked me out." Al rubbed his right shoulder. "I was black and blue and stiff for a week and it was three days before I could raise my arm above my head." He paused momentarily. "When I recovered from the blow, Emile was face down a few steps ahead of me. He must have fallen against the curb." Al rubbed his forehead and Jane wiped her eyes again. "Several guys had run over him by the time I got to him. Two of us carried him to an aid station near the Capitol, but it was too late. He had a broken neck."

"I remember the funeral." Rene said. "Everyone was crying except Tom. He just stared at the coffin and didn't move. You went over and put your arm around him, but he didn't even look at you."

"Well," Al said, "now you know the whole story. When I told him about Emile and showed him the bruise and swelling on my shoulder, he didn't come out and say it, but it was obvious he blamed me." He rubbed a chit in one hand and kept his eyes on his hands. "It's been ten years, but I no doubt remind him of it every day he sees me."

"I remember that you got a check in the mail," Rene said.

Al sneered. "That was our veterans' payment in 1936. It amounted to $568 per person, with fifteen dollars taken out for the train ride back to New Orleans. Roosevelt didn't want to spend the money but Congress overrode his fourth veto."

"Did they send money for Emile?"

"Yes, with the same fifteen dollars taken out for his trip," Al answered bitterly.

"Tom must have gotten his too?"

"He did," Al replied. "I gave his petition to Walter Waters, who organized the Bonus March. He spoke for all of us, though it did little good. Tom's check came the same day as mine. It sent him into a tantrum because it wasn't what the government had promised." Al drained his tea glass. "Tom isn't the kind of man to let the past fade away."

"But I can't believe he'd punish you for something I did." Rene said.

Al slowly rotated his glass in both hands. "The whole Bonus Army idea was a waste. It never would have happened if jobs had been plentiful. But the government didn't care. We were called hooligans and communists. Some were no doubt in the mix, but I never saw any marcher with a weapon or anyone carrying a communist party sign. We were war veterans who wanted a fair shake like we were promised. Instead, we got beaten up by soldiers on active duty and run off like we were bums. American veterans were actually attacked by men who were serving on active duty."

The dismay on Jane's face caught Al's attention. "What is it?"

"I don't like Tom," she answered. "And I've never trusted him."

Al patted the table with one hand. "I've felt that way a few times myself. So perhaps it's time for me to do something else. If I spend the rest of my life working for him, he'll still be the same." He moved the newspaper toward Jane and pointed at a help wanted section. "Welders are needed in the New Orleans' shipyard. This Higgins guy is paying fifteen dollars a day. At that rate I could make twice what I do shrimping." He turned to another page. "Or I could get a job at the Thibodaux Boiler Works. It says they're about to land a big contract to make artillery shells for the military."

Jane tossed an astonished glance at Al. "This is our life. Would you give up what you love and go to work in a dirty, noisy plant? We'd have to move and start over." Her voice grew stronger and her eyes flared. "This is our home. Don't you even talk like that, Al Dugas!"

Al shifted in his chair and wiped his forehead. With the doors shut and dark curtains over the open windows, there was little air stirring to disperse the heat from the stove.

Shaking his shirt to give himself some comfort, Al kept his eyes glued on Jane. "You don't have nice things that I'd like to get you, but a job in the shipyard or a factory would do that." He put his hands together and looked at them, then turned his palms upward. "I don't want to make you work on the boat again. We wouldn't have to be separated anymore if I worked where we lived. We'd have breakfast and supper together and there'd be no more lonely days or nights where we had to sleep alone."

Jane bent forward in her chair, both hands flat on the table. "Don't you think about it for one more second. I don't regret one day of being your wife, and I don't need those things." She grabbed Rene's right hand and squeezed it, staring into his eyes. "Stay here and have a good, peaceful life. The war will be over soon and we'll all be okay again."

Rene stood up and pushed the chair underneath the table. "I have to go see Marie," he said, turning toward the front door and hurrying across the floor before Al or Jane could formulate another reason to stop him.

But Al followed Rene out of the house and caught him short of the road. He looked over his shoulder to determine if Jane was within earshot and placed both hands on Rene's shoulders, his voice barely above a whisper.

"If you want to go, then do it. Your mother and I will get over your leaving. You aren't a kid anymore, Rene. Soldiers younger than you are dying over there. We all knew and liked Ray Anderson, but he did what he thought was right. The odds of war simply caught up with him. You know our opinions and our fear if you go; however, the choice is yours.

"To be honest, I hated the first war, but I wouldn't trade it for anything. Sure, I got wounded, but it showed me that life is precious, and it made me appreciate everything I have--your mother and you, our home, this town, even Tom Savoy. War changes people permanently. People die, and there are often bad times, but hardships make the pleasant days more enjoyable. I don't know how a person can learn the lessons of honor, devotion to a cause, and mutual responsibility any deeper than in a war. If you're sure about going, don't worry about anything. Just go. The worst part is waiting for the separation, but we'll adjust in a week or two and feel proud of you."

5

It was easy to spot Marie's house. Her father, Abe, also a shrimper, had brushed on a new coat of paint in the spring of '41, making the house stand out from others nearby. The house was the same design as Rene's--a rectangle, twice as long as it was wide, with a covered porch across the front, a tin roof and set back from the road by a small front yard. It likewise had an offset doorway into the kitchen from the front room. The houses were versions of the shotgun homes common to New Orleans, except for an additional bedroom.

Waiting in the shadows of the front porch, Marie burst into view and ran to meet Rene in the front yard, grasping him in a prolonged hug that pressed her breasts against his chest. She was a few inches shorter than Rene but their hips and shoulders nearly blended together, and her stomach flexed against his.

They had known each other since grade school but weren't mutually attracted until they turned thirteen when she dared him to dive off a pile of wood in a deep part of the bayou where they often swam. He learned that she liked hamburgers with onions and mustard and that she chewed on her lower lip when concentrating on her schoolwork. She also liked to yell at football games, and as she filled out, he was drawn to the way her hips and legs moved beneath her skirt, and how she put one hand behind his neck and pulled him closer to kiss him. At seventeen, his heart nearly exploded one night when he swore his love for her and she gave him the longest kiss he had ever known.

Marie released him from a lengthy embrace and stood back. "I thought you'd come after supper."

"I got into a conversation with my parents."

She grabbed his left hand and tugged him toward the house. "Let me show you the dress I made for the blessing of the fleet. It's your favorite color. Blue."

He stopped her by grasping one arm. "Not now."

She moved closer and brushed one hand against his face. "Is something wrong?"

"Let's go to the dock."

"Okay."

They followed the clamshell path around the house and out to the wooden dock, which Marie's father had built to launch his flat-bottomed runabout he used for fishing and hunting. The dock sat fifty yards from the house and allowed them an amount of privacy from Marie's mother, who checked on them every five minutes whenever they sat in the front porch swing. When Marie complained about the regular intrusions her mother warned her that she needed to be cautious about boys, including Rene.

The dock was special for them. It was where Rene asked Marie to marry him, though they hadn't set a date.

They watched as the moon edged away from the black horizon and painted a warm swath of light across the smooth water, softening the marsh and ponds that were calm and peaceful, the only noises being a few frogs calling each other and random fish jumping out of the water after bugs.

Marie tilted her head and touched the bottom of Rene's chin with her nose, and he placed both hands at the small of her back and drew her into him. He kissed her and pulled back to look at her in the moonlight that outlined her auburn hair and her face against the nighttime sky.

"Do you like what you see?" She teased.

"Yes, I do, very much."

Rehearsing what he had to say, he felt a tinge of nervousness. They had talked about Ray Anderson and the war, and he had shown Marie the German cans snagged in the Gulf, but she had always changed the subject when he brought up the idea of enlisting. He had joked to her before about joining up but had only mentioned his serious intention to Manny.

"I've been thinking about enlisting."

A change in her expression was visible, even in the darkness. "You're joking, aren't you?"

"No. I've decided to go."

"But you're an only son. They probably won't call you. Your father said so."

"That's no excuse. I feel guilty staying out."

"There's no reason to go. The war doesn't affect us," she claimed.

"Sure it does. You've heard about the U-boats. We also brought in the body of a mariner and another ammunition can this time." Encouraged by his reasoning, he went on. "The newspapers are filled with casualty lists of guys younger than I am. I'm no different than Ray. Besides, after it's over, I don't want to make excuses for not fighting."

"But the war isn't part of our lives."

Rene shook his head. "Then how come the government keeps urging men to enlist? And why do we have German submarines in the Gulf? And why can't we shrimp farther than ten miles offshore?" He swept one arm toward the Gulf. "The subs are there every day, watching. We just don't see them. I wouldn't be surprised if a U-boat fired on us someday. They leave us alone only because tankers make better targets than trawlers."

Marie tightened her grip on his arm. "You're feeding people. Isn't that as important as carrying a gun?"

"My dad keeps saying that," he added, pulling away and looking at the water. "But I don't feel right when fourteen-year old kids can wear aircraft watching armbands and look for airplanes, while I go back to the Gulf and hunt for shrimp. Where's the danger in that? It doesn't balance."

"Rene," she said, drawing him into a quick embrace. "I can understand how you feel, but if you did go, when would you leave?"

"Tomorrow morning, after I talk to Savoy."

She jerked away. "What about our plans to get married this summer?"

"The war won't last long," he explained. "And I'll be back in a year or so. The time I'm away will also give us a chance to save money. Servicemen can take out an allotment and send money home each month, and I'll make mine out to you."

She placed her head against his chest and put her arms around him, and her body shook from a tremor. He traced the outlines of her ears and rubbed her temples with his fingertips, hoping to calm her mood so she would give her consent.

But it didn't work; she took her head off his chest and looked at him. "I'm not interested in money. I want to get married this summer. Isn't there anything I can say that will make you stay?"

"Believe me," he answered. "My going away doesn't change the way I feel about you."

She stepped away and her face hardened. "But you're ruining our plans."

"No, I'm not. I just want to serve first. After Ray got killed, I realized I wanted to go. I dream about it sometime, and I haven't thought about much else during these last two weeks."

"That's obvious," she answered, disappointed.

"I thought you'd be proud of me."

"I am. But I also want us to be together. Why can't you wait six months so we can get married?"

"We'll be together," he said, encircling her shoulders and kissing her lightly, "just as soon as it's over."

She broke away and walked a few steps to the far side of the dock, and he followed, putting his arms around her. But she thrust him aside. "You're throwing everything away," she cried.

He turned her around and placed his right hand behind her head, compressing her hair. It felt cool and silky. He ran one hand inside the collar of her blouse and rubbed the back of her neck and then slipped both hands down until they met the top of her breasts, but she moved them away. He held her and kissed her again, but she didn't respond.

Although he tried to reassure her, his words sounded wrong as soon as he uttered them. "I'll save my money and we'll be married the week I get back. I'll write the date down so you can arrange the banns and get everything ready."

"You don't know how long that will be."

"I bet the war won't last a year."

Her response was flat. "What if you don't come back?"

"Don't talk like that …"

"Well, you might not."

"It won't happen. I promise."

"I wonder if Ray said that too," she countered in a downcast voice.

"Marie …"

"Do you think that mariner kid planned to die?"

"You're not making sense."

"You're the one who's not, and you're ruining everything, Rene," she blurted, pushing against his shoulders.

"It'll work out. Nothing will change. You'll see."

She took a while before answering. "If you leave like this, maybe I will."

"Don't talk silly," he said, reaching for her, but she pulled away again.

"You had this all planned before you got here, and it's like you're sneaking away. Why didn't you have the decency to ask me first? If you really love me, why did I become your last consideration?"

"I had supper with my parents or I would have been here sooner," he replied. "I didn't put you off. I had to talk to them." He grew defensive. "You've always said we should shut out the war," he added, moving toward her, "but I can't do it anymore. And I thought you, of all people, would understand."

She backed up on the clamshell pathway, both of her hands warding him off. "You're putting off our marriage and you won't even stay for the blessing of the fleet. I guess our lives don't mean that much to you after all."

"Please, Marie. I feel bad enough without you blaming me. I'll be back in a year or so."

"You feel bad. Well how do you think I feel? You're cutting me out of your life."

"No, I'm not. Enlisting is not replacing you. I'll be back."

"Then go ahead, but don't expect me to wait." She whirled around and began running toward her house.

Rene called to her but she disappeared inside the back door.

Mad at himself for handling things so poorly, he walked toward the road, forcing down an urge to knock on the door until she answered it. He hadn't expected her to react as she did. Ray's girlfriend even had a going-away party for him. Why Marie didn't feel the same way confused him. Guys were expected to fight. It was the patriotic thing to do. The radio and newspapers put out a daily call for men because the war wasn't going well. Everybody said so. Men as old as forty were being drafted just like the younger ones. She was asking the impossible for him to set aside his desire to protect the country.

He felt like she had cast him off for no good reason. When he got to the road that led to Houma, he stopped and watched her house for a while, hoping she would come out the front door and run to him, but when she didn't appear, or move the curtains to look at him, he turned north and jogged toward Manny's house.

6

The next morning Rene drank a glass of milk and covered two slices of bread with oleo, peanut butter and strawberry jam and made a sandwich. The jam smothered the stale taste of beer still in his mouth, though he had only one bottle. The milk washed his mouth clean and coated his throat, and he put the empty glass in the sink and left the house. It was going to be a full day with Tom and getting ready for the bus trip to the induction center in New Orleans.

The morning atmosphere was already uncomfortable, the temperature was climbing and the humidity seemed to liquefy in his throat. He wore a short sleeved shirt because the day would be hot. Pockets of thick fog lay on the marsh and closed the bayou to boat traffic and Rene could barely make out Tom's black Chrysler parked by the office. Tom seldom missed a full day of work, except for an occasional Mass on Sunday, or to visit his hotel and restaurant in Houma. Weekends and holidays were like any other workday to him.

Tom reclined in his leather chair with both feet on the desk and a cup of coffee in one hand. The diamond ring he wore on the little finger of his right hand reflected a knife-like thread of light when Tom raised his cup for another sip.

"Rene," he said, surprised, "what brings you out so early? I thought you'd be sleeping late this morning."

Rene got right to the point. "I wanted to see you before I leave. I'm going to enlist in the Navy."

Tom's feet popped off the desk and he banged the surface with his coffee cup. "You're what?"

"I'm joining the Navy today."

Tom looked at his desk and appeared to be searching for something, his face breaking into a tight smile. "Well," he muttered, "you could have given me more notice."

"I was on the boat and couldn't do it."

Tom shook his head. "This makes no sense. You'll have a deferment in a short while, and your father needs you. Hell, I need you," he admitted loudly. "You two are my best team. Why would you go away and spoil that?"

"We talked about it last night," Rene explained, trying to stay calm. "He isn't against me going. We also talked about World War One and how both of you wanted to go then, and I feel the same way. I want to fight like you did."

Tom drained his coffee cup, disgust on his face. "Any damn fool can pull a trigger," he claimed, gesturing with his right hand. "You're their only son. Think what that would do if you don't come back. Besides, it won't be long before Washington gives a family's only son a deferment. You're also in a necessary job, so they won't call you. Now be honest. What's the real reason you're going?"

"I just want to--."

"Is your girlfriend knocked up? Is that it?"

"No!"

Tom leaned back in his chair. "If it's more money you want, I can shave some of your operating expenses." He smiled and the skin in front of Tom's receding hairline glistened under the light that hung from the ceiling. A strip of flypaper was tied halfway up the chord, dangling like a loose piece of bark on a tree branch. Tom's shirt collar was damp, and sweat mixed with his shaving lotion, producing a stale odor that reached Rene. "If you stay here, you could be my youngest skipper. But it you go now, you'll be throwing away a great opportunity." He motioned one hand for Rene to leave. "See me tomorrow and we'll talk it over."

"I won't change my mind," Rene warned, standing his ground.

"Then what the hell is bothering you?" Tom demanded in a louder voice.

"I'm not helping the war by staying here."

"But you're wrong," Tom countered. "Every time you bring in a load of shrimp you're feeding soldiers." Tom spun in his chair, stood up and jabbed his wall map at Alabama. "I send a truckload to a

Mobile shipping site every month. When my entire plan for dried shrimp is accepted by the dunderheads in the military, our business will double. So you're part of this war already, and you don't have to wear a uniform." He slapped the desk with one hand and stared at Rene. "Now before you go off half-cocked, you might think about it," Tom cautioned. "Not everyone's rooting for this war. Lindberg spoke against getting involved and lots of people respected him for doing it. Oh hell," he uttered, waving both hands in the air. "The war might not last much longer anyway. The RAF stopped the Germans from invading England and Russia has stalled the Nazi advance toward Moscow. The whole thing may even end before you finish training, and look at what you'll have thrown away if that happens?"

Rene stared at the floor. "I can't get rid of the idea that someone like Ray will be taking my place if I don't go. It bothers me all the time. Fighting in the Navy is what I want."

Tom rubbed his forehead and adopted a somber attitude. "War is no fun, Rene, believe me. It's harder coming back and adjusting than you can imagine. You never look at people the same way afterwards, and you lose a piece of your normal life that you can't ever recover. Your dreams sometimes wake you up, and you harbor thoughts every day of your buddies that didn't come home. Worst of all, you wonder if you could have saved some of your friends."

"I know what you mean about friends," Rene answered. "I think about Ray the same way."

"And you still want to be part of that misery and pain?" Tom asked.

"I think so. Most of the guys in my graduating class have already gone."

Tom exhaled loudly, shook his head and his eyes narrowed as he looked at Rene with a hardened expression. "Let me enlighten you about a few facts." Tom began in a formal and brittle voice. "Are you familiar with the Burke-Wadsworth Bill?"

"No."

Tom took his time answering. "I figured as much. It was enacted in 1940, in time for the war, and exempts individuals who are engaged in essential work for the health, safety or interest of this nation. That means it keeps those people in their jobs during wartime. All strategic businesses are mentioned, and my company is included. In other words, you are already working in support of the critical needs of the nation. That makes you vital to the war effort and, as the owner of this company, you come under my control."

Tom tilted his head and opened his hands. "The law also means that you are to stay in your job." He gave a shrug and knitted his forehead. "The fact is you'd be breaking the law if you tried to enlist, and if you insist on it, I will be compelled to report you to the authorities who will arrest you, fine you, and perhaps put you in jail."

Rene's expression turned sour. "I'm going to New Orleans to enlist. They won't know me there."

Tom answered right off. "I wouldn't do that. They'll check your work records and discover that you're violating the law."

Rene gripped the chair and started to stand up, but Tom motioned him to stay put.

"You can't fight the government," he countered. "If they don't want you, there's not a damn thing you can do about it. You may not like it, but that's the law."

Rene snorted. "I've never heard of it."

"That doesn't matter," Tom responded, leaning forward in his chair. "The truth is you'd better stay here or you, as well as your parents, could suffer from your actions."

Rene started to get up again. "I'm going to ask my father ..."

"Sit down!" Tom demanded. "And listen to me."

Tom gave Rene time to sit, and after staring at him for half a minute, he continued in a less abusive voice. "If you go, you'll cause your father lots of trouble."

"I don't see how."

"I can't train a new deck hand overnight. You know how much there is to learn. You're the best crew member I've got, so it'll take time to break in another one. And with his bad leg, your father can't handle the deck job and run the boat too, so he'll lose at least a month's pay before a new deck hand can be ready to go with him."

"My mom can take my place."

Tom waved one hand. "No women will work on my trawlers as long as U-boats threaten us; your dad may have to miss a couple of trips until another deck hand is ready. I don't see any alternative." He pretended to look over a notebook by turning a page and checking the figures. "I already have enough people in the warehouse, so he won't have any place to work until I can get another man ready."

"That's a lot of money."

Tom didn't even bother to look up. "It isn't my concern. I have a business to run."

Rene searched for an answer. "What about Sam?"

Tom shook his head. "Who'll run the store? Kay fills in only part time. No," he answered. "It won't work."

Rene rubbed his forehead and squinted. "There must be some way."

"There is," Tom replied in a firm voice. "Stay home and let the soldiers fight the war. That way you won't cause your parents a hardship and you'll keep your job and stay alive."

Rene shook his head dejectedly. "You were a soldier with my father. I thought you'd understand."

Tom stood up and pointed at Rene. "I understand that you're only thinking of yourself." He brushed one hand toward Rene. "Go if you want, but I'll turn you in, and when the sheriff brings you back you won't have a job. And I'm not so sure I'll keep your old man either when he can't pull his share of the load. You're a good hand, Rene, but you'd better toe the line, or it'll be rough on you and your parents." He pointed toward the door. "Now I've got lots to do and you're taking up my time. Get the hell out of my sight and don't come back unless you're ready to go to work."

* * *

Al kneeled beside the front flowerbed, pulling high grass that persisted during the warm weather; no matter how many clumps were taken out, it was impossible to get rid of all the roots. He had built a small pile next to his right knee and noticed Rene when he turned to drop more grass.

He began talking and concentrating on his chore before Rene had a chance to say anything. "I need to stay after this grass or it'll take over the flowers and your mother will be upset. Tall grass invites snakes and mice, two things we don't need. If I knew of some poison that would kill the roots without harming the flowers, I'd put it down. But this is the only sure way to save them without digging up everything and starting over in the spring."

71

He adjusted his bad leg to keep his balance and stood up, wiped his forehead with the tail of his T-shirt, and ran his eyes across the front porch. "I need to get after that leak in the kitchen before the rains come this winter and I plan to repaint the rocking chairs on the porch and seal up our water barrel. If I get that done before the thunderstorms, it'll fill up in a few days and we won't have to worry about the supply." He nodded toward the house. "I found a way recently to fix the screen door. I saw an ad in the Montgomery Ward catalog about a brake that keeps the door from slamming. It screws to the door jamb and cushions the impact when it closes."

Al knelt in a new space and began grabbing grass, holding his concentration on the ground. "I'll have plenty to do after you leave. If I need help, your mother can lend a hand," he explained. "We'll make out fine. I only ask that you write us. You're bound to get busy; that's the nature of being in uniform during wartime. But we'd like to keep tabs on you, and it'll ease your mother's mind to read about your duties."

"I'm not going," Rene said, finally getting a word in edgewise.

Al stopped, stood up, and brushed off his pants, "Why not?"

Rene glanced toward the bayou where a pair of seagulls lifted into the air, the wind sustaining them on a slight breeze. It hadn't occurred to him before that birds took off into the wind, just like Joe Christy did with his plane. Boats were affected too. A wind off the stern pushed the boat but a headwind slowed it down, wasting time and fuel.

"He offered me my own boat if I stayed."

"That's the only reason you're staying?"

"Yes," he replied, avoiding his father's eyes.

Al took his time to speak. "What happened to joining the Navy and all the talk you've been giving me for the last two weeks?"

"I've changed my mind."

Al moved closer, his inflection changing. "You're lying. What's the real reason?"

Rene backed away to escape Al's grip. "I've decided to stay. That's all."

"I'm going to ask you one more time and you'd better tell me the truth. What changed your mind?"

"He said I'd be violating my exempt status and I could get in trouble if I enlisted without his permission."

Al broke into a smile as the tension vanished from his face and he broke into laughter. "That bill hasn't been passed yet. Did you believe him?"

"Yes. Why shouldn't I?"

Al clapped Rene on one shoulder. "Do you honestly think the draft board will turn you down? Why, they won't even blink an eye. They don't care about any exemptions, including the so-called strategic jobs law. Nothing is more important, or strategic, right now than someone putting on the uniform."

"But he cited some law."

"What law?"

"It was something about a wartime business and its employees."

Al shook his head. "It has nothing to do with shrimping," he explained. "It applies to heavy industry and manufacturing. His buddies in Houma might not take you because he'll yell at them for stealing one of his employees, but you could go to New Orleans and join up in five minutes." Al blew a gust of air through his nose. "They'd even take me if it wasn't for my leg. If we believe the papers, the age limit for the draft will soon be raised to sixty."

"I'm not going, so it doesn't matter."

Al's voice hardened. "There's more to this, isn't there?" he asked, watching Rene shift from one foot to the other. "If you're staying, I deserve to know the whole truth." Al put both hands on Rene's shoulders and his body odor from working in the sun closed around Rene. "You're holding back; I can see it in your eyes." He gently shook Rene's shoulders. "Get it out, Son. We should never lie to each other."

"My going would mean trouble for you and Mom."

"What kind of trouble?"

"You'll need a deckhand, and it'll take a while to get one ready. Tom said he doesn't want any more women on his boats, so Mom can't go. He said you'd be out of a job for at least a month."

"We'll see about that right now," Al declared, pulling away and starting toward the warehouse, but Rene grabbed one arm and held him.

"There's nothing to talk about. I'm not going. So forget it."

Al flicked one hand at the warehouse. "He likes to shoot off his mouth, but he doesn't mean half of what he says. He's threatened me before and nothing came of it. If you want to enlist, then do it. We'll be fine."

The company iceboat slid away from the dock and the skipper steered into the current on another run to the drying platform. Half a dozen boxes were piled on the back deck. For as long as Rene could recall, he had watched boats that were an integral part of his life, and most of them had been Savoy's. He touched everything in the community through his shrimp boats, his warehouse, and the store. He even functioned as the local bank for the trappers, fishermen and shrimpers who didn't want to drive into Houma and deal with strangers, one reason he kept a floor safe in the store, besides storing his own receipts and money. In some ways, Tom Savoy resembled a ruler more than a boss.

Al raised his voice. "Did you hear anything I just said?"

"What … what did you say?"

"I said," Al repeated deliberately, "it's your mother who doesn't want you to go. No mother enjoys seeing her only son leave home. But don't let it bother you. Deep down she's as proud of you as I am. Don't pay any mind to Savoy's threats. You can't spend time worrying about us. I'll deal with Tom. You have your own life to live."

"I'm going to see Savoy," Rene declared, walking away without waiting for his father to react.

"Don't be too long or you may miss the noontime bus to town," Al called out. "We'll have your favorite lunch, warmed-up shrimp gumbo with potato salad."

* * *

He hadn't gotten far when a patrol plane appeared in the northern sky, climbing for altitude. Airplanes had become a common sight since the turn of '42, particularly for people living near the Gulf. When he was shrimping Rene saw them daily, their propellers emitting a soft whine after the pilots throttled back to slow down and scan the water for outlines of U-boats underneath the surface. Unlike the twin engine Widgeon that the Coast Guard flew, the smaller scout planes were slow and fragile-looking. Compared to the Widgeon and the other Navy aircraft, the Civil Patrol planes appeared to be too small for the job.

An airplane would occasionally drop a bomb on a suspected target and the distant explosion would echo to shrimpers within a mile or two like a muffled clap of thunder. Rene had heard four bombings during June but hadn't seen debris, though one day they cut a swath through an oil sheen eight miles off the beach, but there was no debris in the slick. Rene had wondered at the time where it had come from, but Al said nothing, turned in the opposite direction, added full power, and headed north.

Rene followed the airplane on its path to the Gulf. It was such a slow-moving target that it appeared to be a cinch to hit, especially for someone with a rifle, and it flew so slowly that he wondered if he could outrun it with the runabout at full throttle. The scout plane looked clumsy and helpless, despite the bomb hanging from a rack on the airplane's right wing. The thought of being dependent on an airplane like Joe flew, turned him cold. If a boat became disabled or damaged, it would still float and, if it sank, a man could sit in a raft or swim, while a pilot had no choice but to jump out, parachute to the water, and perhaps drown like the mariner kid.

The sea was where the real war was being fought. He agreed with his father that the country which controlled the sea would win the war

He continued to the warehouse, telling himself that the war wasn't a concern anymore. His parents were more important than putting on a uniform and living with a bunch of guys he didn't even know. Manny was right. There were thousands of others who could don a uniform, but no one else could take care of his mother. God, family, and country, in that order, was the trilogy of his responsibility too, whose duties had been drilled into him from his catechism and now floated through his mind, reminding him that he'd made the correct choice.

Then there was Marie. They had shared too much to cast aside--a collection of mutual ideas, their personal feelings, the physical urges that each stifled and decided to wait on until they got married. He wanted her as badly as he wanted the Navy.

He rehearsed the advantages of staying, but as he approached the door to Tom's office and sidestepped the noose, he wondered why a chill settled in his chest. He swallowed to make it go away, but it lodged in his throat like a fish bone he could neither swallow nor spit out.

7

The Blessing of the Fleet had taken place in previous years at the beginning of the shrimp migration when they left the lakes for the Gulf of Mexico. But when the lake shrimp migrated later that year, Tom decided to move the celebration to July 3rd, a Friday, making a long weekend for the shrimpers and their families.

The blessing wasn't only for Tom's boats but also for a few single operators from Grand Isle, some other men who lived closer to the Gulf and launched out of Oyster Bayou, and one Sabine Indian who had given up hunting and trapping and had a house on a remnant of his historic tribal grounds three miles south of Pat's Landing.

The ceremony drew visitors from Houma and outlying towns and was to be conducted by Father Gruber, the local priest. Although New Orleans and adjacent parts of South Louisiana saw some 7000 Germans already settled by 1830, Father Gruber, along with his parents and one sister, had emigrated to escape the widespread poverty in Germany after The Great War. Though his parents kept him fluent in his native language and English too, the wartime atmosphere of suspicion about some local Germans possibly being spies for Hitler, inhibited his tendency to use German outside of family conversation. As a young priest fresh out of the Notre Dame Seminary in New Orleans, Tom and others in the community squashed opinions that Father Gruber should be restricted to practice only in one of the local POW camps. Now in his third year at Pat's Landing, the criticisms had quieted down because Father Gruber had a sunny, non-combative personality and backed up all patriotic arguments about the war. He also immersed himself in his priestly duties and spoke about the war only when someone else brought it up and wanted his opinion.

The blessing was scheduled for noon but preparations began at daylight. Tom's warehouse was swept clean, space was made for tables and chairs, and he sent the truck to Houma for extra blocks of ice. He was grateful that there was no ration on ice, though he was prepared to bribe the crew with free bottles of liquor if they balked at supplying him.

Many families brought their own special dish for the gathering and since the spring had been ideal for gardening, the harvest was the best in recent years. The variety of choices was abundant--cold shrimp, deep-fried shrimp, chicken and sausage gumbo, potato salad, corn on the cob, fried okra and hamburger casserole, fresh tomatoes and cucumbers sliced together and seasoned with vinegar and pepper, cracklings, fried chicken, pecan and apple pies, and homemade vanilla ice cream.

Jars of ice tea made up for the shortage of Coca Cola that went to the military instead and Tom had prepared for the festival by storing extra cases of beer and several bottles of whiskey from his bar in Houma. Since the long weekend guaranteed three days of celebrations, he expected to sell enough liquor on the side to make a tidy profit.

Although many boats showed evidence of wear and tear over years of shrimping, they were festooned with colorful pennants strung from the wheelhouse to the boom, up to the mast and forward to the bow, forming the outline of a sail. Several boats also sported fresh paint to cover areas of the deck, rub rail, or weathered portions of the wheelhouse.

Activity for the blessing was in full gear by eight and the road had steady traffic heading to Pat's Landing. People set up chairs and arranged blankets on the grass when they could find shade under a tree close enough to the warehouse and dock to witness the goings-on. Several women wore broad hats to shade their faces from the sun that was already heating the air, while others had brought umbrellas to escape the rays. The heat soon began to build, the atmosphere became stagnant, and dust from the traffic was thick enough to cut with a knife. The leaves were lifeless and the air was still. July promised scant relief from the temperature and humidity.

Although everyone was welcome to attend the blessing, coloreds stayed in the rear and were restricted from taking an active part in the ceremony.

Since Friday was a working day, Tom's boats planned to sail into the Gulf after the blessing and spend part of the day shrimping and returning before dark. Tom would have preferred them not to come back for two weeks, but a portion of one day of work was better than nothing.

*   *   *

The idea of a festival queen had arisen with Tom and, after sounding out others in the village, Marie was chosen. At the start of the ceremony, she was picked up half a mile south and transported to the warehouse dock by Al, Jane and Rene in the *Miss Jane*. Marie looked radiant. Her auburn hair was parted down the center and held in place by a blue headband that channeled the hair over her ears and down both sides of her neck, covering the collar of her cotton dress that she had spent a half hour ironing.

People honked their horns and waved when Al steered the trawler up the bayou and nestled into the pre-arranged berth alongside the dock. Then the other boats positioned closer until the gathering of hulls blocked the bayou by forming a continuum of decks and railings that people could cross without fear of falling into the water.

Tom took Marie's hand to help her step off the bow and accompanied her to the designated place in front of Father Gruber. Dressed in a white cassock trimmed in gold, his partially-bald head glistening in the warming sunlight, he made the Sign of the Cross in front of Marie, patted her on one hand, and she turned to face the boats and the crowd that lined the bank.

"Let the blessing begin," she proclaimed.

Father Gruber nodded to Jimmy Breaux, one of his regular altar boys who was also in the Ground Observer Corps and a cousin to Ray Anderson. Maintaining a serious expression, Jimmy moved toward Father Gruber while holding the aspersorium and the aspergillum in both hands.

With all boat and car engines turned off and only a barking dog to interrupt, Father Gruber started the blessing in a clear voice that carried through the crowd. "Oh, God and Father, Creator of the Universe and of the land and the sea, and all the fish that swim therein, we pray for an abundance of shrimp during this season. Let it be a sign of your great benevolence that we may prosper.

"Lord Jesus Christ, you calmed the sea when the apostles cried out for fear of sinking. As you did then, watch over our fishermen and their boats, protect them from harm, and guide them with fair winds through the ever-present and beneficent power of the Holy Spirit."

He then changed from the incantations of the blessing to a local message. "We have come a long way since the early Cajun ancestors came to this land, waded in these waters, and dropped their nets to harvest God's bounty. Instead of stretching our nets from the land, we now venture into the open waters of the Gulf, often now in the face of danger. But we carry those forefathers' spirit of courage and determination with us, the kind of strength that turned a wild marsh into a community for families."

Making the Sign of the Cross, Father Gruber continued. "So we humbly ask you to bless this shrimp fleet in the name of the Father, and of the Son, and of the Holy Spirit. Saint Andrew, Patron of fishermen, watch over those who toil in these dangerous, wartime waters for the greater good of your name and their livelihood."

Taking the golden aspergillum from the Holy Water aspersorium, Father Gruber delivered his blessing, shaking droplets in different directions that encompassed the boats. "In the name of our Lord, I bless this fleet and its crews."

Moving along the row, he sprinkled Holy Water on the vessels and raised his aspergillum, shaking it vigorously and bestowing the blessing on several boats in the second row that he couldn't reach.

Beginning the water journey to the Gulf, the boats separated and carved an opening for Tom, now piloting the *Miss Jane*, carrying Marie plus Father Gruber. After they slipped into the middle of the bayou and were clear of the other boats, Marie leaned over the bow and dropped a small memorial wreath in the water while the onlookers clapped and shouted their approval. Tom then nudged power to the engine and his boat led the slow parade down the bayou, with the remaining boats jockeying for position and blowing their horns in a lingering celebration.

After floating a mile to the south, Tom pulled into an elbow and waited to make a turn-around after all the boats passed on their way to the Gulf. As the third boat went by, Sam waved from the wheelhouse with one hand and held a wine bottle in the other. A broad smile was fixed on his face.

"What the hell are you doing?" Tom yelled, taking on a scowl that matched the sharpness of his voice.

Undeterred behind a wide grin, Sam raised his wine bottle in the air, wiggling it from side to side. "I'm sure you can get along without me for today. Roy and I are going to catch some big shrimp."

Tom shook his head and muffled a reply so as not to be overheard by Father Gruber and Marie. "You crazy Cajun bastard." Then he shouted as the boat slipped further away. "Make sure you're back by dark, and lay off that wine."

Sam waved once more and stepped into the wheelhouse and a dying trail of smoke from his cigarette thinned out as the distance increased between the two boats.

Within fifteen minutes the entire flotilla had passed to the south, and Tom reversed course for the warehouse, still upset with Sam.

But if their luck held, Tom figured Sam and Roy could make a couple of good drags and get back by dark, though he remained uneasy. Sam had a reputation for drinking when he was on the Gulf- -the reason Tom had taken him off as a full-time skipper and put him in charge of the store. The festival atmosphere of the blessing must not have curtailed his thirst. More than anything else, Sam liked to have a good time.

"What the hell," Tom said, not concerned who heard him. "It's a holiday. He has a right to enjoy it and make a dollar or two. I can't blame him for that."

*   *   *

The celebration shifted to the warehouse after the sun washed away the shade and started to bake everyone. Company equipment and parts had been slid to one side, making room for half a dozen tables that held the food, and everyone made their way through the line, choosing their favorites and filling their plates.

Tom had arranged a place for Marie where a dozen chairs were arranged in a semi-circle that also held Tom, some of his friends from Houma and Father Gruber, Kay, and Sarah, Tom's young daughter.

After everyone had eaten and things had slowed down, the conversation turned to the war and Tom didn't hesitate to voice his anger.

"Wilson got us involved in the Great War and Roosevelt did the same with this one. Why Europe couldn't hold back the Nazis is beyond me. We've given England ships, planes, money, and gasoline, everything necessary to survive. What stumps me is how Germany and Italy took the other countries so easily. Europe needs a stronger backbone." He slapped one leg and jabbed a finger in the air. "If you ask me, we should have supplied England and France earlier and stayed out of their fight. Lindberg was right when he spoke against America getting involved. We dived into the last war and it didn't settle a thing. Now, here we go again. It'll be a terrible waste of money and lives."

Father Gruber didn't agree. "But Tom, people are being massacred by Hitler, who doesn't want agreements. He's after the land and its resources, just like the ancient emperors of Rome when they tried to dominate the known world over two thousand years ago. The people are only in his way, just as they were for Aurelius, Caesar and Claudius. If Hitler succeeds, there'll be no one but Germans left on the continent. Their army is close to Moscow right now and, if he wins there, the United States will be his next target."

Tom was disgusted. "We're already a target, at least in the Gulf. And you can blame Roosevelt for that. He never did enough to pull us out of the Depression, he worked against helping veterans of the First War, and now the country is stretched to the limit so badly that we're using women in the factories. Oh, I know," he explained. "We got some money after the Bonus Army went home, but Roosevelt vetoed the bill before Congress overrode him and passed it. He wasn't a friend of veterans then and now it seems like he's trying to lose this war." He warmed to his argument when he noticed more people were listening and had edged closer "I tell you, we're desperate when we have to employ women to take the place of men. Whether we like it or not, the war is on our doorstep. And what help is Louisiana getting from Roosevelt, other than a couple of airplanes, a few volunteers walking the beach with a rifle, and a Coast Guard that wastes time harassing our trawlers instead of looking for U-boats?"

About that time, a man Tom thought he'd seen a time or two in Houma, joined the conversation. He was average in height and a bit slender and wore dark slacks, a white shirt with the collar open and his sleeves rolled to the elbow. He was dressed in an ordinary manner for a businessman on the weekend; however, the shoes caught Tom's eye. They were highly polished, expensive, black wingtips. Tom owned a pair himself but seldom saw anyone else wearing the same shoes in Pat's Landing, though he'd noticed them among businessmen and a lawyer or two in Houma. Recalling his own expense, he figured the shoes had cost the man around twenty-five dollars.

"I think it's the duty of every boy old enough to volunteer," the man suggested. "In my opinion, we're at a critical manpower level. The papers indicate that too. I read where Alexandria sent fifty boys to the Army last month. Imagine," he stressed, "fifty boys from one small town."

"But if everyone went who could go, what would happen to us?" Tom retaliated. "We need men to work the jobs here. I'm having trouble just keeping my own labor force. The military won't be able to fight if they aren't supplied with food and equipment. As I see it, the men at home are doing an important job too."

T. C. Bordelon joined in after becoming frustrated with the conversation. Only twenty-three, he had already served in the Navy and had been discharged after losing a hand during the attack at Pearl Harbor. He helped Sam at the store and was an alternate as a block captain when Sam or Tom needed help.

"I can't speak for you, Tom, but I can for the war. We need every man who wants to go. All he has to be able to do is pull a trigger, walk, and take orders. Manpower is the key to victory. Pearl Harbor convinced me of that. I would have stayed in if the Navy had let me, but I couldn't do much with one hand, not even pass ammunition to the gunners. I said I'd work in the galley as a cook's helper--anything to stay in--but I was turned down."

He took a long pull from his beer bottle and started his story in a somber voice. "I still see those boys in my dreams, the faces of friends I had, and others whose names I can't recall walk through my brain on some nights. I live with them, drink beer with them, sleep with them, and I wonder how the guys who made it out of the attack are doing." T.C. looked at Tom. "It's ironic that you talk about being prepared because on December 7th, it was early in the morning, and lots of those boys who went to war that day died unprepared, barefoot, and in their skivvies. The Japs did it right. We were caught with our military pants down."

He took another drink, wiped his mouth, and settled into the story, taking his time. "I was on the morning watch as the signal officer. Since we didn't use radios much, I was responsible for the messages we sent to other ships by using flags and semaphores. I arrived early to give the night crew time off so they could catch the tail end of breakfast. I used to do that for the night shift because I didn't like to miss a meal either. If you were late for morning chow you had cold toast, coffee and little else, so they were glad to get relieved. Chow and letters from home were the most important things to us.

"We had heard rumors about the Japs stirring up trouble the week before the attack, because a destroyer spotted a Jap submarine halfway between Pearl and San Francisco and radioed Pearl, but we weren't put on alert. We all wondered why. The Sunday of the seventh was like any other sleepy weekend morning. We weren't in any hurry and looked forward to a day of relaxation.

"However, the peaceful morning didn't last long. At first, three planes came in and dropped bombs on the bombing range. That was standard procedure. Pilots were told not to land while carrying live bombs so no one thought much about the explosions. That happened all the time. But I got real curious when more planes showed up behind the first three. I used my binoculars to get a better look, and by God, those planes had the rising sun painted on the fuselage, and their bombs were dropping among ships in the harbor.

"I was on the *Oklahoma*, one of eight battleships on battleship row that morning. Those Jap pilots knew what they were doing and had no doubt practiced from details spies gave them, because the planes turned and headed straight for us.

"Right away, a torpedo plane released a fish that hit us, followed by two more. I saw their trails as they closed in, but all I could do was grab the railing and hang on. If you are close when a torpedo strikes, the shock wave can knock you down and injure you. When those first two exploded, it was like an invisible hand grabbed my shoulders and shook me, and I knew right away that we were in danger.

"We couldn't have been in a more vulnerable situation that morning. The *Oklahoma* was like a sitting duck, because all of our hatches and doors were open in readiness for the admiral's inspection the following day, December 8th. You couldn't have made any ship more defenseless than we were."

T.C. stopped for another sip of beer and brushed his mouth with the forearm of his injured limb, while still holding his bottle with his remaining hand. Talking and drinking beer were his favorite habits. No one said a word while he had another long pull from his fresh bottle and took time to gather his thoughts.

"From where I was on the bridge, I yelled down at the men that we were under attack, but they were already cursing and yelling and clamoring to get out of the galley. When the SOP officer ordered battle stations at the same time, the whole crew realized that this was no goddamned drill, and the lazy sleepers and boys with a hangover swung into action like a hive of bees.

"Although it had only been a minute since taking those fish, the water poured in, trapping many men below deck. About the same time that we were targeted, I saw the *Arizona* take a hit, then another, but I had my own problems and didn't pay attention, because the *Oklahoma* started to list. Since I didn't want to get caught underneath the hull, if it rolled over, I went to the railing, waited until the ship developed a steep angle and jumped twenty feet to the water. I had the code book in my hand but tossed it away as I left the deck. It wasn't going to matter to the *Oklahoma* anymore.

"Being in the water didn't bother me and since I was a good swimmer, I started toward the battleship *Maryland* close by. But about that time, something crashed in the water and tore into my left hand. To this day I don't know what it was, but it was big enough to pull me under with it, for how long, I don't remember. But I finally resurfaced and made it to the *Maryland* where guys pulled me on deck, and before I stood up, I must have puked up a gallon of fuel oil.

"Everybody on The *Maryland* was trying to be useful in some way, so I went over to a gun station and tried to help load ammo, but my hand was broken so badly it was useless. I couldn't grip anything and the fingers didn't respond. But it didn't hurt. I guess I was in shock, but I clearly remember being mad as hell at the Japs and cussing at every enemy plane that passed over us. Afterwards I got to an aid station, the doctors said they couldn't do anything for my hand except amputation. The fingers were broken and the wrist bones were sticking through the skin. It looked more like hamburger than a hand, so they cut it off and sent me home."

He finished his beer and set the bottle on the table next to his chair, holding the neck and staring at the bottle. "I did my time, but I'd go tomorrow if they'd take me back. Over 400 men died in the *Oklahoma*, almost half of the crew. Many simply drowned. As I see it, serving in this war to avenge Pearl Harbor and beat the Japs is the duty of every able-bodied man."

"There's no turning back," the stranger chimed in. "This country is in peril."

"You're right," Tom agreed, trying to place the man's face, but since he stood behind three rows of people, Tom was unable to concentrate on his facial features. "I often wonder how much better off we'd be today if Huey Long had lived. He did more as Governor of Louisiana than Roosevelt's done as President. He gave us free school books, more paved roads, health clinics, and he made the oil companies pay their corporate taxes." He pointed at Father Gruber. "Huey was a man on the move, and Roosevelt recognized that. Things might have been different if Huey was still around. I believe his political enemies had him killed, and our state has suffered ever since because of one crazy man with a pistol. Who knows? Huey might have even become President."

Father Gruber interceded, an astonished look about him. "Surely you don't believe that Roosevelt had Huey assassinated."

Tom held up both hands and tilted his head to one side. "The state would be different if he had lived. That man was on the rise and got things done." Tom pointed to the road. "We'd still be driving on clamshells all the way to Houma if it wasn't for Huey. He was modernizing Louisiana. He was a man of the people, and we've suffered ever since his death." Tom lowered his voice and stared at the floor. "It was politicians or the oil companies that got Huey killed. I'll go to my grave believing that."

"For all his faults," Father Gruber said, "the President is a patriotic man."

"Probably so," Tom answered. "I just think Huey would have been a better war president. But now that we're in it up to our eyeballs, Roosevelt needs to win the war, bring the boys home, and let us get back to a normal life. He says the only thing we need to fear is fear itself. That's horse manure. We need to fear losing this war and this country. We need to fear the damn Germans who might march into this state someday. When you think about it," Tom said, "we're closer to the U-boats in the gulf than we are to our state government in Baton Rouge."

He looked for the stranger who had joined the conversation, but he had disappeared. Tom hadn't gotten his name but was not concerned. The man was probably someone who came for the festival. He shrugged his shoulders, returned to his fried chicken and potato salad and turned to Kay.

"Get me another beer."

* * *

When the last boats came in and the final tendrils of light were blocked by the trees, Sam and Roy weren't among them. Tom maintained a vigil for any stragglers, but the waterway was dark and unoccupied as far as he could see, and no distant engines broke the stillness. He knew Sam hated to navigate the bayou at night, and he planned to give him an ass-chewing when he came in the next day.

Carrying a broom in one hand, Al stepped off *Miss Jane* just as Tom ended his search for Sam.

"Where's the *Gulfstream*?" Tom asked.

"I haven't seen them since they headed for deeper water," Al answered.

"All day long and you never saw any other sign of them?"

"We had two good drags close to shore and didn't have to go beyond three miles."

Rene spoke up. "I saw them head south about two o'clock, but they didn't come back. And I didn't see any boats trailing us coming in."

"Damn him." Tom scowled. "I hope he tied up in the bay. Are you sure you didn't see him inside the islands?"

"There were no boats in the bay," Al answered. "It was so clear offshore that we could see five miles, and unless he went toward Grand Isle, or toward the west and Point Au Fer, we would have seen him."

Tom pointed to the hatch board. "How's the catch?"

"About a hundred pounds."

The haul didn't change Tom's concern. "Okay," he grunted, pointing at Manny. "Get over here and help unload. And stay here until every boat is taken care of. You may as well earn your pay instead of sitting on your butt and doing nothing."

Without making a comment, Manny shot Tom a sullen look that was ignored.

Tom grabbed Al's arm, his face lined with worry. "Are you sure you didn't see any boats tied up? The Last Islands are large enough to hide a trawler on the eastern end. Maybe you missed them."

Al shook his head. "The sky was clear, Tom. If Sam had been in the bay, we would have seen him. I didn't even see another vessel. I asked Woody when we checked with him, but Sam hadn't been by, and he would have been hard to miss if he had. Today's activity was one of the smallest numbers of boats I've seen working since last winter."

Tom mashed his lips over his teeth. "Sam can get out of hand when he's drinking. I need to look for him tomorrow. Would you and Rene go find him in the morning?"

Al looked down the bayou and back to Tom. "He's an experienced guy. I'm sure he's tied up inside Timbalier Bay. You know how he favors that area because he's had good luck there."

Tom touched Al on the arm, his words tinged with emotion. "Al, I have to be certain."

"Sam's a grown man, Tom. He can take care of himself."

Tom edged closer to Al. "I'm asking it as a favor. I'll pay you and Rene double for the shrimp you caught today if you go out tomorrow."

Al closed his eyes. "It's a holiday, Tom. Do you realize how seldom we get to enjoy a long weekend?"

Tom's grip on Al's arm intensified, and the pain in his face captured an intensity that Al hadn't seen since Pierre Savoy's death.

"Please, Al," Tom pleaded, his voice near a whisper. "He's my last living relative."

"Okay," Al finally agreed. "We'll get away at sunrise." Then he let out a chuckle. "He's probably sleeping one off and will meet us on our way out. I know where he likes to go, and I'll head there first."

Tom nodded. "Thanks. I'll make sure you and Rene get a special meal when you come back." Then his face hardened again. "And I'm going to wear my boots tomorrow so I can plant one in Sam's butt for not listening to me. Relative or not, he has to toe the line like everyone else."

Al took the opening to poke fun at Tom. "You might wait until you weigh his shrimp."

"No deal. He knows how I frown on drinking among crews. Unless he comes up with a good catch and an airtight excuse, he's going to be landlocked for a very long time."

8

The next morning dawned cloudless and a light south breeze promised to accompany them until the end of the trip. But it would be a scorching afternoon. The humidity was so prominent already that the air felt warm and damp. It was the kind of day to shrimp in the morning and escape the heat by grabbing an afternoon nap, and then drag later in the day before heading to an inland bay for the night.

But shrimping wasn't on Al's mind as he cleared the island and entered the open water. He had no intention of even setting up for one drag. Finding Sam and Roy and getting in early dominated his outlook for the day.

Rene hunkered down behind the wheelhouse, his knees folded to make a resting place for a *Life* magazine that he leafed through. He was drawn to an ad of a Hellcat fighter launching from an aircraft carrier. The caption read: "There she is, a Jap carrier, and we're taking the battle to the enemy just like we did at Midway. Join up and do your part."

Rene dropped the magazine on the deck and stared at the broad expanse of the Gulf, and his throat tightened like he had something too large to go down. It was a waste of time to look at patriotic ads. He'd made up his mind; family and Marie came first.

Well clear of land now, Rene went to the railing and began a lookout for debris while they searched for signs of Sam's trawler. They paralleled the shoreline, looking for any boat tied up in a bay, but after an hour none had been sighted.

"We'll go further east," Al declared. "Sam claimed that shrimp are more plentiful in that direction because the water is deeper. We'll follow the beach to the east and then go south. Sam laughs about anchoring in a bay because he still favors the old way before the war, stopping offshore wherever he ends up so he could be ready for the next morning. I wouldn't put it past him to be somewhere south of us right now. He snickers at stories about U-boats every time someone mentions them."

* * *

They were southwest of Grand Isle in three hours and met another shrimp boat dragging eastward. Al pulled alongside and shouted their intent to find the *Gulfstream*, and Perry Trahan--a friend of Al's from their school days--came out of the wheelhouse holding a coffee cup in one hand.

"Sam didn't stop by," Perry answered. "He comes in for a drink when he sails our way, but no one saw him yesterday." Then he pointed southward. "But we were three miles south, about five o'clock in the afternoon, when we heard an explosion in the distance, and I high-tailed it toward the beach. You don't suppose he ran into trouble, do you?"

"I can't say," Al answered. "We lost track of him when he came out yesterday and no one saw him after he went toward deeper water."

"Ever since we lost so many ships during May, we pair up when we go near the ten-mile limit," Perry explained "Did another boat go with him?"

"We don't think so. He was alone the last time we saw him, and he's the only one who didn't return last night. He must have made some good drags to stay so late that he couldn't get back before dark."

"Well, I'm sure he didn't go toward Southwest Pass," Perry decided. "No one in their right mind goes there. With the Coast Guard warnings about German mines, and that sector being an active place for U-boats, anyone fool enough to shrimp over there would be asking for trouble."

"I doubt if he'd go there too," Al chimed in. "Sam's a bit on the wild side and a loner, but he's not reckless enough to go forty miles out of his way just to catch shrimp."

Perry pointed toward Rene. "You're about to outgrow your dad."

Al tilted his head toward Rene. "He already has. He's too big to spank anymore. I'm just his helper these days."

Perry concentrated on Rene. "Are you going to join up? Another of my nephews left from Golden Meadow last week."

When Rene didn't answer, Al did it for him. "He's staying to help with the shrimping. He doesn't have to go unless he's drafted."

The change in his inflection was noticeable in Perry's voice. "Well, the boys must decide for themselves." He waved one hand and started toward his wheelhouse. "I hope you find Sam. Good luck."

Al took up a southerly course and called Rene into the wheelhouse. "We'll hold this for half an hour, swing to the west for another hour, then head for home. That should put us about seven miles off the beach. Keep a careful lookout for ships.

Rene sounded dubious. "You don't think he's out that far, do you? All the other boats are at the dock, so in case of trouble, there's no one to help him."

"You've seen Sam's rebellious streak. If he drank much yesterday there's no telling where he spent the night." Al waved his right arm in a broad arc to the west. "Call out anything you see. I'll watch the other side." Then his voice became stronger. "And pay close attention for periscopes. If you see one, give me a direction and distance and I'll turn away from it. I don't think any sub would want to give away his position by firing at us. But stay alert."

The murky water began to change colors half an hour later and it was no problem to see several feet down, past Sheepshead, Blue Runners, and an occasional Amberjack, their silver backs reflecting the sun as they flashed through a shaft of sunlight after an unwary meal. A light breeze and scant ripples made it a perfect day as the *Miss Jane* carved a path through the water with very little pitching or rolling. Not having to handle a drag, mend the netting, or sift through a catch, it was an ideal time to enjoy the Gulf.

A porpoise swam in formation with the boat before tiring from the lack of competition and submerged under the hull and disappeared, only to return a moment later, as if to encourage them to go faster than the seven knots Al maintained. Half a dozen pelicans soared above the stern in graceful circles, riding the developing thermals, their large wings moving just enough to keep them in the air.

Halfway into their southbound leg, Rene called out a spot a hundred yards off the right side, and Al leaned through the door.

"Where is it?"

"Right there," Rene pointed.

After another splash and a tail fin appeared, Al pulled away. "It's just a fish jumping."

"It looked like a periscope before he came out of the water."

"You have a good eye," Al said, "but if you see a periscope, it'll leave a small wake and it won't be moving very fast."

Near the end of their running time on the first leg, a convoy of several ships appeared about three miles away, gray, lumbering shapes moving so slowly that they seemed to be stationary. At that distance Rene couldn't tell if they were zigzagging or following each other, and there didn't appear to be any escort vessels accompanying them.

As they progressed into deeper water, swells rocked the boat and reduced Rene's chances to spot anything. But he timed his scan by concentrating at the top of each crest that elevated the boat and gave him a better interval to hold his search pattern.

After an hour of steering a westerly course, Al turned north, a look of defeat on his face. "I thought Sam might come out here early and drag before the sun got too hot. But I guess I was wrong. We'll head for shallow water." Then he broke into a smile. "It wouldn't surprise me if Sam was already at the dock. He probably tied up late and decided to come in this morning. We could have missed seeing him on his way to the bayou after we cleared the island. If we don't make contact by the time we reach the shoreline, we'll head in. I don't want to extend the day and then run the bayou at night and risk going aground."

A flock of a dozen seagulls floated on the water, waiting until the trawler drew near, then launched into the air, wheeled around and hovered behind the boat, waiting for scraps. But seeing none, they veered away, only to be replaced by another group that was more hopeful than the last.

As the water became shallower and the silt began to reduce Rene's ability to see anything more than two feet below the surface, he relaxed his vigil, but suddenly the boat ran over something that delivered a hard thump against the hull, and Rene leaned over the railing and spied a large piece of wood floating past the stern. There was no need to cry out because Al had already begun to steer the boat in a circle.

"What is it?" he called out.

Rene moved to the door of the wheelhouse and stuck his head inside. "I can't tell, but it's good sized. Maybe a tree trunk."

Al turned the boat in a circle without taking his eyes off the water. "Point it out if you see it again and I'll come around. Stay on the same side because we should pass right by it."

As soon as Al completed a circle and had the bow pointing to the north, Rene called out. "We're almost over it."

Al cut the throttle and joined him at the railing, a long-handled fishing gaff in one hand. "What is it?"

"It's something wooden," Rene said without taking his eyes off the object and reaching for the gaff.

Al seemed sure of himself. "It's probably driftwood or part of an old tree trunk. This is the time of year for them to come into the Gulf." He started for the wheelhouse. "We'd better get going."

"It's not a tree." Rene shouted. "It's painted white."

It was a section of wood three feet long, a foot wide and large enough for Rene to hook one end with the gaff and steady it in the water. But in order to pull it up, he gave the gaff to Al, climbed onto one of the tires hanging over the side and took hold of it while Al steadied it with the gaff. Rene raised his end and Al dropped the gaff on the deck, leaned over the railing and helped Rene lift the piece onboard. One side had no markings and was white, but the other side had red lettering about eighteen inches high, and Rene let out a burst of air as if someone had just struck him in the stomach. Al closed his eyes and put one arm on Rene's shoulders, and both of them fixed on the lettering that spelled *Stream*.

"Maybe they're in the water nearby," Rene cried out, jerking his head one way, then the other.

"We'll look, but I doubt it," Al answered touching Rene on one shoulder. "This could explain the explosion Perry told us about."

"We have to find them!" Rene claimed loudly.

"We'll try, Son," Al said, studying the water. "The current is running from the east to the west. To have a chance, we'll need to follow that pattern. We'll zigzag southeast for an hour, then turn northwest until we hit the shoreline or run out of time. That will let us cover as much area as possible before we start losing daylight and have to go in."

"Okay,"

Al started for the wheelhouse and Rene got back to the railing. "Don't stare." Al reminded him. "Start your scan near the boat by elevating your eyes out a short distance and then back. Hold a steady but slow pattern without fixing on one spot. A body won't be easy to spot in this murky water, so call out anything you see."

At six-thirty, when they hadn't found Roy, Sam, or any other pieces from the boat, Al checked in with Woody and then entered the mouth of the Lower Bayou, and Rene sat on the back deck for the run to the dock, his attention riveted to the wooden piece and the red lettering,

* * *

Several people thought Tom was going too far when he insisted that two small gravestones for Sam and Roy should be placed in the town's cemetery. Since neither body had been recovered, it made no sense. It also went against the idea of a funeral and most people agreed that it was a futile gesture. But Tom bought the markers anyway. They would be nothing but two pieces of stone on the grass, no matter where they were placed. But Tom didn't see it that way. Instead, he was commemorating their lives and their sacrifice. While Sam and Roy had gone out in a shrimp boat--posing no threat to anyone, least of all the Germans--he considered both of them to be casualties of the war. Since they must have had a substantial load of fuel onboard, it was the general opinion that a shell from a sub's deck gun had created the damage. A U-boat had done it for sure. No shrimp boat could blow apart so violently that only small, wooden sections were left.

The service wasn't elaborate. With no bodies or caskets, the simple and stark ceremony consisted of placing the markers side by side, in front of Ray Anderson's resting place, and a brief prayer for the two men was recited by Father Gruber. The entire scene took place in less than ten minutes, a fraction of time that a normal service required, but Tom was satisfied, and without commenting to anyone at the end of the prayer, he walked to his car with Kay and Sarah and drove home.

9

The next week was filled with activity. Since they no longer had the separation standing in their way, Marie and Rene finalized plans to get married. The banns were announced, and after two more readings they were free to have the ceremony.

Anticipating their life together was a pleasant turn of events for Rene, who thought less about the war and more of Marie. Sure of his decision, he concentrated on his future of shrimping and living as a married man and continuing the only work he had ever known.

Tom was likewise relieved and promised him three days off for a honeymoon. But he kept his idea of a wedding present from them--Sam's Lincoln coupe. Tom held Sam's note on the car but wiped out the remaining seventy-five dollars and took the car to a Houma garage, where it was inspected for any mechanical problems and then thoroughly cleaned and waxed and, when it was ready, the Lincoln sparkled like a model fresh off the showroom floor.

Tom also decided to let Marie shrimp with Rene after they got married. He broke his vow about no women because Marie had made numerous trips with her father and already knew how to navigate the bayou and how to handle the engine when making a drag in order to avoid entangling the prop in the net. She was also more adept than Rene at mending holes in the netting. Tom had initially been doubtful but gave in after realizing he would have two top crews by including Manny and Marie, and it gave him a pleasant feeling that Manny would finally be able to earn more money than working in the warehouse. He would crew with Rene until after the honeymoon, then move onto the *Miss Jane* with Al.

Manny welcomed the opportunity but was suspicious about Tom breaking his own rule, because no other Sabines worked on any of his boats. "He may be searching for a reason to run me off. I don't like him and I sure don't trust him."

Rene disagreed. "I'd say he likes the way you work."

But Manny remained doubtful. "He's never done me any favors. I show up to work when other guys get drunk and I don't try to take a nap. All he ever does is yell at me. I've never once seen him smile and say I did a good job. The man's downright mean."

"Remember what the football coach said that a player worth developing will get yelled at because he has value."

"Don't give me that schoolyard crap. Tom's no football coach. He may be the boss, but the man is filled with hatred."

"Look at it this way," Rene went on. "You just got a promotion."

"Big deal," Manny quickly reacted. "He'll find the first thing to complain about and put me back on the dock. You wait and see."

"I don't think so; my father and I told him I wouldn't take the boat unless you came along as part of the crew."

"You said that?"

"We both did."

Manny's face creased into a smile, and he went into a crouch and landed a half-hearted punch on Rene's shoulder. "Okay," he said, "but you better not play big-shot captain, or I'll toss you overboard and let you swim home. I'm taking a big risk by going out with a new skipper. What's more, I'm not going to do all the cooking."

*   *   *

Their boat wasn't a new one. Tom had won it from a Houma shrimper who had gotten behind in a second-floor poker game one night in the hotel, and in order to keep up with the betting, he used his boat as collateral in a game of five card stud and lost on four jacks, when Tom turned up four kings.

The boat was almost identical to the *Miss Jane*, thirty-five feet long, with the same wheelhouse design and the same superstructure. The hull and wheelhouse got a new coat of white paint and the deck railing and roof of the wheelhouse were trimmed in blue. And to limit damage to the hull, when berthing against the dock or another boat, chains suspended a dozen old car tires over the side to serve as bumpers. Matching Tom's other boats, a canvas canopy, tacked to the wheelhouse, covered most of the rear deck and provided shade on a hot day and shelter during a rainstorm.

Copying the habit that Al had established, Rene carried a fifty-gallon drum of gasoline, in case he needed to refuel while working a sector. He also stocked the boat with supplies of canned goods, citrus fruit, potatoes, rice, bread, water, and meat kept on ice in the hold. Everything on the boat was there to maximize dragging time. Like the *Miss Jane,* it had a temperature gauge on the engine block, an oil pressure gauge, and a compass that sat in a water bowl by the wheel. But there was no fuel gauge. That was checked by using a dipstick and estimating the amount the same way Al had always done. The throttle was rigged with twine and a pulley, which Rene replaced after he found two sections that were badly frayed.

*   *   *

In command at the wheel on the first day, Manny guided the boat from the dock and into the bayou. As he worked to anticipate his first turn, the bow swung to the left and threatened to punch into the muddy bank. Standing alongside him, Rene spun the wheel and turned the bow back into the middle of the waterway.

"Don't fight the current," Rene explained. "Lead the boat but always be ready to take out part of your correction. It's a constant battle when you're in the bayou. Think of your own runabout. It turns faster than a trawler because it's smaller, but we need more time and distance to turn. The Fairbanks-Morse engine doesn't have enough power for abrupt corrections, so you have to lead it into a turn. If you expect an immediate reaction, you'll overcorrect."

They approached another jog in the bayou and Manny handled the curve without leaving mid-stream. "Like that?" he asked proudly.

"Good. There's hope for you yet."

"Aye-aye, Captain Smartass," Manny came back.

By the time they reached the mouth of the bayou, Manny had taken the boat around several turns, and his satisfaction was reflected in a confident grin as he reduced power and brought the boat alongside Woody's inspection dock, settling it gently in place, then flashing Rene a broad smile of satisfaction.

They followed the rules laid down by Tom; they were to shrimp in areas no further than seven miles south of the island chain and in a sector no more than ten miles long. That suited Rene because it happened to be the prime shrimping area he'd worked with his father. It was free of worrisome conditions; the bottom was uniform, the area was safely within the ten-mile limit and the sector was so familiar to him that he could shrimp without fear of snagging something on the bottom.

Raccoon Island was one of a handful of barrier islands that formed what had come to be known as the Last Islands, adapted from the French name of Isle Dernieres. It was the westernmost strip of islands that stretched westward from Terrebonne Bay. A longer chain in earlier times, it had been broken into separate parts by hurricanes and tidal action that degraded the shoreline and ushered in the Gulf. Raccoon Island was about five miles long and offered a secure nook to anchor for the night. The passages around the east and western tips were less than fifteen feet deep but passable for trawlers, and random stands of scrub trees and clumps of waist-high marsh grass provided nighttime concealment for crews.

The island had earlier supported the Sabine Indians who lived there until they killed all the deer and moved into the vast marshland where wildlife was more plentiful. From his childhood, Rene had heard stories that a hotel had been built on the island and catered to gamblers from New Orleans and Baton Rouge. The distances from those cities and the difficulty in getting there made the island a refuge from the law and the Cajuns, who fished the surrounding waters, and had used the lights for nighttime navigation.

The hotel had flourished until the middle of the 1800s when a violent hurricane killed nearly 200 people and tore through the buildings, leaving shattered structures and remnants from the storms that turned up now and then and kept alive tales about the island's past; the most outlandish was how guests at the hotel had been entertained with fights between an alligator and a bear, though no evidence had ever been found to validate the story.

After the storm swept the island the only visitors were occasional charter boats from Mobile or New Orleans that anchored near the beach for their passengers to fish, explore the sand dunes, or search for relics from the island's past, watched over by an abundance of seagulls, herons, sand crabs and especially a large number of pelicans that gave them a habitat safe from predators and nested there.

*   *   *

Beginning at the western point of the island, Rene and Manny dragged in water fifteen feet deep and held an easterly direction, which allowed them to set their net against the current and catch the shrimp moving toward them. They navigated in an arc that duplicated the gentle curvature of the shoreline, until they passed the smaller islands that bordered the wide approach into Whiskey Bay and offered them a second opening to the inlet leading to the drying platform a mile north of the beach. If the weather promised good shrimping, they planned to make three cycles to the drying platform and head for home at the end of the second week with several hundred pounds on ice.

Some nervous shrimpers dragged the shallow water within a mile of the beach to avoid a possible confrontation with U-boats, whose warnings were spread by shrimpers at the dock or when two trawlers met offshore. Suppressed by the government that controlled the flow of information through radio and newspapers, no one was absolutely certain where the U-boats were operating. Since Rene had never actually sighted a U-boat, he and Manny worked a safe zone no farther than five to seven miles into the Gulf.

Rene talked it over with Manny and they agreed to copy Al's suggestion; if either one saw a periscope, they would turn immediately and make for shallow water. It had worked for Al and they hoped it would work for them.

"To hell with submarines, Germans, and the war," Manny claimed after going three days without seeing a single periscope or hearing any engines at night. "I'm only interested in shrimp."

They had good luck with the shrimp and the weather. A light breeze each day made working conditions comfortable under cloudless skies and swells under three feet, and they dragged each day until approaching darkness, and then searched for an inlet inside Raccoon Island. They started at first light every morning and used the long summer days that gave them thirteen hours to work. They often ate without stopping, snacking on a banana or a satsuma, a

99

small Mandarin citrus, introduced in the late 1800s from Japan and locally grown south of New Orleans. It tasted similar to an orange and a tangerine. Or they made peanut butter and honey sandwiches.

They took advantage of the long days because both of them had the urge to make lots of money. Rene planned to save his share to get married, while Manny talked about buying his mother a nicer house with a yard, a spacious flowerbed and a front sidewalk that went out to the road, instead of what they had now—thin grass and dirt up to the front porch. And he planned to relocate the clothesline to the backyard, where people didn't have to look at it.

During their first week of work, they gave the boat a thorough inspection. Rene decided to sand the wooden dashboard, brush on a new coat of varnish and lay linoleum on the wheelhouse floor, and Manny discovered that the hatch boards let cold air escape from the hold. He also oiled the block and tackle and winch and spent his spare time mending the net.

What they couldn't fix right away went into the boat's logbook.

Manny learned quickly, so Rene remained mostly at the wheel because Manny no longer needed help with letting out the net and was careful not to bunch it up or jerk on the line when something on the bottom threatened to damage the catcher. At first, Rene had stopped the boat and helped Manny bring in the catch, but after several additional drags, Manny winched up the net, untied it, and opened it on the deck without any trouble.

They brought in abundant catches and their hopes of making good money grew stronger. But during one stormy day, when they waited out a thunderstorm one afternoon, Manny detailed plans for himself and his mother

"I'm going to build another room on the back of the house and buy her a washing machine so she won't have to scrub clothes on a washboard. It makes her hands red. And in another year or two, I'll put a ceiling light in every room, plus one over the front door. And when the war ends, I'll sit on the porch at night, with a cold beer in one hand, and watch the cars and people go by."

His face grew animated from more details. "I'll paint the rooms a soft yellow. She likes yellow. It reminds her of butterflies. I'll buy her a new sofa and a chair, and a porcelain kitchen table that won't scorch if a hot skillet sits on it." He rubbed one arm and kept going.

"When I get married, I'll build a white picket fence around the front yard, like the one at Savoy's house, so my kids won't have to worry about cars, and I'll watch them from my hammock in the shade of a tree." He patted his leg and glanced toward the stern where small rivulets of rainwater ran off the deck and into the bay. "And I'll keep a few cold beers on ice beside me, for whenever I want one. That's what shrimping is going to do for me," he said in a confident manner.

Rene had never before seen Manny so upbeat and relaxed. He normally kept things close to his chest. Though Rene had never asked Manny about his father, Manny's good mood and the lazy day made it a natural thing to do.

"You've never spoken about your dad," he said.

Manny shot Rene an icy stare, but it didn't last, and he finally replied after an awkward period of silence between them. He ran one hand through his hair and yawned, his face gradually losing tension.

"I used to wonder when I was younger and watched you and Ray with your dads," he began. "That was why I started fighting. I would punch the first kid who teased me. I wanted to show everyone that I didn't need a father for protection, that I could stand on my own two feet without any help."

He leaned forward, both elbows on his knees, and stared past the stern. "I heard stories growing up that people said my father was Tom Savoy. They said that was why I got hired and why I was the youngest one to work on the dock. But he's never done me any favors." Manny paused, his mood darkened, and his eyes narrowed. "He uses people like animals. He'd put a mule to work if the mule would make him money," he said, slashing one hand through the air like he was striking at a mosquito. "I do my work and don't talk to him unless I have to. When he's around the docks, snooping to make sure we're doing our jobs, I pretend he's not even there." His words began to come out more slowly, and his anger receded. "My mother has never talked to me about my father. I don't even know who he is or anything about him. She'll probably tell me someday, but I don't let it bother me anymore." He rubbed one forearm without breaking his mood, "I used to daydream about him when I was a kid. It would be nice to know what his name is, where he lives, what he looks like, what he thinks about me." His voice trailed off; he rubbed his forehead and rolled onto his side away from Rene.

The storm was losing its punch, the visibility picked up and the island near the boat became visible. The wall of rain was moving away and, in a few minutes, they would be able to get back to work.

Lying with his back to Rene, Manny ended the conversation. "She's never said anything nice about him, and I don't remember her talking to him, or going near him, so I refuse to believe it's Savoy.

* * *

Manny had never confronted a shark until one day during their second week, so he hadn't learned the practice of eyeballing the catch for sharks and eels. One afternoon, when the last drag was brought in, Manny untied the sack and started to reach into the shrimp, but Rene grabbed him by the shoulder and jerked him back inches away from a three-foot shark.

"Never do that until you look first," Rene warned, pointing to the shark, whose marble eyes glistened above rows of white teeth that resembled a set of saw blades. "Look at his mouth? He'll bite you out of sheer meanness. This is a small sand shark, but he'll still take your hand off with one bite and a head shake."

Rene pulled the net away, grabbed a gaff, hooked the shark by the gills and dragged it onto the deck, and Manny stared in open-mouthed attention as Rene slit the shark's white belly, carried him to the railing, shook the gaff and dumped the twitching body into the water.

Manny watched and pointed in disbelief. "He's swimming away! How can he be alive when you just gutted him?"

"They're tough," Rene answered, cleaning his filet knife with a rag and putting it in the scabbard on his belt. "But he won't get away. A big jewfish or another shark will get him before he goes very far." He drew an imaginary line across the water. "See how fast the blood spreads out? That's a dinner bell for every large fish in the neighborhood."

A blood line thinned out below the surface and trailed behind the boat and was quickly diluted by the current and the repetitious swells.

Manny watched until Rene nudged him. "Let's sort out the fish and stow the shrimp."

* * *

Nearing the end of their second week, their tally stood at sixty-five dollars each, making it a good trip, provided their luck held out. Encouraged by the prospect of more money, they worked until darkness forced them to quit. Long days and quiet, monotonous nights became their routine, until one evening when they stopped barely inside the eastern tip of Raccoon Island, a mile away from their normal anchoring spot.

Rene cut the engine and Manny lowered the mushroom anchor over the side. The tip disappeared in the water, sank lower, and buried itself in the soft, murky bottom eight feet below.

Manny wiped his hands on his pants and entered the wheelhouse as Rene was adding up their tally. "We'll have a full load the day after tomorrow," he predicted. "Then we'll head for home that afternoon."

Manny wiped his brow with the back of his hand. "The first thing I'm going to do when I get there is drink a cold beer. All this water makes me thirsty."

"Just like you Indians." Rene grinned. "All you ever do is drink and lay around. Now I see why Tom yells at you."

Manny had bent over to grab his wooden cot but turned away from Rene and smacked his hip pocket with one hand. "Kiss this Indian's ass, white boy."

Manny carried his cot outside and Rene went down the steps to the engine; his first job at the end of every day was to look it over. He wiped the temperature gauge and removed the oil dipstick and read the level, following the pattern his father had taught him. Then he put on a pair of gloves and inspected the driveshaft, grabbing it, shaking it for evidence of play or signs of wear, running his hands over it until the shaft went through the back wall and connected to the power takeoff outside. He checked the water level in the dry tank and gave the engine a once-over, to make sure there wasn't any evidence of oil leaks or where water might have broken through a gasket.

Since it would be a warm and muggy night, Manny set up the cots and arranged the wooden bars that held the mosquito netting and took an old towel to wipe the windows of the wheelhouse. Continuing his routine, he also went over the net, looking for holes, passing the netting through his hands. But he found none. When he had started working on the docks as a young boy it had been the first job Tom gave him, and Manny became the best net mender in the company.

He had picked up the skill by hiring himself out to shrimpers who came in with damaged nets, and he stayed busy, because he worked at a reasonable rate of ten cents an hour, cheap enough so other crews didn't want to bother with the chore.

Sitting on the back deck, his legs tucked under him, Manny's brown torso mixed with the gray, weathered deck as the sun touched the far end of island and shadows from a nearby clump of tall grass darkened the railing. He smelled the pork and beans and sausage that Rene was heating on the gas stove but kept working until he was called for supper.

They sat on their cots a short time later, balancing the plates on their legs and protected from the mooching seagulls by the overhead canvas. A cool breeze crossed the deck and dried them. Rene stopped eating and watched the pencil-thin arc of sunlight slide into the land somewhere past Texas. With the expanding onset of darkness, the seagulls flew to the land nearby, squatted in dense groups, and maneuvered for their own resting space.

His head down and all his attention directed toward eating, Manny didn't look up. His idea about food was simple--eat it as quickly as possible and clear the plate. Rene was a rapid eater too, but he couldn't keep pace with Manny.

Because of the blackout rule, they didn't light a lantern. No tolerance was allowed, no matches struck in the open; nothing that would make them a target for a U-boat. Though Rene had never known of someone to be charged with a violation, any crews caught breaking the rule could be fined fifty dollars; and for a second one, they were apt to lose their license for the shrimping season and risk jail time too.

Rene had heard that several crews had been warned but guessed the stories had been invented to enforce the blackout. Besides, it would be foolhardy to light a lantern during the nighttime. The darkness was total when there was no moon, and the lack of light obliterated everything further than a few yards. Any flicker of light, even striking a match, was like offering a target to a German gunner.

Rene and Manny lay on their cots in their undershorts. The ocean breeze felt good, though a chill would approach after midnight in the guise of a creeping mist and would make a blanket necessary.

Rene rolled onto one side to look at the stars that were no longer blocked by the overhead canvas. The vast pinheads of starlight didn't follow any pattern he recognized, though several pulsed enough for him to see them flicker against the impenetrable nighttime sky.

Soothing rivulets from the changing tide nudged the boat and floated the keel just a few feet off the bottom, making for a restful evening.

Still restless and wide awake after two more hours, Rene rolled onto his right side and looked at Manny, who laid on his back, both hands behind his head, barely visible only a body length away. In such a pleasant night, it was hard to imagine that the rest of the world was fighting, that shipwrecks covered the seabed, that the armies were scattering men and tanks and airplanes over the landscape in foreign countries. Thoughts of the war reminded him of Sam and Roy, their bodies resting somewhere in the Gulf, but he'd never know where.

His mind drifted to Marie, and the loneliness gnawed at him and spread cold pangs through his chest, and he pictured how he wanted to hold her, her hair against his nose, her hips pressing against his when they kissed, how she smiled and closed her eyes whenever his fingers traced the profile of her breasts. Sometimes she'd let him put his hands underneath her blouse and rub her breasts and stomach, but when he tried to explore lower, she held his wrists, sighing heavily in opposition to his rapid breathing.

As much as he missed her, even for two weeks, he began to feel uncertain if he had made the right choice about the Navy, and a feeling of guilt nagged him like a pebble in his shoe that dug into him with each step. What was worse than not going to the war was making excuses when people asked why he hadn't enlisted. But he hoped his marriage would be the antidote to his doubt and others' comments. After the wedding, he would be too busy taking care of her and shrimping to think about the war. When they were finally together forever, he was sure their future would be the most important thing.

He felt the need to urinate, so he lifted the mosquito netting and planted his bare feet on the cool and damp deck. Careful not to slip, he made his way past Manny's cot and groped for the side of the wheelhouse by extending his arms and trying to avoid stubbing a toe in the dark. He reached the bow, faced the Gulf and pulled down his shorts, and a warm sensation spread through his pelvis.

His own falling water was the only sound he could hear in an otherwise quiet night.

He stared in the distance toward the west but was unable to see anything, though he knew that a dozen shrimp boats were anchored in the same bay. The black nighttime veil created an atmosphere that made it seem like he and Manny were totally alone. Everything was quiet. No marsh dogs barking, no fish jumping, the bay water smooth, and the stars appeared to be within an arm's reach when he looked at them.

Just as he decided to return to his cot, what sounded like a distant clap of thunder caught his attention. He looked toward the south and then the east but was unable to pick out any shafts of lightning. He was prepared to discount it until he heard a muffled explosion and a distant arc of reddish light accelerated into the southern sky.

He hurried back to the deck and shook Manny, who emerged from a sound sleep and grabbed Rene's arm "What the … the hell are you doing?" he demanded, rubbing his eyes.

"Get up," Rene whispered. "Come and listen."

Manny raised the netting and swung both feet onto the deck. "Are you crazy? There's nothing worth hearing in the middle of the night."

But Rene's tone grew sharper. "Come to the bow; hurry!"

Manny stood up and rubbed his eyes "I suppose you've captured a mermaid." He adjusted to the darkness and followed Rene. "If this is a joke, I'm tossing your ass in the water."

Manny stubbed a toe and cursed, and Rene warned him to be quiet, but he cursed again in a lower voice and hobbled to the railing near the bow, his patience gone.

"Show me something or get ready to go swimming."

Rene turned Manny's shoulders toward the Gulf and pointed in that direction. "It's coming from out there. Be quiet and we might hear it again."

Manny leaned over the railing, his mouth half-open, and he turned his right ear toward the water. "I don't hear anything."

The noise then traveled to them again, followed by a secondary explosion a few seconds later.

"That's it."

"It's probably the Coast Guard," Manny replied.

"My dad said they don't go out at night. That must be a U-boat firing at a ship."

Manny stared in the same direction. "How far away is he?"

"Maybe four or five miles. It's hard to tell the way sound carries over the water."

"Maybe it's a ship firing at the U-boat," Manny suggested.

"Perhaps," Rene answered. "The gun sounded the same each time. If it is a merchant ship, I hope they get the sub."

"And I hope they stay out there," Manny volunteered.

"I've heard other shrimpers talk engine noises at night. Some people even say a U-boat is capable of sneaking near the beach and dropping off spies."

Manny gave out a nervous laugh. "You're dreaming."

"My dad and I heard engine noises two weeks ago and he told me it was probably a freighter or a tanker sailing by, but he stayed up all night with a rifle in his hands. And he wouldn't talk about it the next day."

Manny changed his tone. "Could a U-boat get close to us?"

"I don't think so. The water's too shallow. Anyway, he must be six or seven miles out."

Manny wasn't convinced. "How do you know they can't get in here?"

"My dad said so," he replied. "The water's depth south of the island is less than ten feet for a couple of miles. A U-boat would hang up on the bottom."

"Why is he so sure of things? He's never seen a U-boat."

"We've seen pictures of them and read stories. They draft about fifteen feet."

After several more minutes, Manny nudged Rene with an elbow. "Let's get out of here."

Rene grabbed Manny by a shoulder to stop him from walking away. "We can't go anywhere. We'd hit a sandbar and go aground, or hit debris and punch a hole in the hull. We're safe from U-boats as long as we stay behind the island."

Manny turned toward the Gulf. "I wonder if that sub killed Sam and Roy. If it did, I wish we could do something about it."

"So do I, but it'll never happen."

They listened for ten minutes without either one speaking. Then a small arc of light on the far horizon expanded into a brief flash, followed by another explosion, and a sickening, red glow spread across the horizon and grabbed their attention.

"It must be a tanker on fire." Rene finally said. "I don't see how a sub would make a fireball that large."

Manny responded in an emotional half-whisper. "Those poor guys. I can't imagine being forced to jump into the Gulf at night."

"That's what happened to the mariner. They have to jump to get away from the fire. Then fuel spills in the water and ignites and burns them."

"We ought to go help," Manny said.

"Even wide open, we'd need over an hour just to reach them."

"Then we're wasting time; let's go," Manny cried out.

"We can't run at night. Even if we got there, we'd become a target ourselves." Rene explained." We'll head that way first thing in the morning." Back on his cot half an hour later, Rene turned onto his right side that blocked him from looking at the distant glow, but for the remainder of the night, his recurring dream of a U-boat, searching the island with its floodlight, refused to go away. Though he'd move behind a bush or drop down on the far side of a sandy hillock, the light sought him out and made him move.

They started south in the morning as soon as they could see, but Rene cut the engine to idle before they got halfway to the area. A Navy sub chaser was working back and forth over the scene and two patrol planes searched in a pattern at least a mile wide. Rene avoided running through a wide sheen of oil by turning around and returning to his sector of work.

* * *

When they stopped for lunch the last day of their second week, Rene looked at the *Times Picayune* they had gotten from the ice boat that morning. He flattened the page with one hand and propped it up. Not having learned to read much beyond piecing together fragments of a story and captions in the funny papers, Manny peered over Rene's shoulder.

The front page showed a picture of four young Merchant Marine crewmen, their shirts half-buttoned, posing with their arms around each other's shoulders.

Manny nudged him. "Read it out loud."

The story covered the details of a gun battle between a U-boat and a freighter in the southern region of the Gulf. The men pictured were the volunteer gun crew that had spotted the sub north of the Greater Antilles and had braved cannon fire to man the freighter's deck gun hidden at the bow of the merchant ship under a tarp. The U-boat had submerged after the freighter's crew thought they hit the sub with one shell below the waterline, and maybe a second one into the hull, forward of the conning tower, forcing the sub to crash dive so quickly that it stranded one German sailor outside. After the sub went down, the sailor swam away from the oil slick and the freighter picked him up and took him to New Orleans. The article estimated that five German submarines had been sent to the bottom of the Gulf, though confirmation hadn't been made with any of them. But an oil slick in the area had been monitored for several days before disappearing. The gun crew, all volunteers, was given a citation for bravery and a company bonus, while the German sailor was sent to a POW camp in Thibodeaux.

Rene stopped reading and scanned the water, wishing he had been the man who had pulled the trigger and hit that sub.

Manny pored over the comics by running a forefinger along the captions and working out what each character said. Rene wondered if Manny had ever been serious about enlisting, because he didn't appear to care about anything but his mother and making money.

The story of the gun crew reignited Rene's urge to enlist, and he toyed with a simple plan. He would disappear without a word to anyone, with only the clothes on his back, and afterwards write a letter to Marie and one to his parents when he was inducted into the Navy. It was foolproof; by the time Marie or his parents figured it out, it would be too late to stop him.

Savoy would have no one else to blame if Rene acted alone, and his parents wouldn't have to suffer the consequences. He nurtured the idea, and when he was underway again he fell into a rhythm with the rise and fall of the bow and dreamed of how it would feel to be on the flight deck of an aircraft carrier.

But his reverie was shattered when something struck the hull, and he spun the wheel to clear the screw of whatever they had hit, cut the engine's power to idle and stepped outside. Manny was already leaning over the railing, a fishing gaff in one hand, stretching toward the water.

"Do you see anything?"

"Not yet. Check the other side … no, wait. I have something," Manny called out, reaching with the gaff, then raising it and swinging a damaged five-gallon can onto the deck.

It was glossy black, like the ammunition cans Rene had at home, and when he pried the lid off there was a generous amount of brown grease inside. The can was free of seaweed and the wooden handle was in good condition, so it hadn't been in the water more than a few days. He turned the can over, exposing a series of yellow numbers beneath a small swastika.

Manny looked at the can, then at the Gulf behind him. "I thought we were in shallow water where U-boats can't go."

Rene nodded. "We are, but it must have floated in from farther out."

"But we didn't hear any explosions last night."

Rene kept his eyes on the can. "It probably fell overboard." He swung one arm in an arc toward the east. "The Ship Shoal trench is about ten miles from here. The current could have carried it this far in a couple of days."

Manny seemed satisfied. "Oh well, now you have another souvenir."

"And good grease too," Rene declared. He placed the can on the deck and broke into a mischievous smile. "Wouldn't you like to shoot at a U-boat?"

Manny shook his head vigorously. "No way. And I hope I never see one. I'm happy with a slow, wooden trawler. To hell with German submarines."

Rene looked toward the bow. "We could mount our cannon up front like the gun on that merchant ship. Or we could use machine guns. Anyway, the Germans would never suspect a shrimp boat of being armed. And when a U-boat surfaced, we'd let him draw alongside, then fire."

Manny hardened his eyes. "That's the stupidest thing I've ever heard," he said. "We're shrimpers, not sailors." He pointed at the grease can. "Don't use that can as an excuse to start your enlistment crap again."

"I suppose you wouldn't care if the Germans sailed up the Mississippi into New Orleans."

"Yes, I would, but now that I have a chance to make decent money, I'll stay home," When Rene didn't answer right away, Manny went on. "Tell you what; if the Germans come into South Louisiana, I'll fight, but not until then."

"If the war gets worse, the government might come and get you," Rene said. "What would you do then?"

Manny raised both arms. "Let's drop it. You can go if you want. Run out on Marie if that'll make you happy. Go kill Germans. Win a bunch of medals. But leave me alone."

"Aahh," Rene spouted, "forget it."

He went into the wheelhouse, put the boat into gear and took up an easterly heading. Getting ready for the next drag, Manny checked the boards and arranged the lines so they wouldn't be tangled when he lowered them into the water, and he went to the bow and waited for Rene to slow the boat for the drag. Trying to capture Rene's face, he glanced at the windows but the reflecting sunlight blocked his view.

*   *   *

The weekend that Rene and Manny returned from two weeks in the Gulf, Tom Savoy made mental notes on Saturday as he walked to the front door of his company store. The Coca-Cola sign was getting old. Rust bubbles poked through the paint whose letters had disappeared. He planned to ask the salesman for a new one. No matter what was happening overseas, the signs should be well maintained. A new coat of gray was also needed for the wooden porch to protect the wood before the winter rains. Perhaps Manny wanted to pick up some extra change. One section of the roof sat under the branches of a large oak tree and had decayed from being soaked every time it rained, looking now like a gust of wind could blow it off. The warehouse crew should put on a new section. The last note was the parking area; it had numerous holes that needed to be filled with clamshells.

Now that the service for Sam had been held, it was important to get on with life. Tom's grief had been intense, and he had railed at the injustice of the war, yet most of the mourners had watched in polite silence.

He hadn't recognized everyone who attended the service. A couple of men, who weren't from Pat's Landing, had left quickly without talking to Tom or anyone else. One of them resembled the guy he saw at the blessing of the fleet, but he couldn't be certain.

He turned the white porcelain knob on the store's front door that made a loud creaking sound as it opened. So many things to remember; he planned to make a full list. Otherwise, T C., with only one hand, would never do what was needed.

He passed the post office cubicle next to the front door. Its old fashioned, metal bars ran vertically from the top of the partition to six inches above the counter, with room enough to give out stamps and mail but too small for someone to reach inside. Wearing his patriotic pose, Uncle Sam glared from a poster on the back wall, pointing one finger and saying "I want you." Tom had hung the poster where everyone could see it. Two wanted posters flanked Uncle Sam, both so old and yellowed that the pictures and print were difficult to read.

Tom went around a heavily-scratched, glass counter, past a white Simpson scale to the post office cubicle, where he found a single business envelope that didn't have a return address, just like the first one he kept in his desk. The new one had been stamped in Houma two days earlier, addressed to Mr. Thomas Savoy, and like the first one, "Personal" was written in a lower corner. Tom tore open the envelope and dropped it in a wooden vegetable crate underneath the counter that served as a wastebasket.

The letter was half a page long and had been typed on a new ribbon, because the characters were heavily blackened. In keeping with the first letter, there wasn't a heading, date, or other information to suggest the identity of the writer. The body of the letter consisted of two brief paragraphs, single-spaced, with wide margins on both sides. It was impossible to ascertain who sent it since there were no other clues, names or references.

Once again the letter asked Tom if he was interested in making some easy money, payable in cash, and if so, to be in his hotel office, with the back door unlocked, next Sunday night at six o'clock. The second paragraph said a man who had seen Tom before would contact him. It ended by stressing that Tom wouldn't have the chance again if he decided not to show at the prescribed time and place. A caution at the end warned that failure to follow the instructions would nullify all further contact.

While the idea of easy money stirred him, Tom's doubts increased as he reread the letter. The whole thing might be a practical joke, or perhaps a scheme by some loser from the hotel's card games, who had sobered up the next morning and had to explain the loss to his wife. Or maybe someone wanted to get quick revenge with a knife or a pistol, the sort of stuff that happened with regularity in the French Quarter's flop houses. He chuckled at the letter and started to crumple it but changed his mind when his curiosity got the better of him. He smoothed the page, folded it and slipped it into his shirt pocket. It was worth checking out. If it was a disgruntled gambler, he'd give the guy a piece of his mind and tell him not to come back again.

* * *

It was still several hours before Rene and Marie were to be married late that afternoon, and Tom went over his plans. He hadn't balked at giving Rene a few days off for his honeymoon because their wedding was special, and there was no reason to complain over a one-time event. It would not only settle Rene down and get rid of his thoughts about enlisting, but he'd bring in additional money for the company if he turned out to be half as good as his old man.

It promised to be a full day, with the celebration first, then a drive to check on the letter in the evening. He'd have to watch his intake of alcohol at the reception and keep a clear head at the hotel, in case someone was determined to do him harm.

The idea that the mystery man might hold danger, gave birth to a strong sense of caution that nagged at him as he kneeled down to open the safe, which rested against the back wall, and selected the series of numbers. The silence in the store magnified his breathing, and his knees hurt as they did whenever he knelt on them for any length of time. It was the main reason he quit going to church. Since the outbreak of the war, his businesses demanded more of his time, and it was a good excuse to stay away. With the war on and everything being rationed, including his supplies for the boats, Sunday was just like any other work day.

It was going to be another hot day. His armpits were already wet and his beltline was damp.

After opening the safe, he shoved a cloth bag of chits aside that hid a short-barreled .38 revolver. He took it out and rotated the cylinder, making certain each slot held a round, before putting it in a hip pocket. It was a good feeling to be armed and it increased his anger over the letter. No bastard could buffalo him and get away with it. If the letter wasn't intended to be a business deal, he'd be ready to dispense justice. He could always blame it on a robbery attempt.

He shut the safe, spun the combination, grabbed a scratchpad and pencil, and walked around the store, inspecting every aisle. The first one held a rack of coats for the winter, plenty of white boots, long johns and socks. In another area, poles bunched together like giant, horizontal matchsticks, hanging in loops of twine from a rafter. Pots and pans dangled from nails on the back wall next to the canned vegetables, and boat paddles were stacked knee-high beside the back door that opened onto the bayou, where a gas pump stood at the water's edge.

Now that Sam was gone, he and Kay needed to pay more attention to things. T.C. was still learning how the store operated and couldn't be depended on to manage the inventory right away. With a less capable person in the store now, control had to be tighter.

The store had been built in 1900 by Tom's father. It was the first one on the bayou and had competed with the grocery boat that came from Thibodeaux once a week. He later expanded the store and installed a gas pump at the water's edge and secured most of the trade from fishermen, hunters, and trappers who brought their boats down the Lower Bayou. The post office addition came in 1910, bringing more traffic to the store. Tom liked the idea because it afforded him an excuse to snoop through the mail and recognize the pulse of activity in town.

After compiling two pages of notes, he completed his walk-around and left, closing and locking the front door.

10

The wedding activity started when Rene stepped into the green pirogue and took the paddle in his hands. He had spruced up the pirogue with a new coat of paint that gave off a fresh odor. Careful not to snag his suit on the board that functioned as a bench, he waved to his mother, who stood on the dock in a blue dress that nearly matched the cloudless sky. She cautioned Rene to watch his balance while Al pushed the pirogue into the bayou and admonished him not to drown. Since his snug-fitting suit coat restricted movement of his shoulders when he leaned forward to pull the paddle through the water, Rene shortened his strokes but managed to turn the pirogue into the current and start upstream.

"Don't capsize," Jane called behind a giggle. "It's bad luck to swim for your bride."

Rene waved and pulled on the paddle. The summer sun already concentrated its heat on the back of his neck, but he had only a short distance to go to where Marie and her parents waited. She looked resplendent in her billowing wedding dress and wispy white veil that draped over her head and shoulders. One hand keep the veil in place and the other held the hem of her gown to keep it off the ground.

The custom of being transported in a pirogue had been Marie's idea. She wanted to utilize the Cajun tradition that was the custom before the advent of cars when the groom carried the bride to the wedding in a pirogue. Jane had prepared a cushion where Marie was to sit by ironing and folding a white sheet, and Al had tacked the overlapping edges to the underside so it conformed to the wood.

While Rene drew closer to Marie, the events of the previous night rattled through his mind like a disjointed dream, and his head swayed through fragments of the bachelor night that Jay and

George--his buddies from high school--had given him. It had started with several beers from Cheramie's bar, then a ride into Houma, where George ran over a large dog without stopping to see if it was still alive or dead. He also remembered how Jay snickered as he described what he planned to do with the girl he was going to buy. During the half-hour trip, Rene had fallen asleep and didn't wake up, even when the car hit a large bump that sent the front wheels off the ground. He came to later with a dry mouth and an insatiable thirst for a coke, and George offered him another beer, saying it was better to stay drunk than to have a hangover. But Rene turned away, pressed his face against the seat back and closed his eyes, the only way he could stifle the urge to throw up and keep his head from spinning off his shoulders.

At the whorehouse, Jay tried one last time by jerking on Rene's leg to get him out of the car, but he slammed the door in defeat after nearly getting kicked in the chin. They returned to the car a half-hour later, chiding him for missing a great experience. But on the way back home they discussed the odds of catching the clap. George thought it was older women that got it, while Jay had heard that only colored women and Indians became infected, and it didn't occur in white women if they took regular baths at least once a week. Both reached the conclusion that each other was safe since they had chosen white women.

*   *   *

The pirogue nudged the dock and Rene stepped out, steadying it with the paddle in his left hand. Abe Fletcher met him first, looking uncomfortable in his brown suit and white shirt, whose collar was too small and pressed into the fleshy sides of his neck when he turned his head. His black shoes were so new that the vamps had no creases in them. He wished Rene good luck, shook hands, and held a firm grip until Rene relaxed his fingers and let go.

Next, Molly Fletcher hugged him and squeezed his shoulders, but he hardly felt any pressure, due to the arthritis that affected her hands, arms and shoulders. Strands of her hair caught the sunlight and exposed patterns of gray intermingled with dark brown. Her words came out in a throaty whisper, as if she was losing her voice.

She was known to become hoarse whenever she was emotional. "Take good care of her. That's all we ask," she said, pressing a lengthy kiss on one cheek and looking at him with an anxious smile on her face.

"I promise," he answered.

She patted him on one shoulder and stepped back to give Marie room.

Rene planted one foot on the dock while Marie's parents helped her into the boat. When she was settled he pushed away, but before dipping the paddle in the bayou, he leaned forward to help Marie adjust herself in the center of the seat, and as his face brushed the veil, his senses were flooded with the fragrance of her perfume that eased the pain of his headache like a tonic, and he sat back so rapidly that he caused the pirogue to rock and Marie to let out a short cry and caught her dress before it skimmed the water.

"Are we going to swim there?" she giggled.

"Sorry," Rene said emitting a happy grin. "I love your perfume and you, with or without perfume."

"And I love you."

Slipping downstream, the current carried them toward the waiting procession of people and cars near the warehouse. Marie waved when she heard her name from bystanders and carefully turned her head so she wouldn't mess her hair, which was arranged in pampered waves that touched her shoulders. Everything about her looked so fresh and inviting that Rene wondered why he had ever been serious about enlisting.

It was hard to believe that he was getting married to the only girl he had ever loved. But his conviction and devotion strengthened each moment he looked at her, and his headache shrank into a negligible pinpoint as the idea of the wedding made him feel happier than he had ever imagined he could be. He maneuvered the pirogue toward the dock, convinced that nothing could mar his happiness ever again.

Tom had arranged the cars for transportation to the church, with his Chrysler in the lead. George's two-door Ford coupe, sporting a new wax job, was next. Suzie Theriot, the Maid of Honor, who had grown up with Marie, sat fanning herself with George's hat and craning her neck to look at Marie as she took Rene's arm and stepped out of the pirogue.

Tom guided them to his Chrysler and opened the rear door. Marie got in first, careful not to catch her dress as she maneuvered past the door post, while Rene folded her long gown to keep it from dragging.

After they were seated, Rene grasped her left hand and kissed it, but Marie pulled it away and laughed, her face radiant behind a teasing smile. "You have to wait until after the wedding,"

"You look wonderful," Rene said.

"I might say the same about you too," she replied behind a wide smile.

Al and Jane were next, riding in Babe Wilson's 1938 Chevy, a brown sedan with black tires, while the third car--Jay Thibodeaux's Plymouth--was designated for Marie's parents. Babe had acquired his nickname because he had been the most powerful hitter on his high school's baseball team. He was a Mississippi bachelor who had been friends with Abe Fletcher since the Depression, the same year that Babe moved to Pat's Landing and began working on Tom's boats. After closing the door for Jane and Al, he stood by the rear door, wiping his brow with a handkerchief and looking uncomfortable in the persistent heat.

As the procession started Tom crept forward, George blew his horn, and bystanders waved as the cars made their short trip to the church.

When Rene reached again for Marie's hand that rested on the edges of her dress, almost touching his leg, she giggled and pulled away. "It's bad luck before the wedding," she cautioned behind a giggle.

"I love you," he whispered, leaning toward her, but stopping before his face pushed into her veil.

Arriving at the church, Tom drove onto the narrow strip of grass in the front yard and straddled the front sidewalk, leaving enough room for the car doors to open without hitting the statue of St. Andrew who guarded the entrance. Put there after the great flood of '27, he watched over the men who worked in the Gulf. His arms and hands were peeling and the base had several grooves in the concrete from the effects of rain and humidity over fifteen years, and a chalk layer resembling dust covered his head and shoulders, making the statue appear to be crumbling. But St. Andrew had persevered through the destructive power of three hurricanes and dozens of relentless thunderstorms. Some people had called for a new figure to replace the original one, but Tom and several others argued that it should remain as long as St. Andrews is recognizable.

At the same time that Marie disappeared inside the front door and into the vestibule, Rene and George walked around to the side door to await the signal from Father Gruber. Organ music drifted through the door and the half-opened, stained-glass side windows that were adorned with the Stations of the Cross, and the pleasant odor of fresh paint was the result of Al touching up sections of siding that had peeled from the sun and humidity.

Fidgeting before the ceremony, time crept too slowly to suit Rene, who was anxious to get it over with and to be with her on his own terms, where circumstances wouldn't be dictated to them anymore, where they would answer only to each other, and the thought of what the ceremony would bestow on them made him giddy and anxious.

A shrimp boat positioning at the dock caught his attention as the organ music had been muted in anticipation of the wedding march. The sights and sounds of boats, the bayou and shrimping, had been essential in his life for as long as he could recall, and his decision to stay home was an affirmation he would share them with Marie. As he watched George flick a cigarette onto the grass, he realized why he couldn't explain it when George had asked why he didn't leave Pat's Landing and get a good job in the New Orleans shipyard. He was woven inextricably into the fabric of shrimping; it was a benediction of freedom, work, and his life, and now that Marie was to be with him, she would bring a balance that would wipe away his dreams of enlisting.

George was working in the Avondale Shipyards as a welder's helper and Jay hoped to become a machinist. Both were happy with their jobs and expected to make good money, but their plans didn't interest him. He and Marie would live in Pat's Landing. It was home.

On the signal from Father Gruber, Rene and George went inside to the center aisle. The interior of the church was overflowing with decorations. Baskets of flowers were spaced around the altar and small bouquets of daisies filled the window sills. A long, white, cotton runner that covered the center aisle brightened the church's interior and provided an attractive contrast to the brown pews. Presiding over all aspects of the ceremony was an assortment of saints who filled the alcoves and watched from both sides of the church.

A graphic figure of Christ hung on a massive cross behind the altar. The artist had produced a cadaverous Jesus with a concave chest, a spear wound between his ribs dripping blood down to his hips, and a crown of thorns that punctured his scalp in several places, producing multiple rivulets of blood onto his face. There had been strong objections by several parishioners for portraying Christ in such stark detail when the final image of the figure was discussed, because Pierre Savoy and two men on the church committee had insisted on the figure looking real, instead of resembling a department store mannequin. The final decision was to keep the details of his body, but the historical aspect of Christ being nude was turned down, and a fragment of cloth covered his hips and enough of his anatomy so the women were not pressed to explain the nudity to their young children.

All the pews were full and the guests nudged each other for a position to give them a better view when Marie and her father came down the aisle.

Tom and his wife and daughter sat near the center and five rows back with a good view.

Rene searched unsuccessfully to pick out Manny and his mother. He figured they would be in one of the last pews where the Sabines customarily sat. There was no rule against them moving closer to the altar, but the tradition of sitting in the back of the church remained with them and the colored parishioners.

Rene had personally invited Manny and Bootsy after he learned that Molly Fletcher hadn't sent them an invitation, but his reception had been a cool one. Manny had replied that he might be there, but his mother had washing to do, and if she couldn't come, he wouldn't either. Rene tried to convince him that it was a simple mistake but Manny didn't want to talk about it.

*   *   *

On cue with the wedding march, Marie and her father emerged from the vestibule and fell into a slow cadence that allowed Abe, with shorter legs, to stay in rhythm with her. When they reached Rene, he changed places with Abe, took Marie's hand, and they knelt on a ceremonial maroon cushion that covered the third step to the altar.

Now that the wedding was underway, Rene's clothes felt heavy, and nervous twinges played down his back. He wanted to scratch but didn't dare. His headache was gone but an unsettled feeling took its place. He attempted to concentrate on the words of Father Gruber, but his mind wandered to Marie, and he pictured how attractive it would be to embrace when they were undressed. They would have the whole night to love each other, but he wondered if he should wait until the ceremony was over to think about such things. Marriage was a sacrament, and he was uncertain if he violated it by dwelling on their approaching sexual relationship before the ceremony was completed and Father Gruber's blessing made their union official. It wouldn't be a sin when they were married, but he was still single for a few moments. He sought to block the idea by concentrating on the Mass and watching Father Gruber cradle the Mass book as he spoke of the importance of a Christian approach to marriage.

When Marie caught Rene's attention by gently squeezing his hand without taking her eyes off Father Gruber, he wanted to look at her but knew everyone had their eyes on them, so he pressed her hand in return.

They left the church after the ceremony amid a shower of rice from guests who lined both sides of the sidewalk. Tom stood at the Chrysler, looking serious and maintaining the composure of a chauffeur and waiting with the rear door open. But Tom shed his formal airs and gave Marie an embrace, a quick peck on the cheek and grabbed Rene in a vigorous handshake, then poking him in the ribs with an elbow.

"It's too late to back out now," he joked. "From now on, the law, your wife, and the church have a grip on you."

"It feels good." Rene admitted.

"And I hope it remains that way," Tom counseled.

Tom helped Marie manipulate her dress as she and Rene got into the back seat, and then drove them to the reception at the school gym two blocks away. On the way he launched into advice, at the same time noticing through the rear view mirror how Rene had slid closer to Marie and held her in a tight embrace.

"There'll be plenty of time for that later. Save some of your strength for the dancing," he said, prompting laughter from them. He waggled a finger and eyeballed Rene. "You're on the right track to be a good husband. Give her love every day and you'll never have to live with a mad woman. You may not feel that way after you've had a spat over money, cleaning the house, or the kids running wild, but it'll smooth over any bumps you might have." He swung into the parking lot to a space reserved for the Chrysler, shut off the engine and turned around in the seat, a mischievous smile on his face. "Now try to behave until you leave the reception."

After they emerged from the car and started to greet guests that had formed a line inside the gym, Tom returned in a few moments with two glasses of champagne. The cold drink soothed Rene's parched throat, and he drank it in three gulps but told himself to stay away from any more alcohol. Tonight wouldn't be the proper time to imbibe and ruin the excitement coursing through him. He'd heard stories about drunken husbands on their wedding night, and he vowed not to be that kind of groom.

Thanks to Jane and Molly, the gym floor was decorated attractively. The flowers brought from the church now spread among the tables and chairs. Several white, cloth-covered tables were set up past the reception line on one side of the floor and were crammed with food and desserts, each from a housewife who had managed her ration cards and had made her own special recipe. In order to accommodate so many guests, Jane and Molly had borrowed silverware and plates from friends, and Kay Savoy had loaned her large silver punchbowl that served as a dividing line between the food and desserts.

Without anyone watching, Tom emptied a bottle of vodka into the fruit punch. It wouldn't alter the flavor enough to notice but would provide a boost for anyone who took more than two glasses.

The variety of food dispersed their cumulative aromas and filled the building with layers of tantalizing smells, chicken and sausage gumbo, seafood gumbo, fried chicken, steamed soft-shell crabs, deep-fried catfish, fried oysters, cold shrimp on ice, fried shrimp, and steamed shrimp still in their shells, pots of red beans and rice, potato salad, bean salad, collard greens, macaroni and cheese, and okra casserole. The desserts were peach and apple pies and cakes and puddings crowded together on another table. Drinks varied from rice beer in brown bottles, carrot wine and grape wine in gallon jugs, to a few bottles of hard liquor that Tom had collected from his bar, plus a bottle of champagne in a bucket of ice that was covered with a towel.

Chairs ran down the opposite side of the gym and across one end, along the out-of-bounds line, while the band of the same four men, who played at all social functions in Pat's Landing, set up underneath one of the backboards. Three were fishermen; one played the electric fiddle, a second the accordion, the third a harmonica, and the fourth man--a small, wiry math teacher--played a guitar. Only twenty-five, he had been rejected when he tried to enlist because his poor eyesight made him 4-F.

Abe Fletcher had wanted to add a drummer, but the closest one lived in Houma and had asked for thirty-five dollars, an amount that equaled the price for the whole band.

After the guests had passed through the receiving line, Rene and Marie began the promenade that went twice around the gym floor, and then broke up with the bride and groom dancing. Then traditional dances followed; Marie paired with her father and Rene with his mother. Jane had given Rene lessons when he was in high school and still squeezed his left hand whenever she wanted him to turn, a tactic she had used during his first dance lesson at fourteen. Since Marie didn't have a brother the bridal dance with her shoes off was omitted. Instead, she danced with Al, who was also her godfather, and when she and Rene got together again, Marie had a five dollar bill pinned on her veil. The tradition came from earlier times when it was more difficult for those who lived in isolated locations to get into town and buy a present than to give money. The practice continued until Marie's veil had almost disappeared under an array of bills pinned on it.

Tom walked across the floor with two plates of food for Kay and daughter, Sarah, who sat with Father Gruber, and when the priest wiggled his empty glass at him, Tom went back for a refill of grape wine.

*   *   *

Standing alone, Manny watched from outside the gym door, listening to the hum of conversation and debating about going inside.

He was hot and uncomfortable after walking from his house in shoes that he hadn't worn for four months, and strange clothes, starched pants and a white shirt his mother insisted that he wear. The clothes trapped the heat and the shoes squeezed his toes, pressed against the back of both heels and rubbed them with each step. As he watched from beyond the gym, it occurred to him that he had never been to a reception or any other social function in Pat's Landing where everyone else was white. But after a short span of indecision, he moved inside when he picked out a familiar face or two. He went through the door, careful not to bump into anyone, and worked his way toward the line of tables, hoping to avoid calling attention to himself. The last thing he wanted was to get caught in a conversation. His stomach was in knots, and the suffocating air--a mixture of food, cigarette smoke and perfume--was overpowering. His mother didn't wear perfume, and he hated cigarette smoke, so he breathed in short cycles and tried to endure the stifling atmosphere.

But his plan flopped halfway between the door and the food. He had hoped to talk with Rene and Marie, but it appeared hopeless. So many people surrounded him without looking at him that he wasn't brave enough to walk onto the dance floor to get a better look. He felt like he was the only person at the reception who hadn't met a friend or neighbor and was on the verge of leaving, when he saw Jane spooning potato salad into someone's plate.

"Manny," she called out, "I'm happy you could make it. Rene told me to watch for you." She grabbed an empty plate. "Now tell me what you want to eat."

"Some chicken … a little bit of dirty rice and some beans," he answered, holding his attention on Jane and hoping to remain inconspicuous.

Without warning, he was grabbed from behind and turned around to face Rene, who wore a big smile.

"This is a very nice reception," he offered.

Rene glanced toward the door. "Is your mother here?"

"No," he answered, watching Jane put a drumstick on his plate.

When Jane handed Manny his plate of food, it occurred to him that he had seldom eaten out of anything other than a tin plate, and he wondered if Rene knew that. Rene had come to his house many times but had never eaten there, though Manny had shared a meal at Rene's house on several occasions, usually breakfast, during their younger years when they slept outside in the summer. He tightened his grip on the plate and hoped he could maneuver to a chair without bumping someone and spilling his food.

Since he'd always relied on the upturned edge of tin plates, he grabbed his the same way, but drew his thumb back when it protruded into the dirty rice.

The plate was just one more thing they didn't share. He used tin, Rene used real plates, he was a Sabine, Rene was Cajun, and he had no father, while Rene grew up with one. They were friends without actually sharing their lives, other than surface things--work and having a beer once in a while. The community welcomed Rene and his new wife, while Manny lived alone with his mother and could count on one hand the number of times when anyone came to visit them. Rene seemed like a brother most of the time, but Manny couldn't extend that feeling to the wedding reception. Though he knew the opinions that some whites held about Sabines, he was still put out when he and his mother hadn't been formally invited. The cultural gaps would never merge, no matter what happened.

Rene didn't give up. "It's the weekend. Why can't she come?"

Manny wanted to find a chair and eat without making excuses. "She has laundry to finish."

Rene persisted. "Will you be able to bring her after she finishes?"

Manny kept his voice under control but was getting tired of Rene's insistence, and he felt crowded. "I don't think so. She said she can't make it."

He was rescued by Jane handing him silverware wrapped in a white napkin. "Do you need anything else?"

"No; thank you very much."

"You're very welcome."

He turned toward some unoccupied chairs, hoping to be alone without people sitting next to him asking him questions or talking without including him in the conversation, but Rene moved in front and blocked his way.

"How long are you staying?"

Manny shrugged. "Not long. I have to go home and help my mother."

"Make sure you take her a plate of food."

Manny shook his head. "That wouldn't be right."

"What do you mean?" Rene asked. "It's my reception, and I say it's okay."

He looked at Rene as frustration began to creep into his jaw. While it would be pleasant to stay and talk with Marie and share time with them, people might look askance at him, and he didn't want to cause Marie and Rene trouble at their own reception.

"If you say so," he countered flatly, "but I can't stay very long."

Rene pressed for a better answer. "Friends don't eat and run. It wouldn't be polite."

Manny felt people were looking at him and tempered his reaction. "These are your people, Rene, not mine."

He expected Rene to move out of the way, but when he edged forward he rocked onto his heels to avoid bumping into Rene.

"I invited you because you're my best friend," Rene countered, pointing at Manny's chest. "You belong here as much as anyone else."

Manny closed his eyes. "Fine; now please let me eat."

"Okay. But don't leave until Marie comes to say hello."

Tom Savoy appeared at that time and grasped Rene on one shoulder, ignoring Manny, who had to shuffle aside to keep from banging his plate against Tom's belly.

Tom dangled a set of car keys in front of Rene and smiled. "The car's outside, filled with gas, whenever you and Marie want to leave."

"I very much appreciate this." Rene began, but Tom didn't let him finish.

"I can't think of anyone who will take better care of Sam's Lincoln than you. Besides," he added, his eyes twinkling and his face holding a mischievous expression, "It's an investment. On top of that, I don't need another car, so there's no reason to thank me. You'll pay me back by being one of my best skippers and making me lots of money. Men like your father and you keep me in business."

"I'm still grateful for what you've done," Rene explained, glancing over his shoulder. "Please excuse me. I need to find Marie."

Manny had never seen Tom act so kindly toward anyone, even his own wife and daughter. His attitude toward Rene was clearly fatherly and sincere, and he wondered if he had been wrong about Tom.

But he was jolted back to reality as Tom jerked toward Manny with an icy stare blanketing his face.

"What the hell are doing here?" he hissed.

Manny was stunned that such a hateful reaction would surface while people were celebrating a wedding. The stories that Tom might be his father flickered through his mind, and he decided if they were true, he would hate him all the more for not marrying his mother like any decent man would have done. Manny had shaken off Tom's former outbursts as part of his business personality, but the glare in Tom's eyes convinced him that he had been mistaken. His friendly face was a masque. He only pretended to be civil, and after the reception was over, Tom would return to his abusive ways. But for Rene's sake, Manny cloaked his anger in a polite response toward the man he had wanted to be friends with but finally realized that would never happen.

"Rene invited me."

Tom looked him up and down, his narrow-eyed glare returning to Manny's face. "Well, I can't do anything about that now."

Manny's throat constricted, and he quelled the urge to punch Tom. But it would destroy the reception and ruin any further chance to work with Rene. Instead, he forced a weak smile. "I only wanted to offer my congratulations."

Tom was curt. "Okay. You've done it. Now don't stay any longer than the time it takes to eat your food." Tom edged so close to Manny that he could smell Tom's alcoholic breath. "If it weren't for Rene and Marie, I'd throw your ass out right now."

The remark was difficult to shrug off, but it wasn't surprising. Manny had grown up knowing that Sabines seldom mixed with Cajuns on social occasions. He had faced such adversity with his fists during his school years until other boys left him alone. But the encounter with Tom jarred him. He couldn't understand why Tom should be so ugly during an occasion that was meant to be celebrated. Everyone in the room but Tom looked happy and sociable. Manny smothered the impulse to smash his plate of food into Tom's flabby face, because it would damage his own friendship with Rene and Marie.

He wondered if he and his mother should get out of Pat's Landing. Help wanted ads in the newspaper offered jobs in the shipyards in New Orleans and Morgan City. Other than the war, good-paying jobs were all people talked about. A guy named Higgins ran constant ads for workers in his shipyard. With a new job he could work a couple of months, save his money and find a house for himself and his mother. Good wages would allow him to earn enough for both of them, and he could build boats for Higgins and support the war on his own terms without abandoning her. The idea buoyed his spirits because it would take him away from the one person he couldn't stand any longer.

"Mister Savoy," Manny began, the first time he'd ever used the formal way of pronouncing Tom's name. "You don't like me, even though I've done you a good job and never complained." Then he breathed deeply and clenched his teeth. "Fire me if you want. But from now on, you can go straight to hell."

He turned away with his plate and walked toward the chairs but remained ready to spin around and punch Tom in the face if he grabbed him again.

Watching Manny walk away, Tom was struck for a response because it was the first time anyone, other than Kay, had spoken to him like that. Instead of anger, he muttered to himself and turned toward the drink table for another glass of champagne.

"For being half Indian, he's still a damned good kid and full of spunk."

* * *

When the novelty of dancing with others had worn off, Rene and Marie moved onto the dance floor together and she raised her right arm to hold up one corner of her veil.

"Look what Tom Savoy gave us," she gushed, pointing to a twenty-dollar bill. "Most of the others pinned on fives and tens."

"Fine" Rene said, "but I'm more interested in the woman under the veil than I am in her money."

"Do you say that to all the girls?" she teased.

"Just you," he answered, kissing her on the forehead and pulling her closer.

They blocked out everyone but each other, and Rene tightened his arm around her back, their bodies moving to the rhythm of the music. When he tilted his head to kiss her on the ear, her veil teased one side of his forehead, and she pushed against him and breathed onto his neck. He kissed her temple and she pressed her head against his, her lips playing across the base of his neck in a flickering gesture that enflamed his imagination, and he pulled back to look at her and saw an expression of willingness that he had never seen before. Moving closer, he used the fingertips of his right hand to draw tiny circles near the top of her hips, which she responded to by arching her body and pressing into him with each dance step, her back muscles tightening beneath his fingers. Every gesture was received with a sigh, a squeeze, or an effort to stay close.

They stopped dancing and separated, but he held her hands; his head and neck were so warm that he thought only a stream of cold water would lower the temperature inside him.

"Let's leave."

"Okay."

They went over to Jane and Molly who were stacking empty bowls and organizing the silverware, and after embracing both of them, Molly pointed to the other side of the gym where Al, Abe Fletcher and several others sat drinking. "Those two are solving the problems of the world. Go talk to them. They need a break before they run out of steam."

Rene and Marie didn't get very far before they recognized the high-pitched voice of Alex Williams leading the conversation, a talent he displayed every time he had a couple of drinks. He was absorbed by his pet target--Huey Long--who had been disliked by many in southern Mississippi where Alex had grown up. He held the notion that Huey had been a crook who had pocketed much of the federal money earmarked for Louisiana, but Abe argued that Long had done well by giving the people electricity and paving roads in small towns and farming regions. The debate intensified with each new round of drinks.

Alex chewed a bite of fried chicken and talked with his mouth half-open. Since he was enmeshed in his favorite argument, pausing to eat was unnecessary. He had brown eyes behind dark-rimmed glasses and a long shank of black hair that dangled over his forehead, and he perched on the front edge of his chair and leaned forward like someone about to fall on his face. His issue, the coal miners' walkout, absorbed him.

"Roosevelt should toss those strikers in jail," he announced, "but he won't because they're democrats. We need that coal to help win the war. Imagine," he said, in a disapproving manner, wiping his mouth with one hand, "how a few penny-ante union organizers are trying to cripple this country. Those bastards are hurting the war effort and should be brought up on the charge of treason."

Abe didn't agree. "The working man needs to make a living too. If the owners won't pay a fair wage, what else can the miners do?"

Alex shook a fist in the air. "I'll tell you what," he answered. "Put those slackers in uniform and ship them to the fight. Let them get in a tussle that means something."

"Everyone can't enlist, Alex, or we wouldn't have enough men to do the heavy work."

"The heavy work?" Alex scoffed. "The heavy work is fighting the war, not putting in an easy day in the states." He made a fist and concentrated on Abe. "We haven't had one clear victory since the war started."

"What about Midway and Doolittle's group bombing Tokyo?" Al said.

"Tokyo was just a raid and our Midway losses were practically the same as the Japanese. If you ask me, the best we came away with was a draw." He waved one arm toward an open door that looked southward. "We have U-boats prowling the Gulf of Mexico and sinking our tankers before they get around Florida." He stopped for another drink of beer before continuing. "I heard someone in the barber shop last week who said that we'll need to have ten million men in uniform before this is over. If that's so, I wouldn't be surprised if Roosevelt started drafting men up to seventy. It wouldn't bother me to go either. If they'd take me, I'd put my old Navy blues on and report right away. Our nation needs every man who can fight."

Al had avoided getting involved in an argument on Rene's wedding day and when he saw Marie and Rene approaching, he tapped Alex on the shoulder. "Here come the bride and groom. Now mind your manners."

But Alex kept on as if he hadn't heard. "If I was twenty years younger, I'd be carrying a rifle. This nation is in a death struggle, and every young man worth his salt ought to be in uniform."

He slapped Al on one leg and leaned closer to him, maintaining his harsh tone. "When's Rene going to join up?"

Al quelled his anger. "That's up to Marie and Rene. It's none of my business now that he's married."

Alex wrinkled his forehead and jerked backward. "Well, you know how that goes," he suggested, winking. "Boys get married before shipping out because it keeps the little lady home where she belongs and gives him someone to come home to."

"Ask him yourself," Al said, standing up as Marie and Rene reached the group.

"We're going to leave now," Marie said before anyone made a comment, "and we thank you all for coming."

They worked through the gathering, Marie embracing each man and Rene shaking hands, and they came to Alex last. He pecked Marie on the cheek, then pumped Rene's hand and slipped his left arm around Rene's shoulders. He was as tall as Rene and twice as large, with a stomach that pushed over his belt line like an inflated balloon, and his breath was laced with cigarettes and beer.

"When are you going into the Army?"

Rene took Marie by one hand, pulling her toward him and stepping back from Alex. "I'm not. I'm staying here and shrimping," he answered.

Before Alex could formulate a response, Rene guided Marie past the well-wishers and started toward the door. Alex stared after them, his mouth open and his large girth heaving in time with his breathing. He slumped in his chair and wiped his face with a handkerchief.

"I don't believe it," he said in a half-audible voice. "If I was his age, I would have gone during the first week of the fighting. Like the Bible says, we're living in dark days, and if we don't win this war, our nation will never recover."

Al gripped his empty beer glass, the veins in his neck standing out. He didn't want to spoil the reception with a confrontation, but he'd heard enough. "Damn it, Alex, it's his life, not yours or mine. It's for him and Marie to decide."

Alex looked up and blinked his eyes like someone waking from a nap. "But Al, we answered the call in World War One. Why won't he do the same thing now?"

Abe Fletcher stepped between the two and handed Alex a fresh glass of beer just as Al clenched both fists. "Have another drink, Alex."

"Thanks," Alex replied, tipping the glass toward his mouth.

11

They stopped at Marie's house to change clothes. She unpinned the money from her veil and put it in a shoebox, warning Rene of bad luck if they spent it before the honeymoon was over. After he changed out of his suit and she put up her wedding dress, they started for Houma.

They hadn't gotten very far before Marie leaned against his chest and rested her right arm along Rene's thigh, gently rubbing his leg. He kissed her on the back of her neck, closed his eyes for a few seconds, and drew in the enticing scents emanating from her hair, her skin and her perfume. But it also brought about a brief period of inattention, and the car's right front tire went onto the shoulder and dug into clamshells that ricocheted off the fender well like a fusillade of rifle shots. He jerked the steering wheel to the left, got the Lincoln back on the road, and glanced down at Marie, who hadn't bothered to look up.

It had been a long reception and, as the daylight began to fade, he pulled on his headlights and kept the Lincoln at forty--the fastest he could drive safely on the winding, narrow road. The thought of risking an accident from an approaching car, a deer jumping into his path, or a gator crawling onto the roadway, kept him alert.

Strains of Glenn Miller floated from the radio and softened the subtle chattering of the Lincoln's engine, mixing with eddies of warm air dancing through the open windows and encasing them in their precious solitude. The new full moon--now a large, emerging, orange disc low on the horizon--splashed light into the car each time Rene passed a break in the trees that bordered the east side of the road.

Several minutes later, Glenn Miller gave way to Sammy Kay's orchestra playing "The Pearl Harbor Song." And the words, "Let's remember Pearl Harbor as we go to meet the foe," caused Marie to sit upright and stare at the radio with a vexed expression on her face. Tapping his left hand on the steering wheel in time to the music, Rene felt her pull away, so he turned off the radio and put both hands on the steering wheel, waiting through a short, uncomfortable silence that crept between them.

"They play that song so much it's getting tiresome," he remarked.

Marie drew closer, her face inches from him. "You like that song, don't you?"

"Sure. Most Americans do."

"That's not what I mean. I wonder if you still think about enlisting when you hear it."

He reached for her shoulder and pulled her into him. "I've already joined up," he explained, kissing her on the forehead. "And so have you. We've enlisted to work together and supply shrimp for the war. We're both soldiers now."

"Don't toy with me. I want the truth."

He rubbed the back of her neck, kept the other hand on the wheel, and looked at her. "The truth is I love you and have since I was twelve, and I knew then that we were going to have a special life together. Nothing can ever change that."

She planted her face in his shirt and wrapped one arm around his rib cage, kissing him next on top of the head and working down one side of his neck. "I'll never let you go," she declared in a whisper.

"That goes double for me," he said, steering the car back to the middle of the road.

*   *   *

About twenty minutes away from Pat's Landing, Marie still hadn't paid attention to anything outside the car. She kept her head on Rene's chest and rested her face against the pocket on his shirt, and when he adjusted his right arm around her, she nuzzled closer. He kissed her head behind one ear and ran a hand along the bottom of her right breast and she pressed her head firmly against him. When he slid his hand gently upon its curvature, she turned her face into his shirt, kissing his chest through the fabric. He pulled her into him and kissed her on the side of her neck; it was hot from being against him. She reached around his chest and moved closer, her efforts kindling a wave of emotion that lodged in his throat, and he tried unsuccessfully to tell her that he loved her, then got it out the second time and held her as close as he could get her with one arm.

Marie sat up a few miles later and peered through the side window as they neared the southern outskirts of Houma. They drove through an older residential section of pillared homes and circular driveways and bricked flower beds that accented long, well-kept lawns and expensive cars similar to Tom's Chrysler. Every detail of the homes suggested money.

Marie pointed at one house with a broad porch and four front columns. "Isn't that pretty?" she gushed. "Let's get one of those."

Rene wondered how he'd get enough money for such a place. "You should have married a wealthy guy," he remarked, squeezing her.

She answered without looking at him. "No way. You're the right man for me."

They went past the airport but few lights were on. Although the town and airport were thirty miles inland, the blackout rule dominated there too.

"Is that where Joe Christy stays?" Marie asked.

"Yes, unless he's already moved to Grand Isle."

"I wish he could have come to the wedding."

"He said the war doesn't give him weekends off, but he'd try to see us tomorrow."

"Where?"

"At a restaurant across the street from the hotel. If he can get away, he'll be waiting for us at eleven."

Marie snuggled closer to Rene. "That's nice."

Rene laughed softly. "I didn't want it to be too early."

Marie let out a burst of laughter, smacked his shoulder, grabbed his neck, and planted a hard kiss on it, and the Lincoln jumped to the opposite side, forcing him to grab the wheel and get back to his lane.

Because they weren't familiar with Tom's hotel, they drove past the library and grade school, then retraced their path before they found the location. It sat across a side street from the new city hall, on the southern edge of Main. Imposing and official-looking, the white stone building had been built by the WPA in the early thirties and still looked new, compared to the red brick store fronts across the road that sprouted thin layers of dirt and streaks of mildew.

They parked on the side street and entered the hotel. Since the rooms were on the second level, the bottom floor was divided into a bar on one end, a restaurant and dining room in the middle, and the lobby on the other side. A faded red runner from the front door to the reception desk had seen better days, and the overstuffed chairs in the small lobby were sunken and tired-looking.

A short, scrawny clerk rotated the sign-in book and glanced at Marie, then Rene, and a sly grin emerged from his face. He hummed a tune while waiting for the book to be signed, and then took his time selecting a key from a row of hooks on the back wall. He picked one on the top row and winked as he handed Rene the key. "Mr. Savoy said to give you the best room in the hotel. It's very quiet so you won't be disturbed in the morning, if you don't want to get up right away."

Rene grabbed the key and took an immediate dislike to the clerk's attitude, but muttered a quick thank you and picked up their suitcases to follow Marie up the stairs. They turned down a dark hallway and found their room that was two doors away from the alley and a short distance from Tom's office. Marie unlocked the door and swung it open but stopped when Rene reached for her arm. He banged the suitcases on the door jamb as he carried them both inside at the same time, set them down and came back for Marie.

"I won't be able to carry you like this on the boat, so I'd better do it now," he explained. "If I tried it on the water, we may fall overboard."

She giggled and clasped him around the neck.

The room smelled of mildew and floor wax. A double bed rested between two small, veneer nightstands, a lamp sat on one and a Bible was on the other. Rene didn't give the details of the room a second thought as he stopped by the bed, bent down and gently lowered Marie onto her back, still holding her in his arms. She pulled him upon her, kissing him in a prolonged, deep exchange that he had never before experienced. Now that they were finally alone, every gesture took on a different sensation and meaning. When he moved his hands down her back she responded by pushing her hips toward him, her entire body answering the slightest request he made of her. There was no awkwardness between them anymore as he slid his left hand beneath her blouse and worked his way up her stomach, caressing one breast, measuring its fullness with a slight squeeze that ignited a gasp of pleasure and a wide smile from her, and she buried her face into one side of his neck, progressing upward toward his ear in long kisses, while his hand grasped a handful of her hair and cushioned her head. The warmth from her lips drove sensations through him that wrapped around his heart like a pair of soft hands, and his breath came in short, rapid gulps.

It was at that moment that something caused him to look over his shoulder, and a cold surge of disgust hit him and made him promptly release her and stand up. "I forgot to close the door," he confessed.

Marie broke into laughter and ran her hands up his rib cage inside his shirt, leaving goose pimples over his skin. He hurried to the door, closing it and checking the lock, but when he turned toward the bed, Marie had disappeared into the bathroom and shut the door, and it wasn't long before he heard the shower running.

He lay on the bed and stared at the ceiling, holding a broad smile that refused to disappear from his face.

*   *   *

They stayed in bed until nine the next morning, then Marie got up, but Rene stretched across the mattress and took his time to fully awaken. He ran his hand over the warm spot where she had been, a small arc of heat that fit neatly inside his arms and legs.

Marie pulled some hotel stationery from a drawer to jot things down. They had planned to see *Old California*, with John Wayne, after they met Joe Christy for lunch. But the picture had been replaced the day before by a Hitchcock movie, *Saboteur*, starring Robert Cummings and Priscilla Lane. The movie was subtitled "you won't believe it until you see it." Marie was disappointed so they decided not to go. John Wayne wasn't one of her favorite actors, but it would have been better than watching a movie about the war and intrigue.

Since they had a couple of hours until lunch, they went window shopping along Main Street, crisscrossing the street to whatever store Marie's fancy took them. Rene bought her a wide-brimmed hat for two dollars at Estelle's Fine Clothing Shop. He thought it made her look like a movie star, and she picked out a brown suit at Comeau's Clothing Store for him. Then they went inside Delta Furniture where Marie had an old clerk, who looked to be at least fifty-five, show them through all the selections--sofas, chairs, dinette sets and a console radio in a mahogany cabinet. Picking out what caught her eye, she took notes on the prices while Rene added up the amounts in his head, calculating how many pounds of shrimp it would take to pay for everything. The sofa and chair would total a hundred-ten, the equivalent of two weeks of shrimping. She looked at a dinette set for seventy-five, and the radio console was another hundred. By the time they were through shopping, he was already into seven additional weeks of successful trawling just to pay for everything.

They went for lunch to the designated café, whose green-tinted windows were accented with venetian blinds. Inside, a pair of ceiling fans stirred an anemic breeze as Rene set the packages with his suit and her hat near the wall and slid into the booth after Marie. The wooden table was covered with a red and white, checkered table cloth, whose exposed corners were smudged with multiple cigarette burns. He slid the ash tray to the far corner and away from Marie. Half full of cigarette butts, it hadn't been cleaned from several customers.

Entering five minutes later, Joe Christy looked much more distinctive than he did in high school. He'd added ten pounds, most of it on his chest and shoulders, his hair was cut close, military style, and the khaki uniform of the Coastal Patrol made him look older than twenty. Finishing his lunch after fifteen minutes, he set his fork and knife on the plate where his grilled cheese sandwich had been and dumped a spoonful of sugar in his coffee, stirring it vigorously. Then, to Rene's surprise, Joe lit a cigarette. Rene hadn't seen Joe smoke before, though the practice seemed to go with being in uniform. There were multiple ads for cigarettes in the newspapers and magazines, and every serviceman featured appeared to have the habit.

One prominent ad said: "Light up a Julep and light up your life."

But such ads held no appeal for Rene; he didn't even like the smell of cigarette smoke. Nevertheless, he tried to ignore the inconvenience because Joe was careful to blow the smoke out one side of his mouth and keep it away from them.

"So how's married life?" Joe quipped, glancing first at Rene, then Marie, a mischievous smile covering his face.

Marie leaned into Rene and turned red and Rene put an arm around her shoulders. "It'll take some getting used to, but so far it's fantastic," Rene replied. "I highly recommend it for you."

Joe changed his expression and sipped his coffee. "It's not in the cards for me. When I took Cadet Pilot Training at Baton Rouge, I expected to fly patrols. So I'm married to my airplane and the Coastal Patrol until the war is over. My Dad co-signed the note and helped me buy the Stinson Voyager. Most of the pilots in the Coastal Patrol fly their own aircraft, and since they've logged several hours of flight time already, they've advanced faster. After the war I plan to continue flying but, where, I don't know. I'll probably get a spraying contract and work with him.

"Patrolling is a full time job and we stay busy. We're part of Patrol Force Nine. It covers the Louisiana Gulf eastward to the Florida panhandle, and our unit is presently in the process of moving to Grand Isle. The Army also launches patrol planes out of Lakefront in New Orleans. Their range and speed are better than ours, so they fly farther offshore, but we're responsible for watching a big slice of shallow water in the Gulf. On any given day--providing I have enough daylight and gasoline--I might fly from the panhandle of Florida to the Texas border and back, depending on the U-boat activity. My Voyager carries fourteen gallons of gas and burns about four gallons an hour, so I have to figure that into my plans. We're given sectors to fly that are normally sixty miles wide and ten miles long. It's a huge area, but a fraction of the overall war zone because the Gulf is six hundred miles wide. That's the same distance from the shore of Louisiana to Mexico. The Military Defense Zone stops for us at the Florida-Georgia border, but the most critical areas right now are the waters immediately south of Louisiana. I don't hear much of what's happening off the coast of Georgia or Florida, but I can't be concerned. We have our hands full with U-boats here in the Louisiana portion of the Gulf.

"I'm at the airport now for some engine maintenance, but I plan to go out tomorrow. My group should be settled in at Grand Isle in a day or two, right on the beach, and if my engine checks out, I'll be over the Gulf at sunrise tomorrow, looking for U-boats."

Rene was dubious. "They must be hard to find in all that open water."

"They are," Joe admitted. He took a sugar container and placed it in the center of the table. "Let's say this is a U-boat and I'm approaching in my airplane." He raised his right hand and flattened his fingers to represent an airplane. "When we see one we turn toward it, because they can submerge in half a minute. They're skilled at turning into us and cutting off our ability to target them, which gives us very little time to drop a bomb, so we must act quickly. The water distorts their image and makes it difficult to pinpoint them once they get submerged, it's important to bomb them before they descend so deep that the explosion is ineffective. I normally fly about eighty miles an hour, but I slow down to fifty-five when I see one. Shallow water is another problem. The Gulf is muddy close to shore and a sub can hide underneath a pocket of murky water and be darn near invisible in depths as little as fifty feet. At times such as that, we can't find them because they stop their electric motors and lay on the bottom. That's their favorite tactic, to lie on the bottom under dark and then resurface and hunt for ships."

Joe shrugged his shoulders and put the sugar jar back in its place. "Anyway, I stay busy. I actually have two jobs--searching for U-boats and looking for survivors. While we're trying to find U-boats, we also scan the water for debris from a torpedoed vessel because there might be survivors in the water. We use what's called a search ladder. It's a series of big rectangles. We fly four legs of the ladder, one in each major direction, crisscrossing a sector of water the same way. If I find any survivors, I transmit the location so the nearest sub chaser can pick up the men. You may not know it but we lost quite a few ships in the Gulf during May, but I'm not supposed to tell you how many." He tapped his cigarette in the ashtray. "This is important work so I don't have time for a wife. But I'm glad for both of you." He swirled his coffee once more, took another sip and added, "If I was married, I wouldn't be home much. I'm up before sunrise and often working past dark, helping the mechanics. We have one guy who was a piano tuner before joining up. He's good with his hands so they sent him to training and now he's a mechanic. We look out for each other. What I'm doing right now eats up my time," he admitted. "A wife would only be in the way."

Rene squeezed Marie's shoulder. "Marie won't be in my way. I'm going to make her the best deck hand in the Gulf, and we'll be Savoy's number one crew."

"That's great," answered Joe. "I saw an ad that said the farmer who drives a tractor has a weapon just like a soldier. I think the same way about shrimp boats." He unfolded The *Times Picayune*, scanned the front page and pointed to a story that he began to read. "Two Coast Guard signalmen were among the 32 men lost when an Axis submarine torpedoed a ship in the Gulf of Mexico yesterday."

"Where did it happen?" Rene asked.

"It doesn't say. That would inform the enemy and scare the public. Screeners proofread these stories and take out any information that would tip off the Germans. We can't be sure, but it's a good bet the Germans have the capability of listening to our radio transmissions."

He set the paper down, tapped the story with one finger, and his face changed into a frown. "Incidents like this are why I love my job. Our patrols are effective, but we can't catch all of them," he said, pointing to Rene. "Watch yourself out there. We've received reports of U-boats coming as close as a mile from the beach. The Germans know the contours of the bottom and the depths of the water as well as you shrimpers do. One patrol plane dropped a bomb on a U-boat last week, but he got away. He was within three miles of the coast, directly south of Morgan City."

Rene whistled. "That's not very far west of our sector."

Joe continued. "There are some mornings when low clouds or fog ground the planes and the blimp, and U-boats use that limited visibility to pick off a tanker and then submerge before we can get out there to help."

Rene shook his head. "I don't plan to meet one up close."

"I hope you don't either," Joe said. "That's our job, to keep them on the run."

"I give myself plenty of room," Rene explained. "I prefer shallow water where the tankers seldom go. The Gulf isn't much deeper than eighty feet in our sector, but the prop wash from the tankers and freighters still creates silt trails that disturb the shrimp. Anyway, that's what my dad says, and he has over twenty years of experience in the Gulf."

"He's right. We often get a clue where a U-boat is by looking at mud trails. If they're lying on the bottom, we sometimes see a line of disturbed silt behind them that their prop had created. We know if we follow that line to the end of the disturbance, there's bound to be a U-boat sitting there. Or we occasionally get lucky and see the outline of one sitting on the bottom."

Joe turned to the sports page at the same time that Marie gasped, reached for Rene's arm and pointed through the window, and he turned to see an Army guard escorting a half dozen German prisoners getting out of a dual-wheeled truck and coming toward the café. The guard opened the door and the prisoners filed in and took stools at the counter. Rene searched for a reaction from the man and girl working behind the counter but they were unruffled. Instead, the girl worked her way down the line, smiling at them and taking their orders.

All the prisoners wore a baggy, white shirt with black stripes and *PW* stenciled across the back, in four-inch letters. Their pants varied from dingy white to khaki and their rundown boots looked like the same ones they had on when they were captured. There was one heavy set prisoner who was several years older than the rest, but most were in their early twenties. One of the prisoners, whose boot heels were missing, pivoted on his stool toward Marie until an older prisoner nudged him. They exchanged comments in German and the younger one closed his eyes and shook his head, then faced the counter and hunched over his coffee cup.

A few slipped into English when they spoke to the guard, a skinny kid about their age with pimples on his face. He leaned against the counter but held his carbine on his right hip, like the guard riding shotgun in the movie *Stagecoach*. The barrel and wooden stock of his M-1 glistened from a light coating of oil.

Joe nodded toward the prisoners. "We see crews like these guys every day except Sunday. They get that day off to attend church and to rest. Most are Catholic or Lutheran. They're kept busy picking up trash along the parish roads, weeding the ditches and working in the fields. The camp up the road in Thibodeaux has about sixty prisoners of enlisted and non-coms. The officers are shipped to Camp Polk; it keeps the hard-nosed Nazis from making problems for the others. But we rarely hear of trouble with the enlisted men. They're mostly draftees who only want to sit out the rest of the war and go home, though some talk about staying in Louisiana. They're not only happy to be out of the war but prefer the mild winters over the cold in Germany." Joe pointed to a blond near the guard. "You'd be shocked if you knew about some of them. That guy with the boot heels missing went to school in New Jersey. But two years before the war his family moved back to the Fatherland and he was drafted into the German Army. He has no love for Hitler or the war. Listening to him speak, you'd think he was still on our side."

Glancing toward the counter, Marie was surprised to see the same German boy staring at her, so she looked away and put an arm inside Rene's. The prisoner smiled and acted like he wanted to say something, and when he turned toward his food, Marie noticed a wedding band on his left hand.

Still reading the paper, Joe registered surprise and looked up. "Do you remember Allen Mackenzie?"

"Yes." Rene answered. "He played halfback for Houma. Several colleges wanted him but he went into the Marines. A speedy guy like that is sure to be a star when he comes home and plays in college."

Joe's face was expressionless like his voice. "Well, that won't happen. The article says he died from wounds last week while fighting in the South Pacific."

Rene stared at the table and Marie didn't say anything. A soldier's life had been reduced to a few lines squeezed onto a page, as though it wasn't important about what type of person he had been. Most people would read the obituary and know only the bare details instead of Allen, the boy who loved sports, who could rebuild a car engine in two days, who wanted to be a racecar driver and loved dogs.

Stuck for something to say that would mitigate the shock of Allen's death, each one finished their apple pie in silence.

A few moments later, after the prisoners had eaten, the guard told them to load up, and they filed out of the restaurant. The blond German, who had smiled at Marie, was the last one to get into the truck. The guard then closed the tail gate, walked around to the passenger side as the truck's engine coughed twice before catching, then revved up and the truck pulled away, spewing a black line of smoke out of the vertical exhaust pipe above the cab.

At the same time, Marie gave let out a gasp that caught Rene's attention.

"What is it?"

She pointed toward the truck. "The last prisoner, the one with the wedding band?" she said, not waiting for Rene's reply. "He waved at me."

A smile spread across Joe's face as he smashed his cigarette out and picked up the check. "No doubt you remind him of his wife back in Germany," he offered, sliding out of the booth. "The lunch is on me. Enjoy yourselves. I have to get ready for tomorrow. It was nice to see you, and again, congratulations."

*   *   *

The next morning, Rene placed the suitcases by the door and stretched on the bed beside Marie, not feeling the need to leave the room at checkout time because Tom had left instructions with the desk clerk that they could stay as late as they wanted. After going to Mass, they returned for a Sunday dinner, compliments of Tom, which put them in a mood to take a nap, since they had spent more time awake Saturday night than they had sleeping. Rene woke up first and took Marie in his arms but fell back asleep, but two hours later Marie stirred beside him, running her hands down his stomach and kissing him on the chest.

Without having to follow a schedule, Rene caressed Marie's face, undid one button of her blouse and slid his hand upon her right breast, and she arched her back toward him and gave him a lingering kiss, eliminating any hesitation or barrier between them like there had been before they were married. It only took the slightest suggestion from either one to ignite a response, and that awareness surged through Rene in a warm stream of emotion. He kissed her again and explored her stomach, finally moving his hand down further and then upward, in a caressing motion that brought a moan from her.

Rene lowered his head and tugged her skirt down enough to kiss her stomach just below the navel. "I don't want to stop touching you. Yesterday in the café, it was all I could do to keep from kissing you every time I looked at you."

"I feel the same way about you," Marie said, "and I hope you never lose that feeling. I know I never will."

"Don't worry," he reassured her, touching one breast with his lips in a light, flickering gesture. "You're all that's important to me now."

Marie gathered his head in her hands, concentrating on him for a long, silent moment, and then asked, "Are you certain?"

"Beyond any doubt," he answered.

"You don't think we got married too soon?"

Rene wrinkled his face, shook his head and exhaled loudly. "Absolutely not. What makes you say that?" he asked, turning his face toward her breast, but she held his head and made him look at her.

"I saw how you hung onto everything that Joe said about the submarines. Your face changed and you stared at him. And when you read the newspaper you looked at the stories and pictures about the war and didn't go to any other article."

Rene rose up and touched her neck, pausing with his fingertips on her skin, his eyes averted from hers. "It's like Joe said. He's married to the war. But I'm married to you. I can't do both and don't want to anyway. Joe's life is flying airplanes, but it's not mine. I belong with you, and that's how it's going to stay."

Marie pressed her hands against his temples, her eyes roaming over every detail of his face. "Are you sure? I couldn't help but notice your reaction to the news about Allen. The pain in your face was intense, as if you wanted to get revenge for his death."

He pushed through her hands and kissed her in a long, intense union, running his hand down her stomach again, seeking her out, his back stiffening when he found her, and she repositioned one leg for him and held him tightly, her breath coming rapidly.

"You are all I want," he whispered. "That won't ever change."

Marie held his shoulders and glanced toward the door. "Aren't we supposed to check out?"

Rene stood up and began unbuttoning his shirt. "There's plenty of time."

She broke into a smile and started to undress.

12

Alone in his store, Tom munched on a Baby Ruth early that Sunday morning, drummed his fingers on the counter and thought about the last letter. He was ambivalent about its purpose because it could be a trap instead of a genuine offer.

He held his pistol in the light that came through the window and turned the weapon over, looking at each shell in the cylinder and wondering what it would be like to kill a man at close range, to see his face, to watch blood ooze through his clothing, or bubble up through a hole in his skin. And just before he died, would his eyes roll in his head like they did in the movies, and would his neck flop to one side? He didn't have that experience in the Great War because he never was certain if he killed the men he shot at. They were more like cardboard targets on a firing range than people.

He shut the post office door and looked around before locking up. The safe was secure, there was no money in the cash register, the back door was bolted; everything was in order. He snorted when he thought that he might be locking up the store for the last time, but he put one hand on the pistol and pushed away the idea of his vulnerability. He'd know what to do when the time came. He always did.

On the road to Houma ten minutes later, he was already bored. It was too familiar in every aspect--twenty miles of narrow, serpentine roadway, clamshells in the beginning, pavement for the last half and a curve every time the bayou changed its course. It was a nuisance for someone in a hurry but the road was a lifeline for families living along the bayou, the only way to get into and out of Pat's Landing. Clear now of the village, he kept the Chrysler on fifty, though he had to slow down for curves and holes. Each time he hit a bad spot the front wheels bounced against the coiled springs and the front end of the car lurched upward, before settling down in an uncomfortable, see-saw motion.

He watched the scenery go by but its grimness depressed him. The houses along the way were mostly shacks that looked so fragile a good rainstorm could destroy them. Tall grass and weeds threatened to climb onto a few front porches and Tom could see into most of the houses, whose front doors were open to let in fresh air.

About halfway to Houma, where Black Bass Lake was close to the Upper Bayou, a drilling rig sat a quarter mile from the bank. The dark wooden structure reminded him of a giant erector set, tall, slender and fragile-looking. Two boats were anchored near the rig floor, but Tom was unable to determine any of the crew's activities. He had turned down Joe Christy's father two years earlier to invest in a drilling project that would bring up oil from beneath the lake. Benny Christy had talked of a rich future for finding oil in Louisiana lakes and perhaps the Gulf of Mexico, but Tom didn't have faith in the idea. Although Huey Long helped bring the oil and natural gas industry to the wetlands of South Louisiana, there was no comparison in Tom's mind between a few pockets of petroleum to the vast bounty of fish and shrimp in the entire Gulf.

The seafood industry was stable work and he believed things would remain that way. The wildcatters would come and go but the fish and shrimp would stay, just like God had intended. Though Tom grudgingly admitted that the oil field at Leeville and other sites in South Louisiana were helping the war effort, drilling for something you couldn't see was like a fool's game. It wasn't the same as shrimping, which was a sure thing because the shrimp were down there, waiting to be caught. You merely had to pick the spot where they were, lower your net and collect them by the thousands, but drilling for oil and gas was like finding your way down a path while wearing a blindfold.

When an animal suddenly dashed into his field of vision, he jerked the steering wheel to his left and veered to the other side of the road as a skinny mongrel dog got out of the way and plunged into thick saw grass on the shoulder. He brought the car back to the middle of the road and felt grateful that it hadn't been a gator, because even a small six-footer could damage a car and knock it off the road. Hitting a gator would be like driving over a tree trunk. You could kiss your front end and tires goodbye, and you'd better hope the gator wasn't alive when you stopped to check for damages.

He wiped his forehead and turned on the radio, hoping to pick up some music, but there were no stations strong enough to reach him, only static coming from the radio where WWL was supposed to be. It dominated Louisiana's airwaves, especially at night, but its daytime broadcast seldom carried farther than forty miles from the New Orleans site. Tired of searching, he switched the radio off, though all that was left was to stare at the swamp, filled with gators, snakes, stray dogs, maybe a raccoon, and mosquitoes.

He passed the time by dwelling on the latest mysterious letter. Once more the guy didn't sign his name and identify himself. Maybe someone had a grudge he wanted to settle and the letter was a means of maneuvering him into a trap. He searched his memory for the people he had beaten at poker and bourree and half a dozen possibilities came to mind; two men he knew, the others being vague figures he'd never seen before, probably gamblers from New Orleans who planned to make a haul in a small town where the men weren't big-time players. But the idea of violence bothered him. It would be easy for a stranger to walk up and pull a gun before Tom could do anything. That was what happened to Huey Long; a public scene and numerous people near him at the same time. The killer blended in, a harmless-looking, well-dressed man, without anyone being suspicious of him, until shots were fired at a close, deadly range.

But the outside chance that someone wanted to do business with Tom, enticed him. Money from any source was welcome now that the war commission controlled prices and limited his profits, and it irked him that his own government was controlling his company.

He drove by the airport on the south edge of Houma. Except for a few planes of the Coastal Patrol flying out of there, the war hadn't changed it much, though he knew about adjoining land being bought by the Navy for a military base.

The scene changed as he entered the town proper a mile later. Following the main road that paralleled the bayou, he drove past several houses that had been built on the edge of the water, which allowed the homeowners to tie up their boats at their back door. Until the twenties, when the town saw an influx of people who didn't make their living on the water, Houma had a greater population of boats than cars.

He cleared the bayou on a drawbridge just before it rose up for a boat that approached the crossing. Louisiana State statute still gave the right of way to boats. It was one law that Tom agreed with. In his opinion, boats always were and will continue to be the heartbeat of Southern Louisiana's aquatic culture and deserved priority.

His hotel was situated in the downtown section and across the street from the Parish Courthouse, which bordered Main Street behind a wide, green lawn, edged with azalea bushes, flowers and sego palms. A long sidewalk cut through the center of the lawn and formed a concrete circle around a flagpole and a sculpture of a crouching WW I doughboy, his rifle pointing toward an imaginary enemy. The sidewalk continued to a set of broad steps at the front entrance that held four heavy wooden doors. Everything about the building signified strength and order.

After parking in his reserved space, he went inside, where Carol--a chunky, new girl in a loose-fitting dress and mousy brown hair--stood behind the restaurant counter, chatting with two men drinking coffee. She gave a cursory nod to Tom but continued patting her hair and directing her attention to the two customers.

Tom looked the men over before stopping at the end of the counter. They were both dressed in work clothes, had rundown boots, and neither one gave him as much as a curious glance, so he decided they weren't a threat. The letter, after all, had come from one person, and based on their appearance and the way they talked, he wondered if either one was capable of writing letters, because their conversations with Carol included the weather, what they liked to drink, and if Carol had any girlfriends they could meet.

Tom motioned for Carol who excused herself and met him at the end of the counter. "Get me a cold beer and a *Times Picayune,* and tell Sophie to meet me in my office."

Carol disappeared into the kitchen but quickly returned with the newspaper and a beer, and Tom left without giving the two men another thought. With no one to encounter right away, he was beginning to think the letters might be a hoax. It made sense that anyone taking that much effort to contact him would be around a bit early, if for no other reason than to get a good look at him. But no one else was in the restaurant or the lobby.

Nevertheless, he kept one hand on his pistol as he went up the stairs and down the hallway to his office. But seeing no one in front or behind him, he unlocked the door and went inside. He liked the location for its quiet atmosphere and privacy. Other than a random customer to play cards at night, or a philandering husband concealing his tracks, the back door at the end of the hallway was seldom used.

The office held his desk and a swivel chair, two additional chairs arranged at an angle facing the desk, an American flag on a pole, and an identical map of the States like the one in the office at his warehouse.

He uncapped the beer, took a drink and slid open a small drawer on the right side of his desk, placing his pistol inside with the grip facing him. It would be a simple matter of raising the weapon and firing. He liked the plan; the drawer couldn't be seen from the front, so he left it partly open, in case he needed to defend himself.

His devotion to western movies prompted him to see how quickly he could pull the pistol from the drawer, and he practiced several times before he felt confident that he could react rapidly enough to win any confrontation. The perpetrator would have to reach into his pocket, or pull the weapon out of his coat, giving Tom time to fire first.

With half an hour until the meeting time mentioned in the letter, he put his feet on the desk, leaned back in his swivel chair and looked at the paper. Front page stories were about the allies hitting Tobruk and the Russians counterattacking at Kursk. One depressing article quoted Secretary Patterson, who held the view that the war could go on for another five years.

That didn't sit well with Tom. Five more years of price controls would hurt his shrimp business and the draft or the war industries would keep threatening to take his employees.

A knock on the door diverted his attention and Sophie Rougeau came into the office. She was not very attractive. A tight-fitting dress accented her straight-lined, full figure and heavy breasts, and she wore a generous layer of makeup to fill the wrinkles that defied her attempts to look younger than forty-five. Her dark hair was arranged like a bird's nest on top of her head. A stunning brunette when she first met Tom ten years earlier, she had been a bartender, a dancer, and an escort for traveling businessmen, until she convinced Tom to bring in card games and prostitution that would keep the men returning and the cash flow strong.

She crossed the room with a broad smile and took a chair, slowly crossing one leg over the other, giving Tom a generous look at her thighs "Did you want to see me, Mr. Tom?"

"Yes, I did," Tom answered, reaching for a pack of cigarettes on the desk. "I'm expecting someone in a while, so I don't want any interruptions unless the place is burning down,"

Sophie giggled. "I'll see to it." Then she smirked. "Is she a hot one?"

Tom was in no mood for games. "Damn it, Sophie. This is a business meeting."

"Sorry. I'll keep things quiet."

Tom lit his cigarette and blew a cloud of smoke. "Speaking of girls; how's that new one, Carol, working out? I spoke to her today and she acted like she was half asleep."

"She'll do better when she realizes she can't pick and choose her men. She needs to realize it's a job, not a one night stand." Sophie explained. "The guys like her because she isn't thirty yet." Sophie pointed at Tom and smiled. "They're attracted to the young ones who haven't had a passel of kids and put on a lot of weight."

Tom looked at Sophie's stubby legs and recalled how attractive she had been as a young woman. She once had it all--saucy, high-spirited, a well-shaped body, a vivid personality, and an appetite for sex that had matched his own. "I haven't heard much from you lately. Have you been getting any?" he asked, breaking into laughter.

Sophie waved him off with one hand. "Mr. Tom, you know better than that. What would the men want with an old hen like me? They like the young ones with narrow hips, firm boobies and flat stomachs. I'm old enough to be a mother to many of them."

Agreeing with her without saying so, he snuffed out his cigarette and dropped his smile. "How's Kitty working out?"

"She has her good days," Sophie explained. "But now and then she'll change her mind and go home for a couple of weeks, then come back and swear she's seen the last of her husband. I wouldn't count on her staying. She could be a good one if she put a little effort into it, but she needs to warm up to the men and be nice, instead of lying there like a cold fish. If she acted like she was having a good time, she'd have customers standing in line."

"Like you used to do," Tom added.

Sophie cracked a smile. "That was a long time ago."

He dropped all pretense of humor. "You make sure those two girls don't get out of line. When they work the bar they need to be friendly, but they should not make it obvious that they're hustling. I want to maintain the quality of this hotel. This isn't a cathouse in Storyville, and we don't beat up the clients like the whores used to do in New Orleans. They'd better be half decent or they'll find themselves out the door and on the street."

Sophie answered in a flat voice; she'd heard the same admonition many times. "I've got them under my thumb."

Tom folded the paper, set it aside, and straightened in his chair, his voice assuming a business-like manner. "I'm going to look over the books until my meeting," he said, opening the account ledger and selecting a page. "And I'd appreciate it if you'd get me another beer."

Sophie got up and started toward the door. "I'll be right back."

* * *

Tom closed the ledger one hour later, looked at his watch and read more of the newspaper. Except for stories about the war holding his attention, he had trouble concentrating. Whoever had written the letters was ten minutes late. He drained the rest of his second beer and stashed the ledger in a small floor safe at the right side of his desk, spun the dial and prepared to leave. The arrangement now smelled like a setup to get him into Houma so the crook could rob the store in Pat's Landing. Grown men didn't play games with secret, nameless messages.

He decided that the mystery person had been given enough time and was about to leave when there was a knock on the door.

"Come in," Tom said loudly, opening the desk drawer so the pistol would be easy to reach.

The man who came in was dressed in a dark gray suit and wore a hat of the same color, and Tom relaxed some after he saw both of the man's hands. One was empty; the other held a thin, black, leather, zippered notebook. The man closed the door and advanced in an unimposing manner to one of the chairs, sat the notebook down, placed his hat on the notebook and leaned across the desk to shake Tom's hand. His dark brown hair combed to one side, the firm face and hazel eyes looked familiar, but Tom wasn't sure where he'd seen him.

"I'm pleased to meet you, Mr. Savoy. My name is Karl Johnson. I want to thank you for meeting me today."

After hearing him speak, Tom finally placed him as the man who had been in the crowd during the blessing of the fleet, had quizzed him about the war, and had appeared at the wedding reception.

Miffed at being held up, Tom was blunt. "You're late. What did you want to see me about?"

Karl brushed something off a pants leg, appearing to be fully at ease. "I apologize for the clandestine manner of contacting you, but it was necessary."

"Okay. I'm here. But I warn you; if this is a sales pitch, you're wasting your time."

"I'm not a salesman, I assure you, Mr. Savoy."

Tom kept his brusque attitude. "Well, spit it out. I haven't got all night."

Karl glanced at the ceiling fan that turned in a lazy motion. "I'm more or less in the government."

"What part?"

Karl Johnson remained indirect. "You might say we keep track of things."

"Do you mean the Office of Civilian Defense?"

"Something like that, only with a broader range and a different name."

"Well, somebody needs to look after this war," Tom spouted angrily. "My boats are being harassed by those damn German subs, the Price Commission regulates what I get for my shrimp, and I have trouble keeping employees because the government uses my tax dollars to pad the industries. On top of that, if I net more than twenty-five thousand, I lose most of it in taxes. They say it's for the war effort, but I'm already paying in several other ways, plus donating all the scrap metal I can find. In my opinion, Roosevelt and his cronies are thieves," he declared, pointing at Karl. "How am I supposed to run a business when the government works against me by taxing every dollar I make?"

He stopped long enough to light a cigarette, holding in the smoke from a long drag, and when Karl didn't respond, he continued. "I'm not sure we'd be in this mess if Huey Long had lived. Roosevelt doesn't have Huey's spunk and leadership. Huey got things done here in Louisiana." He shook his head and glanced at his desk. "It's a shame how one of our best public servants is being treated after he's gone. In case you hadn't heard, they also turned out the light over Huey's grave in Baton Rouge, claiming it was a necessity of war." His anger increased. "It's a hundred damn miles inland. How in the name of everything holy could a U-boat get up the river and torpedo the capitol? The Mississippi is too dangerous for a sub to navigate the trip submerged and dodge all that boat traffic. The strong current alone would make it a suicide mission. A U-boat wouldn't even get further than the mouth of Southwest Pass. Have you ever heard such a silly excuse? Do the fools in our statehouse think the Germans are planning to attack New Orleans like the British did in 1812?"

Johnson leaned forward in his chair and answered in a controlled voice. "I understand how you feel."

"How can you sit there and say that?" Tom exploded. "You don't know a damn thing about me. We have never sat down and talked, so don't pretend you do."

"I believe we have a few things in common. You are tired of this war," Johnson declared. "Am I correct?"

"Hell yes. What person wouldn't be? The war is on our doorstep and intrudes into our lives. We see Coastal Patrol planes nearly every day and my crews hear explosions and find debris in the water. On top of that, one of my trawlers towed in a lifeboat last week, filled with survivors from a torpedoed tanker." His outpouring grew stronger with his conviction. "You can go back to where you came from, but we have to live with the Germans as our next door neighbors. We are a hell of a lot closer to the U-boats than the politicians in Baton Rouge."

Karl was still unruffled. "I understand; so the question is, would you do something about it if you could?"

Tom was astonished. "Are you crazy? You appear at a couple of social occasions, and now you have the gall to ask me such a damn fool question? I'm no soldier. I can only provide food for the war." He glared at Johnson. "You obviously know nothing about me."

When Johnson zipped open his notebook, Tom reached for his pistol but drew his hand back when Johnson took out a sheet of paper and looked it over.

Then he began a litany that left Tom speechless. "Your father, Pierre, started the company with one boat. He was patriotic and made the maximum annual donation to WW I, and you served with your brother, who was wounded during the first six months. After the war, you and a Mister Walters of Idaho, drew up a petition for the Bonus Army, and your brother died as a result of an accident when some members attempted to flee from a confrontation with the Washington D.C. police. You took over the business after your father drowned in the flood of '27, also expanding this hotel and bar, and you operate illegal card games on weekends and a house of prostitution seven nights a week. You call it an escort service but the girls work for you and your madam, and you control their money by taking a cut of what they charge. You avoid entanglements with the law by paying weekly protection money to the local police and the parish sheriff, who is your second cousin, giving them cut rate prices on booze and allowing them a free service to your girls once a month."

Before Tom could organize a comeback, Johnson kept going. "You have a wife, Kay, and a daughter Sarah. Kay fills in at the store now that Sam is gone. By the way, neither Sam's nor Roy's body was ever found. You distribute shrimp to other destinations in the south, supplied by your fleet of eight shrimp boats and one iceboat. Your crews work two weeks in the Gulf and come in for one weekend. You continually press the limits of your ration cards by bribing your suppliers. You netted twelve thousand dollars for yourself from the shrimping business last year, not to mention three thousand more from your store."

Johnson paused and regarded Tom. "I have more about the finances on your hotel. Do I need to go on?"

Tom didn't know what to say, but the idea occurred to him that he might be in a jam with the IRS and Johnson was a tax agent sent to ruin him. He racked his brain for what they could have about the hotel business. All money to his girls was cash. Sophie kept scant paperwork, and the bouree proceeds were handled like any private card game, though the stakes were often over a hundred dollars.

Tom reached for another cigarette and took his time lighting it and tried to organize a defense in the event that Johnson charged him with anything. But he had little room for maneuvering. The details were accurate.

Finally, he worked up a reply. "Am I being investigated, or are you charging me with something? If so, I'm going to terminate this conversation and get a lawyer."

For the first time Johnson dropped his cold mannerism and chuckled. "No, I merely wanted to demonstrate that we know a considerable amount about you, and despite a shady deal or two, we consider you to be a solid citizen. Your criticisms of the government dragging its feet in the war, coupled with your request to arm your iceboat, make you out to be a patriotic one too."

"Then let's get down to business. It's Sunday, and I want to go home," Tom declared, as Johnson returned the sheet of paper to his notebook. "Explain what you want from me and I'll decide if I can help."

"I work in counterintelligence." Karl began. "It involves tracking people and making decisions that might shorten the war. We have a need to use your iceboat for a couple of trips. We'll pay you for your time and what crew members you need to take."

Tom thought it was a joke. "I don't rent out my iceboat. It's a vital part of my business…"

Johnson cut him off. "We're prepared to pay you six thousand dollars for two trips, three thousand now, and the other half after the second one. The money will not be traced or taxable and will never show up on any record. We need a boat with extra deck capacity, for cargo and seven thousand pounds of diesel fuel, and your iceboat fills our needs. We will require you and two deck hands to transfer the cargo and fuel. They will receive five hundred apiece for each trip. Since the nature of the work must be guarded, do you have two people you can trust implicitly?"

"Six thousand," Tom repeated aloud, whistling and figuring how he could use the money that was equal to six months of profit. He could buy two more trawlers, or expand his business like he planned to do after the war. "I have a couple in mind," he admitted. "One likes only money and the other is itching to get into the war. But for that kind of money, who do I have to kill?" he joked, but quickly dropped his smile when Johnson didn't act amused.

"All we require is that you make two trips into the Gulf and arrive at a specific location at a prearranged time. Your job will be to navigate to the site and then return."

Tom scratched his head. "I can't carry that much fuel."

"I'll obtain a tank at my cost and you can secure it to the deck."

Tom waved both hands in front of his face. "You're going on some kind of a hush-hush mission, aren't you? Well, I did my time in WW I. If you want to go chasing U-boats, get the Coast Guard. They have sub chasers who'll do a better job. I'm not wearing a uniform anymore and I don't want to get my boat shot up."

Johnson zipped up his notebook and propped it up with one hand, ready to get up. "We won't be chasing anyone. We hoped you would cooperate, Mr. Savoy. You have the chance to play a vital role in defense of the Gulf and our country. If you refuse we have an alternate choice, but the distance would be much greater." Johnson opened one hand and sounded congenial. "Why don't you think it over and let me know in a day or two." He took a small notepad from his coat pocket and wrote a number on the slip of paper, handing it to Tom. "You can contact me at this number. Don't try to determine an address because it won't do you any good. When you call say yes or no, nothing else. If you decline you will not hear from me again, but if you accept, we'll meet again and cover more details." He stood up and placed a long white envelope on the desk. "To reassure you of our trust, here is half of the money."

Tom opened the flap and thumbed the bills--fifties and twenties--more cash than he'd ever seen in one envelope. "And what if I don't accept?"

"No problem." Johnson's chilly answer immediately caught Tom's attention. "We know where you live, so we'll come back for the money and you will never hear from us again."

"I need some time to think this over," Tom said. "To tell you the truth, I wasn't prepared for this. I thought the whole thing was a joke."

Johnson pressed Tom in a series or rapid questions. "The war is no joke, Mr. Savoy."

"I know..."

"You're a patriot like your father, right?"

"Yes…"

"Do you want to help your country and be well paid at the same time?"

"Of course I do, but it sounds too…"

"Would you have a problem navigating your ice boat at night?"

"Are you kidding? I grew up working in the Gulf of Mexico."

"Then you are the man for us. I don't need to remind you that we are being threatened by an enemy who is just off our shores. Conditions in the Gulf are worse than what the public hears on the radio or reads in the newspapers. We've never been faced with a challenge like this in our entire history. If we continue to lose ships and men at the rate we did in May, we could be invaded from the Gulf and up and down our eastern coastline, and you and your friends could be fighting from your front doors."

Tom rubbed his forehead. All he could think of was how good another cold beer would taste. "Give me some time to think it over."

Johnson stood up and put on his hat. "Okay, but remember, operations such as this are on a timetable. I can give you twenty-four hours; no more. Call the number on this piece of paper and let us know, or we will consider you out of the plan."

"Fair enough."

Johnson tugged the brim of his hat over his forehead. "You have a chance to do a very great thing for the country by helping to reduce the threat in our coastal waters. Even in my organization, this is a secret operation. Consequently, I will remain someone you don't know. If you choose to go ahead, nothing will ever reach the radio or newspapers and the public will never learn of your actions, but you will have a sense of pride for the rest of your life." Johnson had one hand on the doorknob but stopped short of opening the door. "A word of caution; don't divulge this to your family or friends, not even the two men you pick to make the run, until we are underway, and don't spend the money until after the first trip. Your personal safety depends on following these details."

Before Tom could think of another comment, Johnson turned and left the room, closing the door behind him.

13

The sun edged into the horizon as Rene and Marie cleared the southern edge of Houma and approached the narrow roadway along Upper Bayou. Tall Rozo, resembling thin shoots of bamboo, grew head-high on one side, and thick clumps of vegetation sprouted from mounds of black mud and crowded onto the shoulder of the road on the other.

They rode in silence, Rene with one hand on the steering wheel and one arm around Marie's shoulders. Her head resting on Rene's chest, Marie leaned against him to get closer, kneading her fingers across his stomach, exploring his body and caressing him. There was no need for either one to utter a word in the atmosphere of their mutual happiness.

Despite his contentment, their honeymoon would be over in less than twelve hours, so Rene's thoughts wandered toward work. He needed to prepare the boat for its morning run. Since Tom expected the same out of every crew, they had to be on their way by sunrise, and Rene wanted to be the first one out. He and Marie would be just another object of his loud-mouthed scorn if they weren't ready. He smiled when he thought how shrimping with Marie wouldn't be work. Having her with him for fourteen days and nights would wipe away the tedium. She would be a blessing to the job, and a surge of excitement ran through him. He could hardly wait.

He kissed Marie on top of her head and watched the roadway. Now that the sun was nearly down, nutria, swamp dogs, raccoons, and gators would soon be foraging for food, so he trained his eyes on the road and turned on his headlights. A crushed skunk lay off the right side and two crows hopped away until the Lincoln passed by, then they returned to their meal.

A few half-developed, cumulus clouds lay low on the southern horizon, the sole blot in an otherwise clear sky. The air was so languid that the tall grass, Spanish Moss and leaves on the trees hung lifeless in a serene landscape of soft light that circled the Lincoln as they left the paved roadway and rolled onto the clamshells for the last half of the journey to Pat's Landing.

Marie kissed Rene through his shirt and rose up to look outside. "How close are we?"

"About fifteen minutes more."

"Good," she said. "I'm hungry."

Rene pulled her closer and kissed her forehead. "I'm hungry too, for you."

"I mean real food," she corrected him playfully.

"Right now, you're food enough for me," he replied, running down her cheek with his finger.

She laughed and brushed a hand through her hair, raised up, and caught sight of what looked like a bird at first, until the dark shape developed into a pair of wings on an airplane. It was a mile or so in front of them, in a steady descent toward an expanse of marsh and small ponds.

"What's he doing?" she asked.

Rene slowed down to thirty and watched. "Maybe he's buzzing someone in a boat. Joe's flown low a couple of times and waggled his wings when my dad and I were shrimping. The pilot must see somebody he knows and is doing the same thing."

Marie sat straight upright and her voice sharpened. "It's turning toward the road." She pointed at the plane. "Isn't that smoke trailing behind it?"

Rene pulled over and stopped the car as the pilot banked into a descending turn that put the aircraft on a heading for the road, and its descent rate increased dramatically. "Yes, it is. And he looks too low to land on the road."

The pilot leveled off, banked to his right and flew parallel to the road not more than a hundred feet off the ground. The engine sputtered in loud bursts of temporary power, but the aircraft continued in an unmistakable descent toward the swamp. The pilot fought to keep the wings level, but as the engine caught, tried to die, then regained a small amount of power, he raised the nose just before the airplane struck the ground.

Marie let out a cry when the plane pancaked into the swamp and ricocheted twenty feet back into the air before impacting the marsh again, cart wheeling one time, ripping a wing off and coming to rest on its left side.

"Stay here," Rene yelled, slamming the car door and running across the road.

Realizing that the plane's colors were the same as Joe's Voyager, tears ran down her cheeks. "Could that be Joe?"

"I don't know, but whoever it is needs our help."

He started into the marsh by stepping on a small group of lily pads and hoped to figure out where he could go next, but sank up to his knees in muck that sucked at his shoes. Trying not to slide deeper, he pushed forward a little bit at a time on the uneven bottom and worked his way toward the plane, careful to avoid the sharp leaves of saw grass and praying that he didn't meet any water moccasins.

The plane was only a hundred feet from the roadway, but the soggy marsh forced René to struggle five minutes before reaching the crash site. Soaked with sweat and muddy up to his waist, he worked his way over the right landing gear and pulled himself onto the side of the fuselage by grabbing a broken stub of the wing and then the door handle. The left wing was still attached, though the aircraft's fabric was ripped in several places. The engine was bent upwards and the cowling was peeled back, as if a giant hand had tried to rip it off. Smoke curled upward from the engine but there was no sign of fire, despite the strong presence of gasoline. But a fire wasn't Rene's main concern. It was the limp body of Joe Christy.

Because mud and water had invaded the cockpit on the pilot's side, it was difficult to tell Joe's condition because he was slumped against the far edge of the cockpit in an awkward posture. He wasn't moving, and his head lay on his chest. He appeared to be unconscious, but there was no blood on his clothing or his face. Rene bent on one knee and opened the cockpit door after yanking hard on the handle. He repeatedly brushed one hand across his face to thin out the smoldering engine oil and tried to figure out a way to pull Joe outside.

"Joe, it's Rene. Can you move?" he called out, but there wasn't as much as a hand twitching in response.

*   *   *

At the same time, two miles up the road and heading for home, Tom Savoy turned on his lights to pierce the shadows growing across the road. He didn't want to encounter a dog or a gator and ruin his otherwise pleasant trip. He pressed the envelope of money between his fingers and thought of things he could do with it. Half a year's pay for two trips in the iceboat sounded too good to be true. But the uncertainty over what would happen if he accepted Johnson's offer, punctured every idea running through his mind. But he was wary of the unknown. He'd done his part in the Great War. It was time for others to don a uniform and fight.

Unsure of his decision, the envelope made him think about the deckhands he'd rely on if he went ahead with the plan. Manny talked about money more than anything, other than his mother. If Manny balked at the idea, the temptation of what he could do with several months' pay would convince him. He had a daredevil nature about him, so the opportunity of a nighttime boat ride and very little work should lure him.

Tom didn't have any doubts about the second one. It was common knowledge that Rene avoided talking about the war, but it was only his marriage to Marie that kept him from enlisting. Everyone knew that. He'd jump at the chance to get involved and to have his married life kicked off with a financial cushion. The way Rene counted his chits when he got paid was a dead giveaway. As a newly married man, money would take on a vital role. Marie would see to that. Women can love, but they love money too. It was a tossup whether love or money convinced women to marry, but money didn't hurt in their decision.

Rene and Manny were also young and adventurous, a fine combination for getting involved in a mysterious job.

But Tom considered himself to be a businessman and no longer a soldier. One war had been enough. He was comfortable and doing well, and if things kept going his way, he may wind up owning the largest shrimp company in Louisiana. That would be real success and some cockamamie plan to take an iceboat into the Gulf in the middle of the night, paled against what he had already accomplished.

The whole plan sounded to him like a recipe for disaster.

He let go of the envelope and turned the steering wheel enough to miss a hole in the road, calculating that he could make the same amount of money that Johnson offered him at his hotel, if Sophie would keep his girls working four tricks a week. Wars came and went, but sex would never disappear. Men would be men, no matter what happened. His girls were soldiers in the sexual war and he was the commander, and the victims were men who opened their wallets to satisfy their lust. It was the type of generalship that appealed to him, not the military version.

He placed the envelope on the front seat and glanced toward the road again as a column of pale smoke a mile ahead caught his attention. A car was stopped on the shoulder. Drawing closer, someone was standing in the roadway and waving both arms in the air. He figured it was the driver with car trouble and decided to stop. If he was needed, he could go for help in Pat's Landing. But as he drew closer and recognized the Lincoln and Marie, and saw the broken fuselage of the airplane, he pulled in behind the Lincoln, skidded to a stop and jumped out.

"It crashed in front of us," she cried, running toward him and pointing at the scene. "Rene's trying to save the pilot."

Prodding her by the shoulders, Tom rushed her to the Lincoln and made her get inside. "Drive for help. I'll join Rene."

He launched into the swamp and sank up to his waist, cursing the mud and slogging forward, grabbing lily roots and whatever he could to get him to the airplane. Muddy and out of breath, he reached the site to find Rene bent halfway into the cockpit, tugging at the pilot's seat belt.

The smell of fuel was overwhelming and Tom spat in a futile effort to rid himself of the stench of leaking gasoline. It floated around the fuselage and formed a dangerous sheen on the puddles of water. Tom stretched across the side of the fuselage, squeezed his shoulders into the open door behind Rene and shook him on one shoulder until Rene stopped to look up, a frantic expression embedded in his face.

"It's Joe Christy!" he shouted, turning back and tugging on the buckle at Joe's waist.

"Grab his arms so I can reach him and I'll help you lift him out." Tom said. "We need to get him away from here before the plane catches fire." He held Joe's left shoulder and moved him backwards. "Push the instrument panel away from his arms."

Rene repositioned Joe so his head pointed toward the door and raised Joe's arms upward for Tom to reach him and they began to move Joe from his pinned position.

"Pull on his belt," Tom directed. "But be careful about his stomach. We don't know if he has internal injuries." They slid Joe halfway out the door and got a look at his face. "Is he breathing?" Tom asked.

"I can't tell."

"Joe, can you hear me?" Tom said.

Rene searched for a sign, but Joe's face had no expression. "His eyes aren't moving."

Tom slid off the side of the plane and took Joe with him. "Go easy with his legs. We don't want to aggravate any injuries he may have."

Clear of the aircraft, they stumbled in half steps as they made their way toward the road. Tom held Joe by the shoulders and Rene had his legs, dragging Joe's back through the water at times when they sank in a hole or stepped into a soft part of the marsh and lost their footing. After several minutes of frustrating progress, they reached the road and crossed to Tom's Chrysler, exhausted, muddy and fully spent.

Tom opened the rear door of his car and didn't hesitate. Getting his car filthy didn't faze him. He thought Joe's breathing was shallow, but it was hard to tell. The best thing they could do was get him to the medical clinic. Joe's face had lost some of its color; his eyes were narrow slits and his neck had a strange twist below his chin. "We can't wait for Marie," he explained, moving Joe's shoulders onto the back seat of the Chrysler and positioning his legs together. "There's no other place we can take him. She'll know what we did."

*   *   *

After getting Joe to the Houma Clinic--the only medical facility in the small town--they sat in the chairs next to the examination room, their pants caked with mud, their hands and arms up to their shoulders also covered. Neither one had thought about cleaning up. His legs pressed together and both hands clasped in his lap, Rene stared silently at the green wall across from him, while Tom found his way to the clinic's small office and returned with two cups of coffee, but Rene didn't want any.

"He loved to fly," Rene uttered, barely above a whisper. "He was protecting us. He fought the war with his airplane instead of a rifle. He wanted…" His words trailed off, and his eyes remained fixed upon the wall.

The doctor emerged from the exam room after twenty minutes, wearing a grim face. "I'm sad to tell you that there was no hope," he explained in a somber voice. "His visible injuries were mostly bruises. He had two fractured ribs and a punctured lung, but they didn't threaten his life. His neck was broken. There was nothing anyone could do. He was beyond help when you got to him. At the speed he had to be going when his airplane hit the ground, his chances of surviving were very slim. I see the same conditions with victims of head-on car wrecks. The sudden stop snaps the neck when a person slams into the dashboard."

Tom closed his eyes and nodded. "Thanks anyway, Doc."

"Did you know him well?"

Tom gritted his teeth and Rene looked away, rubbing his eyes.

"Yes. He was one of our local boys," Tom answered, biting his lip.

"It's a shame. The paper seems to be full of such stories these days." The doctor rubbed his forehead. "I wonder when this war will end."

"So do I." Tom echoed, glancing behind him. "Can you tell me where I might find a phone?"

"Use the one in the office," the doctor answered, pointing to the same room where Tom had found the coffee.

Tom held up one finger as he walked away. "I'll only be a minute."

Inside the office, Tom closed the door, took out the note Karl had given him and picked up the phone, getting a quick response from one of the local operators. "Number please."

Tom thought the woman's voice sounded like someone he knew, but he wasn't in the mood for chit chat. "Central, give me 324 J."

The phone rang three times before Karl Johnson answered. The experience of burying relatives and friends, and now another local boy, was something Tom didn't want to endure anymore. He had seen dead men before, but never had he been personally involved in trying to save a young man he knew well. He didn't smell the odor of marsh mud caked on his arms. Instead, it was the stench of another person's death, an experience he never wanted to repeat.

He wanted to find Karl Johnson and have the meeting right away, but he didn't know where he lived. Anyway, details didn't matter to him anymore. Whatever Johnson had planned was fine with him.

"Yes, damn it," he said, when someone picked up the phone, but he spat out the words before Karl could say anything. "And the sooner the better!"

He slammed the phone down without waiting for an answer and strode from the room.

14

Rene guided Miss *Marie* past a sunken wreck four miles off the coast, and after noticing the current against the bow, he set an easterly course that would take them to a good location. Other than dragging familiar areas, he watched for seagulls or pelicans diving into the water--an indication they were going after a school of shrimp. Numerous seabirds meant good luck. He throttled back to maintain a manageable speed that would not pull too hard on the net and kept a lookout for obstacles. A plastic statue of the Blessed Virgin Mary rested on the dashboard next to him. Mary was Marie's favorite saint. Anything she wanted was okay with him.

Since the water wasn't more than twenty feet deep, he stayed ready to react in case the boards picked up too much mud or ran into something heavy on the bottom. He also watched for other boats that might have dragged nearby and had stirred up the muddy bottom. But no other trawler was closer than a half mile and the water ahead was undisturbed.

Because the shallow waters of the Gulf were often filled with silt, it was difficult to see anything deeper than a few feet below the surface. So Marie was ready to act if they had a snag that could damage the doors or rip the net. It was not possible to predict when they'd run into something, because the strength of the current could roll objects several miles in a few days from where they had sunk.

It was their third day together on the boat and Rene was still catching up on his lost sleep from the enjoyment of being married and the constant attention they gave each other. It was exhilarating to give her a kiss or a prolonged caress whenever the urge took hold of him and to receive the same from her. Their lovemaking only whetted his appetite, and since he continually felt it must be fulfilled, such intensity made him wonder how two people could ever lessen their love for each other.

Rene rehashed the information which Tom had divulged the night before he left Pat's Landing. They were late getting underway on Monday because Tom had pulled him into the office and used the excuse that the boat wouldn't be ready for an hour. Giving him a few sketchy details, Tom outlined the trip that Karl Johnson had detailed after following him to Pat's Landing the night before. The trip sounded impossible at first, but the more Rene concentrated on it, the better it seemed. He would make a hunk of money for merely riding offshore and handling a few boxes, and the trip would provide the opportunity to get revenge for Sam's, Roy's and Joe Christy's deaths. In Tom's opinion, which Rene echoed, the trip now became a military operation.

Because Joe's funeral was on a weekday, Rene and Marie were unable to attend, but Tom had promised to give him the details when he returned in two weeks.

Rene thought about the rendezvous plan and wanted to share it with Marie but remembered Tom's warning of personal harm, including the loss of Rene's job, if he told anyone. He alternated between thoughts of Marie and the upcoming mission. Money and love vied for his attention, and the thought of having both of them thrilled him.

It was a mild day. An easterly breeze promised limited visibility, while a north wind would push out the humidity and clear the skies until southerly breezes took over again. A few ragged clouds hung low in the sky and forecasted calm seas and warm, humid nights for a day or two. It was like rolling dice to depend on the weather, especially in the summer when the Gulf was unpredictable. Shallow water extended only a hundred miles out to the Continental Shelf, and the deeper water often brewed up violent squall lines. One day the water would be bathtub-calm, until thunderstorms developed by noon with waves six feet high, winds of sixty miles an hour and torrential rain limiting visibility to less than a hundred yards.

However, the current weather was a secondary concern to Rene, who was still adjusting to the wonder of having his own boat. *Miss Marie* was in like-new condition. The wheelhouse smelled of paint and new linoleum, and the boat had been cleaned, spot-painted in places and gotten ready for them over the weekend. Utilizing blue, the Blessed Virgin's color, Manny had painted the boat's name on the bow. Tom had discovered Manny's talents when he was thirteen and used him to paint the names on all of the boats.

The wheelhouse and cabin were packed with canned goods in cabinets, while along the back wall were pots, skillets, clothes, a suitcase, oil skins and a gas burner for cooking.

Marie brushed against Rene as she came into the wheelhouse for a drink. Despite having jeans rolled above her ankles, wearing white boots, a loose blouse that draped over her hips and her hair tied in a ponytail, she lit Rene's senses when she closed a cabinet door and started to pass between him and the wall. He slipped one hand around her waist and pulled her into him, planting several kisses on her neck, and she briefly rested her head on his shoulder, then laughed and pulled away when his hand traveled toward her thighs.

She moved toward the door, smiling. "Get back to your job. I don't want the captain to fire me on my first week,"

"That won't happen, because the captain loves you."

"Is that permitted in this crew?"

"I spoke to him personally, and he approves of the relationship."

"He seems like a nice guy."

"You'll wrap him around your little finger if you're nice to him."

*   *   *

Their first week of work helped Rene recover from the aftermath of Joe's crash. Before their departure that following morning, they had spent the night in Marie's old bedroom. It had been strange for Rene because he felt like an intruder, and the two of them in her old single bed didn't offer much chance to sleep. Their own house wasn't furnished for them but would be when they came back. Abe, Molly, Jane and friends planned to work on it every day.

Prior to heading out, Rene had filled the hold with the maximum amount of ice that would let them work independently. He planned to avoid meeting other boats and chatting so he could share his time only with Marie. They would drag in the western sector that ran from Raccoon Point to Point Au Fer and pick isolated spots to anchor at night not favored by other crews.

July was hot and muggy. Daytime temperatures climbed into the nineties, with oppressive humidity and bathtub-calm seas. When they didn't encounter a thunderstorm, Rene kept the cabin doors and windows open, hoping any disturbed air would rustle through the cabin and cool them off. But the only relief came past midnight when sea breezes lifted moisture off the water and eventually covered the boat with a morning layer of dew.

Because she had made numerous trips with her father, Marie was efficient as a deck hand as well as handling the boat. She knew how to manipulate the boards, and the story about Sam getting his hand caught in the winch made her doubly cautious. She was careful about letting out the boom, lowering the net and watching for the lines to slacken after the boards touched bottom. Rene had early qualms about her ability to haul in a full net, but she brought it out of the water on her first try, swung it over the deck and untied the sack with ease.

She was likewise a natural at handling the boat, at recognizing the current, when to keep pressure on the net during a drag, and avoiding slack lines that could snag in the prop.

As they settled into a routine, one of the best times happened each day when they sat on the deck and picked through a catch, tossing away crabs, sand trout, sheepshead and young snapper that wouldn't make a decent meal. She had heard about Manny's close call and was cautious when picking through a catch. No matter what the size was, any shark was a threat. A catch also was a dinner bell for seagulls and sometimes pelicans that hovered above the stern, flapping their outstretched wings, waiting to catch fish or scraps tossed overboard. With the trawler's engine shut off, the only other sounds than the birds came from the rigging brushing the wheelhouse, or the boom creaking when the boat rocked between swells.

Marie's loose-fitting shirt caught a breeze as she got up to toss a couple of sand trout toward several pelicans loitering on one side. But before one could wheel toward the fish, four seagulls dived on the prize and climbed off the water, the winner avoiding others flying alongside, harassing him to drop his catch.

* * *

When Rene washed down the deck one day after the shrimp were put on ice, Marie approached him from behind and encircled him with her arms, spreading her fingers across his stomach. He held the hose away, turned into her and placed an arm around her shoulders, sharing a brief kiss.

"How do you feel?"

She smiled self-consciously. "I don't hurt as much today. I think it'll be okay."

"I don't want to …"

Marie squeezed him and pecked his forehead. "I know. But it's passing." She looked over the water where seagulls trolled behind the boat, patrolling for whatever had been washed over the stern, and her eyes met his. "I wanted you so badly last night but the pain was still there. I'm sorry."

Rene dropped the hose and cupped her face in his hands. "We have the rest of our lives to catch up."

She laughed and hugged him again. "We'll be old then and I'll have gray hair."

Rene kissed her forehead. "You'll always be young to me."

Their days evolved into a routine of shared work, and Rene took care to choose a private nightly spot inside the islands. The idea of talking with his father and Manny was the last thing he wanted. His father would no doubt remain in the background, but Manny might work up a joke to embarrass Marie.

*   *   *

On their eighth night out, Rene found a secluded area inside the eastern tip of Raccoon Island and dropped anchor with the stern facing the Gulf. That way, the wheelhouse would block anyone from seeing them when they were on their cots. They anchored just in time to eat and enjoy the last threads of daylight. Marie fixed fried chicken on the gas stove and they ate under the protection of the tarp that ran from the roof of the wheelhouse and was tied to a pole at the stern. After eating, Marie washed the plates and utensils, Rene dried them, and they decided to take a swim. Provided the bottom wasn't populated with debris, or thick with silt and mud, it was a good way to wash off the heat, the smell of shrimp, and sweat.

Rene had set up their cots in the cabin earlier in the week because they were concerned about their privacy, but the arrangement became unworkable. The room blocked most of the breeze, despite opening all the windows in the wheelhouse. So he moved the cots outside, used extra blankets for padding and cobbled together a mosquito bar so the netting would reach across both of their cots.

Before joining Marie, Rene went to the fo'c'sle, where he was confident she wouldn't look, and brought out the bottle of rum that Tom had given him, breaking his own rule about alcohol on his boats. He stopped at the wheelhouse for a pair of glasses, then walked to the hatch and scooped ice into them. It didn't attract Marie's attention because they often got ice to cool their drinks. He also pulled a bottle of coke out of the ice and carried everything back to the wheelhouse.

Marie was busy arranging the blankets and hadn't paid attention, so when he approached, she looked puzzled.

"Where did you get the coke?"

"Tom gave it to me when I told him I needed something for our second anniversary." Rene said. "But he warned me not to depend on other cokes. Most of them go to the military these days."

"But our second week isn't over yet."

"I couldn't wait. Besides, we have a whole bottle to drink. We may as well get started."

They clanked their glasses in a toast and Marie took a sip, wrinkled her nose, eyeballed her glass and rotated it in her hand. "How much rum did you put in it?"

"Just a little. Do you like it?"

She tried another sip and licked her lips. "It's sugary and makes my throat warm."

"Good," Rene said. "I hope you're warm tonight."

She put an arm around his neck and gave him a kiss. "I don't need rum to warm up for you."

Marie took another drink and turned the glass in one hand. "It doesn't have a heavy feel like beer, and the coke makes it taste smooth."

"Tom gave me a bottle but said to go easy so I wouldn't have a drunken deckhand."

Marie let out a laugh and brushed back some hair dangling in front of her eyes. "I'm surprised that he broke his own rule about alcohol on the boats."

"I promised to be careful." Rene replied, and then defended him. "He yells and acts mad most of the time, but he's been generous to us with the car, the extra money, the use of his hotel, and fixing up our boat. I think he wants to make things go right." He realized that he'd said too much and quickly added. "You know, with the company."

Marie kissed him again. "It was thoughtful of you." She ran her hands underneath his shirt and rested them at the small of his back, a come-hither smile spreading over her face. "You know what, sailor? I feel warm all over right now."

She took his glass with hers and put them in the wheelhouse, then returned and led him toward the cots. There was barely enough light to determine the shape of her body as she pulled him upon her, kissing him and progressing over his neck and down his chest, ending at his stomach. Then she moved upward and brushed his left nipple with her tongue. One of her hands slid over his shorts, and he felt like an unusual surge of electricity had invaded him, because it was the first time she had taken the initiative. He sat up to take off his shirt, and then held her in an unhurried embrace, stroking her back down to her hips.

But Marie suddenly stiffened and turned her head to one side, as if she'd heard something.

"Don't worry," Rene said, sliding her underpants off and running one hand up her legs. "The closest boat is half a mile away."

He fell asleep thirty minutes later with her head in the crook of his right arm, the motionless boat supporting them as if they were in their new house and shuttered from the rest of the world.

He dreamed about being alone in the trawler and trying to get up the bayou, but he couldn't pick up speed, despite pulling on the throttle string until his fingers hurt. He thought he was getting close to Pat's Landing because he heard the sound of a diesel engine. Yet the harder he tried, the slower the boat went, and the sound of the engine didn't change.

He woke up and opened his eyes. Everything but the outline of Marie's body and the boat's railing was cloaked in darkness. When he raised his head to look around, Marie nuzzled closer and continued to breathe deeply. Adjusting to align his body with hers, he felt a light coating of dew when he reached underneath the mosquito netting and touched the deck.

Fully awake now, he was surprised that the engine sound in his dream had not stopped but appeared to be a short distance away. It held a steady rhythm and a low rpm that sounded like it was idling.

He shook Marie, who stirred against him and didn't awaken until he shook her again.

"What?" she asked, still half asleep.

"Listen," he whispered.

Marie yawned and rubbed one eye. "What am I supposed to hear?"

"Concentrate," he said. "Do you hear that? It's not very far away."

She was silent for a short time before replying. "I hear something."

"It's the same engine noise that Manny and I heard on our last trip."

She rose up and looked at him. The outline of his face and hair was all she could see. "Are you sure?"

He answered quickly. "I'm positive."

"But who's out there? No one goes shrimping after dark."

"Those are the diesel engines from a German U-boat."

Marie rose onto one elbow and looked seaward. The whole world was black beyond the opaque railing and the moon was a pencil-thin slit disappearing into the Gulf.

"They don't sound like very big engines," she said.

"That's because they're two or three miles away."

"But why would they come so close to the beach?"

"They might be patrolling."

Marie was skeptical. "It's probably the Coast Guard. Why are you so sure it's a German sub?"

He turned and faced the Gulf. "I heard them the first time with my father, and this is the same sound that Manny and I heard. Other people have heard them too, because Tom asked me the last time in if I'd seen any signs of U-boats. Remember what Joe said? They submerge in the daytime and come up at night when it's too dark to be spotted, and when very few airplanes are flying, so they have more freedom to look for tankers and cargo ships. If they aren't hunting at night, they surface to charge their batteries by turning all their lights off and sitting there with their engines idling. I've never heard of patrol planes flying at night, so it must not be dangerous for them.

"Why do they have to come up?"

"They can't run their diesel engines underwater, so they surface, run at idle and charge the batteries that power up their electric motors. They can only run their diesel engines when they're on the surface. I read a story about them in The *Saturday Evening Post* last month."

Marie wasn't convinced. "My dad never mentioned them."

"He probably didn't want to scare you and your mother."

"They must operate in very deep water."

"I don't think so. One rumor says they sometimes come close and sneak spies ashore."

Marie's voice sharpened. "Now you're starting to scare me."

"It's the truth. Some people say the subs can come within a mile of the beach, surface, and listen to us at night. It's been in the newspaper..."

She cut him off. "Must you keep reading about the war?"

"Well, you can't wish it away," he said in a matter-of-fact tone. "The story was recently in The *Times Picayune*. The Gulf and the entire East Coast are being watched every day by German submarines. That's why Tom wants to do something about them," he hinted, then wished he could take back what had slipped out.

Marie became immediately suspicious. "What does that mean?"

Rene tried to sound nonchalant. "He's mad about the Coast Guard restricting the shrimpers to sectors and making the crews report to the coast watchers," he explained, hoping it would satisfy her. "You know how Tom complains. We can't go into deeper water and get the large shrimp because of the subs, and that costs him money. He lets off a lot of steam because there's nothing he can do about them."

Marie kept probing, "You said he wanted to do something about them. What did he mean by that?"

"Just that he's put out about them," he answered. "Griping is his way of blowing off steam."

Marie reached for Rene and held his face between her hands and her words were filled with determination. "You can't get the war out of your mind, can you?"

"It isn't that..."

"Oh, yes it is," she insisted, interrupting him. "I see how you look at the stories in the papers, staring at the pictures and ads like a magnet is pulling you toward them. And when you go through one section you don't stop until you find another story like the last one. Then you go back into that faraway trance again."

Rene rubbed one side of her neck and removed her left hand from his face, kissing the palm. "The war is part of our lives. It's taken some of our friends. We can't ignore it, can we?"

"No, but it's become an obsession with you."

"No, it hasn't."

She slid closer, shivering and pushed against him. "I love you, Rene, and I'm your wife. Please don't lie to me."

"How can I put the war aside?" he asked. "It affects everything we do. I've tried everything, but when we pick up German oil cans and hear their engines, it's like they're living with us." He turned her shoulders and held her face inches from his own. "I guess you're right. I can't forget it, but it's not an obsession." He kissed her on the forehead. "My only obsession is you."

She buried her head in his chest. "Hold me, Rene."

He rubbed her shoulders and hoped to calm her. "They can't come in here. We're safe," he said confidently.

"I'm worried more about you than the Germans and U-boats."

"Nothing's going to happen. They aren't able to get within two miles. The water's too shallow."

"It's not the U-boats I'm worried about," she stressed. "I'm afraid you still want to enlist."

He kissed her on the forehead again. "That won't happen. We're married, remember? I love you more than anything else."

She still persisted. "You should listen to yourself talk about the war. You get excited and your voice changes. I couldn't help but notice it in the café."

"Ray, Joe, Roy, and Sam were all people we knew. I wanted to enlist and fight for them before we got married. But that's in the past. I don't have that urge anymore."

Because he didn't admit his excitement about the coming week and Tom's decision to use him and Manny on a secret nighttime trip, the guilt of keeping it from her sat on his mind like a weight he couldn't remove.

He leaned closer and kissed her on the cheek. It was damp under her eyes, then he kissed the top of her head and they sat entwined in a silent embrace. He felt her heart thump against his chest, and a twinge of guilt swept over him.

It was so quiet that he could hear her breathing, until the distant rumble of the engines continued to reach him the darkness, reminding him that the Gulf belonged as much to the Germans as it did to the shrimpers.

She finally sat up, her face indistinct, her eyes two black indentations. "I want you to be happy more than anything else…"

"I am," he answered, but she overrode him.

"If you want to go, I won't try to stop you. I… won't say anything this time."

"I'm not going anywhere. Put that out of your mind."

"I want you to be happy…"

He held her and kissed her on both cheeks. "There is nothing in this world that can keep me away from you."

When they kissed, salt from her tears seeped into his mouth, and not long afterwards the rhythmical movement of their bodies flexed the legs of the cot. The depth of her breathing increased, she kissed his left ear and filled him with a conviction that made the sounds of the engines disappear in a mutual wave of gratification.

15

Tom edged the iceboat from the dock at six o'clock and started down the bayou. He had explicit directions to be at the rendezvous site by darkness, and since the trip was estimated to take three hours, Karl said showing up late would cause the meeting to be cancelled. By the time he reached the Gulf, the sun would be setting and the iceboat would become more difficult to see, which gave him a veneer of confidence. The rest of the trip could be made in encroaching darkness, away from the prying eyes of the Coast Guard.

Tom didn't like Karl's heavy-handed control but realized it was needed. He scanned the horizon to the south and shuddered when he contemplated what life would be like if the Nazis won the war. Much as he hated the taxes he paid, the Nazis would no doubt be worse by taking over the company and forcing him to report to them. He looked at his watch; he would be on time. He wasn't about to lose the money and the chance to deal out a bit of revenge too. He smirked when he thought about the surprise the U-boat crew would get tomorrow.

But for now, the fly in the ointment could be a harbor patrol boat from Grand Isle that might stop them and question why they were heading offshore so late in the day. But his explanation would be simple. The iceboat's normal route to the drying platform consisted of looping around Raccoon Island and into the estuary of an adjacent inlet. The facility sat on the edge of an old channel that trappers and fishermen still used. Just as he had covered his tracks in Pat's Landing with Al, Tom planned to explain that he was bound for the platform now, instead of early in the morning, because the Chinese were running low on supplies and he needed to straighten out a few personnel problems with them and needed to use the weekend because the iceboat makes other runs during the week.

The more he rehearsed it the better the story sounded. He'd also have the Coastal Patrol over a barrel. They were military and would understand that he had a business to run, rules to follow, and things to do just like they did.

He had thought out every phase of the preparation, except confronting the patrol late in the day. Carrying an extra fuel tank on the back deck and supplies flooding the deck, was a new twist. Woody would cooperate at the inspection dock but convincing the Coastal Patrol ate at Tom's nerves. All the foodstuff had been taken care of-- three sacks of potatoes sat near the door to the fo'c'sle, boxes of canned goods, bread, cheese, meat and coffee sat in the middle of the deck, and the extra fuel tank was supported by timbers bolted to the rear deck and filled with diesel fuel. A three-inch hose, with a coupling that would marry with the U-boat's equipment, lay by the tank.

Clear of the houses two miles south of the warehouse and out of sight from town, he eased the iceboat to the right hand side of the bayou to provide room for any trawlers on the way to the dock. Meanwhile, Karl walked around the port side of the wheelhouse and opened a small box, taking out a sextant, then holding it up to his face and comparing his own height with the roof of the wheelhouse.

Tom challenged him. "Why do you have a sextant? I know where we're going."

"I have to fix the sub's precise position," Karl answered. "I'll relay the numbers to the Coastal Patrol tonight and they'll carry out a raid on any U-boats who use the same location."

Tom didn't challenge Karl's reasoning, but the idea that U-boats would hide in the same spot every night, struck him as ludicrous. Nevertheless, Karl paid the money, so Tom kept silent. Karl glanced around the wheelhouse. "Where are the weapons?"

Tom pointed to a bottom drawer at the floor and behind a wooden chair. "I have a pistol and shotgun hidden down there under a blanket in case the Krauts get nosey and start making trouble."

"That's good planning," Karl said. "I'm sure the Germans will look the boat over before the transfer. We can't be too careful. And if we need the weapons, it'll be a simple matter to take them in hand." Karl then asked. "Are all the weapons loaded?"

Tom kept his eyes on the bayou as the boat approached a curve. "Of course they are," he answered, holding back the urge to laugh. He couldn't recall ever carrying a rifle, shotgun or pistol that wasn't loaded.

Karl pressed with more details, "Did you check out the boys so they know how to operate each weapon?"

Tom held back a sarcastic reply. Everyone he knew in South Louisiana was familiar with firearms. Hunting was a way of life, not a hobby. "No problem there. They were used to firing rifles by the time they were eight years old."

Karl looked past the door jamb toward the stern. Manny and Rene were not in sight.

Moving closer to Tom, one hand in the pocket of his pants, Karl took out a small box that looked like it might have contained a ring and handed it to Tom, who was reluctant to take it. But Karl pushed it into his hands.

"Hide this in a safe place."

The box was too light to give away any clues, so Tom shook it but didn't detect any movement. "What the hell is this?" he bellowed, his patience worn thin.

Karl put a finger to his lips. "The boys don't need to know right now."

"Why not?"

"You probably won't have to use it."

Tom raised his right hand that held the box and cocked his arm. "Tell me now or this damn thing is going into the Gulf."

"It's three cyanide pills," he admitted, patting the pants pocket on his left leg. "I have one too."

Tom shot a critical glance at Karl. "What gives here? You said we'd have cooperation with the U-boat."

"We plan for every contingency," Karl countered. "That includes being double-crossed by the sub's captain."

Tom didn't want to ruin the mission, but he suspected Karl of playing a two-sided game. "And what's going to happen afterwards? I've seen what the government can do when they change the rules. It happened with the bonus march and the flood of '27. Are we going to be double-crossed by our own government again?"

Karl elevated his binoculars, looking for planes or boats that might detect them. "We plan for whatever happens in our job," he answered, maintaining his concentration with the binoculars. "The pills are for you and the boys if the Germans resort to violence. They look at these supply runs as a chance to remain in the Gulf a while longer, so I doubt they will harm us. They certainly don't want to capture us because a submarine's quarters are limited so they won't take prisoners; hence, the pills." He lowered the binoculars and touched Tom on one shoulder. "I don't believe any harm will take place, but in my business it's best to prepare for everything." He broke into a thin smile and patted Tom again, "After the job is over, you and the boys will never hear from us again. Instead of dwelling on what can go wrong, look at the bright side. If the ruse is successful, the Germans won't be so brazen with their U-boats anymore. Keep in mind, Mr. Savoy; you're doing the country a great service."

Tom changed the subject, "Did you pay them?"

"Not yet," Karl answered, reaching into a pocket and withdrawing two white envelopes. "I'll do that now." He turned to leave the wheelhouse but stopped at the door and looked at Tom, his tone commanding again. "Don't forget; the Coast Guard hasn't been told about this plan. If a patrol boat stops us, tell them I am a new-hire and you're taking me to the drying platform."

Tom held his tongue. Karl needed to relax. Every aspect of the job had been covered.

Tom was sorry the iceboat didn't have a radio because he could answer a patrol boat's call, tell his story and continue without the patrol boat stopping them. But he didn't begrudge them for doing their job. They were like the block captains walking the streets and keeping the lights out, only their territory was the Gulf.

* * *

After receiving their envelopes and counting the money, Manny and Rene watched Karl eyeball the boat like he was a Coast Guard inspector conducting a seaworthy inspection.

Manny brought up their good fortune. "What will you do with your share?"

"Marie and I need furniture, and I plan to save the rest. How about you?"

"I'm giving it to my mother. She needs it more than I do. Now that I'm shrimping with your dad, I plan to fix up our house and get a car. We've never been to New Orleans. But when I have a car, I'll take her there any time she wants to go."

The bayou widened as they neared the Gulf, and butterflies fluttered inside Rene's chest. He looked at Manny but his face was difficult to read. Although they had grown up together, Manny's personal life was something he never talked about. Time and again Manny had picked a fight with kids who said derogatory things about his mother, and Rene had learned at an early age to respect that part of his personality.

"Don't you want anything for yourself?" he asked.

Manny shook his head. "A car and a new engine for my runabout; that's all."

"I don't understand," "Rene admitted. "When I talked about enlisting you said the war didn't affect you, that your mother needed you."

Manny followed a pair of seagulls floating past the stern and took his time to answer. "That's how it was until Joe got killed and Tom talked to me. Then I changed my mind. You can call it an accident, but Joe wouldn't have been flying that day if it hadn't been for the war. The Germans killed him just as sure as I'm standing here. And after the U-boat attack last week, I realize that the war is a greater threat to us now. If the Germans have spies in Louisiana, they may be living near us, watching us, waiting to pounce on Louisiana. Tom's given me a chance to do something about it. Besides," he admitted, "my mom can use the money."

Rene held the same opinion. The war was too close to ignore any longer. He hadn't slept as well with Marie as he had when he was shrimping with his father. The subs were out there… waiting… threatening every vessel in the Gulf. And the threat convinced him of his decision. He may not be wearing a uniform, but he was making the rendezvous in the names of his friends that the war had taken.

He'd managed to get away without Marie suspecting anything by saying that Tom needed help with the run to the drying platform. She had agreed but didn't like him being away for the entire night. While his story had worked, he wasn't sure about the next time. Things would be different if he tried the same version. But he brushed the future aside for the time being and felt the money in his pocket. He'd hide part of it and bring it out gradually, until the second trip was over. Then they'd celebrate with a movie, a dinner in Houma and another night in Tom's hotel. He'd ask for the same room so they could relive their weekend honeymoon.

*   *   *

They emerged from the bayou as the sun set and were passed through the inspection station after Woody checked off the supplies and heard Tom's explanation about Karl going to the drying platform. Although Tom felt guilty for lying to a friend, he put his personal feelings aside. They would be facing open water for an hour and a half, and a sub chaser's crew may not be as cooperative as Woody.

A few minutes later they were making ten knots in open water; no patrol boats were in sight, and Tom's spirits lifted. The visibility was a good ten miles and every minute took him closer to the destination. Since the sub chasers couldn't make more than twenty knots at full power, Tom's confidence grew, because once they reached the rendezvous site it would take the Navy vessel three hours to come from their base at Grand Isle. By then the rendezvous would be completed and the ice boat would be on its way home.

In open water now, Tom doused the lights on the wheelhouse, the mast and the aft deck. The white iceboat was enough of a silhouette without added illumination. After putting the island behind him, he recalled how Fort Jackson, on the Mississippi, had a gun battery stationed on a hill overlooking the river and had fired at what they thought was a U-boat slipping upriver. But no wreckage was ever found. It was a good idea to protect inland waterways, and he wondered why a gun battery hadn't been placed on Raccoon Point or other Louisiana sites from Cameron to Grand Isle. Like the coast watchers, the crews could rotate every two weeks and provide protection for the tankers who sailed within five miles of the beach.

But he scowled at his idea; it would have gotten denied like the letter he had submitted for his iceboat. After the first sign of sub activity in the Gulf, in early '42, he had written the War Department and proposed that they give him a fifty caliber machine gun, mounted in the bow, plus a two-way radio, and he volunteered to cruise along the ten-mile limit and look for submarines. However, the answer came in a terse letter that insulted his patriotism and still burned in his memory.

> *Dear Mr. Savoy,*
>
> *Thank you for your interest in our national defense, but bear in mind that our military, the Coast Guard and the coastal volunteers are capable of defending the Gulf Coast against enemy activity. There is no need for additional civilians to be involved. You may rest assured that the federal government and the military are doing everything possible to protect you and win this war.*
>
> *Your concern and patriotism are to be commended.*
>
> *Sincerely,*
> *The War Department*

An actual person hadn't even signed the letter. He was adding up the other abusive things that the federal government had done to him when Karl came into the wheelhouse and eyeballed the course.

"How much do we have left?"

Tom didn't look at him when he replied. "Five or six miles."

Karl glanced at the compass and then through one of the windows. "Why are you on a course of south by southeast?"

Tom held his temper. "I'm holding a few degrees eastward. With no moon tonight, the Gulf appears to be calm, but the current can fool you. We ought to come to the shoal in about forty-five minutes," he said, looking at his watch.

"How can you be certain?"

Tom explained about time, distance, and speed and the effect of the current on their course. It seemed apparent from his nitpicking that Karl knew very little about boating or navigation. He struck Tom as a desk type who had never gotten his feet wet, probably a city boy, and a government goon too. Because Karl looked to be about thirty-five, Tom wondered why he wasn't in the military since he fancied himself a patriot. Being in intelligence was clearly a less important job than carrying a rifle.

Karl scanned the Gulf to the south with binoculars but kept talking in a matter-of-fact manner. "I didn't want to bring this up until now, but there's been a change in our plans."

Tom squeezed the wheel, his anger rising. "What the hell do you mean?"

Karl raised one hand. "It will make a big difference and might even give us a better opportunity to gain their confidence the second time. The change came from our German source. The crew wants to meet a contact they can trust, so I'll be the first one onto the sub. It's a lucky break for us. Since I speak German, I can move about on the sub's deck and gather more details for the second rendezvous instead of sneaking around." He paused, and then added, "I've never seen a submarine, let alone ever been on one. Of course, the Germans don't know that."

Tom wasn't comfortable with Karl's explanation. He didn't know if the change came from the Krauts, if it was a plot hatched by Karl, or if the Krauts planned to sink the iceboat after the transfer of food and fuel. He didn't trust Karl beyond getting paid for the rendezvous. Double agents had to be natural liars. Tom shuddered to think what could happen if Karl favored Germany over America. He knew little about Karl beyond a handshake and two conversations and was heading to a rendezvous with a guy who claimed to be a double agent but on the American side. Karl hadn't shown him any identification to prove who he was, so Tom was glad he had his personal .38 laying in the top drawer. If things went badly, he'd at least have a chance to shoot Karl.

Tom checked the time; they had been running in the open water for fifty minutes. "We're almost there."

"How can we be sure?" Karl asked.

"Ship Shoal is a mile wide and three miles long. Rene and Manny will sound the bottom, and when they measure forty feet we'll be there. The trench is the only nearby area where the water is that deep." He reduced the engine and pointed at the wheelhouse door. "Tell them to get ready with the rope."

With the iceboat moving slowly, Rene lowered the weight of two discarded automobile brake rims with a rope looped through them. They sank quickly out of sight while Manny let out the line, which stopped a few inches beyond the third knot.

"Twenty-five feet," Rene called out.

"Okay," Tom acknowledged.

He added a slight amount of rpm for a minute and called for another sounding, and this time the rope descended to the fourth knot.

"Pull the rope up and wait another minute," Karl suggested. "The Sub needs room to maneuver."

"Hold off until I say so," Tom directed. He increased the power for a short span and went to idle again. "Okay. This ought to do it."

The rope stopped just past the fifth knot, and Tom was satisfied. He maneuvered the bow around to point northeast and held low RPM to neutralize the current's flow and to keep the boat stationary.

Karl left the wheelhouse and walked around the starboard side, looking at the water and crossing the deck to push against the fuel tank, which prompted a smirk from Tom. He wondered about Karl's sudden interest in the iceboat because he hadn't lifted a finger to help when the boat was loaded at the dock.

Swallowed by darkness, the ice boat was a small, fragile feature on a giant seascape where the dark water merged with the black, canopy of sky. Other than the lights coming from the iceboat's dim instrument cluster, the only illumination came the untold thousands of bright, pinheaded stars overhead.

Tom checked his watch by the dim light from the boat's compass. It was a few minutes past nine. They were on time. The starboard side pointed to the shoal and gave the sub an approach path. He had done everything asked of him and was ready and looked in all directions, but there was no sign of the sub.

Karl stood at the railing and watched while Tom remained at the wheel, fidgeting with minor corrections in the heading that kept the ice boat in position so the U-boat would not rise up and smash them. Then he returned to the wheelhouse and barked out more instructions. "I'll meet the crew and assure them that everything is okay. You and the boys will no doubt be frisked for weapons, and I expect the boat to be given a careful going over. I'll go aboard in the meantime and you start the transfer of food and fuel." He raised both hands toward Tom. "Try not to get fidgety while I'm on the sub. And don't become anxious if you hear me talking in German. I imagine few of their sailors can speak English. We may joke around some because I'll do that to relax the crew. So keep calm if you hear us laughing." He motioned toward the back deck where Manny and Rene stood by the railing. "I've already spoken to the boys, but I must remind you not to speak to any of the sub's crew. I'll be your go-between for everything."

"Got it," Tom said, but vowed that Karl would be the first one to die if the meeting was a trap. The night wasn't half over and Tom already had his craw full of Karl. He had taken more orders from him than any other person in the last ten years.

After waiting fifteen minutes without anything happening, Karl went over the plan with Manny and Rene once again. Even with an abundance of starlight, Rene strained to focus on anything past the stern. Beyond that, the water appeared to flow into a coal-black sky that absorbed everything. From magazine pictures of submarines, he guessed it would be impossible to spot the dark gray U-boat before it got close.

Standing at the rail with Rene, Manny pointed into the darkness. "What's that?"

Rene looked in the same direction but saw nothing. "Where?"

"About fifty yards off the stern," Manny said. "It looks like a rowboat, and it's coming straight at us."

"I don't see…"

"Right there!" Manny insisted, pointing again. "Look at it!"

Rene picked it out as the small boat stopped, and he wondered if the rowboat might be survivors from a torpedoed ship, but the sea convulsed into a frothy wave that rocked the iceboat, causing both Manny and Rene to grab the railing. A loud hiss that sounded like a whale exhaling flooded the deck as the sub cleared its ballast tanks and the hull rose out of the water. It surfaced less than ten feet from them, like a formidable sea creature rising from the depths. Its menacing profile was three times the size of the iceboat, and its dark hull and conning tower blended perfectly with the dark water. What had resembled a rowboat at first, turned out to be the conning tower, alive now with sailors climbing down to the deck. The first two manned the gun on the foredeck and another took up a position behind the four machine guns on the back portion of the conning tower. They moved so quickly that Rene fought a brief surge of panic and wondered if he and the others were about to be killed.

When the U-boat edged sideways and stopped six feet from the iceboat, one sailor tossed a line from the foredeck onto the bow of the iceboat and another aft of the conning tower lobbed a rope onto the rear deck. While Manny and Rene secured the lines, a third sailor planted a walkway from the sub to the iceboat.

In less than a minute the sub was tethered to the ice boat and the U-boat crew was in position to start the transfer.

Rene was struck by how lethal the U-boat appeared. The hull didn't protrude higher than a few feet out of the water, and from the conning tower rearward, the aft deck narrowed into a slender fantail that was designed to create a minimal wake. Other than a large ring for tying up, the bow had no raised structure to give it away. Except for the conning tower, that appeared to rise about seven or eight feet above the deck, the submarine rode low in the water and displayed a sleek, dark profile.

Karl spoke in German and started to cross onto the U-boat, but stopped when a sailor blocked his way and lowered a rifle at him and pointed the weapon in Karl's face, so he raised his hands while the sailor frisked him. Satisfied that Karl wasn't carrying a weapon, the sailor moved to Manny and then Rene, frisking them both. He didn't look much older than Rene but had a substantial beard that hid most of his face. His black oilskins outlined his body against the iceboat's white railing, and he stood so close that Rene was struck with the odors of cigarettes, sweat, wet leather, the penetrating stink of rancid food, and the sailor smelled like he hadn't taken a bath in a month.

Tom had initially reached for his pistol when he noticed the weapon being aimed at Karl but put it back when he saw it was only a precaution. After all, it wasn't every day that a German submarine met Americans off the coast of Louisiana.

The sailor left Karl for the wheelhouse and raised his rifle at Tom, who held up one hand and pointed at the bow. "I have to control the boat."

The sailor jerked the weapon toward the roof of the wheelhouse. "Up," he ordered.

Unfazed, Tom kept a grip on the wheel with his left hand. "The boat," he insisted. "I have to keep it straight, so go ahead, you damn Kraut, and search."

The sailor looked toward the bow, finally nodded in agreement and frisked Tom. Then he nosed around the wheelhouse, looking on the floor and opening two drawers, but ignoring the bottom one with the weapons when he found none in the others.

Waiting at the railing with Manny, Rene heard Karl talking to someone in the conning tower, while a pair of sailors made a quick inspection at the fuel tank and moved forward to the boxes in front of the wheelhouse, running their hands over each one, feeling the sacks of potatoes and finally returning to the sub.

The quiet night was suddenly punctuated by a screeching whine of compressed air as one of the sub's diesel engines started up, causing the U-boat to give off a noticeable shudder that traveled the length of the hull, followed by the second engine that fired up and settled into a rumbling pattern with the first one, their combined exhausts snaking onto the iceboat and covering the deck in a pungent, odor that was nearly thick enough to taste.

At a signal from a man in the conning tower--that Rene guessed to be the skipper--Karl walked back onto the iceboat to Rene and Manny. "Start the fuel first. It will take longer." He pointed to the forward portion of the deck by the sub's conning tower. "The fuel port is near the forward wall. A sailor will be there to help you. Be careful on the deck," he cautioned. "It's slippery and wet. You don't want to fall overboard with these vessels so close to each other."

Rene crossed onto the U-boat and followed a sailor to the fuel port. Other than his heart beating rapidly from being on an enemy warship, vibrations from the diesel engines pierced his feet and resonated through both legs and made walking precarious. The entire hull hummed like a huge, breathing animal. The deck was about eight feet across at the conning tower and narrowed to a point at the bow. He searched for handrails as he made his way but saw none, so he moved in a deliberate, flat-footed pace. One misstep sideways could pitch him into the water.

Manny leaned over the railing of the iceboat and extended the fuel hose by swinging it in an arc until Rene caught it and coupled the hoses, then Manny started the gasoline motor to pump the fuel into the U-boat. According to Karl, the fuel would give the crew several extra days of patrol time, depending upon how often the diesel engines were run. But Manny didn't bother with the details. All he wanted was to get back to the warehouse. He wondered if he and Rene had made a mistake by volunteering. If it hadn't been explained that the trip was a set up to fool the Germans, he never would have come. He remained wary, suspicious and very cautious, unable to rid the thought that Americans were dying in the Gulf of Mexico and the very U-boat he stood on could have been responsible for the deaths of Sam and Roy.

He was also bothered that they were helping the Germans but fought to dampen his uneasiness by knowing a bomb might take out the sub in the morning.

With the fuel running and no leaks around the connection, the sailor guarding Rene went to the walkway when Manny approached with his first sack of potatoes. He bent down to get under the barrel of the deck gun that was aimed at the iceboat, and as he eased past, Rene slid against the conning tower wall to give him room. Manny took half-steps with the bulky sack until he came to the galley hatch immediately aft of the conning tower and below the machine gun deck. The sailor accompanying him rapped on the door and as it opened, a wave of red light rose into the air. Manny then lowered the sack onto the top step of an aluminum ladder where a sailor reached for it. When he leaned closer to the ladder he was confronted with a wall of smells that nearly made him vomit--a thick, stifling mixture of fuel, old food, burned meat, engine oil, body sweat, and the smell of toilets so prevalent that it hurt to breathe. At the same time, band music drifted from inside the sub in a flowing rhythm and melody that sounded familiar. He wasn't certain but believed it was "Dancing in the Dark."

He pulled away from the hatch just as someone inside raised a bucket of food scraps and handed it to the sailor on the deck, who emptied the bucket into the Gulf and returned the bucket to the person standing on the ladder.

Manny stood up to adjust his eyes and to replenish his lungs with fresh air and started toward the walkway, accompanied by the same guard. Passing amidships, he was surprised at the low profile of the U-boat's conning tower. If he jumped from where he stood, he could possibly stretch an arm above his shoulders and grab the thickly-soled boots of the German manning the machine guns.

The second trip with another sack of potatoes wasn't any easier. Although his rubber boots gave him some traction on the slippery, metal-slotted deck of the U-boat, the steady vibrations running through his legs made it difficult to plant his feet and feel the deck for support.

Karl was ahead of him, standing with one of the crew, smoking a cigarette and talking. Since their conversation was in German, and the throbbing diesel engines drowned out most of their words, Manny didn't pay attention, even when Karl and the German shared a burst of laughter. He was more interested in avoiding the noxious flow of diesel exhaust coming from the stern and the odors from inside the sub. If all submarines smelled the same, he didn't know how anyone could live in such an awful place, particularly when they were submerged. Even marsh gas didn't make his throat tighten as much as did the rank air of the U-boat.

*   *   *

Tom remained at the wheel and kept the iceboat in position; it wasn't difficult in the calm seas and a light breeze. Now that his night vision had improved, his fingers tightened around the wheel when he watched Manny slip sideways and correct his balance to avoid pitching overboard. Evidently, the others on the U-boat failed to notice, or they didn't care. After all, it would be one less American to kill after the transfer. He patted the pistol in his pocket and felt more secure now that he was armed. The one fear, however, that kept running through his mind, was how the iceboat was tethered fore and aft to the sub. If something went wrong, he would be helpless to try to pull away. He didn't dwell on it, but in the event of trouble, they were trapped.

Tom kept reminding himself that everything would be fine as long as both boys did what they were told and if Manny kept his temper under control.

Karl came into the wheelhouse and opened a drawer, looking for something. "Where are your cigarettes?"

"I have two packs in the top drawer."

"They aren't for me. The sub's skipper wants them." He took Tom's arm in one hand and drew closer. "This gives me an idea for the next trip."

"Take both of them. I have a pack in my shirt pocket."

Karl paused before leaving. "We'll need two more cartons next time. It'll give me an excuse to come back to the iceboat. The Germans are watching our every move."

Tom couldn't imagine what Karl had in mind and didn't ask. All he wanted was to get clear and go back to Pat's Landing. He was nervous and jumpy about being so close to the enemy and filled with more tension than he could ever recall during the Great War.

* * *

Rene knelt by the fuel port and watched Manny carry supplies back and forth, while Karl worked his way from one sailor to another, offering cigarettes. Now that he had adjusted to the darkness, the design of the U-boat amazed him. He could cross the deck at its widest part in just a few steps. It wasn't much more than a dozen feet wide at the conning tower. The boat was shaped like a fish--tapered at the bow and the stern. Even the rounded, leading edge of the conning tower was designed to slip through the water with a minimum amount of drag. The entire U-boat appeared to resemble the fuselage of an airplane more than a boat. The conning tower and the deck gun were the only parts of the vessel that would interrupt the flow of water over the smooth, unobstructed deck when the sub was submerged. The entire boat appeared to be designed without one right angle that could interrupt the flow of water.

He guessed the U-boat to be about two hundred feet long. Its deck sat so low in the water that it created a slim profile. He ran his hands past the fuel port and felt a length of tubing in a shallow groove and felt a hinge that was part of a folding snap rail. Everything about the boat's shape, design and dark gray color made it a dark and deadly weapon.

Karl touched him on the shoulder. "The skipper wants you to help carry the supplies. A crewman will stand by the fuel hose until the transfer is complete."

Rene crossed the walkway and grabbed a box of bread. Since there were ten more boxes remaining, he and Manny altered their timing so they wouldn't pass each other on the narrow walkway. As Rene went back and forth he realized that no one would survive if the Germans decided to kill them. The deck gun was pointed at the iceboat's bow, there were rifle-carrying guards at the walkways and the conning tower and the machine guns were pointed at the rear deck of the iceboat. To make matters worse, several sailors stood on the bridge of the conning tower, watching the goings-on, while two more with binoculars scanned the sea and sky in opposite directions. The iceboat crew was outgunned and outnumbered in a white, slow, cumbersome boat that carried no weapons to match a fraction of the sub's firepower.

He concentrated on his trips and tried to put their grim situation out of his mind.

After all of the supplies were transferred, Rene went back to the fuel port and Manny returned to the gasoline engine. When the fuel tank was empty, Manny killed the engine and Rene uncoupled the hose, then held it up while Manny came to the iceboat's railing to pull the hose onboard and, when the slack was taken up, Rene let go of his end.

He stood up and turned toward the walkway when the sailor standing beside him spoke in English. "You did a good job."

Rene was too startled to reply so the sailor kept talking.

"I went through high school in Pittsburgh. My family came over in thirty-five. I was pulled out of medical school in Berlin and drafted."

Before Rene could react, Karl came up and took him by the arm. "Let's go."

As they crossed to the iceboat Rene noticed a sailor untying the forward line, and when he released it from the U-boat, the bollard retracted into the hull.

Manny met them at the wheelhouse door as the walkway was pulled onto the sub, and Karl turned to wave to the sub's crew as Tom added power and turned the bow toward the northwest.

"We're getting the hell away from here," he scowled.

"Why? It's too dark to risk returning to the beach," Karl cautioned.

"We're not going that far," Tom replied. "I want to put enough distance from them so they can't spot us anymore. I've seen enough Germans to last me a lifetime."

Karl didn't like the idea. "Without forward visibility we could run over debris and damage the boat."

Tom pointed through the front window. "I'm getting out of their sight. If they change their mind about us, they won't know which way we went. And once we're out of this shoal, the water becomes too shallow for them to follow us." Tom indicated the course with a jerk of his head. "We'll be closer to the beach where it's safe." He nodded to Rene, who stood by the wheelhouse door, staring back at the sub. "You and Manny go stand in the bow and yell if you see anything in our way. I'll maintain five knots."

Karl was uncomfortable. "It's dark as Hades. No one knows where we are, so we'll get no help if we hit something."

Tom's reaction was blunt. "Calm down. We won't be moving fast enough to do serious damage to the hull. This area was free of obstacles when we came out and I'm following the course we used then. Besides," he added in a confident tone. "This boat only drafts six feet, and after we clear the shoal the water will grow shallower by the mile. The Krauts don't know this area like we do so they won't take a chance on running aground."

Karl dropped his criticism and handed Tom a slip of paper that noted the rendezvous' position. "I estimate that you and I are half a mile apart. My calculations place the spot north of your figures." He made a square in the air with his left forefinger. "We'll draw a grid half a mile wide and a mile long. That ought to narrow it for the planes."

"When will they come out here?"

"Tomorrow morning," Karl answered, "This latitude and longitude will be their target."

Tom let out a burst of air. "If you're so sure, why make another trip?"

Karl put the paper in his shirt pocket. "We want to pin down their position."

"But you're talking about a large area. A half-mile of water isn't a small target," he countered. "And I'm not sure another sub will choose the same location on a different night."

"I'll know that when I get the next message. That's why we need another trip." Karl replied impatiently. "Half a mile of water could hide ten subs. The target area needs to be smaller. One more trip, Mr. Savoy, and your job will be over. I guarantee it."

"We're not through with this one," Tom warned. "We still have to dodge any early morning sub chasers; and don't forget Woody. It's not normal for me to come back the next day, and he knows that," Tom explained, pointing at Karl. "He'll want to know why you didn't stay at the platform. I only hope he buys the excuse that you quit when you got there."

16

During the second day back on *Miss Marie,* Rene had the uneasy feeling that Marie doubted his story about a run to the drying platform and questioned why Tom chose them and why it was important to spend the night when a daylight trip made more sense. It bothered him that he lied to her, and the aftermath was like an itch he couldn't scratch.

His skin crawled when he remembered that night. But he welcomed the money and the pride of finally being involved in the war. It was a soldier's duty to do his job and, since the mission had required secrecy, it was critical to withhold the details from her. When it was all over they'd celebrate with a bottle of champagne and a comfortable night in Tom's hotel.

He had given Marie fifty dollars of the money and planned to tell her the whole story as soon as he returned from the second trip. He wondered if the three of them would be so famous that the newspaper would write about their exploits, like the tanker gun crew that fought off a U-boat near the Lesser Antilles. It would be thrilling to be welcomed by the mayor of New Orleans and given a medal.

He lined up for the first drag of the day just as Marie came to the wheelhouse, her face drawn and tired-looking. "Will you work the net today?" she questioned in a dispirited tone. "I don't feel good."

"Sure," Rene agreed, pointing over the bow. "Hold this course; due east."

She moved behind the wheel and rubbed her eyes, her voice apologetic. "I didn't sleep more than two hours last night. I couldn't get those engines out of my mind."

He gave her a long hug, his hands massaging her lower back in a slow rhythm. Since their first day out, the catch had been good and they were due for a profitable two weeks, if they continued with the same luck.

They headed east where the Gulf was not as shallow toward Grand Isle. Deeper water meant possibly finding larger shrimp, though there would be more boats to compete with. But he wanted a change of scenery as much as Marie did and a few nights in one of the many coves in Terrebonne Bay appealed to him.

They would also be closer to the patrol base at Grand Isle, where the coastal planes flew from. But he made a point not to bring up Joe Christy. Their occasional airplane sightings were reminders enough without piling on more details that would upset her.

*   *   *

The shrimping had been so successful that they stopped at midday and anchored in Terrebonne Bay, several miles west of Grand Isle and inside an island that stretched for a mile. He had heard stories about the Barataria pirates and their settlement farther east and on the northern shore called Lafitte's Landing. It was now a village of a few hundred Indians, Cajuns and Creoles, most of them claiming to be a direct descendent of Jean Lafitte or one of his band. The locals regarded other shrimpers and fishermen, who didn't live near Barataria, as intruders. They couldn't enforce their opinion on outsiders because no one could lay claim to the open water, but the locals regarded the Gulf waters south of them as their private domain. It had been Lafitte's a long time ago and the locals persisted that they had inherited it from him.

The island chain ran westward to Grand Isle and had offered a multitude of openings for Lafitte to avoid detection from American warships and Mexican pirates. The hillocks and dunes between Barataria Bay and the Gulf provided natural protection for Lafitte, whose low-profile skiffs hid in bay-side water that was too shallow for the English warships to enter.

The Gulf had seen Spanish, then English, French, Mexican, American vessels and now German U-boats. But all Rene wanted was to shrimp in peace and spend quiet nights with Marie, free to swim in the bay, to enjoy the night and free to love each other in solitude, witnessed only by the stars and God.

They stopped after a late lunch and a profitable drag. It had been a fine day. They had caught a bounty of shrimp that averaged twenty-five to the pound, a quarter-size larger than the shrimp in the shallow waters off Raccoon Island. If his luck held out, he'd have a fine two weeks of work. The Lafitte shrimpers would just have to put up with him working on the edge of their waters. Shrimping in the eastern area of his sector separated him from most of Tom's other boats, but Tom wouldn't complain after he saw the poundage they'd bring in.

The following day the sun was low on the western horizon and Rene entered Terrebonne Bay again some fifteen miles west of Grand Isle and dropped anchor inside a sheltered inlet. In order to take advantage of a fresh breeze that was rare for so late in the day, they sat on their cots and ate boiled shrimp and Cole slaw.

Marie was first to notice an advancing mass of densely-packed storm clouds forming in the southeast and edging toward them. "Did Tom give you any weather warnings for this week?"

Rene scooped up the last of his Cole slaw and cleaned his plate with a slice of bread by pushing the crust into the juice. "He didn't say anything other than wishing us luck and telling me to get to work."

She looked at the sky again, her face showing concern. "Don't those clouds look like a storm system?"

"Yeah," he agreed, "but it'll be a small one. Most of the southeast storms don't last very long." He glanced skyward, studying the clouds. "It can't be serious or we'd see lightning." He reached for her and pulled her into an embrace. "The only storm I know about is inside my chest," he said, running his hands inside her shirt and up her back.

Later that night he was still awake after Marie had fallen asleep, her head on his chest and one hand on his stomach. The last time he looked at his watch it had read midnight. Every now and then he rubbed Marie's shoulder, which prompted her to arch her back and scoot closer to him. He was filled with satisfaction and a deep longing to hold onto their routine and could think of nothing he'd rather do than live on the boat with her, shrimp every day and dwell in their private world, safe from the war, and he vowed to make the next rendezvous his last one, no matter what Tom or Karl said. The money was good, but it was a pittance compared to the happiness they shared.

She turned over, put a leg across him, kissed his chest, and he had a fresh surge of desire. It was surprising how little time it took to recover and to want her again. But he closed his eyes and tried to sleep. They both needed rest. Fatigue could cause mistakes during work, and he'd never forgive himself if he became the reason she got injured.

The wind shifted out of the west and ruffled the tarp, but he liked the coolness it delivered and fell asleep.

He dreamed fitfully about airplanes and submarines traveling through the rain. The last dream placed him on a battleship, where he stood at the railing, looking at the wake of a torpedo that approached the ship, and at the last second the captain maneuvered out of its path and the torpedo barely missed the bow.

He woke up feeling as if he had only slept a short time and held up his left hand to check the time just as a gust of wind snapped their canopy and made the sound he had in his dream. Then a stronger one followed, and the air was saturated with moisture, and then the first sheet of rain slammed into the boat, ricocheting droplets through the mosquito netting. He shook Marie, who only pushed against him. He rose up and looked to the south. The beach wasn't more than fifty feet away but was obscured by rain and darkness.

He shook Marie again. "We have to get up."

"Why?" she asked, half asleep. "It's only rain."

The wind shifted, a gust nudged the bow toward the island and waves began to slap against the hull. He scanned the dark sky toward the south, looking for lightning. There wasn't any, but the weather was clearly worsening.

He planted a kiss on her forehead and pulled her into a sitting position, his voice filled with haste. "The wind is strong like a bad storm is coming. We'd better get dressed in case we have to move."

Marie reached for her clothes in a wooden orange crate under the cot and Rene pulled on his pants as the rain hammered the canopy in wind-driven sheets that popped the canvas above their heads. The boat rocked enough that the net swung back and forth and the mast creaked in the wind.

They went to the wheelhouse and got into their rain slickers and Marie put on a broad-brimmed cap that would keep her head and face dry.

Rene's directions were crisp. "I'll tie the catcher and net to the railing. You take the cans of food off the shelves and put them on the floor. Make sure the gas stove is in a corner and braced so it won't turn over and I'll fold the cots and put them in the cabin. We'll take down the canopy after everything else." He pointed toward the engine compartment. "Check the bilge pump and make sure it's sucking water. If it's too dark down there, get the flashlight in the top drawer at the wheel."

She started her chores and he went outside for the cots, folded them and carried them to the cabin. Wind-driven rain was now falling in large drops that bounced off his slicker and smeared onto his face, forcing him to wipe his eyes. Trickles worked around his neck and slipped into his shirt, but the slicker pressed against his skin and kept the rest of his body dry.

He questioned how a storm could have developed so rapidly without any warning and then remembered that they had avoided other boats for the last two days. Some crews would have looked south around Raccoon Island for him, but since he hadn't told anyone where he was going, they wouldn't know where to start. With no radios on the shrimp boats, a healthy respect for developing weather was the only means available. It wasn't unusual for a storm in the southern Gulf to intensify and move northward with little warning. He figured that was what had happened.

But instead of being a large thunderstorm, the weather behaved more like a hurricane; the wind came in consistent streams and there was no sign of lightning or thunder.

He thought about heading west but it was too dark to move. They had to wait for daylight. He wiped the water off his watch. It read five o'clock. It would be an hour until he'd have enough light to navigate. Running in the open Gulf wouldn't be easy, but if he remained in the bay, or attempted to flee west through shallow water, he'd run aground. Once they got offshore he'd stay within reach of land and try to make the mouth of the Lower Bayou. For a brief moment he wondered if they could ride out the storm where they were, but it didn't last. The island would break the heavy waves, but the stronger winds, sure to come with the hurricane, would capsize the boat or run it aground.

For the present they were protected by the barrier island, and if the storm didn't intensify, they could use the boat for shelter. But in case things got worse, they were a short distance to the island if they had to abandon the boat.

Heavy rain beat on the wheelhouse and made talking difficult as he sought Marie's advice. "Should we stay or try for the bayou?"

Marie chewed on her lower lip and watched the wheelhouse windows flex inward from a strong gust of wind that struck them. "What do you want to do?"

"It can't be any worse to the west. If we stay here and run aground, the boat might get torn apart."

"Then let's get going."

"Let's roll up the canopy before it tears off."

Working in the driving rain, they untied two corners near the deck and Rene held the tie down ropes while Marie undid the other end. As soon as she loosened her end, the canvas bucked and twisted, nearly tearing away from Rene, who went to one knee to avoid being knocked off his feet and losing the cover.

"Grab a corner," he yelled. "We'll roll it together."

The wind blew his slicker up on his shoulders and rain pelted his back while he rolled the canvas in small sections, and Marie kept pace with him until the tarp wasn't at the mercy of the wind anymore. They carried it to the cabin and stuffed it inside and then used a smaller canvas cover for the hatch board to protect the shrimp from water collecting on the deck. Marie smoothed it over the board while Rene clamped one side at a time, sliding the slats into the grooves and securing the canvas. If seawater broke over the railing, the canvas would keep a majority of it out of the hold, saving most of the shrimp and reducing the threat of flooding the hold and putting the boat in danger of sinking.

Before following Marie to the wheelhouse, he looked over the deck for anything that needed to be tied down, but everything was secure. The gasoline barrel was roped to the stern and unused tubs were tied together. The only thing loose on the boat would be the anchor when he pulled it up, but it was heavy enough to stay in one place.

Making his way to the wheelhouse, a pocket of wind slammed into the boat that pitched the bow upward and shook the hull, causing

Rene to lose his balance and fall to one knee. If additional waves bottomed the hull against the mud line, it couldn't sustain repeated contact without splitting and tearing apart. And stronger winds were certain to come. The shallow water where *Miss Marie* lay anchored was in danger of being scooped up by high winds.

Marie held onto the wheel with both hands, her feet spread apart to keep her balance.

"We can't take many more like that one," he said. "We have to head west and get ahead of this storm."

"But it's still dark," Marie answered in an anxious voice.

He put one hand on the wheel, pulled her close and kissed her wet, cold lips. Soggy tendrils of hair hung from her face. He cursed himself for not recognizing the signs of the encroaching storm--the abrupt wind shifts during the evening, the wall of dark clouds that was sure to approach, and a significant drop in temperature. If he had acted sooner they could have made an hour's headway last night and stayed ahead of the marauding rainstorms that were now pummeling them and destroying their visibility.

He added power and shifted into reverse and felt a tug on the anchor line, but not enough to tear it loose from the bottom.

"When I pull up the anchor you turn the wheel and bring the bow to the south. We'll face the wind and waves until we have enough light to follow the coast."

"Okay," she answered, nodding with quick jerks of her head.

Outside again, the rain beat on his shoulders and arms as he yanked on the anchor and pulled it out of the mud. Not bothering to coil the line, he dropped the anchor and got back into the wheelhouse to help Marie, who had shifted the boat in gear and had the bow swinging to the left.

They were on the edge of a narrow inlet with scant room to maneuver, and if they became grounded they would be at the mercy of the storm. If that happened, he was concerned that the Fairbanks-Morse engine wouldn't be powerful enough to get them free. A gust came over the bow and flexed the windows and the boat pitched downward and settled into a trough. Pointed south now, the bow sliced into the wind but still absorbed much of the storm's energy.

The worsening conditions tore at Rene's confidence. He had never been trapped before by such weather. "This seems like a good position," he said, though Marie didn't reply or look at him. "Hold it steady and I'll go lower the anchor."

When he let out the anchor the ten-foot marker stopped at the edge of the water. Although it was only a slight difference, their new location gave them deeper water and less danger of bottoming out. They should be alright unless the storm increased and bigger waves crashed over the narrow island that separated them from the Gulf.

They didn't have long to wait before pockets of light began to squeeze between the rain cells, and they had been dressed for less than an hour when the bay began to take shape. In a few more minutes there would be enough light to parallel the beach.

Marie huddled against Rene and squeezed him around the waist, and he put one arm around her and they watched the rain pour onto the foredeck. His spirits rose a bit as the horizon grew lighter, so he talked about other things than the storm.

"It's such a good haul of shrimp that I'm surprised Tom doesn't tell more crews to work this area." He surveyed the bay as Marie held him in a silent hug. "One nice thing about storms is that the shrimping is improved afterwards. No one has ever explained why, but the shrimp become more active."

To get rid of a cramp, he flexed his left arm that held the wheel and shook his hand. "I'm going to sleep late tomorrow when this is over."

They were momentarily safe, but stories he'd heard from other shrimpers gnawed at him. Every sunken shrimp boat that he knew about, except Sam's, had gone down in a storm. A stubby, wide-hulled trawler with a small, underpowered engine didn't stand a chance in waves ten feet high and winds over sixty. In calm seas the best a shrimp boat could do was ten knots, if it carried a light load, had a clean prop and was being pushed by a tail wind.

Looking over the wheelhouse and cabin, he shined the flashlight into the engine compartment and caught his breath. Although the rain had let up, they were taking on water. Marie broke away and went to cycle the bilge pump because there appeared to be twenty or thirty gallons in the bilge. If no more came in, the pump could get rid of the water in fifteen minutes, but Rene wasn't confident about keeping more out. He had closed all the openings and the hull had been freshly caulked when they first took the boat, but no shrimp boat was watertight. The only alternative was to stay on the pump and get away from the storm.

Rene started to relieve her but she refused. "I can do this. You handle the boat."

"Okay," Rene agreed, returning to the wheel, "but tell me when you get tired and I'll take over. Once we get in the Gulf we'll head west and get on the weak side of the storm," he said, trying to sound confident. But he couldn't overcome his doubt; the storm had him rattled.

He cursed under his breath for not staying closer to Raccoon Island that would have given him a chance to run inland. Whatever happened now would be his fault.

"Don't worry about me," she answered without looking up.

He wanted to leave right away but the sky was black in the west. They needed half an hour more. When a large wave hit the bow, he felt the anchor move off the bottom and added power. But when the hull bounced like a cork, he had no doubt any longer that the storm was a hurricane. A new pattern of wind-impacted rain, driven by a howling stream of storms, hammered the boat.

He was thankful now that he'd taken on extra ice. Its weight gave the boat a lower center of gravity that helped keep it upright and could possibly save them from capsizing.

His visibility dropped to a few feet beyond the bow and he depended on pressure through the wheel to tell whether the bow was swinging left or right. He judged by instinct because the bouncing compass was useless to pin down a hard direction, so he alternated his concentration from inside to outside, then back inside, struggling to keep his equilibrium and sometime sensing that the boat was moving sideways when it wasn't.

He looked in the engine compartment where Marie worked the pump, her shoulders flexing back and forth in a constant rhythm.

"How are you doing?"

She gave a rapid wave of her left hand without looking up, and her effort made him determined to battle his own uncertainty that gripped him each time the boat rolled or nosed into an approaching wave. Her shoulders struck the wall now and then, but she regained her balance without losing her grip on the pump handle.

Rene had seen the close-up work of only one other hurricane when he was ten, a developing mass of rain, wind, and one tornado that dropped out of the clouds and took aim at Pat's Landing. But instead of the village absorbing a direct hit, it skipped over the bayou and turned to a westerly course over the marsh, leaving behind broken tree limbs, piles of leaves, and many dead animals, but no serious damage. He had heard the account of the killer hurricane early in the last century that blew down the walls of the hotel on Raccoon Island and killed several people. The entire island was flooded, many animals drowned as sea water pushed a mile inland, killing most of the plant life for two years and also coming close to wiping out the population of Grand Isle, which convinced many of the survivors to move inland.

Rene could have gotten a warning from the Coast Guard if he had a radio, but Tom always bristled when crews asked for them. He called them expensive frills that didn't make shrimping any easier and didn't improve the company's profit. Instead, the iceboat was their communications lifeline. It kept the crews supplied and brought them newspapers. Tom had argued that radios would take the crews' minds off their jobs because they would be yakking to each other and only doing half a day's work.

Rene hoped that Manny and his father had made it to the dock. Al customarily anchored within a stone's throw of the channel, in case he had to move during the night and get in quickly, and Rene blamed himself for not following his father's sensible practice. He was sure he would hear about the foolishness of wandering away from the other boats. Right now, his parents were most likely boarding up windows, taking in the potted plants on the porch, tying the swing to the railing, filling the lanterns with coal oil, making sure the skiff was staked down and securing anything that would fly around when the winds hit.

Since no one could be certain where to look for them, he was sure both families would hold a vigil by saying the rosary and lighting candles after the storm passed, but it was too dangerous now for any boat to venture out and look for them.

During a brief lull his mind wandered, and he closed his eyes and imagined himself outside their house, a cold beer in his hand and

Marie stretched out next to him, like a cat napping in the sun, her skin warm when he touched her.

"Rene," Marie called out, nudging him on the shoulder.

He opened his eyes, stunned that fatigue had controlled him. "Huh," he uttered.

"Shine a light on the pump," she said.

He had just looked at the water five minutes ago, or maybe it had been ten. He wasn't sure. The flashlight beam showed the water to be six inches high and surrounding the base of the pump. Marie went back to work, and the handle squeaked in a faster rhythm as she fought to gain control over the water.

He rubbed his eyes and shook his head to get rid of the cobwebs; he looked outside, and his heart raced. Tendrils of battered, gray clouds were approaching the black, watery sky around the boat.

"Marie," he shouted, "it's getting light!"

She shrieked when she looked outside and came up to him, planting a hard, sweaty kiss on him.

"Let's get out of here. I'll pull up the anchor and you take the wheel. Then get back on the pump. We'll clear the channel, hug the coast, and follow the shoreline to the west."

He pulled the slicker's hood over his head, though he knew the wind would blow it off. Now that he could see to fight the storm on better terms, he grew more determined. He stepped outside the wheelhouse and protected his face with one arm from the rain that drove the slicker against his chest but kept his concentration on the deck, despite wind gusts that threatened to knock him off balance.

The anchor rope was frayed from where it had rubbed on the top of the railing, and in another hour they might have lost it. He pulled the anchor off the bottom on the second try, brought it aboard and got back into the wheelhouse to take the wheel from Marie, swung the bow toward the mouth of the inlet, pulled the throttle string and brought the engine to full power.

As the bow edged into the open water, he saw the face of the hurricane for the first time. The entire Gulf was in motion; row after row of frothy waves lined up parallel to the beach, waiting to roll over the bow and onto the land. The dark clouds had white edges that shook as if being driven by a gigantic fan and the surface of the water disappeared about fifty yards off the bow as the rain fell in torrents against the wheelhouse windows. A momentary gap appeared, followed by another sector of rain, as if the sky was being wrung dry. Bloated clouds raced past the windows like unearthly demons, and a succession of eight-foot waves, resembling foam more than water, waited for their turn to strike the boat. Everything ahead of him was in motion, except the nearby island off his starboard side, and though the beach was saturated with water, bits of sand whipped into the air and splattered against the boat and into the marsh grass.

As the bow dipped, rose up and jolted with each wave, Rene edged past the island until he had a wide berth and then turned to the west. One mistake in judging the distance would take him into shallow water where *Miss Marie* would beach like a stricken fish. They no sooner got on a safe course than the boat was struck broadside by the waves and rolled to one side, then returned upright, and he struggled to hold an angle from the shoreline, like a crab swimming against the current, as continuing waves of rain limited his visibility.

Temporarily stable, he figured he could handle the storm and get to the bayou. "We're going to be all right," he shouted to Marie, who swayed from side to side, depending on where the boat was rolling.

Her eyes wide and her hair matted against her forehead, she turned halfway toward him and nodded without smiling.

He maneuvered with each blast of wind and rain and thought he had the waves figured out. The high rollers lost some of their punch in shallower water by breaking up on the bottom, so the odds of them enduring were good as long as he could hold the same direction without beaching. But it was only a minute or so before he had to turn toward open water and took on the waves directly. The boat lurched downward, and then rose on the swell, forcing Rene to grip the wheel and keep his balance, and Marie lurched sideways and struck the wall without interrupting her pumping.

He returned shortly to his planned course and was heartened by their progress as Marie came to him and pointed at the floor where the water was mostly gone for the time being.

"I'm hungry," he declared. "My stomach is growling."

Fighting to keep her balance without falling over, Marie searched the floor and held up a jar of peanut butter and one of honey. "This is all I can do right now."

"Fine," he agreed. "What's left to drink?"

"I'll find something."

She spread peanut butter on three slices of bread, topped with honey, made him a triple-decker sandwich and opened a bottle of warm Nehi orange soda. She wasn't hungry but shared the drink with him. The peanut butter stuck to the roof of his mouth and the bread balled up, so he crushed it between his teeth, luxuriating in the honey's sweetness that reminded him of a world outside the storm that was waiting for them. The storm surely had everyone at home awake, praying to lessen the wind and water, that the tornadoes stayed away and hoping things would soon return to normal.

He gave Marie another drink and they exchanged a quick kiss, but she hurried back to the bilge pump; the water was coming in again.

The storm grew closer an hour later and the wind started to shift northwest and hit the boat head on. The change in direction created new swells that caused the prop to come out of the water at each crest, and then settle into a trough, making it impossible for Rene to hold a steady course. There seemed to be no end in sight; with each successive swell, he got out of one, only to face another. Dark waves pushed layers of froth that resembled boiling water, and the sky was filled with fast-moving clouds, unleashing pockets of rain that struck the wheelhouse and sounded like bullets, and the roaming storm clouds hung so low that he thought he could reach up and touch them.

The waves increased until some crests were even with the windows of the wheelhouse, and when the boat nosed into them, layers of foam slithered onto the deck like angry serpents. Each wave washed the deck and eventually ran through the openings along the rails, and for a few minutes Rene disregarded the struggle to make headway and turned the bow into the rollers.

He said a silent *Hail Mary* and looked at Marie, who fought to stay upright, her right arm working the pump without any letup in her rhythm.

"I don't see how it can get worse than this," he yelled.

If she heard him, she didn't show it.

But he had no sooner said that when he realized he was wrong. Rain-wrapped when it struck the boat, a large waterspout hit them without warning. He hadn't seen it coming because it was the same color as the water. Powered by a strong gust of wind, it whirled in an angry dance across the surface and moved over them in a sudden burst of wind. Struck broadside by the funnel, the boat lurched to one side and the bow swung to the left. The wheelhouse door shook on its hinges and canned goods rolled past Rene's feet as the boat listed in a slow, sickening motion.

Marie screamed and braced against the wall and Rene fell to one knee before pulling on the wheel and standing again. After a sudden, dramatic drop in noise and wind, the waterspout disappeared as quickly as it had arrived and headed toward shore, pulling more water into its rotating shaft.

Marie righted herself and came over for a hug, shaking as she grabbed him in a tight embrace.

"Are you okay?" he asked, pulling back to look at her.

Instead of speaking, she kissed him; her lips salty from tears.

He forced a smile and tried to sound confident. "We're going to make it."

She broke away and went back to the pump; the water was threatening again. He thought about changing jobs with her but suspected the high seas pressuring the wheel would overwhelm her, and capsizing would be disastrous. Swimming--even with a life jacket on--was no guarantee they would survive.

He concentrated on the waves and lost track of time until he checked his watch several moments later, surprised that it was past nine o'clock. Not long afterwards he looked through the windows in disbelief and wondered if fatigue made him hallucinate, because a wide cleavage in the storm had opened a pocket of blue sky between two massive squall lines. The visibility grew to half a mile, the waves slackened and the boat stabilized.

He steered toward the north and a shot of adrenalin surged through him when he recognized the mud line and a patch of marsh grass on the arm of Raccoon Island. Shaped in a gentle curve on the south side, it was unlike any other island in the chain.

Helped by a tailwind, they had traveled through fifteen miles of the storm.

The wind shifted to an easterly direction and pushed the boat toward the inlet, though Rene was cautious about taking a direct course, because rain quickly obscured the island once again and foam broke over the stern. He swung to the west instead and held a wide arc to avoid going aground.

"I see the island." he shouted. "We'll be at the inlet in less than an hour."

She climbed the steps from the bilge and came to him in a crouched posture, with her eyes closed, as if she had something hidden in her hands. Guilt took hold of him because she had been doing the harder job, and from the beginning he had wondered if she would hold up. But she had shown toughness and fortitude that he hadn't ever seen in her.

"You can stop now," he said, reaching for her shoulders. "We'll be able to make the mouth of the bayou. It won't matter if we go aground now because we could use a plank and row the rest of the way home," he said, laughing.

She buried her head in his chest, tremors cascading into him, and when he reached for her hands she broke into a sob, pulling them away and holding both palms against her chest. He turned them over and saw a broken blister the size of a quarter at the base of her right thumb; the loose skin had collapsed and blood matted an inner layer. And she had two smaller ones on her other hand that had also ruptured.

He kissed her on the forehead. "I'm sorry. I should have given you some gloves, but I didn't think about it."

"I didn't either, but I'm alright," she answered in a quivering voice. "They really don't hurt that much."

He looked at a drawer by the wheel and shook his head. "It was my fault. I should have traded places with you."

She forced a weak smile. "I couldn't have handled the boat like you did," she admitted, looking at her hands and shrugging.

He situated her behind the wheel. "Well, you can now. We're in calmer water," he noted, gesturing through the window at the outline of the island. "Keep to the left of that point and it'll take you into the bayou. Maintain this distance from shore or you might run aground and I'll take care of the pump." He pulled a pair of soft gloves from the drawer and handed them to her. "Put these on." Then he went to the pump.

In less turbulent water and smaller waves now, he set up a cycle where he'd bail for a few moments then check on Marie. The water was not the threat that it had been so he was able to lower the leakage in the hull and reduce the chance of killing the engine by the water causing an electrical failure.

After a short routine of pumping, it was clear what she had endured. Half-enclosed and bending over the engine, that emitted heat waves like a hot oven, he was already sweating. Escaping gases infiltrated his nose and made breathing difficult; but the worst were the acrid odors of burned engine oil and gasoline, and the only way he could breathe without choking was to keep his mouth open.

Besides the putrid atmosphere, the waves struck the hull close to his head like battering rams. While he was at the wheel, he had been more occupied with the noise from the rain and wind, but the waves hitting the hull now dominated his attention. He concentrated on cycling the pump so he wouldn't have to think about them, but it wasn't easy.

After what must have been a long time, he looked at his watch. He had only been working fifteen minutes but it seemed like an hour. He turned toward Marie and caught a profile of her determined face, her lips mashed together, her gloved hands constantly making adjustments with the wheel and her feet spread apart to keep her balance. Rene straightened up and went to her, slipping both hands around her stomach and pressing his body closer, kissing her repeatedly up and down the back of her neck.

"That's awful down there. I don't understand how you stood it as long as you did." He kissed her again and she took one gloved hand and ran it quickly through his hair, then grasped the wheel again.

"You didn't know. Anyway, it's not important now."

"I can take the wheel for a while. The water has slacked off and you can rest."

But she drew back and looked at him with an expression of resoluteness that he'd seen in her that night on the bayou, when she'd made up her mind about him leaving for the war. "I'm okay. I don't need a break, but you'd better get back to the pump."

"Yes, Ma'am," he said, breaking into an obedient chuckle.

Her eyes danced as she jerked her head toward the bilge. "Go to it, sailor."

* * *

When they entered the bay where most of Tom's crews usually anchored for the night, the island broadened out eastward and blocked most of the waves, and the storm showed little more now than gusts from a thunderstorm, so Rene opened the front window and flooded the wheelhouse with fresh air.

Woody's inspection station at the mouth of Lower Bayou was damaged from the storm and had been abandoned. Its roof was ripped in places and the door hinges were broken, so they continued toward home; however, several minutes later, they approached another shrimp boat that had capsized a short distance away. Its partly-exposed hull looked like the belly of a giant fish and protruded out of the water so far that starboard side was visible from a hundred yards, including the metal support for the prop.

But there was no sign of life.

"Whose boat is it?" Marie asked, as they closed the distance to the boat.

"I don't know. I can't read the name because part of the bow is covered with leaves."

"Can we get closer?"

"No," Rene cautioned, motioning for her to steer clear. "We may go aground in the mud."

"Maybe they took refuge on the island?"

Rene searched in the light rain but couldn't pick out details yet. Since the land rose several feet on the western end, there was a chance the crew might have made it ashore and hunkered down behind a sandy hillock. He called out to let the survivors know help was near, but the falling rain shortened the range of his voice. He climbed onto the roof of the wheelhouse to get a higher angle and a broader picture and took a kneeling position but was unable to read the name of the boat. He couldn't stand up without something to brace himself because the wind blowing across the wet hull might knock him into the water, and since they couldn't safely draw the boat close to the capsized hull, their only option was to head toward Pat's Landing.

As he began to climb down, he glimpsed black striping on the stern; there was only one shrimp boat in the fleet with that color. It belonged to Earl Morvant and his young son, Giles, who had quit school in his sophomore year to shrimp with his father. At sixteen, Giles was still too young to enlist but told everybody in Pat's Landing that as soon as he turned seventeen, in six more months, he was joining the Navy. Meanwhile, he crewed with his father and helped look for enemy airplanes as a volunteer with the Aircraft Warning Service when he was home every other weekend.

Rene cursed Tom Savoy for not putting radios in the boats. At least he would know if the crew had been picked up. They had no choice now but to continue on to Pat's Landing and hope Earl and Giles had been found.

When he moved to the corner of the wheelhouse he saw something at the mud line on the far side of the boat but couldn't make it out. It was either a large animal or a person lying at the water's edge. He cupped both hands around his mouth and shouted several times but got no reply, and a new splash of rain crossed the capsized boat and hindered his ability to pick out better detail.

Marie handed him a towel when he came into the wheelhouse. "Did you see someone?"

"I'm not sure. It looked like a person by the water, but I can't be sure."

She turned the wheel and looked toward the island. "We have to find out."

Rene stopped her turn and brought the bow around on a line that would keep them headed up the bayou. "We'll go aground if we try to get closer."

Marie's face contorted in pain. "Maybe we could..."

"It's impossible. We'll tell Tom what we found and he'll send a boat out as soon as the weather lets up."

They entered the bayou as the winds receded, the clouds dispersed, and pockets of blue sky opened above them, followed moments later by the morning sun. Streaks of light cut through the cloud wall and a rainbow formed along the beach not far behind them, its northern arc of colors touching the marsh half a mile ahead. The bayou quieted down, the wind stopped, and the visibility increased to a mile in every direction.

Rene unwound the throttle string and shifted the boat into neutral and took Marie's hand. "Come and see this."

The only sounds were the engine idling and soft rivulets of water slapping the hull, as if the eye of the hurricane had been tamed just for them. A vast circle of deep blue developed above them, ringed by gray clouds, whose vertical columns ran downward nearly to the water and were stacked up like bricks in a wall.

But the quiet serenity of the eye was brief. New whitecaps soon appeared off the stern, driven by the wind that now came from the north. Rene put the boat in gear and headed inland. They'd have the peaceful eye for a while before the waves and wind redeveloped. Ten minutes later the sunlight vanished and the turgid mass of clouds gathered over them, rocking the boat, but the waves were restricted by the narrow bayou and incapable of threatening their progress.

Rene held Marie with one arm and gave her a quick kiss on the forehead. "We did it," he said, his face splitting in a wide grin. "We'll be at the dock in less than two hours."

Fatigued and sore all over, she leaned against him and closed her eyes.

*   *   *

Tom had gotten out of bed with the first sign of the storm and spent the morning pacing the floor, shouting orders, tying up his boats as they straggled in and securing loose equipment in the warehouse.

Rene and Marie had no sooner tied up at the dock when he stepped onto the boat, his face aflame. "Where the hell have you been?"

Rene shut down the engine and choked off a reaction to Tom's attitude. He had expected curiosity but not anger. "We couldn't get away until daylight."

"Where did you anchor?" Tom insisted.

Rene looked at several people on the dock, including Marie's parents, but there was no one related to Earl and Giles, so he ignored Tom's question.

"Have you heard anything of Earl and Giles?"

"No," Tom answered quickly. "What about them? They aren't here either. But when they get in, I'm going to give them an ass-chewing they'll never ..."

Rene interrupted him. "They capsized north of Raccoon Point, not far from the mouth of the bayou. We couldn't get to them because the water is too shallow. We didn't see any signs of life. I called out but got no answer."

Tom was doubtful. "Are you sure they had capsized?"

"The keel is out of the water and the boat is lying on its side."

Tom shook his head and rubbed one cheek, gritting his teeth. "How do you know it's their boat?"

"It has black striping," he said. "Is there any other local boat that you know of with black striping?"

Tom's face shed its angry expression. "It has to be them. I wonder if they anchored too far away to make a run for it. Or maybe they took on water and lost the engine. Anyway, we'll take my runabout and get down there as soon as this wind drops." He gestured toward the stern. "How much shrimp do you have?"

"About three hundred pounds, but some might be ruined. We took a lot of water over the deck."

"Let's get you unloaded as soon the rain stops." He waved one hand to a pair of his dock hands who stood by the bow of *Miss Marie*. "Find Manny and tell him to unload the shrimp."

The southern part of the hurricane was not as fierce as the northern phase, and after an hour of waiting, Tom, Rene and Manny were in Tom's flat-bottom runabout, slipping over the bayou at twenty-five miles an hour, bucking a stout breeze, though nothing like the winds that had hit earlier. The rain squalls had moved westward and blue sky was expanding far offshore.

Nearing the open water of the bay, Tom cut back on the power and slowed down after a wave broke over the bow.

The memories of the hurricane sat on Rene's mind--the waves, the wind, the roar of the storm, like an animal trying to devour them, the pressure on his hands and arms as he fought the wheel; finally, Marie's blisters and their bloody texture plagued him. The storm had also taken a physical toll; every time he shifted his weight, pains shot through his shoulders and back.

Since the runabout drafted less than a foot, Tom reduced the engine to idle and approached the *Shrimp King*. He slipped around the hull by a section of deck that wasn't submerged and called out, but there was no answer. So he moved into the current and came back to the bow. The wheelhouse windows above the water line were shattered and the mast was snapped like a broken tree limb.

Tom yelled again, swung wide and drifted at idle toward the island. Now the body that Rene had seen was visible, face down, arms spread apart. Tom shut off the motor and Manny used a pole to guide the runabout nose-first onto the muddy bank. Being the first one to get out, he stepped close to the body of Earl Morvant, who lay on his stomach; the left side of his face was exposed and both arms reached beyond his head, as if he had made one final attempt to grab the safety of the bank.

Tom took charge. "Ease him over. Put his legs together and cross his arms over his chest. We'll carry him that way."

As they moved Earl onto his back, two sand crabs fell off the side of his neck, and gouges were visible in the skin where they had been chewing.

"Sonsofbitches," Tom shouted, kicking them into the water.

Carrying him by one shoulder, with Manny on the other and Tom holding Earl's legs, Rene couldn't avoid looking at Earl's face. His skin was ashen like his lips and his puffy, bloodless face. His mouth was partly open and both eyes were half-closed, like he was about to fall asleep. He gave off a sickening mixture of bodily fluids, mud and marsh water, and Rene turned his face away and tightened his throat to keep from throwing up.

After arranging Earl in the runabout, they worked their way to the sunken portion of the trawler and found Giles floating in a pool of water behind the wheelhouse. One shoulder was in a strange angle and his skull was visible through the hair on the left side of his head.

Tom bent lower and examined the blow. "From the looks of his injury, the poor kid must have died right away."

*   *   *

They learned from news on the radio the next day that the hurricane had formed north of Cuba and had struck Louisiana a glancing blow with winds of seventy-five. After hitting the coastline close to Grand Isle, the storm paralleled the shoreline a few miles inland and veered westward toward Beaumont, then turned northeast, dissipating into a group of thunderstorms in northern Arkansas and finally breaking apart among the foothills of the Ozarks.

Since it had been a small hurricane that moved rapidly, the following day was serene, with a mild, dry morning, bright blue skies and a light breeze off the Gulf.

It was time to get back to shrimping, but Tom held the boats at the dock until the funeral service for Earl and Giles could take place.

Rene and Marie spent one day repairing equipment on their boat. The *Miss Marie* had absorbed little damage, considering how long the storm had tossed them about. The catcher was wind-battered and one board was split, the net had a foot-long tear, and two rub rail tires had slammed against the hull until they ripped away. But the vital parts of the boat that allowed them to safely operate the trawler--the engine, shaft, prop, mast and rudder, power take off and boom--were serviceable.

*   *   *

The funeral occurred two days later at ten in the morning, under scattered clouds that formed on the heels of ground fog that shrouded the bayou early but dissipated in time for the service. Two more plots in the community graveyard were filled, both on the left side of Joe Christy. Although Earl and Giles had died from the results of the hurricane, it seemed fitting for them to lie next to Joe Christy.

Al read a Bible passage and Father Gruber gave the final prayer. "Heavenly Father, we ask a blessing for Earl and his son, Giles, two decent men who plied the Gulf in honest, hard work. We humbly implore you in the name of Saint Andrew, the patron saint of all fishermen, to grant them grace and forgiveness. Their last hours were spent working to feed this country in a war against our godless enemy." He sprinkled holy water on both caskets and clasped his hands together in prayer. "Watch over these men as they enter your kingdom and offer them life everlasting in the name of the Father and of the Son and of the Holy Ghost."

After Father Gruber closed his prayer book and blessed the caskets, Tom asked for a brief period of silence and then spoke to the fifty people in attendance. "We have food set up for everyone in the warehouse. Please come by. I'm sure Ellie would appreciate you stopping to say a word or two. There is no need for anyone to do anything but share good memories of these two brave men. Earl was a steady hand and a good father and Giles was a faithful son who planned to enlist on his birthday." Tom lowered his head. "I'll miss them both. Please take time today to honor them. We can all start back to work tomorrow morning."

* * *

Rene suspected that Tom was holding his anger back, because later that day, after the mourners were gone and the warehouse was cleared of chairs and tables, he took Rene into the office, lit a cigarette and pointed at him to take a seat.

He then began in a concerned, normal tone. "Are you ready to go in the morning?"

"Yes. Marie's loading supplies right now, and I plan to be the first one out."

"Tell me," Tom said, his voice dripping with sarcasm, "where did you anchor the night before the storm?"

"We went east. The shrimping was poor, so we moved to Terrebonne Bay."

Tom flicked ashes from his cigarette into the tray on his desk "Weren't you catching anything by Ship Shoal?"

"Yes, but the count was only in the forties. We also wanted more privacy than we had north of Raccoon Island."

Tom started to bare down. "Why didn't you stay with the other shrimpers?"

"We wanted to be alone. The shrimping was larger where we went and I didn't see any problem..."

Tom interrupted in a hardening manner. "The problem was that you did not communicate with the other boats. Do I need to explain it to you, after you've grown up working with your father? My boats work a common sector and stay in contact and are supposed to anchor in the same general location at night in the event that another boat needs help. This has been my rule for ten years and I don't want it broken."

"Maybe we could get radios."

Tom shook his head. "I petitioned the War Procurement Board two months ago but was turned down. Equipment like that is going to the military. I tried to get Baton Rouge to help, but I wasted my time talking to them."

Rene attempted to explain. "All we wanted was to be alone and ..."

Tom slammed the desk with one hand and glared at Rene. "No one cares about what you do at night. Play with each other and walk around naked if you want. No one is spying on your love life. The other crews don't give a tinker's damn what you do on your own boat, but I do, and you'd better stay with the others unless you want me to put Marie ashore."

Rene tried to reason with him. "The storm was an exception. I don't see any harm in what we did."

Tom's face reddened and he smashed his cigarette in the ash tray, his lips tightening. "Do I need to remind you that we have another trip coming up? If you aren't there, I'll have to find someone else, and that'll screw up the plan." His voice grew more demanding. "If it wasn't for that, I'd fire you right now for not following my orders," he snarled and pointed at him. "You are stubborn like your father, and I won't stand for it. Do I make myself clear?" he demanded, sitting immobile as a stone and waiting for an answer.

Rene wanted to tell Tom where he could stick his threats, but it would only make things worse. He thought about the five hundred dollars and what he and Marie could do with it and swallowed his anger.

When Rene didn't answer right away, Tom shouted. "Do you understand me?"

Rene nodded but didn't speak, and Tom sat back in his chair, his frustration ebbing away.

"Okay," he responded, closing his eyes and taking a deep breath. "You and your dad are my best skippers. Let's keep it that way." He rubbed his forehead and continued. "I know I sound mad, but damn it, I'm more concerned about your safety than I am angry." He glanced at a calendar that hung near his chair. "I'll offer an excuse to hold you back for a day when you come in next month because we make our second trip on a Monday night. It'll give us cover for our next run if you complain about a driveshaft vibration, or a steering problem-- anything that will delay you from going out right away."

"I'll work on it," Rene complied.

Tom lit another cigarette, his favorite move when he was agitated. It kept his hands busy and gave him time to think. He blew a long column of smoke in the air and regarded Rene behind the gray film that rose above his forehead.

"There's another thing to consider. I run a business that requires insurance, and with the war on, the War Shipping Administration has increased my marine policy. My rate is reviewed every three months, and when I inform them about the *Shrimp King*, they'll raise my rates again. I have to watch the bottom line, and you could have made it that much worse by losing your boat. Higher rates mean less pay for you and the others." He smashed his half-smoked cigarette and rubbed his right thumb against his forefinger, crushing the butt. "There's more to this business than waiting for the boats to return. That storm could have cost this company plenty. Thank God it wasn't worse."

"I guess I never considered that."

Tom broke into a smile. "Well, now you understand. So let's put this behind us," he suggested. "Go have a good two weeks with Marie. By the way, how's she working out?"

"She can do the work of a deck hand and skipper the boat too." Rene bragged.

"And perform the duties of a wife, I bet," Tom implied, his eyes twinkling.

Struck for a comeback, Rene gave a shrug, said nothing, and left the office.

"And stay in communication with the other boats," Tom yelled.

17

The after-effects of the hurricane were everywhere; broken tree branches still held pockets of Spanish Moss, Rozo plants had been sheared off by the wind, hordes of leaves were scattered in the bayou, dead birds floating among them, and several deer stood on the levee to escape high water in the marsh. But the hurricane wasn't all bad. The rains saturated the marsh and replenished a myriad of ponds, giving the nutria, muskrat, alligator, and fish a better habitat.

There was very little noise to mar the quiet landscape, other than the soft chugging of the trawler's engine when Rene picked his way down the bayou.

The weather had returned to normal, as if the hurricane had never happened. The morning atmosphere was so serene that a permanent peace seemed to have been declared among the sky, wind, and water. The air was dry and comfortable, and despite the rising temperature, the visibility was unlimited under a bright blue sky that ran down to the horizon.

The sunsets during their first week painted the bay in a shimmering bronze and the shrimping became so good that they nearly filled the hatch in four days. The hurricane seemed to have invigorated the shrimp, which were medium-sized and in dense schools, and Rene and Marie worked until approaching darkness at the end of each day forced them to find a spot north off Raccoon Island and anchor for the night.

While Rene didn't mention the submarines, the war surfaced again during one long drag six miles south of the island, when one tanker and a freighter went by on their way toward the Florida passage. They seemed to be so cumbersome and slow that is was hard to be sure they were even moving.

Marie noticed Rene watching the vessels and didn't try to hide her frustration. "Let's go back to shallower water so we don't have to look at them."

When he didn't answer or look her way, she pressed her lips together and stared at the water.

Although he kept looking for the ships, their appeal had diminished. Now that he had Marie with him on the boat, living in Pat's Landing didn't agree with him. If Tom wasn't poking around, others wanted to talk with him, which robbed him of the time to spend with her. He had tasted the thrill of being with her without interruptions and relished it. Her presence heightened his appreciation of the Gulf- -of porpoises nosing around the boat and following off the stern during a drag, of an occasional turtle surfacing for air, exhaling and diving again, of seagulls and pelicans maneuvering for morsels and swooping for scraps tossed overboard.

Nothing bored him now that they were together and belonged to each other.

Since she needed no assistance anymore, Rene stayed in the wheelhouse and helped only when the net came out of the water with a heavy catch, or when the boards swung wildly and might injure her. Their days were pleasant and their nights were covered with stars, as if the heavens had been swept clear just for them, and the moon sprinkled soft light across the water, outlining the inconsistent shoreline of tall grasses and open spaces of sand.

In the wake of Tom's criticisms, Rene became more careful about where they anchored. His favorite spot was along the channel not far from the tip of the island and a short run to the mouth of Lower Bayou, providing him with easy access to the Gulf or the channel. Always searching for privacy, he chose a small cut where tall Rozo obscured them from the bayou on the north and sand dunes and scrub trees on the island protected them on the south.

They used their quiet time at night to talk about their plans for the house. It needed painting, an oak tree on the south side had developed branches that scraped the house during high winds, and clumps of weeds around the foundation threatened to choke out the grass. But Rene didn't consider any of those chores as drudgery. Instead, he looked forward to the privacy of living together in their own house, closing the door and shutting out everything, including the irritating noise of submarine engines.

They also rehashed the hurricane. Talking about the hazards reminded him that Marie often slept fitfully from the same bad dream. She'd wake up and take hold of him until he whispered that no storm was threatening them.

But on quiet evenings, when meager ripples brushed the hull, he rested beside her, his arms cradling her, and he wondered why he had ever wanted to join the Navy. Although each additional day of being married strengthened his contentment, the occasional nighttime chatter of diesel engines still reminded him of the war.

One more trip, he vowed, and he was through with the war forever.

*   *   *

Their first week sped by in a common routine of working until sunset, anchoring at the inlet in time to beat darkness, grabbing a bite to eat and settling onto their cots. But during the late hours one night, they heard the engines again.

Their rumbling woke Marie up, and she rolled onto her left side and reached for Rene, but he wasn't there. She got up and found him at the stern, looking toward the Gulf.

She came up behind, put her arms around him, and kissed him on the back of the neck. "Can't you sleep?" she asked, yawning so wide that her eyes closed.

He answered in a hushed voice, as if someone else might hear him. "I'm wondering about those engines."

"Why?"

"I'm curious how long they'll stay in our area," he answered, holding his watch at an angle to read the time. "They've been idling for two hours. You'd think they'd move after a while."

She looked seaward and then back at him. "Why are you concerned? They have nothing to do with us."

He spoke without looking at her. "They might. Did you read the story in the *Saturday Evening Post* that we got from the iceboat two days ago? It mentioned how Nazi spies could sneak into the United States from German U-boats that would come close to shore and drop men in black rubber boats, who then meet up with other spies already here."

"You don't believe that," she said skeptically.

"Well, it could happen. South Louisiana has no cities on the Gulf, so it would be a cinch to land undetected at night. The coastal watchers can't see every mile of beach, and on a moonless night our visibility is limited to less than a hundred yards.

She looked toward the Gulf and took her time answering. "That must be the sound of the Coast Guard or a merchant ship, not a submarine," she said.

"Don't forget the oil can we netted last week. It had a black swastika on top. That didn't come from any other vessel than a U-boat." He pointed at the Gulf without looking at her. "If the Coast Guard anchored in open water at night, they would be an ideal target for a sub. I'm positive," he stressed, "we're hearing the engines of a German U-boat."

She hugged him without saying anything and pressed her head against his chest before breaking the silence, her face nearly touching his. "I thought you were going to forget about the war."

Rene recalled Karl's warning about keeping the rendezvous a secret. But Marie was a part of everything he did. If the war intensified, he worried that the U-boats might decide to shell the bays where the shrimpers spent their nights, though it would be wasting ammunition on a target that couldn't fight back. He didn't like keeping his activities from her, and his vows came to mind--sickness and health, rich or poor--four conditions that touched everything in their marriage.

"I've tried to block them out most of the time, but I can't do it tonight," he answered in a subdued voice.

Marie let out a cry and went back to her cot and Rene remained at the railing, staring at the midnight sky filled with stars, all seemingly aimed at him. Despite the late hour and a warm breeze out of the south that flowed over his arms and neck, the air would grow cool before morning and the boat would be covered with dew. He searched until he found the Milky Way directly overhead, stretching out like a giant, gauzy canopy. The outer edges reminded him of angel hair that his mother used every year for decorating their Christmas tree.

Somewhere down the beach a seagull cried and another one answered.

While Tom's warning about secrecy disturbed him, he wasn't in the military, he didn't wear a uniform, and his love for Marie was more important than his allegiance to Karl and the mission. He wanted it to succeed, especially for Joe Christy's memory and for Earl, Giles, Ray, and Sam. But his marriage would be of longer duration than a war that was bound to end in the near future. It spread death, while he and Marie sowed happiness, and later a family.

The engines changed power settings and the noise receded and appeared to be moving away. He looked at his watch. The U-boat had stayed in position for three hours, ample time to charge its batteries or to set up an attack. He stared at the Gulf but saw only a weak half moon rising above the eastern horizon. The U-boat would sneak away without a trace and he wondered if it was one of the subs responsible for American deaths.

He went to the cot and sat down instead of joining Marie under the blanket, and she rose up and rested her head on one arm since he didn't slide in with her.

"Why can't you forget about those submarines?" she insisted in a tone that announced her aggravation.

Rene took his wallet out of his hip pocket and rested it on one leg. "Because some things have changed for us."

"No they haven't," she countered. "We still have each other and the war can't touch us."

He reached into his wallet for the three hundred dollars and handed them to her. "It already has," he said.

After counting the money a confused look blanketed her face, so he began with the earliest details of the plan, and they didn't sleep for the rest of the night as he explained about the rendezvous, Karl, Tom, Manny, and himself.

18

Tom sat at his desk and stirred a cup of dark roast coffee, the only kind he'd drink. He liked it black with three spoons of sugar ever since his first cup at fourteen, but it took a while until the sugar dissolved. He glanced at his new gold-plated Bulova wristwatch that he had bought two days earlier, discounted fifty percent because the jeweler had taken a liking to Tom's newest girl, Carol. Selling the watch at a reduction gave the jeweler two free visits to her.

Tom compared his new watch with a clock on the office wall. Their times matched, which highlighted his frustration at Karl's failure to be punctual once again. He looked at the letter that didn't have anything written except the time--three o'clock.

"Damn Germans," he complained out loud. "The whole race isn't worth the ammunition it would take to blow them to hell." At least he was pretty sure Karl was a German. And being an American citizen didn't hide Karl's ancestry. He still exhibited the cold, Teutonic eccentricities--an overbearing personality and a dictatorial manner of speaking.

Tom rehashed their first trip, which had gone smoothly, but he worried about the next one over the weekend. Navigating in the dark was the worst aspect, but changing the date and time was out of the question, according to Karl. Tom had suggested another night when there was adequate moonlight, but Karl had rejected it, in spite of Tom's warning of how going aground on a sandbar, or running into debris from a past sinking were disastrous possibilities. In any event there wouldn't be a proper explanation that the Coast Guard would accept without checking up on their story, and the result would be an arrest, the end of the mission, and jail.

Tom acknowledged the need for secrecy, but the tension on the first trip had been overwhelming enough to give him stomach cramps, and it bothered him that the next submarine skipper might decide to blow up the iceboat after taking on the fuel and supplies.

Getting into the location for the rendezvous had been nerve-wracking, but seeing the U-boat surface alongside had been frightening. If the sub's captain had miscalculated by as little as ten feet, the iceboat would have been rammed from underneath, cracked open like an egg and sunk. He hoped the next captain would have the same careful approach as the first one. Karl hadn't mentioned anything about the other sub, but it didn't matter. A Kraut is a Kraut, and since it had been impossible in the darkness to read the markings on the first U-boat, all that mattered was that the next skipper was as careful and friendly. If he misjudged during surfacing there would be no chance to move away in time, because the boat was as black as night and would not be visible until it lunged out of the water next to the iceboat.

He would never get used to being tied up to a U-boat and didn't like a sailor pointing a rifle at him. On the last trip he had kept his pistol available for quick action, and a thorough search would have turned it up and ruined the entire trip. So he decided the next time to keep it in the back of a drawer behind the knives, forks and spoons where he could still reach it quickly.

He checked his watch again, lit a cigarette, and smiled at the time in the wheelhouse during the first trip when he'd craved a cigarette. Instead of lighting it, he put it between his lips. The Nazi guard would probably have shot him if he had struck a match then, even if he had cupped his hands to absorb the light. Everything had been draped in darkness, except for a vague shaft of red light that came from the galley hatch, but it didn't render the men on deck more visible.

He thought about the money he'd make on the second trip and what he would do with it. He'd open a New Orleans bank account under his daughter's name, making it difficult to trace. The total dazzled him and the opportunities were tantalizing. He'd improve the business and move to New Orleans, perhaps buy a house on St. Charles Avenue and get a new car every year, or when the government allowed the automotive companies to resume their annual production schedule. He'd promote Al to manage the business, but he'd visit the warehouse occasionally and keep in touch the rest of the time by telephone. As a successful businessman's daughter, Sarah would get a good education at a private school run by the nuns and would eventually attend Newcomb College. He thought also about traveling to Cuba or the Virgin Islands as soon as the war ended.

The nagging problem was the food and fuel that went to the U-boats. Although the scheme was a setup to damage U-boat operations, he was worried that the supplies may contribute to the sinking of an American ship. But instead of feeling guilty about cooperating with the enemy, he looked at it as a business activity. He provided the boat and personnel, and Washington, or some other federal spook organization, paid for his services, making up for World War One, the Bonus Army lie, and the flood of '27. The payoff helped balance things out. Some facets of war were a business, such as American industries being paid to produce tanks, ships and planes, only he rented his iceboat to the government for a price and expected to get it back undamaged.

Although Karl was working for a government agency and no doubt being paid a handsome salary, his job wasn't any more vital than guiding the iceboat to the rendezvous.

*   *   *

Tom announced "come in" to a knock and Karl entered, careful not to slam the door. He was dressed in his customary dark suit, white shirt, black tie and carried the same notebook. Anyone on the street who saw him would no doubt think he was a banker or a lawyer about to have an afternoon drink in the hotel bar before heading home.

Tom was silent as Karl took a chair and opened his notebook. He didn't like to wait on people and didn't like being told what to do--two things Karl rubbed in his face. So he began in an angry mood.

"You said three o'clock. You're ten minutes late."

Karl didn't look at his watch when he replied. "I walked around the block twice, checking traffic into the hotel. It just slacked off. We don't want our work to become known."

Tom wasn't impressed. "It's the middle of the damned afternoon and half the town of Houma is taking a nap. I couldn't schedule a business meeting with people at this time of day if I wanted to. Surely you know that if you live in New Orleans."

Karl flashed a weak smile without answering the question. "It's too late for lunch and a bit early for the evening drinkers, a perfect dead time, which is why I planned our meeting for now."

Tom gave up. "Okay. What have we got to talk about? I thought we were to maintain minimum contact, but since you called this meeting, has anything changed?"

"First things first," Karl said, taking the money from his notebook and placing it on Tom's desk, which Tom counted by fingering the fifties. He put the money in the desk drawer and leaned back in his chair. He was becoming a rich man at the government's expense.

"We've received information," Karl began, "that activity in the Gulf is going to increase, which changes our plans. It's been decided that two trips are not sufficient. We need at least a couple more that will involve another location that you can reach in no more than an additional half hour."

Tom sat upright, his eyes growing hard. "Now just a minute. We agreed on two trips, not four."

Karl took his time answering in a confident voice. "Tom, this war is at a turning point, and the Gulf is playing a vital part. Much of the fuel that powers our planes and tanks comes out of Corpus Christi, Houston, Beaumont, and Lake Charles. The Gulf of Mexico has always been considered the soft underbelly of the States and needs protection. Intelligence sources have recently picked up information that the Germans have a contingency plan to invade through the Gulf and Louisiana in particular. If they carry out that plan, we have the responsibility to defend ourselves as best we can. The coastline from Mobile to Galveston has no cities capable of spreading the alarm if the Germans came ashore. They could put several hundred men on land before anyone would know about it. New Orleans, Baton Rouge, Lake Charles, and Beaumont are all inland and are soft targets. Except for the Coastal Patrol and volunteer observers, Louisiana is wide open and somewhat defenseless, and U-boats may in fact be the lead element in the plan.

"So your continued participation will be helpful in battling the submarine threat. It will be a shot in the arm to convoys and the Atlantic supply system. Two more trips will help us pinpoint other places the U-boats use and will save American lives. Think about that, Tom. Your unarmed iceboat could help turn the tide of the war in the Gulf."

Tom wasn't convinced, but Karl's upbeat attitude made his head swell. He pondered his answer by lighting up and staring at his desk. "But you said this would be just two trips..."

"I know, but things change. War isn't a neat business. You were in the Great War. Surely you recognize that."

Tom remained dubious. "Maybe the war is a business for you but shrimping is our livelihood, not fighting the Krauts. That job belongs to the government and the military."

More determination shadowed Karl's response. "This war is the business of every citizen of this country," he replied. "You are already involved through your business, and your idea for dried shrimp is being considered by two states as we speak. I can help that situation if you cooperate."

Tom's attitude grew more stubborn. "In case you haven't looked, I don't wear a uniform. Our agreement was for two trips. I don't intend to make any more."

Karl was unfazed. He closed his notebook and rested it on his lap and regarded Tom as a shopper might look at a piece of furniture, his face void of expression.

"We'll discuss this after our second trip. Think it over. I'm sure you'll decide to help."

"Don't count on it," Tom shot back. "I'm sticking my neck out as it is. Ever since the Great War the government has been pushing me around. Well, I've had enough. Sure," he admitted, "the money is good, but I didn't sign up just to help you, and who's to say you won't want six or eight more trips? That's the military's favorite trick. They ask for volunteers and before you know it you're trapped in something more dangerous than you ever imagined."

Karl patted his notebook. "I hope you'll change your mind. As I've mentioned before, this is a clandestine operation that German intelligence thinks is being carried out to their advantage. They made the request for more rendezvous, and that gives us a chance to pinpoint more of their U-boats." Karl's tone took on a steely edge. "If you refuse to cooperate, I cannot protect you. This plan was set up to make you look like a collaborator to the Germans. Unknown to you, their agents have come into your hotel before this plan kicked off. They no doubt know your routines and where you live. You might pose a threat to them if you refuse to cooperate, and it wouldn't be difficult for them to keep you and your two helpers quiet."

Tom glared at Karl and sat silent, his throat so tight that he wouldn't be able to express his anger without screaming.

Karl grew apologetic. "Such things are beyond my control; however, I may be able to warn you if I got word of their intentions. Our government is a large organization and I'm just one of many following orders, and I'm not privy to everything that's planned." He clenched one fist and leaned toward Tom. "But we can put a crimp in the U-boats' operations when we pinpoint their other locations. You needn't worry about being paid. The money will be there. Your continued cooperation will negate any action taken against you, Rene, and Manny." Karl paused to let his words sink in and then carried on. "This is a secret operation that few know about, and it has to stay that way. But you and the boys can be proud for playing an important role."

Without responding, Tom clasped both hands and rested his chin on them, his eyes fixed somewhere on his desktop.

"I'll see you Sunday at the same location and time," Karl said, standing up and cradling the notebook in one arm. "War is a dirty business, Tom, but think of the good you're doing for your family, your grandchildren, and the people of Louisiana." He walked toward the door, and then turned around. "I almost forgot. We'll be carrying an additional half dozen cans of fresh water. Our sources tell us that the sailors are on water rations and are allowed only one cup per day."

*   *   *

Lying on his back underneath the boat, Al grabbed *Miss Marie's* driveshaft and ran his hand along the shaft until it went through the hull behind the engine and transmission housing. "I don't feel anything that would produce a vibration," he volunteered, shaking it back and forth for good measure, but it didn't move. "Does it happen all the time?"

"No," Rene answered. "It's smooth during a drag but comes on at full power. It sounds like a bearing might be wearing out."

"Maybe so," Al guessed. "Have you noticed any grease on the driveshaft?"

"No, but it could get worse, couldn't it?"

Al wasn't overly concerned. "The vibration may be an indication of only a minor problem, not a breakdown. Bearings last a long time after they start to leak. You won't see one break apart. These engines aren't run hard like an automobile. Most of the time we're pulling less than half of the available power." He stood up and wiped his forehead with a handkerchief. "A worn bearing is not serious enough to keep you out of the Gulf. Apply power a little bit at a time, avoid full throttle and I'm sure the boat will get you through two more months before it has to be replaced."

Tom stood by, watching Al's reaction. "I'll have Babe take a look at it. Maybe he can find the problem," he decided. "I'll leave it out of the water until he examines it tomorrow. It's better to be safe than sorry."

Al faced Tom, "Rene should go back to work tomorrow."

Tom dismissed Al's comment by waving one hand. "I'm going to keep him here for one more day. I don't want to take a chance on him breaking down. I'd lose two whole days; one to go get him and another to repair the boat if he broke down offshore. I'm going to hold him here until Monday noon. He can go out then."

"He'll lose two days of work," Al challenged, but Tom brushed it off and changed the subject.

"Good things are about to happen," he hinted. "I'm planning to buy another iceboat, and I'll need a crew. I'm considering Rene and Manny." Before Al could react, Tom kept talking. "I know this is sudden, but I'm making another run to the drying platform tonight, and I'm taking Rene and Manny along. It'll give me another chance to see how they work together. We'll be back in the morning and Rene can go out the next day."

Al's face clouded over. "What in God's name is…?"

"Cool off, Al," Tom said. "I'm running the company, not you."

"When did all these things take place?" Al asked, both hands on his hips.

Tom swung one arm toward Rene. "The company is doing well and we're in a position to expand the fleet." He let his comment sink in for a moment. "I know this comes as a surprise, but the Price Commission let me know a week ago that I can get ten cents more per pound for the shrimp." He pointed at Al. "That means we're about to grow, and I'll need a warehouse manager. I hope you'll take the job, Al. It'll mean more money too."

Al didn't know how to react. "This is kind of sudden ..."

"Yes, it is. But think it over. If things keep going well, I'll need help, and I want you to be that man. You know the business as well as I do and the men respect you.

Before Al could respond, Tom motioned to Rene and Manny. "You two come with me. We have a few things to do before leaving."

* * *

A short time later, on his way home, Rene waved to Marie as she stood on the front porch, wearing the green dress that she had bought on their honeymoon. It was tapered at the waist and had full-length pleats running just below her knees. She held a wide smile as she crossed the road and ran to meet him in the yard, her body forming into his. Her cheeks were damp when she tilted her head to kiss him again, harder this time, and she held him until he removed his arms from her shoulders and broke away.

He ran his hands down the small of her back, and her muscles twitched beneath his fingers. "I'll spend all my afternoons at the dock if you meet me like this every time I come home," he joked.

She had a look of pain on her face. "You're going, aren't you?"

He looked toward the warehouse and nodded.

"Why didn't you tell him you were staying? You said you would," she insisted in a louder voice.

"I said I'd think about it," he replied, moving toward the house with an arm around her shoulders and coaxing her to walk with him. "Wait until we get inside."

She turned on him when they closed the front door, her face in a frown. "This is a joke, isn't it? You're not really going. Tell me I'm right."

"We're leaving at six o'clock," he said flatly.

"Why must it be you?" She cried in a higher voice.

He hadn't expected her reaction. The plan was perfect--he was being paid and finally had a part in the war. "I can earn nearly half a year's pay. Think what that money can do for us?"

She grabbed his arms and shook them, "It won't matter if you get killed."

"We're giving them diesel fuel and food. They have no reason to harm us; they think we're helping them."

"But you told me the whole thing is a trap."

"It is, but they won't discover that until they get bombed," he said confidently.

Rene followed her into the kitchen and put his arms around her as she leaned over the sink. "We'll only spend an hour with them, and I'll be back early in the morning. I'll be okay," he insisted, kissing her on the back of the neck. "And we'll go back to the Gulf the next day."

Marie placed a hand on his arm, the strain covering her face. "You're all that's important to me," she said in a husky voice. "The money won't be any good if you don't come back."

"I'll be fine." He patted her on the shoulder and kissed her on the forehead. "I'll come home with another five hundred dollars and we can buy more furniture and fix up the house the way you want."

Marie was baffled. The whole scheme was sewn with menace, and the war that had been put in the background by their wedding was now an octopus wrapped around them. She was surrounded by despair and fear while he bragged about the second trip. He mentioned the importance of the rendezvous, but they were empty words that withered before her fears. He would be gone overnight for only the second time since their marriage, and she had come to despise the war that had invaded their lives.

Rene looked at his watch and then at her.

"Be careful," she said. It sounded foolish, but she couldn't think of anything to change his mind and didn't want him to leave on the backside of an argument.

He rubbed her shoulders and hugged her. "Don't worry. The Germans don't bother the shrimp boats. They know we're..."

"Don't talk about them," she cried, kissing him in a hard, sustained embrace, until his body relaxed and his hands gently nudged her back. "I know. You have to go."

"But I'll be back in time for breakfast. If you want to sleep late, I'll be quiet coming in, and the man sliding into bed and kissing you will be me."

She mashed her lips together in a forced smile. "I'll be waiting."

"If you can't sleep, stay in your bathrobe," he winked, "and be ready."

"Sure," she said, "but I won't be hungry."

"Do you feel okay?"

She shrugged. "I'm a little queasy if I eat in the morning," she said, then forced herself to be in a brighter mood. "Just hurry back."

She held him until he backed away, then kissed her one more time before turning toward the door, and as he went outside she went to the front window and watched him walk away, proud of herself that she hadn't cried, but it only lasted until he left their yard.

19

Tom coaxed the iceboat into the current under Al's scrutiny, but instead of waving as he sailed by, he pretended to be too busy with the boat to look Al's way. It eroded Tom's patience that he was being challenged about decisions regarding his own business, even if it came from Al, one of his oldest employees and friends. He looked straight ahead until the boat was turned into the bayou and the stern finally blocked Al from his sight.

Since Tom could see a mile or more downstream, traffic wouldn't be a problem and they'd make good time. Apart from a pair of fishermen in a runabout and one guy walking the levee, there was no other activity. He wasn't concerned with storm debris any longer because the current had washed leaves, branches, dead birds, and animals clear of his path, except for a few carcasses of deer and one wild dog on the levee, sending out a putrid stench that made him catch his breath as he went by. Turkey buzzards and crows vied for their share of the meat and an eating space on the deer.

Karl pulled two cartons of cigarettes from a sack and handed them to Tom, who put them in a drawer by the wheel. They would be easy to reach, another reason for him to grab his pistol in the event of trouble. He trusted Karl as long as he could monitor his movements, but he planned to stick the pistol in the back of his belt when the opportunity was good.

Karl was guarded. "Bear in mind; this crew will no doubt know what went on the day after our first trip, so warn Manny and Rene to be careful. We can't afford to make mistakes tonight."

"I've already talked to them," Tom said quickly, miffed at the idea that the presence of two dozen Germans, soon to be within a stone's throw, required any warning.

"Hide the sextant after I make the final reading. It might make the Germans nervous if they see me fixing their position."

"For all I care," Tom scowled, "you can toss the damn thing overboard."

Holding the sextant in one hand, Karl looked at it, then at Tom. "Then what would we do on the next two trips?"

Tom ignored the question and kept his eyes ahead of the boat.

After no answer, Karl bristled. "I need to know if you talked to Rene and Manny about two more runs."

"Not yet. I'll do that after tonight."

"This can't wait. It's important. Stopping at two runs would jeopardize our entire plan. We must keep pressure on the U-boats."

Tom raised one hand and shook it near Karl's face. "Don't worry about the boys. They like the money and will do what I say."

"Then you're set for two more trips?"

"As long as you keep the money coming," Tom answered.

His response drew a short lecture. "Oh, the money will be there, but I hope you see the importance of what we're doing. If we can discourage U-boats from having free rein in the Gulf, we will significantly reduce the losses to our tankers and freighters and save lives."

"Maybe so," Tom said, "but we can't operate secretly forever. I've already been questioned about running the iceboat at night. Sooner or later, people will find out. And I can't swear that the coast watchers at the inspection site will take my word indefinitely. How many times do you think Woody is going to buy the lie that you're going to the drying platform? Sooner or later he'll smell a rat."

Karl remained matter-of-fact. "By then we'll have accomplished our goal and Germany will consider the price too high to stay in the Gulf. After a period of time, perhaps even years, I think the story of these rendezvous will leak out, and you three will enjoy the appreciation of everyone in Louisiana."

After being given a pass by Woody's replacement at the inspection point, who bought the same story about Karl, Tom rounded Raccoon Point and scanned the open water for signs of the Coastal Patrol. But since nothing caught his eye, he set up a course for the rendezvous. "I just want to be able to tell this to my grandkids," he admitted. "I've already seen enough of the damn Krauts to last me a lifetime."

Karl broke into a grin without taking his eyes off the water. "I feel the same way. You three may not wear uniforms, yet you're fighting alongside a million other guys. The public might never know what we're doing, but you'll have the satisfaction. That's what counts."

Tom had one more question before Karl left the wheelhouse. "You never said if the bombs got the first U-boat, so how are you sure we won't be meeting the same one tonight?"

"There's no way to tell," Karl explained. "Bombing missions occur every day. Even if one of our planes racked up a lucky hit, the number of the U-boat may not be known, or we may not be able to confirm the kill. But odds say this will be a different one."

*   *   *

The sun had nearly touched the horizon to the west when Manny came into the wheelhouse. "The hose is stretched out and ready. I laid it along the railing so we can rig it up faster this time."

"Good job," Tom said, looking for a friendly response, but Manny's face was impossible to read, so Tom tried to be humorous. "It's going to be as dark as an African night out there."

But Manny acted as if he hadn't listened.

It struck Tom that he had never heard Manny laugh while in his presence. The awkward scene he had with him at the wedding reception ran through Tom's mind and agitated him like an itch he couldn't scratch. He decided to apologize about his rudeness that day and gathered the words he wanted to say, but Manny left the wheelhouse before Tom got them out.

"Be careful tonight," he called after Manny as he turned the corner of the doorway and disappeared from sight.

Manny was a lot like Bootsy, headstrong, vindictive and unforgiving. From the time he turned thirteen, Tom had been smitten with Bootsy, who was the same age but looked five years older, with a body that was well-rounded in the right places, making every boy in school talk about her. Tom was sixteen when it happened the first time, in a dark corner of the warehouse--lingering kisses that led to blind groping between them, followed by an intense coupling that ignited sweaty, emotional vows of affection from both of them. One time was not enough for either of them. He made better arrangements in the future, hiding in the iceboat after the crew had gone home, then in the back seat of Pierre's car several times, once at the end of the dock on a particularly dark summer night, and finally the sofa in Bootsy's house one afternoon when her father and mother had gone fishing in the marsh.

He was captivated at first, but as Bootsy became possessive, Tom grew cautious about a long-term relationship because she had quit school after her sophomore year and had taken a job in Emile's restaurant and had become the object of gossip. He continued to see her but less frequently, especially after she did little to quell the rumors about them. The following spring, when he was ready to graduate from high school, he and Kay were sharing the idea of marriage and, other than an occasional sexual time, Tom and Bootsy had grown apart.

The break came when Bootsy told him she was pregnant the same week he and Kay finalized their plans to be married. Tom's suspicious nature led him to question Bootsy about the father, and when he asked her to swear that he was the one, Bootsy pulled a knife and tried to stab him, but Tom grabbed her wrist and forced the knife out of her hand.

After their confrontation, she never approached him again and continued to work at the restaurant, though the boys who had tried to flirt with her kept their distance behind her icy formality that daunted them, and the larger her stomach got, the more distance she was given by male customers. The week after Manny was born, Bootsy and her baby moved into a small rental house that Pierre Savoy owned, where she raised Manny alone by working at the restaurant and taking in laundry, her principal customers being the Savoy family.

Tom heard stories after Manny's birth that he was the father but did his best to discount the rumor. Bootsy had tradition against her too, in case she tried to indicate Tom. Sabines and colored women rarely fingered a white man as the father, though it wasn't uncommon to see mixed-blood children in South Louisiana.

After his wedding, Tom tried to put the past behind him, but the idea that Manny might be his child never left his conscience, and he reduced the rent on Bootsy's house as soon as he took over the company upon Pierre's death.

During later years, he thought of Bootsy when she had been young and attractive, and Tom watched Manny grow up with his own similarities. One of his favorite pastimes was to observe Manny from the office window and dwell on their common traits. Manny confronted kids who angered him, like Tom had done, and his short temper also flared if he was heckled. He used Manny around the house and the warehouse as soon as he was capable of doing chores, paying him generously, but never making overtures to befriend. Instead, he hid his feelings by speaking as harshly to him as he did to the rest of the warehouse crew. He was cautious about displaying favoritism toward him which could spark the old rumor that he hadn't heard since Manny had turned twelve.

As Manny grew up, it haunted Tom that Bootsy may have been truthful with him about being Manny's father, because Bootsy never married, and it was known that she had turned down several men who proposed. He had bouts of regret because the lingering idea that she might have been the woman for him, invaded his dreams and influenced his marriage to Kay, which evolved into one of convenience more than emotion. Kay lacked sexual impulsiveness when she was aroused and didn't have the intensity during their love making that Bootsy had shown.

After the four trips were over, Manny would have money to spend, and Tom planned to advise him about buying his own trawler. As the owner of his own rig, Manny could keep a higher percentage of the profit and make a better life for himself and Bootsy. And since Tom controlled the net price of shrimp, he could pay Manny a small percentage in the guise of extra ten-dollar chits and no one would be the wiser. It would be the same as dropping the house rent that Tom had done for her. No one would ever know that he'd helped them, and his action would give him relief from his sense of responsibility.

*   *   *

Breaking Tom's reverie, Rene entered the wheelhouse. "How much farther is it?" he asked.

"Another ten minutes."

Tom expected him to go back outside, but Rene lingered, taking in the spacious wheelhouse, its details and equipment. "We're going to have a big company one day," Tom boasted. "People will buy our shrimp from Houston to Mobile and will be able to walk into a grocery store and pick up a box of Savoy Shrimp. That's my goal," he bragged.

Rene ran his hands over the large water bowl that enclosed the compass and admired the varnished wooden panel that housed the engine's tachometer, fuel, temperature, oil pressure gage, and the large leather captain's chair. Rene had loaded and unloaded cargo on the iceboat numerous times but had never looked over the wheelhouse. "A boat this large must take a lot of experience to handle."

"It does," Tom answered. "But you've become a good skipper, and who knows, you might be its captain if things work out."

"That'd suit me," Rene answered. "Being home at night with Marie would be a blessing."

"None of us can get through life alone," Tom said. "We can all work together and make this company grow. Save your money," he counseled. "After the war, I plan to go public with the company and you'll be able to make a nice profit if you invest in it. Who knows? You might make enough to retire and move to Florida when you get older. I aim to put our shrimp in cities throughout the south and become a rich man," he boasted. "So rich I won't be able to count all my twenty dollar bills in one day."

Rene wasn't as upbeat. "I just want this war to be over so Marie and I can live in peace."

"It'll happen," Tom assured him. "And when that time comes, thanks to what we're doing right now, you'll know that you helped make it happen. You can be mighty proud. The public might never learn about us, but you'll have the satisfaction of knowing that you did your part to win this war."

Tom looked at his watch. "It's time for you and Manny to take measurements. We're getting close."

Five minutes later, working the weighted rope, Rene called out forty-five feet--the adequate depth for the sub to maneuver alongside the ice boat and surface. In addition to what he had done on the first trip, Tom felt in the drawer to make certain his long fish-gutting knife was within reach. His favorite knife gave him a degree of comfort. Karl seemed a bit jumpy, if that was his actual name, so an extra weapon could come in handy if they were double-crossed by the submarine's crew. And if the Kraut guard found the knife, he couldn't complain. It was natural to have knives on a fishing boat.

20

Marie left her house before dark and walked along the bayou, imagining what Rene was doing at that moment. She had paced the floor after he left, and her nervous energy multiplied until she obeyed the urge to get outside, hoping a walk might dispel the upset feeling she'd been having recently. Shadows from the chinaberry and oak trees lengthened in front of her as she made her way beyond the warehouse and past Al, who was weeding a flowerbed. He had his back to her, so she went by without acknowledging him. As she followed the bank for a short distance, the bayou landscape and the canopy of trees along the way were being draped in the darkening and calming atmosphere of early evening.

Ever since Rene told her the details of the rendezvous, her sense of security had been shattered. Except for the patrol planes and coast watchers, who would spread the alarm if the Germans invaded? The trawlers were helpless with no radios, and there was nothing to slow the Germans down but mud and marsh. If his mission was really important, perhaps the actions of Rene and the others would make the U-boats more vulnerable to an attack from the air. But she felt no consolation that both of their lives were disrupted by the war. It was an invasion of their privacy and she hated it.

But while she was fearful for Rene, her pride for him was almost equal to her caution. He could have let someone take his place but chose not to, and she took comfort in the hope that his action would go toward protecting the country. But above all, she admired his bravery.

She didn't agree with all the secrecy but liked the idea of saving the lives of soldiers and sailors. In her opinion, it was on a par with the tanker gun crew on the Atenas that had fired on a U-boat and had then been taken to New Orleans to be congratulated on the steps of City Hall by the mayor. From what Rene had told her, he and Tom and Manny seemed more heroic than that tanker crew, because they were confronting an enemy without any training or adequate weapons.

The warm gulf breeze gradually put her in a better mood; the frogs croaking and cicadas buzzing lifted her spirits, and she made plans for his special breakfast when he got back.

*   *   *

Al had gathered a pile of weeds and stopped when he saw Marie approach. "What takes you out so late?" he inquired.

"I was restless and felt like a walk," she answered, hoping to avoid questions about Rene.

Al tossed the weeds across a small coulee that drained water from his yard, stood up, and brushed his hands against his pants. "Did the groom abandon you for the night?"

Marie caught a cry forming in her throat but forced a smile. "Something like that."

Al put an arm around her shoulders and tugged her in the direction of the house, nodding his head toward the front porch. "Jane has fresh pecan pie on the table just waiting to be eaten. Let's go have some."

"I'm not really hungry."

"Try a little piece and a glass of milk," Al coaxed. "It'll tide you over until he comes back, and it'll make Jane happy."

She leaned against him but kept her face down and her emotions in check. "Okay," she answered.

Once inside, Al pulled the blinds behind him after shutting the front door and checking the other windows on his way into the kitchen. "We don't want the block captain on our case again," he quipped, winking at Marie and showing her to a chair.

Jane gave Marie a hug, placed the pie on the table and began cutting three pieces. But before she got to the third one, Marie held up her right hand. "Please make mine smaller. I'm not very hungry."

Jane trimmed her slice and put a fourth piece on a saucer, wrapped it in wax paper and placed it beside Marie. "Give this to Rene when he comes home. It's his favorite."

Marie took a bite but found it difficult to swallow. The tension made her throat tighten, so she sipped her milk and tried to relax.

But Al's prodding didn't help. "How long has Tom had that drying platform?" he asked Jane.

"More than fifteen years. Don't you remember? You helped him build it."

He dug out another bite of pie. "I can't recall when he's ever made a night run out there, let alone twice. It's foolhardy not to wait until daylight. Since it's larger than a trawler, the iceboat might tempt a U-boat to take a shot at him."

Marie jammed her fork into the pie crust, broke it into small pieces and stared at the saucer, praying that neither one would ask her any questions about Rene.

But Jane noticed Marie's odd expression and patted her on the arm. "Does the pie taste okay?"

Marie trimmed off some crust and pie filling onto the fork and placed it in her mouth. The crust felt like cardboard, but she forced herself to chew. "It's good," she responded, hoping her approval wouldn't require her to eat the rest of it. "It's just that I haven't been very hungry for a couple of days."

Jane put her fork down and looked at Al, who didn't catch Jane's expression right away, but he finally let out a grin, set his fork in the saucer, and looked at Marie.

Not waiting for Al to speak, Jane began probing. "Are you eating breakfast each day?"

"Maybe a small glass of milk," she offered in a flat voice. "Food seems to ball up in my stomach if I eat before noon."

Jane formed a wide smile and Al looked at Jane again, then Marie, and back at Jane, his eyes twinkling, and Marie's confused expression brought out a joyous response from Jane.

"Don't you know?" Jane cried excitedly, grabbing one of Marie's hands and squeezing it several times.

Dwelling on Rene, she hadn't let thoughts about herself get in the way. "Know what?"

"Honey," Jane answered, her reply interspersed with laughter. "I think you're pregnant!"

"I don't know," she answered. "I feel normal after noontime, and the queasiness goes away."

"You have the classic symptoms," Jane insisted, sliding her chair closer. "Now tell me; does bacon make you nauseated?"

"It did this morning," Marie confessed, anxious now for Rene to come back so they could go to Houma and find out for sure.

"Food and nausea make it a sure thing," Jane added, reaching to give her a brief hug. "I think congratulations are in order." She looked at Al. "What do you say, Gramps?"

Al chuckled as he slid his fork under the last morsel of pie. "Here you are, unable to tell the father because he's out playing boat skipper with Tom." He shook his head and smiled. "It serves him right if he has a sleepless night for abandoning you at such an important time."

Marie choked back a gurgle that sounded like she had something stuck in her throat, and her eyes welled up. She looked at the clock on the wall. Rene had been gone nearly three hours. According to what he had told her, he should be finished at the sub and on his way back in half an hour.

"Are you okay?" Al asked. "I was only joking about him not being here."

Marie wiped her eyes and wondered what harm it would do to tell them. Of all people she could imagine spreading the story, his parents would be the last ones do so. What was a family for if not to share each other's problems?

"Marie, what's wrong?" Jane asked, rubbing Marie's forearm and nearly crying herself.

It would all be over in a few hours and he'd never have to do it again. So it didn't seem dangerous to be speaking about it now.

"Don't worry about Rene," Al suggested in a soothing voice. "One night away from you won't kill him."

"Don't say that!" she blurted out in a loud voice.

Al started to apologize but was cut off.

She closed her eyes and pounded both fists on the table. "He's not where you think he is," she burst out, giving way to convulsive sobs.

Al responded immediately. "What do you mean?"

"They didn't want anyone else to know."

"Know what?" he asked in a stronger voice and leaned toward her.

They listened in stunned silence as Marie detailed the mission and its intention.

When Marie finished, Jane uttered a cry of desperation and looked toward Al, who shoved his chair back and knocked it over as he stood up.

"Damn that Tom Savoy!" he bellowed, charging into the bedroom and coming back in less than a minute, wearing a jacket, a rifle in one hand and a box of ammunition in the other. He opened the box onto the table and loaded the rifle, jamming the extra shells into a jacket pocket.

"You can't do anything tonight," Jane cried, but Al headed for the front door as if she hadn't said anything.

He turned toward them, his face distorted in anger, and he spat out the words in a hoarse voice. "The hell I can't. I've put up with Tom for years and swallowed more than my share of his meanness. It's time someone gives him what he deserves." He shook the rifle above his head. "He'll not endanger our son and get away with it."

Looking quickly at Marie, then Al, Jane challenged him. "This is silly. The Gulf is six hundred miles wide and you have no clue where they went."

Al kept talking as he closed a button on his jacket. "I have two things working for me. I've heard those engines, so I have a good idea where they are. And the iceboat will stand out like a beacon against the darkness."

Jane made a last-ditch effort to stop him. "It's pitch black out there. How are you going to find your way?"

He answered without looking at her as he felt for the shells in his left pocket and set the rifle on safety. "I've spent my whole life in this marsh and the open waters and I know them like I know myself," he said, raising one hand toward Jane. "Now don't you worry. I'll be okay."

Jane tried another angle. "Why not let the Coast Guard handle it?"

"They don't run at night," Al replied. "Even if they did, I'll be there before they could put together a crew and clear the beach."

"At least wait until daylight," Jane pleaded, unable to think of anything else to say that would stop him.

He went through the front door, without looking at Jane or Marie, slamming it on his way out, his words trailing behind him as he took fast strides across the grass. "I'll be back with Rene by then."

21

Spewing a prolonged hiss, its ballast tanks blew clear and the U-boat surfaced, creating a wave that rocked the iceboat, and the diesel engines came on, one at a time, then the sub slipped to one side until its hull aligned with the iceboat. Seconds later, sailors appeared on the conning tower bridge and others climbed out of the galley hatch, charging to their battle stations as if enemy contact was imminent. One man took a position at the deck gun, a second one inserted a shell into the barrel, and another got behind the quad machine gun station on the rear deck of the conning tower. Three others, with weapons in hand, took up security points on the deck.

"More guards than before," Karl commented before leaving the wheelhouse. "Be careful. This crew looks jumpy."

"We're in the middle of the Gulf with no friends around," Tom snarled. "The damn Krauts are nervous and you tell me to be careful. That's just what I don't need."

The first indication of tension came with a sailor shouting directions to Karl and pointing a weapon in his face and frisking him while Karl held both hands above his head. Two more submariners crossed onto the iceboat and did the same to Manny and Rene. Then the sailor who finished frisking Karl, snooped around the aft deck, looking behind the fuel tank and several other places, finally entering the wheelhouse, and pointing his rifle at Tom's chest.

"Up!" he ordered in a brisk voice, raising the muzzle into Tom's face.

"I have to keep one hand ..."

The sailor stabbed the barrel in Tom's chest, his order becoming more insistent the second time, and Tom braced his left leg against the wheel and raised his other arm. As he was being frisked, he realized how much more aggressive this sailor was than the one on the previous trip. Since Karl hadn't mentioned anything that went wrong on the first rendezvous, Tom figured this could be a less experienced crew, which would explain the sailor's apprehension. But Tom's temper simmered when the sailor poked him again and pushed him aside by using the barrel of the rifle, and then looked around the wheelhouse, running his hands into the corner, down to the floor and feeling along the shelves. After he finished and went to the door of the wheelhouse, Tom slipped his right hand into the drawer and withdrew his fish-gutting knife, sneaking it into his belt at the small of his back. It would be a quieter weapon than the pistol.

After a few more uneasy moments the operation began, and the harsh, confrontational atmosphere settled into a routine similar to the first one. Rene hooked the hose to the fuel port and Manny started the pump for the transfer, and then went forward for the first sack of potatoes. He had extra trips to make because Karl had included additional sacks of onions and extra cans of water. The sailor guarding Manny followed him across the walkway and stopped by the deck gun, letting Manny make his own way to the galley hatch. Upon Manny's return for another sack, the sailor stayed on the sub and relaxed his guard, and Tom guessed that the rest of the rendezvous would go smoothly.

After seeing Rene at the pump on the stern and Manny on the walkway, about to retrieve his third sack of potatoes, the routine reminded Tom of the first trip, and he breathed a little easier, though his German guard, who didn't appear to be older than eighteen, remained fidgety, as if he expected trouble. He stuck his head out the wheelhouse door as Manny went by and looked toward the bow, then whirled his rifle back toward Tom and stared at him.

Karl came across the walkway and entered the wheelhouse unexpectedly, alarming the guard who hadn't heard him coming. Karl quickly raised his hands and said "cigarettes" several times and pointed to the drawer in front of the wheel, and the guard edged back to give Karl room. He took out the two cartons of Lucky Strikes, tearing open one end and handing a pack to the guard. He stuffed it into a shirt pocket, then aimed the rifle at Karl, who backed off, his hands raised. The guard then opened the drawer and ran one hand inside, and with his concentration diverted momentarily from both of them, Karl eased a step back and stood in the doorway, holding the cigarettes in his right hand while he waited for the guard to watch him leave. Standing on the guard's other side, Tom gripped the knife in his pants and concentrated at a point near the base of the guard's rib cage, where he planned to bury the blade if the sailor made an aggressive move toward Karl or himself. But the guard withdrew his hand from the drawer.

Though the guard had found nothing, the tension was so strong that Tom could taste it, and he vowed that no matter what happened, this would be his last mission. Shrimpers had no business playing military games. It had been a mistake to get entangled in a scheme that the government gumshoes should be conducting themselves. He was no longer a soldier.

Shortly after leaving the wheelhouse, Karl returned and opened the drawer next to Tom. "These extra cigarettes should quiet things down after I give some to the captain and spread a few packs among the crew."

But Tom wasn't impressed. "I should have tossed you out of my office when you first came to see me," he admitted. "This is madness. I'm through with you after tonight."

"You're doing fine," Karl answered, as if he hadn't heard what Tom said. "This will be over in a short while and we'll be on our way."

Karl crossed onto the U-boat and disappeared around the far side of the conning tower and climbed up to the bridge, where the skipper met him and shook his hand. Glancing through the wheelhouse door, Tom was able to pick out figures more clearly now that he had grown accustomed to the darkness. According to the plan, the whole thing should be over in less than a half-hour.

The combined chatter of the U-boat's diesel engines idling and the gas-driven pump transferring fuel, constructed a pattern similar to the first trip, and much of the tension Tom felt began to ebb away, except for the overwhelming firepower of the U-boat that made him feel vulnerable and helpless. If things went wrong, they would be no match for the sub's weaponry. They were at the mercy of the enemy and he was a prisoner on his own boat, and that realization hit him harder than any battlefield memory he had from the Great War.

He silently said an *Our Father* but doubted the prayer would do him any good, because he had agreed to the trips primarily for the easy money, and it made his prayer seem hollow.

22

Al guessed at the bearing to the U-boat after passing the tip of Raccoon Point and heading in the direction of Ship Shoal. He had swung wide of the inspection station and bent down while praying that the substitute coast watcher, filling in for Woody, wouldn't take a shot at him. He had passed the station at the runabout's full speed of forty miles per hour, and if the guard had yelled at him, he couldn't tell because the engine noise blocked out all other sounds. But he planned to stop on his way back and explain the reasons for his actions.

Nothing mattered now except bringing Rene home alive.

After twenty years of shrimping and committing the water depths to memory, Al knew Ship Shoal was the likely area where the sub would be. Other than Marie's explanation of the time it took to reach the rendezvous, he had no other clues to guide him.

The noise of his engine running at full power drowned out any chance to hear the U-boat's diesels, but he'd contend with that later. He was still close enough to shore to be within rifle range, so he kept a low crouch and rose up only to adjust his course. After putting a mile between himself and the beach, he shut off the motor and listened and tried to pick up the distant rumble of the sub's engines that would pinpoint his heading. He was sure he had the correct site in mind, the same area where he had heard the engines before. He started the engine and pressed on but planned to stop at intervals and listen again.

From his long experience of shrimping, he knew that the sea floor on the east and west sides of Ship Shoal was shallow and presented a hazard for a submarine to navigate without going aground or colliding with an old shipwreck. Except for tankers that had been torpedoed south of Barataria Bay, Grand Isle and other areas of deeper water to the east, he didn't know of any ships being sunk closer to the local sector than four miles.

In spite of the darkness, he was in luck so far. The sea was as smooth as a huge black mirror and allowed him to run at full speed, but there was no way to see debris in the moonless night. Putting that aside, he kept his hand on the throttle, utilizing every bit of energy and speed that the engine could produce, his left hand gripping so tight that his fingers began to ache.

He figured to be at the site within thirty minutes and rehearsed his plan. Since the runabout was painted navy blue and would be impossible to see, he'd approach close enough to pick off the German crewmen with his rifle, if he had to resort to violence. The runabout also had a low silhouette that put the dark night in his favor, unless the Germans homed in on the muzzle flashes from his rifle, or isolated him with their spotlight. Otherwise, he would be an elusive target. Not only would the small boat be difficult to spot, the U-boat's diesel engines would smother the runabout's noise and the crack of his rifle. He began to feel confident; he would practically be invisible and silent…and, if necessary, deadly. But he needed to wait until the transfer was completed. If it came down to trading shots with the Germans, he'd be courting disaster and endangering Rene and Manny. The best bet was to loiter until the iceboat pulled far enough away to be out of range; then he'd pull alongside and deal with Tom.

One way or another, he'd have it out with him for his abusive, oppressive ways, and if he had lied to Rene and Manny and lured them into danger, only to line his own pockets, the Gulf was a huge body of water, and was capable of holding another victim for the crabs and scavengers.

After traveling several miles, the darkness made it difficult to find his way because the water and sky merged into an indistinguishable horizon. While he knew the general heading from listening to the engines in the past, he guessed about the current's direction and speed. With only his instincts to guide him, he cut the engine for the third time and listened for the gurgling diesels. They seemed to be dead ahead. He started the engine, picked up speed for a few moments, and then killed it to get another bearing. On the move again, he kept the stern pointed toward the handle of the Big Dipper and hoped he was going in the right direction.

After stopping for the fourth time, the engines sounded much closer, so he kept the runabout at a slower speed and proceeded warily, still unable to pick out any shapes. But he took a handful of bullets out of a backup cardboard box and stuffed them into his left pants pocket, giving him a total of forty shells. If things went to hell, all he needed were targets.

Knocking off Germans would be like old times again.

* * *

Manny had completed his last trip to the sub when he cleared the walkway and started toward the fuel tank. The sailor guarding the deck adjacent to the conning tower motioned for Manny to stop and then accompanied him. Waiting for the transfer to be completed, Manny noticed that his own guard had remained beside Rene, and it surprised him that an additional sailor was also guarding Rene.

The pump picked up speed from the lack of diesel fuel and Manny shut it off and waved to Rene that the transfer was over, and Rene kneeled down and disconnected the hose to the U-boat's fuel port, raised it above his head and tossed it into the water for Manny to pull it onto the iceboat.

About the same time that Tom congratulated himself on another successful trip and a great payday, he heard Karl speak what sounded like a demand in German from his position on the conning tower, and a seaman, who had worked his way unnoticed toward the ice boat's stern, leveled his weapon at Manny.

"Come outside, Tom," Karl ordered. "We don't want any trouble."

Another sailor, who had taken up a position close to the wheelhouse, stepped through the door, raised his weapon in Tom's face and made a gesture for him to go outside. Before moving ahead of the sailor, Tom reached into his beltline, pulled out his fish knife and held it against his right leg. He cleared the doorway and saw two additional sailors escorting Rene onto the iceboat, and the realization hit like a hammer blow.

As the three of them were herded onto the deck, Tom said a silent *Hail Mary*, then gathered his anger and hatred in a deep breath and yelled toward the conning tower at the top of his lungs. "This whole thing was a setup from the beginning, wasn't it?"

"You've made a good amount of money, and now we're going home," Karl answered. "I wouldn't call it a setup. You just helped us out."

"You and this sub and Hitler and your money be damned," Tom yelled, noticing at the same time how Manny's guard prodded him to move closer toward Rene, placing them within an arm's reach of each other. "I'll see you in hell."

Karl's reply shed all pretense of civility. "Take it easy and you'll live. You did us a favor, and we don't kill civilians without a reason. Since you have no radio you won't be able to contact anyone for several hours, so if you cooperate, we'll call it a draw and you'll be free to go."

"You don't kill civilians, huh? Tell that to the survivors of the *Robert E. Lee*. That was a passenger liner, and one of your U-boats torpedoed it and drowned a hundred civilians."

"Calm down," Karl warned. "It was carrying munitions. That made it a warship."

Tom was flabbergasted. "A warship? It was an old banana boat that happened to be carrying a few passengers."

"This isn't getting us anywhere, Tom."

"Karl isn't your real name, is it?" Tom yelled over the idling diesels.

"It doesn't matter anymore."

"Did you ever live in America?" he shouted. "Are you one of those turncoat bastards who moved to Germany before the war? Did the Krauts recruit you to spy on the people who taught you in school and on friends who thought you'd grow up to be a decent American?"

Karl remained unaffected. "Save your breath, Tom. You have a long voyage home."

But Tom kept didn't stop. "I suppose the money is worthless. Did your Kraut leaders pay us in counterfeit bills too?"

"You were paid in fine American money," Karl answered. "Compliments of your government; now go have a good time spending it. The mission in the Gulf is winding down for our U-boats. I have done a job for my country, the same that you three have done for yours. We are even, so let it go at that and we can depart on equal terms. By the time you get back to the dock, we will be far away and you will be free to go about your business."

Tom reached into a pocket and tossed the envelope onto the deck. "Take your blood money and go to hell. I'm no traitor to my country."

Karl remained calm. "Whatever you say."

But Tom wasn't through. "You never contacted Grand Isle, did you? And no planes bombed our rendezvous site, did they? We're just pawns in your damnable chess game."

"You acted in the best spirit of your country. You have nothing to be ashamed of."

Tom gathered every ounce of hatred he could muster. "Oh, yes I do; and I hope you and all of the other Kraut bastards rot in hell, you turncoat, Nazi sonofabitch!"

During Tom's outbursts, Manny had eased half a step closer to one guard, who had diverted his attention toward the conning tower and had taken his hand off the trigger housing of his weapon. Recognizing an advantage, Manny grabbed the weapon's stock and rammed it into the guard's face, turning him with the other arm and holding the guard's body as a shield while he fired the weapon in a wild, erratic burst that bounced off the wall of the conning tower and forced the men on the bridge and the machine gunner on the deck to scramble for cover.

When Tom's guard started to intervene, he shoved the fish knife deep into the sailor's back, twisting the handle so the blade would rip into his lungs. Then he pulled the guard backward, using his body as a shield, and dodged into the wheelhouse before the startled sailors beside Manny could draw down on Tom. Instead, they first chose Manny and fired, lacing rounds across his stomach, shoulders and neck, crumbling Manny and his guard together onto the deck, the weapon falling at the guard's feet.

Rene screamed Manny's name and kicked the sailor next to him in the crotch and fell upon him, reaching for his weapon that was under the sailor's body. But his attempt was futile. The fourth sailor, standing over Rene, hit him in a vertical butt stroke with the stock of his rifle that crushed the base of Rene's skull at his spine and splayed his lifeless body across the legs of the stricken sailor, who lay trying to catch his breath from Rene's kick. He jerked his feet from beneath

Rene's body and rose up on his hands and knees, retching from the intense pain.

The machine gunner on the conning tower deck sat upright just as Tom disappeared in the wheelhouse and tried to shut the door. He ignored the three dead bodies, swiveled his weapon toward the bow of the iceboat and aimed at the wheelhouse, walking a burst along the wall and through the half-opened doorway. He quickly adjusted his aim and his second burst tore into Tom and knocked him backward against the iceboat's wheel. He tried to speak Manny's name but was unable to cry out as additional rounds tore into his throat and disintegrated his spine.

The firing ceased in a matter of seconds and the U-boat captain barked orders to retrieve the fallen crewmen; their bodies were secured and the sub backed away fifty yards. On the captain's next order, the gunner on the four-inch deck gun fired a shell into the fore deck at the iceboat's water line, then traversed left and sent a second round into the aft section, both shells tearing large holes in the hull that caused the iceboat to explode, break apart and sink stern-first in less than two minutes.

Nothing was left but a pool of burning fuel and several large pieces of floating debris from the severed hull, and the U-boat turned to the southeast and retreated.

* * *

Al yelled Rene's name when he saw the muzzle flashes and heard the sounds from the machine guns. He jammed the throttle to full power and bent toward the site, as though his posture would get the runabout there faster, rapidly accelerating to full speed. From the initial noise of the answering quad machine guns and brief reports of other gunfire, he figured the site was less than half a mile away. He gripped his rifle and cursed Tom Savoy and the Germans, and jolted in desperation when the successive burst of machine gun fire raked the wheelhouse. He stopped the runabout and tried to pick out the U-Boat's profile that would give him a target and leaned forward, resting his elbows on the forward seat and, after adjusting for the runabout's sway, he drew a bead and rapidly squeezed off three rounds, but the engine noise didn't let him verify if he'd struck the sub, hit someone, or if the rounds fell into the Gulf. So he added power and moved closer for a better shot.

At the same time that he stopped and fired, the iceboat's silhouette flashed into view as the first shell from the deck gun smashed into the forward section of the hull, followed by a second round that produced the explosion.

Concentrating on the growing fire that engulfed the iceboat, Al cried out his son's name and mashed the throttle to full power, not caring anymore what might be in his path. The runabout lurched forward, picking up speed, skimming over the smooth water too fast for Al to be able to dodge objects in the darkness, and as he bent forward to grab his rifle, he ran into a large piece of floating debris. An instant later, the runabout lurched into the air, flipping the right side toward the water and slamming into the surface, at the same time, catapulting him out of the boat and tossing him head-first into the gulf.

AFTERWORD

Reggie Arcenaux looked at the clock. Marie Dugas had taken two hours to tell her story, and now he was late for the party. But he had never heard such a jumbled bag of details and references to people, actions and dates, and yet he had mixed feelings. So many others had sworn their stories were true that his lawyer's instincts cautioned him to remain dubious. Perhaps Marie had made up things from reading magazines and talking to other people. At her advanced age it would be natural to cobble snippets together from rumors, gossip or a faulty memory of happenings seventy years in her past, and then eventually believe them to be true.

But he had also taken ten pages of notes for the first time, and she had threaded events together with so many dates and newspaper articles that he had scribbled dozens of statements that needed to be researched. Doris Boudreau, the city librarian, would stay busy for a week just tracking down the dates of newspaper and magazine articles he needed to read.

"As I said before," he began in a cautious tone, "you have used certain people's names, and some of your opinions of them aren't complimentary. If you have fabricated anything, you could be subject to a libel charge." Then he dug in deeper. "For instance, how do you know what happened that night? You didn't mention anyone else being at the scene of the explosion, and you don't have any witnesses I can contact."

Marie went on as though Reggie's opinion didn't matter. "I suppose the explosion caught the attention of other ships who called the Coast Guard, because one of their vessels found Al the next morning. He had broken some ribs and had a fractured arm. At least that was all anyone could see. But as it turned out, he had internal injuries too.

When they brought him back to Pat's Landing he called for me and Jane and told us what had happened and spoke about the gunfire from the U-boat and the deck gun blowing up the iceboat. His story should be proof enough for you. He couldn't describe other details because he was thrown into the water and didn't recall anything until he was picked up the following morning."

Reggie scribbled something on a sheet of paper. "Where can I contact him to verify your story?"

Marie winced and took her time to answer. "Oh, he's not alive. Even if he was, he'd be way past a hundred. Anyway, Jane and I heard his story before the ambulance took him to the medical clinic in Houma. But he died before they got him to there. He's buried in the town's cemetery with Tom, Rene, and Manny, beside their stone markers that signify their graves. No one ever found the bodies or any evidence of them. I suppose the explosion was the reason." She dabbed her eyes with a Kleenex, clamping it in one hand, her voice faltering. "Our son, who died in Vietnam, lies next to Rene's headstone, and when I pass on there's a plot for me so I can be with him. The only good years Rene and I had were growing up and being married in that small town, so I want to go back and be with him and my son and the others. It's a beautiful old cemetery. Some of the remaining families keep it up by mowing the grass and pulling weeds."

She returned to the story and her voice smoothed out. "Except for a piece of the iceboat's railing, nothing was ever found, though the search lasted for three days. Kay Savoy saw to it that four trawlers covered the area as far west as Point Au Fer." She paused and breathed heavily, fighting for control. "Shrimping can be a hard life. You have to feel it in your bones. I loved it because I worked with my husband. But after the accident, I never stepped on the deck of another trawler. I recall an old adage about life at sea that said there are no flowers on a seaman's watery grave." She pushed her lips together and hardened her eyes. "But there are flowers on my husband's grave, Mr. Arcenaux. And as sure as I'm sitting here, his spirit, as well as my son's are under those gravestones, and I visit them several times a year to set flowers and say hello. In the spring I put azaleas there, sprigs of honeysuckle for summer, amaryllis in the fall, and hothouse roses in the winter." Her face took on a warm expression. "Rene loved roses. He planted two bushes in the front of our house." She glanced toward the office door as though looking for someone. "During my last visit to the cemetery I drove by the old place and saw the big rose bush blooming in the flowerbed. It was a shoot from one Rene had planted near the same spot he chose so many years ago."

When Marie grew silent with her eyes fixed on the carpet, Reggie finally spoke up. "You've told me a very interesting story, Mrs. Dugas, but I need concrete evidence."

"Two weeks after the funeral," Marie continued as if Reggie hadn't said anything. "A pair of FBI agents came to the house. I told them what Rene spoke of that night on our boat and it didn't surprise them when I brought up Karl. According to them, he had been under suspicion for quite some time. The agents said his real name was Karl Heinrich. The aim of the operation wasn't to supply U-boats but for him to elude arrest for espionage and to escape to Germany. No agents knew about the rendezvous until the night of their second trip, and by then it was too late to capture him. Karl was an American citizen who had become a double agent for Germany. He was influenced by his father who was a member of Abwehr, a German espionage ring that operated in the States during the war and recruited him. The entire operation was an elaborate front for him to get away and to avoid arrest and a trial for treason."

Reggie didn't stop probing. "Forgive me, but it sounds improbable. Except for two U-boat logs that were never recovered, the Naval Archives has records of most U-boats that entered the Gulf of Mexico during World War II. Of those twenty-four boats, only one was known to have been sunk; U-166, and it was identified by a National Geographic team that found the vessel and descended to identify it. From the others who did the research for the family, I don't recall anything in the logbooks about a sub picking up an agent and taking him to Germany."

But Marie didn't falter. "Surely you don't have information on the U-boats that were lost in the Atlantic. Karl might have been on one that picked him up and then went down on its way back to France."

Reggie was about to challenge her when he recalled the incident with the merchant ship *Atenas*. He couldn't remember the sub's number, but the U-boat's skipper had omitted firing on the ship and had backed off when the ship's gun crew found the range with their deck gun and fought him off. Karl might have been taken on board a U-boat and his name not entered in the logbook.

Another possibility existed that some U-boat records might not contain every minute detail of each boat's action during a patrol, especially if an attack failed. Although each U-boat captain was supposed to keep a daily log, another skipper could have omitted sinking an unarmed iceboat that posed no military threat in order to save face and avoid criticism from the German High Command.

Reggie picked up his pen after turning off his portable recorder. "Tell me your home and work phone numbers where I can reach you."

"Oh, I'm too old to work anymore," she said.

She gave him her home number and added, "I'm there every day, except when I go to morning Mass on Wednesday, Saturday, and Sunday."

He wrote down her information and leaned back in his chair, studying her face. Her demeanor had remained unchanged from the beginning. She hadn't wrung her hands or twitched in her chair when he asked questions, and she had held constant eye contact with him, except when covering tender memories that temporarily took control of her emotions. He had been able to punch holes in other people's stories, but she hadn't faltered or corrected herself on any details, and he had run out of questions.

"I'll talk to my clients and let you know their decision. However, I must caution you. What you have said doesn't lead me to other witnesses. That's something the families have stressed. As you can imagine, they want justice but also validation."

"I want justice too," Marie agreed. "It may not be a Christian thing to say, but I hope Karl Heinrich died a horrible death. He was a traitor and caused hardship for the community. His scheme killed my husband and set in motion the chain of events that changed Pat's Landing forever. A week or two after the incident, the story went around that local shrimpers were collaborating with the Germans, and hateful letters were mailed to Kay, Jane and me, filled with awful threats. I'm certain the events were magnified into wild rumors that some believed. Anyway, the same story persisted long after the war ended. If you ask me, your clients are acting on gossip and innuendo more than truth. In my opinion, they're wasting their money to offer a reward. No one is out there who will refute me.

"The rumor was vicious and changed things for all three of us. Kay Savoy sold the shrimp company six months after the incident, and not two months later it burned to the ground. No one knows where she is now. Some said at the time that she would never come back. I don't know how much she knew because she didn't talk to anyone. But those awful stories had to hurt her.

"My mother-in-law, Jane, moved back to Texas after the incident but sent me annual Christmas cards until she died in 1955. She was only fifty-six. She never remarried and never mentioned the event in her letters or cards. I'll always believe that remorse shortened her life. As for Manny's mother, she left right after the service for Tom and the boys. No one knows where she went, but she used to come back at special times, then leave without talking to anyone. Until five years ago, a small crucifix on a chain would be draped over Manny's gravestone at Christmas." Marie paused and focused on her wrinkled hands and bony fingers that showed the ravages of arthritis, and when she continued her voice was tinged with regret. "That traitor changed our lives in other ways too. Losing the shrimp company crippled Pat's Landing, so now all that's left is a smelly Pogie plant and a heliport for oil companies who fly their people offshore. The plant provides a few jobs but the community isn't what it used to be. With the docks and warehouse gone, there was no place to unload the shrimp, so the commercial shrimpers and families moved to Grand Isle, Morgan City, or Delcambre. Over half the town moved away.

"Houma lost a lot too. The Navy built a blimp base on the airport in '42, but after the war the base was no longer vital and it was closed. All that's left now are crumbling foundations where the blimp hangar was, a few dilapidated buildings, several helicopters supporting the oil companies, and the old runways. The parish road to Pat's Landing is still there, but pipe yards, oil field businesses, Cajun restaurants, and seedy bars have squeezed out the marsh and destroyed the beauty I knew as a girl."

"If the place meant so much to you, why did you leave?"

"I had to raise my son. Rene and I hadn't saved much and, as I said before, I had to find a job. We moved to New Orleans where I worked for Mr. Higgins until the war ended and the contracts dried up. So I moved to Lafayette. My son graduated from USL. Now it's called the University of Louisiana. He joined the Army in 1966 and wanted to be a pilot like Rene's friend, Joe Christy, but he was killed in a helicopter crash a month and a day after going to Vietnam."

Reggie's face and voice softened. "I'm sorry for your sacrifice. By losing both your husband and your son in a war, you've suffered more than your share of sorrow and pain."

Her face brightened, and a smile emerged through the wrinkles. "Oh well, I'm better off than a lot of folks. I still have my health and my religion, and every morning I thank the Lord that I'm still here."

"Amen," Reggie echoed, shuffling papers on his desk and placing the recorder in a drawer. "You have a compelling story, but I can't say it validates the rumor. Seventy-five years is a long time to track people down and get facts. At any rate, I'll contact the families and let you know their answer, though I doubt if they will offer you any money."

Her face assuming a defiant look, Marie reached for her two canes and leaned heavily on one, then the other, finally standing up, but depending on the canes for balance and support. "I didn't come here for the money, Mr. Arcenaux. They can keep it. I had to let you know that my husband, just like Manny and Tom Savoy, acted because he thought he was helping win the war. In the summer of 1942, we lived with the daily thought of a potential invasion into South Louisiana. Tom, Manny, and my husband were not traitors. No red-blooded American would have done what the rumor implies. They were asked to help this country but were lied to and, unknown to them, became victims in a diabolical scheme that fooled everybody and ruined the community. I pray that Karl Johnson or Heinrich, or whatever his real name was, has a special hot seat beside the Devil."

Reggie patted her on one shoulder and helped her to the door in half steps that matched her laborious, flat-footed pace. "I believe you. But it isn't my decision. I'm only the attorney. The families will examine the details in your story and I'll call you next week."

Before he could shut the door, she turned toward him. "I hope my story gives them some peace. I'm still asking God for my own because I should have stopped Rene from going. That makes me partly responsible for what happened. If I had only..."

Reggie interrupted her and shook his head. "Put that out of your mind. From what you've told me, your husband was doing what he thought was best for the country. He knew the risks but did his duty like a soldier."

She motioned one hand toward him but still held the cane. "Anyway, thanks for your time, and God bless you for listening."

He patted her on one shoulder and smiled. "Why, thank you, and you are very welcome."

Reggie had no sooner closed the door than his phone rang. It was difficult to hear because the music from the band and the multitude of background conversations at Smitty's Bayou Club nearly drowned out Ed Touchet's voice. "What's been keeping you, Reggie? We need our festival king to get here."

"I have a couple of clients who pay me three-fifty an hour and won't go away." Reggie explained. "The case has brought me a bunch of wild stories, and I just heard the best one."

Holding the phone closer, Ed raised his voice to overcome the noise of an electric accordion nearby. "Well you'd better get here before the shrimp is gone, the beer runs out and all the pretty girls go home."

"I'll be there in ten minutes," he answered. He put his cell phone in his pocket, grabbed his sport coat off the hook and closed the door behind him.

Printed in the United States
By Bookmasters